THE LURE OF MAGIC,
THE CLASH OF ARMS . . .

Called upon to face a human-devouring beast, a
swordwoman and a sorceress find that men not monsters
present the greatest challenge. . . .

Fleeing a plague-stricken land, a lone swordswoman
must battle wizard and demon to save a treasure beyond
price. . . .

Can bard's sight free a wizard from an earth magic
prison?

She was a gullrider, sworn to protect her people. But
when the monster kraken began its reign of terror,
could she alone master the one weapon that might
prove the kraken's doom?

These are but four of the eighteen tales of flashing
blades and fantastic sorcery included in this latest
collection of—

SWORD AND SORCERESS

SWORD AND SORCERESS IV

AN ANTHOLOGY
OF HEROIC FANTASY

Edited by
Marion Zimmer Bradley

DAW BOOKS, INC.
DONALD A. WOLLHEIM, PUBLISHER

1633 Broadway, New York, NY 10019

Copyright © 1987 by Marion Zimmer Bradley.
All Rights Reserved.
Cover art by Jael.

Introduction © 1987 by Marion Zimmer Bradley.
A Tale of Heroes © 1987 by Mercedes Lackey.
The Woodland of Zarad-Thra © 1987 by Robin W. Bailey.
The Weeping Oak © 1987 by Charles de Lint.
Gullrider © 1987 by Dave Smeds.
Blood Dancer © 1987 by Diana L. Paxson.
Kayli's Fire © 1987 by Paula Helm Murray.
The Ring of Lifari © 1987 by Josepha Sherman.
Rite of Passage © 1987 by Jennifer Roberson.
The Eyes of the Gods © 1987 by Richard Corwin.
Fate and the Dreamer © 1987 by Millea Kenin.
The Noonday Witch © 1987 by Dorothy J. Heydt.
Redeemer's Riddle © 1987 by Stephen L. Burns.
The Tree-Wife of Arketh © 1987 by Syn Ferguson.
Spell of Binding © 1987 by Richard Cornell.
Storm God © 1987 by Deborah Wheeler.
Die Like a Man © 1987 by L.D. Woeltjen.
Death and the Ugly Woman © 1987 by Bruce D. Arthurs.
Bloodstones © 1987 by Deborah M. Vogel.

DAW Book Collectors No. 714.

First DAW Printing, July 1987

4   5   6   7   8   9

PRINTED IN CANADA

TABLE OF CONTENTS

INTRODUCTION

Well, it's been another year, and here we are again. I tend to think of these volumes as a magazine in paperback format, appearing yearly, and dedicated to the proposition that sword and sorcery fiction, once the most sexist of all fields of fantasy, must not be confined to tales of power and pillage, with a seamy underside of rape, which at one time comprised about eighty percent of sword and sorcery fiction—including that written by women.

Peopled with mighty-thewed heroes (what are thews anyhow? I'm sure the dictionary would tell me, but I honestly don't think I want to know) and shrinking (or shrieking) maidens whose main function was to stand about screaming, or to be distributed to the heroes as bad-conduct prizes, these stories usually followed a general philosophy (if you can call it that) of "Ho, hum, another day, another dragon, another damsel in distress." Yet they were good fun, and even women enjoyed the adventures, though we deplored the philosophy behind them.

This series started out with only one major rule; that, without resorting to feminist rhetoric, we would present women as central to their own adventures, neither as victims nor as bystanders to the men's deeds. In the first volume, we found far too many stories of rape and revenge—a category which seems to have dwindled virtually out of existence; this year I received only one such story, and that was written by a man. But then, even men no longer fantasize the rapist as brave or heroic, but as the sickly, impotent psychopath he usually is.

On the other hand, we have tried very hard to avoid

the female adventurer who is merely the male adventurer
dressed up in long hair and skirts with a girl's name; we
have also tried very hard to avoid the story where the
only plot is that a woman Challenges Men's Magic (or
mystique) and proves that she *can too* be a camel driver, a
wizard, a mercenary or swordswoman, a dragon tamer;
this story is simply no surprise to anyone in this day of
female astronauts and women climbing Everest. Nor is
it surprising to me—or, I hope, to my readers—that
women should succeed or even excel as thieves or soldiers; if this still surprises—or satisfies—anyone, that
reader is living in the Dark Ages. After all, of my three
children, only the girl won a varsity letter for any sport.
While her brothers were content to excel in mathematics
or art, my tall, athletic daughter gained a varsity letter in
fencing—not a sport notorious for woman champions,
though perhaps aptly suited to them. One of the (women)
writers of these volumes holds a black belt in Kung Fu;
and there are among them university professors, farmers,
animal trainers, and even a few who have the courage to
be housewives and mothers; probably the most unpopu-
lar profession in this day and age.

On the other hand, women in society and in female
achievement and education enjoyed (and despite the best
efforts of a few misguided women, still mostly enjoy) one
major and unqualified advantage in our country. They
were not expected or required to drain off a lot of energy
or initiative learning how to throw, kick or chase various
kind of balls around some field or other. Women have
been and mostly are free to concentrate on more serious
tests of the human spirit. An enormous amount of male
energy is still taken up by these balls (and believe me, I
did not intend the pun, but if it fits. . . .)

The only thing sillier in my opinion than the sight of a
group of supposedly adult men kicking, throwing or chasing some kind of ball around a field or court is the even
sillier sight of adult males sitting on their flabby and
under-exercised backsides watching *another* group of supposedly adult males kicking, chasing, throwing or batting
some such inflated hunk of plastic around some field or
other. The cynic who defined golf as "a good way to ruin

a perfectly good walk" had obviously never seriously contemplated the phenomenon of Monday Night Football. This is a waste of the human spirit unequaled by anything in history with the possible exception of the hairdressing industry or the following of the plots of soap operas. The hunger for adventure is still there in the best of us (despite the best efforts of Barbara Cartland and her competitors), and the purpose of these volumes is to fill it.

As a child I thrilled to the exploits of Maurice Herzog climbing Annapurna, and Francis Chichester sailing single-handed along the Clipper Way; now these feats (and many others) have been duplicated by women, and even the most porcine of male chauvinists find it impossible to deny them. But with our own adventure stories come our own *cliches*.

The first of these volumes was based upon "rape and revenge"—a category which has fortunately declined. The second volume rather overdid the various changes which could be rung on the Sacrificed Maiden story.

This year I discovered a new cliche which came in so often that I got tired (in this one year) of reading it; the thief waking up with a hangover, having spent or gambled away all her profits for her last endeavor; or sometimes it was someone meeting—always in a tavern of some sort—a tired-out, hard-bitten, gray-haired, old or middle-aged mercenary, looking for a way to make One Last Haul and retire. I have bought, and will continue to buy stories of this kind, just as detective novels will continue to feature the hard-boiled (on the surface) private eye with a heart of solid marshmallow; but they must be more subtle. If I recognize the plot on the first page, I reach for my handy rejection slip, and often don't bother to read on through the slimy employer who hires the unlucky lady to steal the ill-gotten gains of Bogus the Barbarian, or to heist the hoard of the Horde; not if it is already obvious to even the inexperienced reader that the dame is being set up as the sacrifice demanded by the Guardian of the Treasure in the booby-trapped stronghold, so that Slimy Employer can get away with the goods.

This kind of story is perhaps the modern equivalent of the much-overworked governess novel—the one we've all read a hundred times; where the not-very-bright heroine goes as governess, or maybe companion, to the isolated old house at the edge of the moors and is lured into the old wine cellar by the Sinister Byronic Hero who heads the household.

This kind of story has all but vanished in the twentieth century, due to the decline of governess candidates without enough worldly wisdom to come in out of the rain. The potential governess now holds a degree in Early Childhood Education, or went to Katherine Gibbs and can type eighty-four words a minute. And even if she did end up in the sinister old house on the edge of the moors, and the Sinister Employer tried to lure her into the old wine cellar (whether on murder or seduction bent), she could pick up the phone and call the cops, or take the first Greyhound bus out of the place.

So there's hope that even a hired, middle-aged mercenary may learn to recognize a trap when she sees one, or develop enough brains in her long career of knocking around the world to come in out of the rain or stay out of the hands of Bogus the Barbarian and his various evil magicians and shills.

But I don't want to take all the fun out of reading or even writing these things. I think we all enjoy the glorious old stories—in fact, the story of the guy who makes it back home in spite of the devil, the deep blue sea, and all the bad guys, is still around, whether you call him Ulysses, Two-gun Tex, or Travis McGee. So if I read one of these things in utter fascination, and only afterward recognize, "Well, son-of-a gun, if that isn't the old story of the Heist of the Hoard again," that's fine; but if I spot it on the first page, all it gets is a rejection slip. We can still fall in love with a lovable thief, whether called Robin Hood or Tessie the trickster. But Tessie must have Robin's lovable qualities, not just a generic reshuffling of well-tried plot elements.

Believe it or not, even after four volumes, I still greet every day's haul of manuscripts with enthusiasm; my secretary now slits the envelopes for me, but I still dive into them with delight. After all, the payoff for reading nineteen stories about dragons straight out of Anne McCaffrey may well be that the twentieth will be something like "Kayli's Fire," in this volume. Every now and then you find a prize. It's like pearl diving. Most of the time when you wrench open the shell, all you get is a wet, smelly oyster which isn't even good to eat.

But the hundredth time you get the pearl.

I've done the diving—and you get to read the pearls.

About half the stories this year are by men; which should surprise no one. Men, after all, created the sword and sorcery category; although I still get the odd letter (usually from a very odd person,), who asked me how I *dare* print "women's fantasy" by men? (Although this kind of person usually calls it "wimmin's fantasy" and asks if I am going to let "wimmin's fantasy, which should be by and for strong womyn, and written by womon only" be taken over and co-opted by men.

Well, I'm afraid that I'm just looking for good stories; and women who object to men writing about women should remember that during our first thirty years or so, women sf and fantasy writers had to write mostly about men. Are they seriously trying to say that no one can write about a character not of one's own gender? How sad. (And how stupid.) There was Leigh Brackett's splendid Eric John Stark, for instance—one of the great sword and sorcery heroes of all time. And C.L. Moore's incomparable Northwest Smith.

Fantasy is always the poorer for any attempt to limit its scope. In fact, if it can be limited, it's not fantasy at all.

Granted, some female characters created by men are pure wish fulfillment—and I hate to think whose wishes they would fulfill. There are the modern Heinlein "Girls" (one still can't call them women) who have grown up and learned to cuss—but they're still Podkayne of Mars under the skin; little girls, and I think they were more attractive before they learned to cuss or to have a self-conscious sex life. But that's neither here nor there; the important thing is that there are many fine writers whose characters are neither mighty, broad-chested heroes, nor shrinking maidens screen-tested only for their Fay Wray-ish screaming power, but plainly and simply *human*.

I think, for instance, that it would be hard to create a more simply human and believable character than B.D. Arthurs did in "Death and the Ugly Woman." And I doubt if Robin Bailey's Cymbalin in "The Woodland of Zarad-Thra" could be bettered by any woman writer, whatever her political correctness.

But then, I have a constitutional detestation for apartheid, even when it's disguised as women's space. Or, as they'd probably say, *wimmin's space*.

When it comes to politics, my version is always, "A plague on both your houses." Any attempt to mix art and politics makes for bad art and bad politics—or why are so many dancers and choreographers, the petted darlings of the system, defecting from that paradise of political art, the USSR? And any attempt to put politics into fantasy fiction should be treated with the utmost contempt—not to mention the editor's ultimate weapon, the rejection slip. If you want to write a political treatise, hire a hall—or have the decency to *package* it as a political tract and hand it out on a street corner to the already converted. Don't try to sneak it into your story.

On the other hand, if you write with conviction and honesty, your views will be clear enough. Not one of these stories descends to rhetoric (which, after all, is defined as the art of making the worse cause appear the better, or the finer art of telling lies) but I think they embody a consistent view of women in adventure fiction. And that's what it's all about, isn't it?

—M.Z.B.

A TALE OF HEROES
(Based on an idea by Robert Chilson)

by Mercedes Lackey

"Misty" Lackey made her profesional debut in SWORD AND SORCERESS III with the much-liked novelette "Sword Sworn" which introduced Tarma and Kethry. Misty recently sold a three-novel series to DAW Books. I can't wait. Female adventurers tend to travel in pairs (like nuns?)—usually mixed pairs; one swordswoman and one sorceress. In this story, they face a problem rather more domestic than most, and some dedicated feminists may find the solution untenable; but to each her own. The haggis shortage is not yet imminent. (Haggis is a Scots dish comprised of liver and oatmeal which is very much an acquired taste. There's a proverbial statement that it's a good thing we don't all like the same things— think what a haggis shortage there would be!)

(If this story doesn't suit you, try the next story; Robin Bailey's "The Woodland of Zarad-Thra, which is superficially founded of the same elements, and raising much the same questions, yet is about as different as any story could be.

"**M**iles out of our way, and still not a sign of anything out of the ordinary," Tarma grumbled, her harsh voice carrying easily above the clopping of their horses' hooves. "For certain, no sign of any women in distress. Are you—"

"Absolutely certain," Kethry (the swordswoman's partner) replied firmly, eyes scanning the fields to either side of them. Her calf-length, buff-colored robe, mark of the traveling sorceress, was covered in road dust, and she

13

squinted in an attempt to keep that dust out of her eyes. The chilly air was full of the scent of dead leaves and dried grass. "It's not something I can ignore, you know. If my blade Need says there're women in trouble in this direction, there's no chance of doubt: they exist. Surely you now that by *now*."

It had been two days since they diverted from the main road onto this one, scarcely wider than a cart track. The autumn rains were sure to start before long; cold rains Tarma had hoped to avoid by getting them on the way to their next commission well ahead of time. Since they'd turned off the caravan road they'd seen little sign of habitation, only rolling, grassy hills and a few scattered patches of forest, all of them brown and sere. The bright colors of fall were not to be found in this region—when frost came the vegetation here muted into shades more like those of Tarma's worn leathers and Kethry's traveling robes than the carnival-bright colors of the farther north. In short, the trip thus far had been uneventful and deadly dull.

"I swear, sometimes that sword of yours causes more grief than she saves us from," Tarma snorted. "Magicians!"

Kethry smiled; she knew very well that the Shin'a'in swordswoman was only trying to get a rise out of her. The magic blade called "Need" that she carried had saved both their lives more than once. It had the peculiar property of giving weapons' expertise to a mage, or protecting a swordswoman from the worst magics; it could heal injuries and illness in a fraction of normal time— but it could only be used by a female. And, as with all magics, there was a price attached to Need's gifts. Her bearer must divert to aid any woman in need of help, no matter how far out of her intended way the sword pulled her. "You weren't saying that a few weeks ago, when Need and I healed that lung-wound of yours."

"That was then, this is now," her hawk-visaged partner quoted. "The moment is never the same twice." A bit of fresher breeze carried the dust of the road away, but chilled both of them a little more.

Kethry shook amber hair out of her eyes, her round

face full of amusement. "O wise sister-mine, do you have a proverb for *everything?*"

Tarma chuckled. "Damn near—Greeneyes, these fields are cultivated—left to go fallow just this year. I think there's a farm up ahead. Want to chance seeing if the owner'll let us pass the night in his barn? Looks like rain, and I'd rather sleep dry without you having to exhaust magics to keep us that way."

Kethry scanned on ahead of them for possible danger, using magic to smell out magic. "It seems safe enough—let's chance it. Maybe we can get some clue about what Need's calling us to. I don't like the way the air's chilling down, sybarite that I am. I'd rather sleep warm, if we can."

Their ugly, mottled-gray battlemares smelled the presence of other horses, even as the sorceress finished her sentence. Other horses meant food and water at the least, and a dry and warm stable at best. With the year being well into autumn a warm stable was nothing to scorn. They picked up their pace so abruptly that the huge black "wolf" that trotted by the side of the swordswoman's mount was left behind in the dust. He barked a surprised protest, and scrambled to catch up.

"That's what you get for daydreaming, lazybones," Tarma laughed, her ice-blue eyes slitted against the rising dust. "Don't just look stupid, get up here, or we'll leave you!"

The lupine creature—whose shoulder easily came as high as Tarma's waist—gathered himself and sprang. He landed on the carrying pad of stuffed leather just behind her saddle; the mare grunted at the impact, but was unsurprised at it. She simply waited for the beast to settle himself and set his retractile claws into the leather pad, then moved into a ground-devouring lope. The sorceress' mount matched her stride for stride.

Strands of raven hair escaped from Tarma's braid and blew into her eyes, but didn't obscure her vision so much that she missed the sudden movement in the bushes at the side of the road, and the small, running figure that set off across the fields. "Looks like the scouts are out," she grinned at her partner. "We've been spotted."

"What? Oh—" Kethry caught sight of the child as he (she?) vaulted over a hedge and vanished. "Wonder what he made of us?"

"We're about to find out." From the other side of the hedge strode a heavy, muscular farmer, as brown as his fields; one who held his scythe with the air of someone who knew what an effective weapon it could be. Both women pulled their horses to a stop and waited for him to reach the road.

"Wayfarer's Peace, landsman," Tarma said when he was near enough to hear her. She held both hands out empty. He eyed her carefully.

"On oath to the Warrior, Shin'a'in?" he replied.

"Oath given," she raised one eyebrow in surprise. "You know Shin'a'in, landsman? We're a long way from the plains."

"I've traveled," he had relaxed visibly when Tarma had given her pledge. "Soldiered a bit. Aye, I know Shin'a'in—and I know a Sworn One when I see one. 'Tisn't often you see Shin'a'in, and less often you see Sword-Sworn oathed to outlander."

"So you recognize blood-oathed, too? You're full of surprises, landsman," Tarma's level gaze held him; her blue eyes had turned cold. "So many, I wonder if we are safe with you—"

He raised his left arm; burned onto the back of the wrist was a five-spoked wheel. Kethry relaxed with a sigh, and her partner glanced sidelong at her.

"And I know the Wheel-bound," the sorceress replied. " 'May your future deeds balance all.' "

" 'And your feet ever find the Way,' " he finished, smiling at last. "I am called Landric."

"I'm Tarma—my companion is Kethry. Just out of curiosity—how did you know we were she'enedran?" Tarma asked as he moved up to walk beside their mounts. "Even among Shin'a'in, oathsisters aren't that common."
He was a big man, and muscular. He wore simple brown homespun, but the garments were well made. His hair and eyes were a few shades darker than his sun-darkened skin. He swung the scythe up gracefully out of the way, and though he eyed Tarma's beast-companion warily, he

made no moves as though he were afraid of it. Tarma gave him points for that.

"Had a pair of oathbound mercenaries in my company," he replied, "That was before I took the Wheel, of course. Brother and sister, and both Sword-Sworn as well, as I recall. When you held up your hands, I recognized the crescent palm-scar, and I couldn't imagine a Shin'a'in traveling with any but her oath-sister. If you've a wish to guest with me, be welcome—even though—" his face clouded "—I fear my hearth's cold comfort now."

Kethry had a flash of intuition. "Grief, landsman—your Wheelmate?"

"She waits the next turning. I buried what the monster left of her at Spring planting, these six months agone."

Their host walked beside their mounts, and told his tale with little embellishment.

"And there was no time for me to get a weapon, and little enough I could have done even had there been time. So when the monster headed for the babe, she ran between it and him; and the creature took her instead of the child, just as she'd intended." There was heavily veiled pain still lurking in his voice.

"Damn," Tarma said, shaking her head in awe at the dead woman's bravery. "Not sure I'd've had the guts to do that. What's this thing like, anyway?"

"Like no creature I've ever heard tell of. Big; bigger than a dozen horses put together, covered with bristly brown hair—a head that's all teeth and jaws, six legs. Got talons as long as my hand, too. We think it's gotten away from some mage somewhere; it looks like something a nasty mind would put together for the fun of it—no offense meant, sorceress."

"None taken," Kethry met his brown eyes with candor. "Lady knows my kind has its share of evildoers. Go on."

"Well, the thing moves like lightning, too. Outruns even the lord's beasts with no problem. Its favorite prey is women and children; guess it doesn't much care for food that might be able to fight back a little."

Kethry caught her partner's eye. *Told you,* she signaled in hand-speech. *Need knows.*

"The Lord Havirn hasn't been able to do anything about it for the time being, so until he can get a hero to kill it, he's taken the 'dragon solution' with it."

" 'Dragon solution'?" Tarma looked askance.

"He's feeding it, in hopes it'll be satisfied enough to leave everyone else alone," Kethry supplied. "Livestock—I hope?" She looked down at the farmer where he walked alongside her horse. He kept up with the beast with no trouble; Kethry was impressed. It took a strong walker to keep up with Hellsbane.

He shook his head. "People. It won't touch animals. So far he's managed to use nothing but criminals, but the jails are emptying fast, and for some reason nobody seems much interested in breaking the law anymore. And being fed doesn't completely stop it from hunting, as I well know to my grief. He's posted the usual sort of reward; half his holdings and his daughter, you know the drill."

"Fat lot of good either would do us," Tarma muttered in Shin'a'in. Kethry smothered a smile.

They could see his farmstead in the near distance; from here it looked well-built and prosperous; of baked brick and several rooms in size. The roof was thatch, and in excellent repair. There were at least five small figures gathered by the door of the house.

"These are my younglings," he said with pride and a trace of worry. "Childer," he called to the little group huddled just by the door, "do duty to our guests."

The huddle broke apart; two girls ran into the house and out again as the eldest, a boy, came to take the reins of the horses. The next one in height, a huge-eyed girl (one of the two who had gone into the house), brought bread and salt; she was followed by another child, a girl who barely came to the wolf's shoulder, carrying a guesting-cup with the solemnity due a major religious artifact. The three children halted on seeing the wolf, faces betraying doubt and a little fear. Plainly, they wanted to obey their father. Equally plainly, they didn't want to get within a mile of the huge black beast.

Tarma signaled the wolf silently. He padded to her right side and sat, looking very calm and as harmless as it is possible for a wolf to look. "This is Warrl," she said. "He's my soul-kin and friend, just like in the tales—a magic beast from the Pelagir Hills. He's wise, and very kind—" she raised one eyebrow with a comic expression "—and he's a *lot* smarter than I am!"

Warrl snorted, as if to agree, and the children giggled. Their fears evaporated, and they stepped forward to continue their tasks of greeting under their father's approving eye.

The guesting ritual complete, the eldest son—who looked to be no older than ten, but was a faithful copy of his father in miniature—led the horses to the stock-shed. It would probably not have been safe to have let him take ordinary battle-trained horses, but these were Shin'a'in bred and trained warsteeds. They had sense and intelligence enough to be trusted unguided in the midst of a melee, yet would no more have harmed a child, even by accident, than they would have done injury to one of their own foals.

Just now they were quite well aware that they were about to be stabled and fed, and in their eagerness to get to the barn they nearly dragged the poor child off his feet.

"Hai!" Tarma said sharply; they stopped dead, and turned to look at her. "Go gently, warladies," she said in her own tongue. "Mind your manners."

Landric hid a smile as the now docile creatures let themselves be led away at the boy's pace. "I'd best help him, if you think they'll allow it," he told the Shin'a'in. "Else he'll be all night at it, trying to groom them on a ladder!"

"They'll allow anything short of violence, providing you leave our gear with them; but for your own sake, don't take the packs out of their sight. I'd hate to have a recompense you for broken bones and a new barn!"

"Told you I soldiered with Shin'a'in, didn't I? No fear I'd try *that*. Take your ease inside; 'tis poor enough, and I beg you forgive the state it's in, but—"

"Landric, no man can be two things at once. Better

the house should suffer a little than your fields and stock. Clean plates won't feed your younglings," Kethry told him, following the oldest girl inside.

There was a musty smell inside, as of a house left too long unaired. Piles of clean clothing were on the benches on either side of the table, the table itself was piled high with dirty crockery. There was dust everywhere, and toys strewn the length and breadth of the room. The fire had been allowed to go out—probably so that the two-year-old sitting on one corner of the hearth wouldn't fall into it in his father's absence. The fireplace hadn't been cleaned for some time. The kitchen smelled of burned porridge and onions.

"Warrior's Blade, what a mess!" Tarma exclaimed under her breath as they stepped into the chatoic kitchen-cum-commonroom.

"It's several months' accumulation," her partner reminded her, "And several months of fairly inexpert attempts to keep up with the chores. Guests or no, I'm not going to let things stay in this state." She began pinning up the sleeves of her buff-colored traveling robe and headed toward the nearest pile of clutter.

"My thought entirely," the swordswoman replied, beginning to divest herself on her arms.

Landric and his son returned from stabling the mares to a welcome but completely unexpected scene. His guests had completely restored order to the house; there was a huge kettle of soup on the once-cold hearth, and the sorceress was making short work of what was left of the dirty dishes. Every pot and pan in the kitchen had already been washed and his oldest girl was carefully drying and stacking them. The next oldest was just in the last steps of sweeping the place out, using a broom that one of the two had cut down to a size she could manage. His four-year-old son was trotting solemnly back and forth, putting things away under the careful direction of—the *swordswoman?*

Sure enough, it was the hawk-faced swordswoman who was directing the activities of all the children. She was somehow managing to simultaneously change the baby's dirty napkin, tickling him so that he was too helpless with giggles to fight her as he usually did; directing the four-year-old in his task; and admonishing the six-year-old when she missed a spot in her sweeping. And looking very much as if she were enjoying the whole process to the hilt.

Landric stood in the door with his mouth hanging open in surprise.

"I hope you two washed after you finished with the horses," Kethry called from her tub of soapsuds. "If not, wait until I'm through here, and you can use the wash water before you throw it out." She rinsed the last of the dishes and stood pointedly beside the tub of water, waiting for Landric to use it or carry it out.

"This was—not necessary," he managed to say as he hefted the tub to carry outside. "You are guests—"

"Oh come now, did you *really* expect two women to leave things in the state they were?" Kethry giggled, holding the door open for him. "Besides, this isn't the sort of thing we normally have to do. It's rather a relief to be up to the elbows in hot water instead of trouble. And Tarma adores children; she can get them to do anything for her. You said you know Sword-Sworn; you know that they're celibate, then. She doesn't often get a chance to fuss over babes. But what I'd like to know is why you haven't hired a woman or gotten some neighbor to help you?"

"There are no women to hire, thanks to the monster," he replied heavily. "Those that didn't provide meals for it ran off to the town, thinking they'd be safer there. I'm at the farthest edge of Lord Havirn's lands, and my nearest neighbors aren't willing to cross the distance between us when the monster is known to have taken my wife within sight of the house. I can't say that I blame them. I take the eldest with me, now, and I have the rest of the children barricade themselves in the house until we come home. The Gods of the Wheel know I'd be overjoyed to find some steady women willing to watch them and keep the place tidy for bed, board, and a bit of silver, but there isn't anyone to be hired at any price."

"Now it's my turn to beg your pardon," Kethry said apologetically.

"No offense meant, none taken," an almost-smile stretched his lips. "How could I take offense after this?"

That night Tarma regaled all the children with tales until they'd fallen asleep, while Kethry kept her hands busy with mending. Landric had kept glancing over at Tarma with bemusement; to see the hash-visaged, battle-scarred Shin'a'in warrior smothered in children and enjoying every moment of it was plainly a sight the had never expected to witness. And Warrl put the cap on his amazement by letting the baby tumble over him, pull his fur, tail and ears, and finally fall asleep using the beast as a mattress.

When the children were all safely in bed, Kethry cleared her throat in a way intended to suggest she had something touchy she wanted to ask their host.

He took the hint, and the sleepiness left his eyes. "Aye, mage-lady?"

"Would you object to my working a bit of magic here? I know it's not precisely in the tenets of the Path to use the arcane, but—"

"I'm a bit more pragmatic than some of my fellows. Nay, lady, I've no objection to a bit of magicking. What did you have in mind?"

"Two things, really. I'd like to scry out this monster of yours and see what we're going to be up against—"

"Lady," he interrupted, "I would advise against going at that thing. Let the hired heroes deal with it."

"While it takes more women and children?" she shook her head. "I can't do that, Landric—even if it weren't against my conscience, I'm geas-bound. Anyway, the other thing I'd like to do is leave you a little help with the children—something like a cross between Warrl and a sheepdog, if you've no objection. It won't be as bright, or as large and strong, but it will be able to keep an eye on the little ones, herd them out of mischief, and go for help if need be."

"How could I object? The gods know I need something like that. You shouldn't feel obligated though—"

"Balance the Wheel your way, and I'll balance it in

mine, all right?" The twinkle in Kethry's eyes took any sting there might have been out of her words.

He bowed his head a little. "Your will then, mage-ady. If you've no need of me, I'm for bed."

"No need, Landric, and thank you."

When he'd left, Kethry went to the stack of clean dishes and selected a dark, nearly black pottery bowl.

"Water scrying?" Tarma asked, settling herself on one side of the table.

"Mh-hm," Kethry replied absently, filling it very carefully with clear, cold water, then bringing it to the table and dusting a fine powder of salt and herbs from a pouch at her belt over the surface. "For both of us—you may see what I'd miss."

She held her hands just above the water's surface and chanted softly, her eyes closed in concentration. After a few moments, a mist-like glow encircled her hands. It brightened and took on a faint bluish cast, then flowed down over her hands onto the water, hovering over it without quite touching it. When it had settled, Kethry took her hands away, and both of them peered into the bowl.

It was rather like looking at a reflection; they had to be careful about moving or breathing, for the picture was distorted or lost whenever the surface of the water was disturbed.

"Ugly rotter," was Tarma's first comment, as the beast came clear. "Where and when?"

"I'm past-scrying; all the encounters with the would-be heroes thus far."

"Hm. Not having much luck, is he?"

That was an understatement, as the monster was making short work of a middle-aged man-at-arms.

"It looks like they feed it once a week," Kethry said, though how she was able to keep track of time-passage in the bowl was beyond Tarma. "Oh, this is a mage. Let's see how he fares."

"Huh, no better than a try with a sword."

Magics just bounced off its hide; the mage ended up traveling the same road as the fighters.

"It's a good bet it's a magic creature," Kethry concluded. "Any mage worth his robe would armor his own toys against magic."

After watching all the trials—and failures—they both sat silently.

"Let's think on this a while. We've got enough information for now."

"Agreed. Want to build Landric's little shepherd?"

"*That* I could do in my sleep. Let's see, first I need a vehicle—"

Warrl got to his feet, and padded over to Tarma. *Let me hunt,* he said in her mind.

"Warrl just volunteered to find your 'vehicle'."

"Bless you, fur-face! I take it there's something within range?"

"He says 'maybe not as big as you were hoping, but smarter'."

"I prefer brains over brawn for this task—"

Warrl whisked out the door, and was back before a half-hour was up, herding an odd little beast before him that looked like a combination of fox and cat, with human-like hands.

"Bright Lady, that looks like a Pelagir Hills changeling!"

"Warrl says it came from the same place as the monster—when *that* got loose, apparently a lot of other creatures did, too."

"All the better for my purposes." Kethry coaxed the creature into her lap, and ran softly glowing hands over it while she frowned a little in concentration. "Wonderful!" she sighed in relief, "It's Bright-path intended; and nobody's purposed it yet. It's like a blank page waiting to be written on—I can't believe my luck!" The glow on her hands changed to a warm gold, settled over the creature's head and throat, and sank into it, as if absorbed. It sighed, and abruptly fell asleep.

"There," she said, rising and placing it beside the hearth. "When it wakes all its nurturing instincts will be imprinted for Landric's children; as bright as it is, he'll be able to leave them even with a fire burning on the hearth without them being in danger."

She stood, and swayed with exhaustion.

"That's more than enough for one night!" Tarma exclaimed, steadying her and walking her over to the pallets Landric had supplied. "It's definitely time *you* got a little rest! Greeneyes, I swear if I weren't around, you'd wear yourself into a wraith."

"Not a wraith—" Kethry yawned, but before she could finish her thought, she was asleep.

They left the next morning with the entreaties of the four youngest children still in their ears. Despite the distraction of the new "pet" they still wanted the two women to stay. None of the six had wanted Tarma, in particular, to leave.

"I'd've liked to stay," Tarma said, a bit wistfully, as she turned in her saddle to wave farewell.

"So would I—at least for a bit," Kethry sighed. "Need's not giving me any choice though. She's nagging me half to death. All last night I could feel her pulling on me; a few more days of that and I'll start chewing furniture. Besides, I had the distinct impression that Landric was eyeing me with the faint notion of propositioning me this morning."

"You should have taken him up on it, Greeneyes," Tarma chuckled. "You could do worse."

"Thank you, but no thank you. He's a nice enough man—and I'd kill him inside of a week. He has very firm notions about what a wife's place is, and I don't fit any of them. And he wouldn't be any too pleased about your bringing up his offspring as Shin'a'in, either! You just want me married off so you can start raising a new clan!"

"Can't blame me for trying," Tarma shrugged, wearing a wry grin. The loss of her old clan was far enough in the past now that it was possible for Kethry to tease her about wanting to start a new one. "You *did* promise the Council that that was what you'd do."

"And I will—but in my own good time, and with the man of *my* choice, one who'll be a friend and partner, not hope to rule me. That's all very well for some women, but not for me. Furthermore, any husband of mine would have to be *pleased* with the idea that my oathsister will be training our children as Shin'a'in. I didn't promise the

council, she'enedra," she rode close enough to catch
Tarma's near hand and squeeze it. "I promised *you.*"

Tarma's expression softened, as it had when she'd
been with the children. "I know it, dearling," she replied,
eyes misting a trifle. "And you know that I never would
have asked you for that—never. Ah, let's get moving;
I'm getting maudlin."

Kethry released her hand with a smile, and they picked
up their pace.

They entered the town, which huddled at the foot of
the lord's keep like a collection of stellat-shoots at the
foot of the mother-tree. The ever-present dust covered
the entire town, hanging in a brown cloud over it. Warrl
they left outside, not wanting to chance the stir he'd
cause if they brought him in with them. He would sneak
in after dark, and take up residence with their horses in
the stable, or with them, if they got a room on the
ground floor with a window. Taking directions from the
gate-guard, they found an inn. It was plain, but clean
enough to satisfy both of them, and didn't smell too
strongly of bacon and stale beer.

"When's feeding time for the monster?" Tarma asked
the innkeeper.

"Today. If ye get yerselves t' the main gate, ye'll see
the procession—"

The procession had the feeling of a macabre carnival.
It was headed by the daughter of Lord Havirn, mounted
on a white pony, her hands shackled by a thin gold chain.
Her face bore a mingling of petulance at having to undergo the ceremony, and peevish pride at being the center of attention. Her white garments and hair all braided
with flowers and pearls showed the careful attentions of
at least two servants. Those maidservants walked beside
her, strewing herbs; behind them came a procession of
priests with censers. The air was full of incense-smoke
battling with the ubiquitous dust.

"What's all *that* about?" Kethry asked a sunburnt
farmwoman, nodding at the pony and its sullen rider.

"Show; nothing but show. M'lord likes to pretend it's
his daughter up for sacrifice. But *there* is the real monster-

fodder," she pointed toward a sturdy farm-cart, that contained a heavily-bound, scurvy-looking man, whose eyes drooped in spite of his fate. "They've drugged 'im, poor sot, so's the monster knows it'll get an easy meal. They'll take milady up the hill, with a lot of weepin' and wailin', and they'll give each of the heroes a little gold key that unlocks her chain. But it's the thief they'll be trying to the stake, not her. Reckon you that if some one of them heroes ever *does* slay the beast, that the tales will be sayin' he saved her from the stake-shackles, 'stead of that poor bastard?"

"Probably."

"Pity they *haven't* tried to feed her to the beast—it'd probably die of indigestion, she's that spoiled."

They watched the procession pass with a jaundiced eye, then retired to their inn.

"I think, all things considered," Tarma said after some thought, as they sat together at a small table in the comfort and quiet of their room at the inn, "that the best time to get at the thing is at the weekly feeding. But *after* it's eaten, not before."

"Lady knows, I'd hate being part of that disgusting parade, but you're right. And while it's in the open— well, magics may bounce off *its* hide, but there are still things I could do to the area around it. Open up a pit under it, maybe."

"We'd have to—" Tarma was interrupted by wild cheering. When peering out of their window brought no enlightenment, they descended to the street.

The streets were full of wildly rejoicing people, who caught up the two strangers, pressing food and drink on them. There was too much noise for them to ask questions, much less hear the answers.

An increase in the cheers signaled the arrival of the possible answer, and by craning their necks, the two saw the clue to the puzzle ride by, carried on the shoulders of six merchants. It was one of the would-be heroes they'd seen going out with the procession; he was blood-covered, battered and bruised, but on the whole, in very good shape. Behind him came the cart that had held the thief. Now it held the head of something that must have been remarkably ugly and exceedingly large in life. The head just barely fit into the cart.

The crowd carried him to the same inn where the two women were staying, and deposited him inside. Tarma seized Kethry's elbow and gestured toward the stableyard; she nodded, and they wriggled their way through the mob to the deserted court.

"Well! Talk about a wasted trip!" Tarma wasn't sure whether to be relieved or annoyed.

"I hate to admit it—" Kethry was clearly chagrined.

"So Need's stopped nagging you?"

Kethry nodded.

"Figures. Look at it this way—what good would Lord Havirn's daughter *or* his lands have done us?"

"We could have used the lands, I guess—" Tarma's snort cut Kethry's words off. "Ah, I suppose it's just as well. I'm not all that unhappy about not having to face that beast down. We've paid for the room, we might as well stay the night."

"The carnival they're building up ought to be worth the stay. Good thing Warrl can take care of himself. I doubt he'll be able to sneak past that mob."

The carnival was well worth staying for. Lord Havirn broached his own cellar and kitchens, and if wine wasn't flowing in the fountains it was because the general populace was too busy pouring it down their collective throats. Neither of the women were entirely sober when they made their way up to their beds.

A few scant minutes after reaching their room, however, Kethry *was* sober again.

The look of shock and surprise on her partner's face quickly sobered Tarma as well. "What's wrong?"

"It's Need—she's pulling again."

"Oh, bloody Hell!" Tarma groaned and pulled her leather tunic back over her head. "Good thing we hadn't put the candle out. How far?"

"Close. It's not anywhere near as strong as the original pull, either. I think it's just one person this time—"

Kethry opened the door to their room, and stared in amazement at the disheveled girl huddled in the hall just outside.

The girl was shivering; had obviously been weeping. Her clothing was torn and seemed to have been thrown on. Both of them recognized her as the inn's chambermaid. She looked up at them with entreaty and burst into a torrent of tears.

"Oh, bloody Hell!" Tarma repeated.

When they finally got the girl calmed down enough to speak, what she told them had them both incensed. The great "hero" was not to be denied anything, by Lord Havirn's orders—except, of course, the lord's daughter. *That* must wait until they were properly wedded. That he need not languish out of want, however, the innkeeper had been ordered to supply him with a woman, should he want one.

Naturally, he wanted one. Unfortunately, the lady who usually catered to that sort of need was "inconvenienced" with her moon-days. So rather than pay the fee of an outside professional, the innkeeper had sent up the chambermaid, Fallan, without bothering to tell her *why* she was being sent.

"—'m a good girl, m'lady. I didna understand 'im at first; thought 'e wanted another bath or somesuch. But 'e grabbed me 'for I knew what 'e was about. An' 'e tore me clothes, them as took me a month's wages. An' 'e—'e—" another spate of tears ensued. " 'E was mortal cruel, m'lady. 'E—when I didna please 'im, 'e beat me. An' when 'e was done, 'e threw me clothes at me, an' 'e yelled for me master, an' tol' 'im I was no bloody good, an' what did 'e think 'e was about, anyway givin' 'im goods that was neither ripe nor green? Then me master, 'e—'e— turned me off! Tol' me t' make meself vanish, or 'e'd beat me 'imself!"

"He did what?" Tarma was having trouble following the girl, what with her thick accent and Tarma's own rising anger.

"He discharged her. The bastard sent her up to be raped, then had the bloody almighty gall to throw her out afterward!" Kethry was holding on to her own temper by the thinnest of threads.

"I've got nowhere to go, no ref'rences—what 'm I

going to do?" the girl moaned, hugging her knees to her chest, still plainly dazed.

"She'enedra, get the brandy. I'll put her in my bed, you and I can sleep double," Kethry said in an undertone. "Child, worry about it in the morning. Here, drink this."

"I *can't* go back 'ome. They 'aven't got the means to feed the childer still too little to look for work," she continued in a monotone. "I bain't virgin for two years now, but I been as good as I could be. I bain't no lightskirt. All I ever wanted was t' put by enough for a dower—maybe find some carter, some manservant willin' t' overlook things; have a few childer of me own." She was obviously not used to hard liquor; the brandy took hold of her very quickly. She mumbled on for a bit longer, then collapsed in Kethry's bed and fell asleep.

"I'd like to skewer this damned innkeeper," Tarma growled.

Kethry, who'd been checking the girl for hurts, looked up with a glower matching Tarma's. "That makes two of us. Just because the girl's no virgin is no excuse for what he did. And then to turn her out afterward—" Tarma could see her hands were trembling with controlled rage. "Come look at this."

"Ungentle," was a distinct understatment for the way the girl had been mauled about. She was bruised from knee to neck, ugly, purple things. Kethry took Need from beneath the bed and placed it beside her, then covered her with the blankets again.

"Well, that will take care of the physical problems, but what about the bruising of her spirit?"

"I don't have any answers for you," Kethry sighed, rage slowly cooling. "But, you know, from the way she talked, it isn't the rape that bothers her so much as the fact that she's been turned out. What we *really* need to do is find her somewhere to go."

"Bloody Hell. And us knowing not a soul here. Well, let's worry about it in the morning."

In the morning, it seemed that their erstwhile charge was determined to take care of the problem by attaching herself to them.

They woke to find her busily cleaning both their

swords—though what she'd made of finding Need beside her when she woke was anyone's guess. Tarma's armor lay neatly stacked, having already been put in good order, and their clothes had been brushed and laid ready. The girl had both pairs of boots beside her, evidently prepared to clean them when she finished with the swords.

"What's all this about?" Tarma demanded, only half awake.

The girl jumped. Her lip quivered as she replied, looking ready to burst into tears again. "Please, m'lady, I want to go with ye when y' leave. Ye haven't a servant, I know. See? I c'n take good care of ye both. An' I can cook, too, an' wash an' mend. I don' eat much, an' I don' need much. Please?"

"I was afraid this would happen," Kethry murmured. "Look, Fallan, we really *can't* take you with us. We don't need a servant—" she stopped as the girl burst into tears again, and sighed with resignation. "Oh, Bright Lady. All right, we'll take you with us. But it won't be forever, just until we can find you a new place."

" 'Just until we can find you a new place.' She'enedra, I am beginning to think that this time that sword of yours has driven us too far. Three days on the road, and it's already beginning to seem like three years."

Fallan had not adjusted well to the transition from chambermaid to wanderer. It wasn't that she hadn't tried, but to her, citybred as she was, the wilderness was a place beset by unknown perils at every turn. Every snake, every insect was poisonous; she stayed up, kept awake by terror, for half of every night, listening to the sounds beyond their fire. Warrl and the mares terrified her.

They'd had to rescue her twice—once from the river she'd fallen into, once from the bramble thicket she'd *run* into, thinking she heard a bear behind her. For Fallen, every strange crackle of brush meant a bear; one with Fallan-cutlets on his mind.

At the same time, she was stubbornly refusing to give up. Not once did she ask the two women to release her from her self-imposed servitude. No matter how frightened she became, she never confessed her fear, nor did she rush to one or the other of them for protection. It was as if she was determined to somehow prove—to herself, to them—that she was capable of facing whatever they could.

"What that girl needs is a husband," Kethry replied wearily. "Give her things to do inside four walls, things she knows, and she's fine, but take her out here, and she's hopeless. If it weren't for the fact that the nearest town is days away, I'd even consider trying to get her another job at an inn."

"And leave her open to the same thing that happened before? Face it, that's exactly what would happen. Poor Fallen is just not the type to sell her favors by choice, and not ugly enough to be left alone. Bless her heart, she's too obedient and honest for her own good—and, unfortunately, not very bright. No solution, Greeneyes. Too bad most farmers around here don't need or can't afford woman-servants, or—" she stopped with an idea suddenly occuring to her. Kethry had the same idea.

"Landric?"

"The very same. He seems kind enough—"

"No fear of that. He's Wheel-bound. When he took that tattoo, he took with it a vow to balance the evil he'd done previously with good. That's why he became a farmer, I suspect, to balance the death he'd sown as a soldier with life. Did his children look ill-treated?"

"Healthiest, happiest bunch I've seen outside of a clan gathering. The only trouble—"

"—is, does she know how to deal with younglings? Let's head for Landric's place. You can talk to her on the way, and we'll see how she handles them when we get there."

Two days of backtracking saw them on the road within a few furlongs of Landric's farm. Landric's eldest spotted them as he had before, and ran to tell his father. Landric met them on the road just where it turned up the path to his farmstead, his face wreathed in smiles.

"I had not thought to see you again, when the news came that the monster had been slain," he told Tarma warmly.

"Then you also know that we arrived just a bit too late to do the slaying ourselves."

"If I were to tell the truth, I'm just as grateful for your sake. The hero had a cadre of six hirelings, and all six of them died giving him the chance he needed. I would have been saddened had their fate been yours. Oh, that little pet you left for the children has been beyond price."

"If we'd gone down that thing's gullet, you wouldn't have been half as saddened as I!" Tarma chuckled. Out of the corner of her eye she saw Kethry, Fallan, and the children entering the house. "Listen, you're in the position to do us a favor, Landric. I hate to impose upon you, but—well, we've got another 'pet' to find a home for." Quickly and concisely she laid out Fallan's pathetic story. "—so we were hoping you'd know someone willing to take her in. She's a good worker, I can tell you that; she's just not suited for the trail. And to tell you the truth, she's not very flexible. I think we shock her."

He smiled slowly. "I am not quite *that* stupid, Sworn One. You hope that *I* will take her in, don't you?"

"Oh, well, I'll admit the thought did cross my mind," Tarma smiled crookedly.

"It is a possibility. It would neatly balance some wrongs I committed in my soldiering days. . . ." His eyes grew thoughtful. "I'll tell you—let's see how she does with the younglings. Then I'll make my decision."

By the look in Landric's eyes when they crossed the threshold, Tarma knew he'd made up his mind. It wasn't just that Fallan had duplicated their feats of setting the place to rights, (although it wasn't near the task they'd had) nor was it the savory stew-odor coming from the kettle on the hearth, nor the sight of five of the six children lined up with full bowls on their knees, neatly stowing their dinner away. No, what made up Landric's mind was the sight of Fallan, the youngest on her lap, cuddling him and drying his tears over the skinned knee he'd just acquired, and she looking as blissful as if she'd reached heaven.

They stayed a week, and only left because they'd agreed to act as caravan-guards before all this began and would be late if they stayed longer.

Fallan had been in her element from the moment they'd entered the door. And with every passing day, it looked as though Landric was thinking of her less as a hireling and more in the light of something else.

"Are you thinking what I'm thinking?" Tarma asked her partner as soon as they were out of earshot.

"That he'll be wedding her before too long? Probably. There's mutual respect and liking there, and Fallan loves the children. She even likes the little beastie! It's not a life that would appeal to me or you, but it looks like exactly what *she* wants. There've been worse things to base a marriage on."

"Like the lord's daughter and her 'hero'?" Tarma grimaced. "I don't know whether to feel sorrier for him or her or both. From the little I saw and heard, she's no prize, and m'lord is likely to have made an arrangement that keeps the pursestrings in his hands and out of her husband's."

"Which is hardly what he'd have counted on when he went to slay the monster. On the other hand, we have reason to know the man is an insensitive brute. They deserve each other," Kethry replied thoughtfully.

"As Landric and Fallan do. There're your real heroes, the people who keep coping, keep trying, no matter how many blows Fate takes at them. Nobody'll make a song about them, but they're heroes all the same," Tarma said soberly, then grinned. "Now, if we're going to get *our* desserts, we'll have to earn 'em. Let's ride, She'enedra— before that damned sword of yours finds something else it wants us to do!"

THE WOODLAND OF ZARAD-THRA

by Robin W. Bailey

The first story chosen every year for an anthology to some degree sets the tone of the whole volume. Since Misty Lackey's "A Tale of Heroes" was domestic, my following choices were an attempt to balance this by external heroism and adventure; since it featured a time-honored convention of a soldier paired with a sorceress of gentler style, I decided to balance it by a totally different style of contrasted women.

These two wholly different stories in a sense set the tone of this year's book.

Robin Bailey appeared in the first of these Sword and Sorceress volumes, with "Child of Orcus," the story of a female gladiator who challenged death, not in the abstract as all gladiators do, but, like Orpheus, in the particular. At first I thought "Robin" as it often is, in this country, to be a female name because Bailey's heroine did not fall into any of the traps for woman characters delineated by men, weak creatures, or such wild wish-fulfillments as never bore sword on land or sea.

I state that this is the mark of a writer who need not be defined by gender at all; if I so define him, it is only to say to other writers, "Go thou and do likewise." Now, not content to create a female gladiator, Bailey has taken on the difficult and challenging task of creating a protagonist saddled unwillingly with a baby; it's difficult, as *women* writers never tire of pointing out, to go out and have adventures in the intervals between changing diapers. Robin Bailey adds a unique perspective to this singular dilemma; and while he does not solve the story exactly as a woman writer might, I do not think his solution will annoy or offend our female audience. Although many of the writers in this volume (including the editor) are mothers, I can't remember a problem of this type which has been better handled.

Robin Bailey, since his first appearance here, has published two novels entitled *SKULLGATE*, (October 85) and *BLOODSONG*, (April 86).

T he icy wind howled mournfully and whipped the driving snowflakes into a churning, pelting frenzy that stung Cymbalin's face and eyes. Though she was clothed from head to toe in garments of fur, she felt as if the very marrow in her bones was freezing. Only the small, struggling bundle deep inside her several tunics provided any warmth at all, but she took no comfort from it. She lurched through the storm, clutching the damnable little brat as it nipped and gummed her swollen breast. Time and again she had thought to abandon it beneath a bush or in a drift. It occurred to her that it might yet suffocate inside the thick furs, and she would be free of it.

If only it would go to sleep and leave her alone for awhile. She was sore from its constant feeding, and she was weary to the point of falling down. Cymbalin peered up desperately through the looming trees as she trudged onward. The bleak, gray sky segued toward darkness as the goddess, Night, folded stygian wings about the earth. Yet Cymbalin dared not stop. To fall asleep, she knew, was to freeze and die in this wintry forest.

The child began its incessant crying once again. Its body felt hot against her flesh. Fever, she wondered fearfully? Visions of plague-twisted forms and funeral fires still tormented her. She saw again the flames that leaped so high and danced with such hellish, crackling glee among the piles of infected corpses, some of whom had been her friends. She had been lucky to escape from Ischandi before the king's soldiers could quarantine the city. But had she escaped the disease? Was this squawling spawn of her own foolish loins even now poisoning the air she breathed?

Gods, how had she ever been so stupid as to let a mere lieutenant swell her belly? All the pleasure she'd taken from his sleek, hard body had faded from her mind when she'd discovered she was with child. He'd laughed and told her it was her problem, not his. Then he'd walked away.

As long as possible she'd tried to hide her condition. Finally, though, even the squad commander had noticed her increasing weight. That had brought a swift end to her mercenary service. And since she'd become unable to fulfill the term-year of her contract, they'd sent her off without so much as a copper coin to buy a meal.

If only she'd thought to cut her lover's throat before she left. The memory of his blood might have assuaged her aching thirst. She scooped up a handful of snow and pushed it into her mouth.

"Shut up!" she snapped at the wailing child. "Stop your screaming!" It was as much a plea as an order. It had no effect at all, and she tried to shut her eyes to the shrill, plaintive sounds.

She had stolen and whored her way to Ischandi after her discharge in hopes of finding an herbalist there with skill enough to shrivel the seed in her body without poisoning her in the process. But her pregnancy had been too far along by that time. None of the reliable practitioners would help her, and no matter how desperate, she'd known better than to deal with the back-alley quacks.

She'd stayed in Ischandi, pilfering enough to afford a decent midwife. The child had been not three days old when the cry of plague went up through the city, sending everyone into a panic and the soldiers of the King of Shardaha racing to seal off the city from the rest of the countryside.

Now she cursed the impulse that had made her seize up the infant along with her sword, but there had been little time to think. The disease had struck with frightening speed, claiming a score of lives in that first night. Ignoring the ache in her loins, she had gone to the window to watch the trundle cart roll by with the corpses. She had seen the oozing blood and pus, the red sores

that pock-marked the faces. And she had seen the pyres
at the center of the city waiting to receive the dead.

Then she had run as fast as her weakened body and
the burden next to her breast would allow her. She had
seen plague once before. There would be no safe place in
all of Shardaha, she knew. As it had infected the city it
would infect the king's soldiers, and they would carry it
throughout the land.

So it was out of Shardaha she headed, toward the
border and neighboring Rhianoth.

The baby's crying reached a sharper note, snapping
her out of her reverie. She cursed and rocked the child at
the same time, opening the neck of her garments a little
to give it fresh air. *Shut up, shut up,* she wished, ignoring
the cold wind on her exposed skin. *At least you feed,
ungrateful wretch. Two days, and not a bite for me!* She
clutched the hilt of her sword, then the dagger sheathed
beside it. Perhaps it would be better to kill the little
noisemaker now, quickly. They were surely doomed to
feeze before they got through this forest. She would at
least have a few hours' peace before her gods claimed
her.

She gazed upward. Encased in winter ice, the tall trees
reared defiantly against the sky. The blackened branches
wove a crystal lace above her head. As the woodland
grew more dense, a canopy formed, a roof that kept out
some of the biting wind and snow. She strained to see in
the nearly total darkness, fearing roots that might trip
her or holes that might swallow her up, but a greater fear
of the plague compelled her limbs. She ignored the com-
plaints of her muscles and pushed onward.

Cymbalin had studied maps during her time in the
army of Shardaha. She wasn't sure, but it was possible
she had entered the huge forest that grew along the
border between Shardaha and Rhianoth. That gave her
some small hope, but every step she took seemed a
major labor.

She stopped suddenly and stared at the ground. There
were footprints in the snow. How long she had been
following them she couldn't recall; she had been too
dazed, too lost in her thoughts. She uttered another

curse. The steps were widely spaced, the pattern irregular. Each one had made a roiling mess of the unblemished snow. Cymbalin swore loudly this time. Someone had come this way recently, running as if devils were chewing their heels.

It wasn't the cold, then, that brought a chill to her spine. Whoever came this way might be infected with the plague. She might even now be breathing air that had issued from tainted lungs, inhaling pestilence. She examined her hands for any sign of the red splotches. They appeared clean and pure, if pale from the cold. But she was again aware of the warmth of the babe inside her tunic and an earlier fear that the child might also be diseased. She shivered, uncertain what to do. Finally, she gripped her sword's hilt for reassurance and trudged after the footsteps. The path was narrow, and short of plunging into the undergrowth, there was no other way for her to go.

Her stomach growled pitifully, but there would be no appeasing it this night. At least, the infant had quietened.

Cymbalin heard the girl long before she saw her. At first, she had thought the baby had begun to whimper again. But it hadn't been the child. The sound grew louder as she followed the footsteps until, at last, she spied a fur-clad figure prone upon the snow.

The girl shook with plaintive sobbing in a manner that reminded Cymbalin of the convulsive twitching of Ischandi's plague-victims. She clapped a sleeve over her mouth and nose and stopped, considering a retreat along the forest path. But there was only disease back that way, so she gripped her sword's hilt and decided to tread a wide course around the stranger.

But then the girl lifted her eyes, and Cymbalin saw it was not plague, rather a terrible fear that caused such shivering. She met that imploring gaze and studied the ivory face that regarded her from within an ermine hood. Gleaming tears had frozen, forming tiny pearls on her cheeks and lashes.

The girl raised a hand in supplication. "Please!" she moaned. "Dear gods, take it and leave me alone!"

A necklace glimmered on that mittened palm. Even in

the darkness the jewels shone with their own inner radiance, burning in sets of gold.

Cymbalin put aside her trepidation and took a step closer. The girl gave a choked cry, cowered and thrust her face into the snow, covering her head with her arms as if to ward off a blow.

But Cymbalin only touched the girl's shoulder. "I won't hurt you," she promised softly. Then, she jerked her hand away, aware that the death sickness could be transmitted by a touch. She wanted to console this younger woman and ease her fear, but there was no point in taking foolish chances. "You don't need to be afraid of me," she said, folding her arms around herself and under the bundle within her clothes. "I won't rob you."

The girl looked slowly up again and tried to crawl backward through the fleecy whiteness. Hysteria gleamed in her eyes. "I won't go back!" she spat, raking the air with her nails. "Kill me right here, but you won't take me back!"

There was fire in the speech, but the anger died quickly. A fresh flood of tears burst free, and the girl threw herself forward in the snow again, trembling.

Cymbalin gritted her teeth, biting back foul language. It was enough she was saddled with one baby. She looked contemptuously upon the weeping heap at her feet, so representative of all she detested about her own sex. She had a mind to just get up and leave the stupid girl to freeze. Yet, she recalled those words spoken in such terror! If something or someone threatened that one, then there might be danger on this trail for Cymbalin, too.

Better to find out now what it was.

She had tried gentleness. This time, she knelt, lifted the girl's chin and dealt her a rough slap. "Enough," she growled. "Stop that blubbering and look at me, or I'll really redden your cheeks."

But the slap had the wrong effect. The fearful girl only wailed louder.

Then, the infant next to Cymbalin's breast began to cry as well, perhaps awakened by the violence of the blow or by its mother's angry voice. But those small peals accomplished what Cymbalin's threats could not. The girl sat up suddenly. Her tears ceased, and she stared wide-eyed at Cymbalin.

"A child!" the girl whispered incredulously. "You have a child inside your clothes. Bring it out. It can't possibly breathe inside all those furs!" She extended her hands. The necklace shimmered with the movement, dangling from one fist.

But as she reached to touch the squirming lump within Cymbalin's tunics, the older woman slapped her hands away. The ornament flew, and the girl scrambled to retrieve it from the snow.

"Little fool!" Cymbalin snapped. "If I bring it out the cold will freeze its blood, and the chill air would fill its lungs. Now, tell me your name, and say what in the nine hells you're doing out here all alone. Do you run from the plague, too, or from something else?"

The girl clutched her prize to her breast, eyed Cymbalin with the look of a desperate beast, a look that gradually faded. Then she opened the neck of her own garments and dropped the necklace within.

"Plague?" she said, tilting her head, looking puzzled. "I've heard nothing about plague. My name is Iella." She crawled on her hands and knees through the snow, closer to Cymbalin. Again she reached out to touch the baby within the furs, and again Cymbalin slapped her hand away. Iella pouted and stared away into the dark recesses. "I've been a prisoner of Zarad-Thra. He claims these woods."

Another sharp chill raced up Cymbalin's spine, a sensation no winter garment could keep out. She hugged her child and rose to her feet. *Zarad*. That was a Shardahani word, both a name and a title. It meant wizard.

"I thought that you were one of his demons until I heard the baby cry," Iella continued. "Zarad-Thra didn't send you to bring me back to him?"

"My name is Cymbalin," she answered, shaking her head. "And some men have called me a demon." She forced a smile. "Usually as they wiped blood from scratches on their faces."

Iella got to her feet, dried her tears with a sleeve and

walked a slow circle around Cymbalin. Glistening ice
clung to the long strands of blond hair that spilled from
beneath the ermine hood. Against the pallor of her skin
her eyes shone like black fire. Obviously, hunger had
taken a toll on her once voluptuous form. Iella was gaunt
and frail-looking.

"You could pass for a demon, yourself," Cymbalin
remarked.

"I've never seen a woman who carried a sword," Iella
said with a trace of awe. "Can you use it?"

Cymbalin frowned, trying to swallow her prejudices.
Where she came from the woman *had* to fight right
alongside their men. The villages were too small and the
raids too constant to allow the luxury of the softer life for
anyone. A woman either fought with her father or husband, vanquishing the enemy, or she became a piece of
chattel passed from one warring tribe to another at fate's
whim.

But in this part of the world the women seemed to
take pride in their weakness. It was more than she could
fathom.

"I use it well enough," she answered at last.

"What about your child?" Iella said, stepping closer to
Cymbalin. Her eyes darted to the lump the baby made in
the older woman's furs, but this time she kept her hands
to herself. "Does it have a name? Is it a boy or a girl?"

Cymbalin backed away reflexively, uncomfortably aware
that she had been rocking the infant, trying to calm its
crying. "It has no name," she muttered. "It came into
this world uninvited and unwelcome. It's a burden, that's
all. A *thing*. I don't dignify things with names."

An expression of shock flickered across Iella's face.
"That's a hard attitude," she snapped. Then, she softened. "Let me hold it." She held out her arms.

"I told you," Cymbalin said, keeping Iella at bay with
a glare. "The cold would surely kill it. Now, think about
your own hide. If there's a wizard in these woods, then
we'd best make tracks as fast as we can for Rhianoth."

"I could carry the baby," Iella persisted. "That would
free you to use your sword if Zarad-Thra attacks."

That seemed reasonable, Cymbalin thought, brushing

her hand against the weapon at her hip. Yet, she would have to unfasten several belts and remove several garments to get at the child. Her gaze raked through the dark corners of the forest, then along the branches of the trees, searching for any sign of danger. "We seem safe enough," she said finally. "I'll carry it a little farther."

Cymbalin turned away and started along the path again. She'd wasted too much time in talk, and she was growing cold from idleness. She set a brisk pace, finding some hidden well of strength within herself, refusing to show weakness or fatigue before a girl she'd found blubbering upon the snowy ground.

To her surprise, though, Iella showed no difficulty keeping up with her.

After awhile, the child fell silent. The crunch of their footsteps in the snow and the labor of their breathing made the only sounds. Cymbalin felt the baby's feathery breath upon her breast and realized the infant was dozing. She sighed with relief, grateful for a respite from the little mouth's sucking and pulling.

"That necklace," she said at last to Iella, hoping conversation would help her to forget the leaden weariness growing in her legs. "Where'd you get it? It was beautiful."

Iella clutched the ornament within her furs where it rested near her breast. Cymbalin saw the motion and smirked. *A babe at my breast and cold stones at hers. Which has it worse?* The thought flickered through her head before she could push it away. She certainly knew who had the greater treasure, and the stones would warm with the heat of Iella's body.

Iella seemed to hesitate. Then she said, "An admirer gave it to me. I was wearing it when Zarad-Thra stole me away."

Cymbalin bit her lip at mention of that name again. "Tell me more about this man, Zarad-Thra," she said. "If he's a threat to us, I'd better know something about him."

"Zarad-Thra is no man," Iella answered glumly, "but an evil creature of magic, a beast with monstrous appetites."

The words of a true victim, and a cowardly one at that.

Cymbalin scoffed privately, making a face, secure in the knowledge that Iella's fur-lined hood prevented the girl from seeing the expression.

"I was a tavern dancer in Shalikos," Iella continued. "Men came from all around to watch me." She hesitated again, then smiled. "Oh, I had my admirers, and they all gave me things—expensive things—but I never gave myself to them. Not to one of them. She ran a hand over her breasts as she spoke and clutched the necklace once more. She let go a long sigh. "Several nights ago Zarad-Thra came to the tavern. I didn't know him then—he was just another man, I thought." She wrapped her arms around herself as if the cold had suddenly penetrated her furs. "But when I left to go home, he was waiting for me in the alley. His eyes burned with red fires; I couldn't look away from him!" She swallowed hard, and fear drew her mouth into a taut line. "The next thing I remembered was waking deep in his cave somewhere in this forest."

"You call him *zarad*," Cymbalin interrupted. "Did you see his power? What gods does he worship?"

"Gath," she answered with a shudder. "the Chaos Lord. Zarad-Thra prays at an ancient tree that grows at the very heart of these woods. He performs sacrifices there." She shuddered again, and her eyes swept the gloom around them. "That's why he took me captive. Do you know what day this is?"

Cymbalin considered, then nodded with understanding. "The day of the spider," she said softly, "in the month of the spider and the year of the spider." She didn't need much knowledge of magic to appreciate that such a time would be sacred to Zarad-Thra. The spider was special to the Chaos Lord. Some claimed it was Gath, himself, who created the small creature to weave a small piece of order out of the vast churning abyss he ruled. In Cymbalin's memory there had never been a cult to Gath, but there were tales of his individual worshipers. For them this would be a night of power and purpose.

"You were to be his sacrifice," Cymbalin guessed.

Iella nodded. "I lived a chaste life and guarded my

virtue." See where it has led me? When I think of some of those handsome boys who vied for me. . . !"

Even as she said it, Cymbalin suspected Iella was something less than chaste—at least, in the classical sense. Perhaps it was a certain tension in the lower lip as she said handsome *boys*. Or perhaps it was just a note in her voice that couldn't quite be disguised, a note of experience. Still, Cymbalin allowed a small grin. It was the first hint of humor her new companion had shown. And anyway, who was she to judge? She thought bitterly of the baby she carried. After all, she, too, had a taste for the *boys*.

"But if his power is so great," Cymbalin asked, attempting to turn her thoughts from her problems, "how did you get away?"

Iella squeezed her eyes shut and clapped a hand over her mouth. For a moment she said nothing. Then words came hissing between clenched teeth.

"All this afternoon Zarad-Thra slept in the embrace of a mandrake powder, resting for the ritual he expected to perform tonight.' She gave Cymblain a furtive glance, and the fear was there once more in her eyes. "He locked me in a small tunnel, but while he slept I managed to work an old iron nail loose from a little bed he'd provided me." She swallowed hard again, and all the color fled from her cheeks as she talked, whether from the cold or the memory Cymbalin could not decide. "At dusk he came to fetch me, but the drug must have still worked in his veins for he was slow and careless." She faltered, staring at her right hand. "I drove the nail into his eye. It was horrible! He screamed, and there was all this blood!" She rubbed the hand over her sleeve as if to wipe it clean. "I pushed him out of my way, and ran. I must have run for hours. Then, when I heard you coming along the path I thought you were a demon, and I lost all hope."

Cymbalin shivered. The smart thing to do would be to leave this baggage as far behind as possible. She had no desire to get caught between a wounded wizard and his prey. She increased her pace, hoping Iella might fall behind. But the girl stayed right by her side.

When they had gone some distance Cymbalin finally stopped to rest, having succeeded not in losing Iella but only in exhausting herself. She cursed the pain in her legs and the flabby soreness of her breasts and her general weakness. She opened the necks of her tunics, peered down and tried to see her baby, but it was too dark and the garments too close. All she accomplished was to wake the child. It did not cry, but pushed its small mouth to her nipple again. Cymbalin groaned softly in anger and anguish; there was little or no milk left in her breasts, nothing remained but a strange yellowish fluid that had frightened her when she had first noticed it. There was nothing to do, though, but bear the suckling.

Iella spied a partially exposed log just ahead and guided them to it. They sat, and Cymbalin almost resented the girl. Itella seemed in far better shape than a tavern girl had a right to be, almost unaffected by their swift, steady progress, even eager to move on. Cymbalin felt her own fatigue more acutely and scowled.

"You're tired," Iella observed. "Let me hold the baby for awhile. It must be heavy after you've carried it so far."

Cymbalin wrapped her arms around the infant, feeling it wriggle inside her furs. It felt too warm, and again she thought of fever and the plague and knew the taste of fear.

"Let me hold it," Iella persisted. "We can think of a name together."

"No name!" Cymbalin snapped, pushing Iella backward off the log when she reached to unfasten Cymbalin's belt. "I told you once. Call it my *burden* if you have to call it anything. Or my *sorrow*. By any name, it's only trouble to me."

Iella rose to her feet and brushed snow from her garments. Anger smoldered in her dark eyes, and her hands curled into fists. But then, the fists relaxed, and the girl sat down again meekly. "If the small thing is such a burden to you, then give it to me and get on with your selfish life. I'll give it a home and plenty of love. It would be wonderful to have a baby if I didn't have to take a man in the bargain!"

Cymbalin glowered at the stupid girl, got to her feet and started off through the snow without looking back. A wet crunching on the path behind her, though, told that Iella still followed. She muttered an insult that would have colored a soldier's cheeks and trudged on through the darkness and the trees.

Then, she hesitated and stopped.

A small flame hovered in the air directly in her way, flickering warmly against the woodland gloom. As she watched, it began to spark and twist. It flared suddenly brighter, crackled and writhed, taking a strange, unnatural shape, a nearly human form.

Cymbalin caught her breath. A hideous face leered at her through a mask of fire. The hellish warrior floated on the air, blocking the path. It extended a clawed hand; there came a burst of flame and dark smoke from the creature's palm, and suddenly it bore a great, burning sword. A venomous grin split the monster's lips.

Fear spread through Cymbalin, an unworthy paralysis that gripped her heart and squeezed. Her own sword shone redly in the dancing flamelight that sheathed her foe. Its steel edge seemed pitifully inadequate against the demon's weapon. She had not even been aware of drawing it, but she deepened her stance without thinking, turning aside to offer the narrowest target and to pull her child away from her sword arm.

From the corner of her eye she spied Iella. The gutless little bitch had prostrated herself, weeping and pleading, on the ground.

"What do you want of us?" Cymbalin hissed, hating the feeble sound of her voice as the words chattered through her teeth.

The demon's grin widened, revealing slender fangs that dripped with lava heat.

A sharp pain burst behind Cymbalni's left temple. She groaned aloud as one eye seemed to draw involuntarily shut. The demon sucked her memory, her knowledge, her experiences, pausing here and there to gnaw on a detail, to chew on her hopes and dreams. She could not resist the mind-fangs that ground and swallowed her perceptions and spit them out again.

Then, her pain ended, and the demon spoke to her in the Shardahani tongue. "I am the Plague you fear and flee, human-woman. One touch from me and your brain will burn with the fever and sickness will feast on your body."

Red splotches rose on her sword hand as the demon spoke. The splotches turned to boils that popped and sent thick, yellow pus running into her palm. Cymbalin screamed and dropped her sword and held her hand as far from her face as she could.

"My master is Zarad-Thra," the demon continued. "Step from my path, and I will remove the plague, take the Iella-thief and trouble you no more."

At his word the boils healed and vanished and the red blemishes on her skin faded away. Cymbalin sagged to her knees, sobbing with relief, unconsciously clutching her baby at the demon's feet.

The vision gave a low chuckle, floated around her and moved toward Iella. A raw, high-pitched shriek ripped from the terrified girl, snapping Cymbalin from her own hysteria. A hot desperation filled her. She snatched up her fallen sword, rose and swung with all her might.

The blade passed through shoulder, spine, ribs.

Unharmed, the demon turned to face her, laughter bubbling on its lips. Again, Cymbalin raised her sword, but this time her fiery opponent brought his own weapon up. The blades met, and a spark leaped from the creature's sword and raced down the length of steel to touch her hand. Cymbalin gave a sharp, choked cry as the shock knocked her off her feet.

The child within her tunics let out a terrific wail. Tiny hands began to knead and claw her tender breasts. Iella whimpered uselessly on the snow, petrified by her fear. Cymbalin lifted painfully onto one elbow as the demon floated over her.

"Do not interfere, human-woman," the demon advised. Cymbalin felt the heat of his weapon's point near her face. "The Iella-thief deserves its fate. It has robbed my master and blinded his eye. Now it would use you to save it from its destiny. But you have not the power to fight me."

"It lies!" Iella screamed. "I didn't rob anybody. Zarad-Thra wants to sacrifice me. Don't let it take me, Cymbalin, kill it!"

Cymbalin glanced toward her sword, knowing she could not reach it. "That necklace!" she shouted, filled with equal measures of fear and anger. "Where did you get it?"

Iella"s eyes widened, and she crawled backward a pace through the snow. "I told you! An admirer gave it to me. I was wearing it when Zarad-Thra took me. The demon lies!"

Laughter drowned Iella's next words, and the demon flared brighter with its mirth. "Oh, my master chose well! You have earned the Chaos Lord's embrace to endanger this human-woman and her spawn with such lies. Well you knew your fate when you came to Zarad-Thra and volunteered to save him on this night of nights. But it was all a ruse." The demon turned and spoke its speech to Cymbalin. "It drugged my master, and thinking him asleep did that which it truly came to do—help itself to Zarad-Thra's treasure, for it is a thief well-known in these parts. But Zarad-Thra is no ordinary human, and its drug was inadequate. Still it was enough to befuddle him, and when he stumbled after it, it drove a small gold dagger into his right eye and fled with but a single ornament." The demon looked down upon her, and there was almost a pity in its gaze. "Then it found you and thought your pathetic sword might defend it from a wizard's wrath."

"It lies!" Iella shrieked again. "Cymbalin!"

"The necklace!" She shouted in answer. "Stolen from a wizard? Gods damn you, stupid little bitch!"

The demon answered with a grin. "They have. She will be with Gath this night, wedded to Chaos."

"Take her then!" Angry at her helplessness, Cymbalin flung a handful of snow at the creature. "And leave me and my child alone!"

An inhuman sound rent the night. The sword fell from the demon's hand, touched the fleecy ground and vanished with a hiss and a bit of smoke. The creature clawed at his face where her handful of powder had showered it. A sizzling mist exuded between its taloned fingers.

Cymbalin stared, disbelieving. Then she began to move. She didn't understand, but she realized now that the demon's feet had never touched the snow. It was a thing of fire, and snow was wet. Was that why it affected the demon so? Or was it that the demon was evil and the snow was pure? She didn't know or care. She was ignorant of magic. All that mattered was she had a way to strike back.

She scooped a double handful of snow and hurled it at her tormentor. Another shriek was her reward. Doglike, she flung it, working her arms like shovels.

The air filled with a snapping and popping and a thickening, stinking vapor. With a final howl the demon drew up into a tiny spark, no more than a cinder, and winked out.

Cymbalin collapsed on all fours, panting with fatigue and relief. The baby wailed and kicked. Without thinking, she wrapped one arm around it to support its weight. Slowly, her eyes adjusted to the renewed darkness. Then, she heard Iella's sobbing. Crouched in the snow, she looked at Cymbalin and began to crawl toward her.

"Thank you," she said between gasps. "Of course, it lied. . . ."

But Cymbalin was on her feet. She caught Iella's hair in one hand, jerked the girl's head up and dealt her a vicious slap.

"A damn thief!" she shouted, striking her again. "I don't even mind that. Gods know, I've stolen, too. But you could have helped me fight that thing!"

"How?" Iella whined. "It's not over! I should have killed the wizard, but the dagger missed his throat and I lost my nerve. Now he won't stop until he has his sacrifice."

Cymbalin put her foot in Iella's chest and pushed her over. "You disgust me! Guts enough to steal from a drugged pigeon, but in a fight you're worth less than this suckling at my tit." She wiped her hands on her sides and spat. "Find your own way through his wood, Zarad-Thra can have you."

She spun around, retrieved her sword and sheathed it. Without another glance for Iella, she walked away, rocking her child with a gentle moton. Its tiny, shrill mewling still pierced her ears unpleasantly, but at the moment she was just grateful to be alive to hear it. She drew a deep breath and let it out slowly.

How far to Rhianoth, she wondered, letting her anger ebb. How far to the end of this cursed forest?

When she heard the footsteps rushing up behind her, she knew without a doubt it was Iella. She turned, curling her hands into fists to drive the girl away. Too late, she saw the thick, ice-and-snow covered branch that whistled toward her head. Pain and fire exploded in Cymbalin's brow. Even as she fell she wrenched her body so she didn't fall on the child. The last thing she saw before the blackness claimed her was the fearful desperation on Iella's face as the thief bent over her.

"I didn't know his power," were the last words she heard. "I didn't know about this terrible night."

When she awoke she was instantly aware that she was alone. Utterly alone. The baby—her burden—was gone. Only the cold and the wind nipped at her bare breasts and belly. She sat up slowly and gathered the layers of her many tunics about herself and tied the belts that kept them closed. She lumbered to her feet, feeling like a broken doll.

On the ground she spied Iella's club and several drops of her own blood. There was no sight of the child-thief. A warm stream trickled into her eye. The cut on her head was not severe, but gods, it bled. Iella had probably thought her dead. She wobbled unsteadily on her feet and waited for the dizziness to pass.

A smoldering rage grew within her. Cymbalin fastened on her sword belt, noting that her dagger was missing. One more debt to collect from Iella. It took a moment in the darkness, but she found the younger woman's tracks. They led back the way they had come, and Cymbalin followed. Her breasts felt flabby and empty as they bounced inside her clothes; she drew her garments tighter to restrain them. Her thoughts churned, and her anger swelled. Her blade hissed from its sheath.

Iella's tracks abandoned the main trail and led into the deep woods. Snow fell down Cymbalin's neck as she brushed aside a low limb, but she paid little attention. She kept her eyes on the foot-shaped impressions in the snow and thought of nothing else.

The trees loomed around her. It was impossible to see the sky through the snow-covered lacework of branches. She bent low to see Iella's tracks. She didn't know how long she followed them, but the fear began to gnaw at her that the girl was lost, wandering without direction. No matter, Cymbalin thought, she had to follow. She increased her pace; her fingers clenched and unclenched around her sword's hilt.

Suddenly, she stopped. Off to her right came a sound. She strained to see in the dark. The sound repeated, the snap of a limb, the crunch of a booted foot in unbroken snow. Cymbalin hesitated only a moment, then abandoned the tracks and started off in the direction of the noise.

Even in the gloom there was no mistaking the ermine-clothed form of Iella. The thief trudged quickly through the snow, casting furtive glances back over her shoulder as she hurried. Her face was sheened with fear-sweat, and her eyes were wide. Her arms, however, were empty.

Cymbalin stepped from behind a tree and blocked the path. The point of her sword came to rest on a fur-clad shoulder. Iella stopped sharply, then leaped back. She clapped a startled hand to her rounded mouth, her eyes widening even more.

"The child, you worthless little slut," Cymbalin demanded. "Where's the child?"

Iella said nothing, but bolted to her right between a pair of ancient trees. Cymbalin moved faster and intercepted her, fist-first. Iella tumbled to the ground.

"Where's the baby?" Cymbalin shouted again, seizing Iella by the collar, dragging her to her feet.

"You heartless bitch!" Iella shouted bitterly. "What do you care about a damned baby? It was a burden to you, trouble. That's what you said. You wouldn't even give it a name. Well, I've done you a big favor!"

Cymbalin shook the girl until Iella's head rolled around on her shoulders. "Where, gods damn you, where?"

Iella managed to twist free, stumbled and fell. "Zarad-Thra needed his sacrifice," she managed desperately. "I wanted to live. You said you didn't want the baby. So I—I traded it. I took it to the wizard and bargained to save my life!"

A red rage filled Cymbalin. "He accepted? But you blinded him!"

Iella got her feet under her and crouched in the snow. Gone were the girl's tears. Her eyes burned with a desperate feral hysteria. "A baby's virgin soul weighed against the likes of me? Of course he accepted, you fool. It's a far greater prize for his god, great enough to buy off his vengeance if I'm out of his wood by dawn. So I'm free, and you're free, too, without that little baggage to slow you down."

Cymblain advanced on Iella, caught the front of her garment and slammed her against the bole of a tree. "You stole my child," she shouted. "I saved your cursed life, and you repay me this way." She slammed Iella again with ever greater force. "Nobody steals from me, Iella. Whether I wanted the child or not—nobody steals what is mine!"

"But we're free now," Iella screamed back. "We're both free!"

Cymbalin felt a sudden impact and a sharp prickle in her belly. She glanced down as Iella withdrew the dagger she'd taken from Cymbalin's weapon belt. The treacherous thief stared in surprise, and Cymbalin thanked her gods for the many thick tunics she wore and for Iella's weak arm. The blade had barely penetrated enough to break her flesh.

"If it's freedom you want," Cymbalin hissed, releasing the girl and stepping back, "I'll give it to you."

Before she could say more, Iella's eyes narrowed to hateful slits. She raised the dagger and leaped at Cymbalin with a manic shriek.

The older woman stepped aside with contemptuous

grace, drawing her sword in a smooth, flashing arc, showering the white snow with a black spray. Iella was dead before she hit the snow.

Cymbalin stared at the small patch of powder that dissolved under the fountaining throat-blood. Then, she retrieved her dagger from a still-clenched fist.

There was only her baby to think of now. She spied Iella's tracks once more and began to follow them through the dense undergrowth back, she hoped, to Zarad-Thra and her child.

Her child. Even as she ran with all her speed those words jumbled over and over in her head, hammering at her, tormenting her. She remembered the baby's warmth at her breast, and her fear that it had the plague. She recalled its crying and its constant suckling. She hated the child. But she hated herself more for hating it.

Low branches caught her hair as she ran; unseen brambles scratched her face as she bent to keep the tracks in sight. Her thick garments saved her scores of cuts and scrapes, but time and again she tripped and fell on an unseen root or slipped in the snow. Each time she scrambled breathlessly to her feet and chased in the blackness after Iella's footsteps.

She wondered at the time, too. How long had she lain unconscious? How long ago had Iella made her shameful bargain? By the witching hour, she knew, Zarad-Thra must make his sacrifice. That much of magic she was sure. Was it after midnight? Was she too late? The questions pounded her. She ignored her weakness, ignored the building pain in her thighs and ran faster.

At the heart of the woodland, Iella had told her, at an ancient tree, there Zarad-Thra would make his offering to the Chaos Lord. But where in the nine hells was that? The trees were as numberless as the stars she couldn't see; the gloom between them far deeper than the night sky itself.

Then, a tiny familiar crying touched her ears. Over the sound of her own heavy panting she nearly missed it, but it came again and she stopped. Faint and distant, but it was a better beacon than footprints. In fact, she realized, she didn't know if the tracks led to the tree at the woodland's heart or to the cave Iella had spoken of. She moved in the direction of the noise, her heart thumping in her chest.

She had heard that cry once before and rejoiced to be alive. Now she rejoiced that her baby was alive.

She wound her way among old trees and gnarled bushes with one arm before her to sweep the limbs from her face. She made no attempt at stealth, but ran as fast as she could toward the sound of her infant's crying.

Then, suddenly, the cry became a wail, and Cymbalin's heart seemed to stop. She paused only for an instant, then ran on. The wail repeated and dissolved into a raucous, unmistakable bawling. She thanked her gods again for their mercy. Had the sound ended completely, it could only have meant the wizard had made his sacrifice. But her baby was not yet dead, and little lungs proclaimed it to the entire forest.

Through the thick trunks ahead a light suddenly flickered. It occurred to her first that it might be another demon, but she ran on, smug in the knowledge that while there was snow she had no fear of such creatures. As she drew closer, though, she realized it was no demon, but a bonfire glowing in the distance.

Over the crying of her baby there rose a chanting. Cymbalin didn't know the language, but she knew she had found her wizard. She burst out of the woodland into an immense clearing. Suddenly, there was a moon and stars to light the world. Her shadow raced far ahead of her as she ran toward the bonfire and a huge giant of a tree— the only thing that seemed to grow in the clearing.

But Cymbalin stopped again, brought short by shock and disbelief. A scream of purest rage ripped from her throat. In the red light of the fire she saw her child and the slender nails that held it crucified to the black trunk.

As if in answer, the baby's wail reached a new note.

The chanting ceased. A cloaked figure materialized from the far side of the roaring flames, seeming almost to step from them. She could not clearly see his face, but she could fell upon her the menacing gaze of his one good eye.

Shouting curses, she ran at him.

The wizard brought up one hand. His voice was like a blast of thunder in her skull; lightning crackled in his gaze. The word he spoke made no sense, but its power rushed through her, freezing her muscles before she could swing her blade.

Zarad-Thra smiled and spoke again in a tongue she understood. "Iella told me you were dead."

So low did he speak, almost to himself, that the whimpering of the child nearly drowned his words. Cymbalin heard that whimpering; it filled her soul with anguish. "One more lie to add to her charge," she managed.

Zarad-Thra took a step backward in surprise. "You can speak? You resist my spell?"

Cymbalin strained against whatever power held her. The crying of her child was a saw-edge on her soul. But try as she might she could not move. The wizard's icy gaze bound her with a strength greater than chains.

Zarad-Thra stepped closer again, sure of his power. He chuckled and swept back the concealing hood, revealing the new leather patch he wore. "Yes, she was a treacherous one, wasn't she? Why, she fooled me for days, loving me, cajoling me, claiming she wanted to be my acolyte before she finally made a move for my treasure." His smile faded, and he sighed. "Of course, I was probably too gullible. My sacrifice had come knocking on my door, saving me the need to go, shall we say, hunting. I wanted to keep it entertained until this night."

Cymbalin forced out the words. "The only entertaining she'll do now is for the dead in hell!"

The wizard raised an eyebrow, then shrugged. "What a shame. I'd looked forward to paying her a visit when my business allowed it." He touched his patch. "But you prove quite a surprise. We must talk more, though I'm afraid the hour is getting late." He started to turn away.

"Stop!" she shouted. "Leave my baby alone or I swear I'll make you pay!"

Zarad-Thra gave her a harder look. "Quite a surprise! Few men can even blink in the grip of that spell. You manage not only speech, but threats!"

She felt his gaze on her again, and the magical bonds drew tighter, seeming to squeeze the air from her lungs.

Tears oozed down her cheeks as she struggled against him. The sword dropped from her numb hand.

But then, the fire popped loudly, sending up a fountain of hot ash and sparks. An ember settled on the baby's neck, and it let go a high screech of pain.

Whether that cry broke the wizard's concentration, Cymbalin didn't know. Perhaps, it just filled her with the final desperation she needed to break the spell that held her. Zarad-Thra turned at the sound, and she found herself free to act. She snatched up her weapon and swung even as he spun back to her.

The point scored him across the face as he dodged away. Dark blood spattered the snow. His own pain-cry rose on the night as he stumbled back, clutching the ruin of his other eye. "I'm blind!" he screamed. "You've blinded me!" He whirled and ran sightless, straight toward the raging flames of the bonfire, and she thought he meant to destroy himself. At the last instant, though, sensing the heat, he threw up his hands and lurched across the clearing toward the woods, leaving a black spoor to stain the snow's purity.

She wasted no more time on the wizard, but rushed to her baby. The iron nails protruded grotesquely from its tiny hands, and she wrenched them away. The infant shrieked, but she rocked it in her arms and made consoling sounds. Bitterly, she hurled the bits of iron into the fire.

Blood oozed from the holes the nails had made. Cymbalin knelt by the flames and examined the punctures with all the skill she had learned on the battlefield. Its tiny fingers curled and opened; fortunately the nails had been driven between the bones. She pressed snow into the wounds until the bleeding slowed; then she cut strips from her innermost tunic which was not of leather, but of a softer, woven fabric. From that she made bandages.

It was the best she could do. She prayed to her gods that it was enough. The child's crying softened to a whimper. She rocked it by the fire's warmth for a long while, holding it to her bare breast. It didn't feed, though, and that scared her a little.

Her *burden,* she had called it, her *sorrow.* She shook her head slowly, not knowing yet what to do, not knowing what would become of her. She couldn't soldier, not with such a small one. And she didn't want to thieve.

Cymbalin stared beyond the fire into the blackness. There was no sight or sound of Zarad-Thra. She sighed. That was the life she knew: fighting a foe, vanquishing an enemy. What other life was there for her?

She didn't have the answer.

But she got up, wrapped her baby inside all her tunics again and tied the belts so they supported the child's weight near her nipple. Its crying had ceased at last, and it was almost pleasurable to feel its warmth next to her flesh, even to experience its mouth when it began a tentative suckling.

She started off through the snow with a brand from the fire to light her way. As the woods and the miles passed behind her, as she neared the border of plague-infested Shardaha, all thoughts of Iella and Zarad-Thra faded.

The night had been a dream, she told herself, a restless nightmare, a brief fever. She dwelled on it no longer, but gave her attention to more important matters.

And by the time she crossed into Rhianoth, her child had its name.

THE WEEPING OAK

by Charles de Lint

Dryads belong more to the category of fantasy than of sword and sorcery; but they are seldom well handled; I can't think of a good fantasy involving dryads since A. Merritt's classic WOMEN OF THE WOOD: long out of print. Until this one, that is.

Charles de Lint was born in the Netherlands and is presently a citizen of Canada. A full-time writer and musician, he makes his home in Ottawa, Ontario.

As a musician, he plays traditional and contemporary Celtic music on fiddle, bouzouki, guitar and bodhran (an Irish goatskin drum). His writing includes novels, short stories, poetry and non-fiction. He is also the proprietor/ editor of Triskell Press, a small publishing house that specializes in fantasy chapbooks, art prints, and *Dragon fields*, a magazine of fantasy stories that appears on an irregular basis.

The recipient of the William L. Crawford Award for Best New Fantasy Author of 1984 for THE RIDDLE OF THE WREN presented by the International Association for the Fantastic in the Arts, he has written many novels including *HARP OF THE GREY ROSE* (1985).

She found him in Avalarn, one of Cermyn's old forests, the one said to have been a haunt of the wizard Puretongue, though that was long ago. He lay in a nest of leaves, sheltered in a cleft of rocks. Above them, old oaks clawed skyward with greedy boughs, reaching for the clouds.

"I know you," he said, dark eyes opening suddenly to look into her face. They glittered like a crow's.

"Do you now?" she said mildly.

He was a reed-thin feral child and she felt an immediately kinship with him. He had her red hair, and the same look of age in his eyes that she had in hers. He could have been her brother. But she had never seen him before.

"You lived in an oak," he said.

Angharad was a tinker with the blood of the Summerlord running through her veins, which was just another way of saying that she had a witch's *sight*. She rocked back on her heels as the boy sat up. A small harp was slung from her shoulder. Her red hair was drawn back in two long braids. She wore a tinker's pleated skirt and white blouse, but a huntsman's leather jerkin overtop. A small journey-pack lay by her left knee where she'd set it down. By her right, was a staff of white rowan wood. Witches' wood.

"Are you hungry?" she asked.

When he nodded, she drew bread and cheese from her pack and watched him devour it like a cat. He took quick bites, his gaze never leaving her face.

"I lived up in the branches of your tree once," he said, wiping crumbs from his mouth with the back of his hand. "I'd hear you playing that harp, when the moon was right."

Angharad smiled. "You heard the wind fingering on oak tree's branches—nothing else."

The boy smiled back. "So you *were* there, or how would you know? Besides, how else would a treewife play the harp of her boughs?"

His voice was soft, with a slight rasp. There was a flicker in his eyes like fool's fire.

"What's your name, boy?" she asked. "What are you doing here? Are you lost?"

"My name's Fenn and I've been waiting for you. All my life, I've been waiting for you."

Angharad couldn't help smiling again. "And such a long life you've had so far."

The boy's eyes hooded. A fox watched her from under his bushy eyebrows.

"Why have you been waiting for me?" she asked finally.

Fenn pointed to her harp. "I want you to sing the song that will set me free."

Angharad crawled through the weeds with the boy, keeping low, though out of whose sight, Fenn wouldn't say. The foothills of the West Meon Mountains ran off to the west, a sea of bell heather and gorse, dotted with islands of stone outcrops where ferrets prowled at night. But it wasn't the moorland that he'd brought her to see.

"That's where he lived," Fenn said, pointing to the giant oak that stood alone and towering in the halfland between the forest and the sea of moor.

"The wizard?"

Fenn nodded. "He's bound there yet—bound to his tree. Just like you were, treewife."

"My name is Angharad," she said, not for the first time. "And I was never bound to a tree."

Fenn merely shrugged. Angharad caught his gaze and held it until he looked away, a quick sliding movement. She turned her attention back to the tree. Faintly, among its branches, she could make out a structure.

"That was Puretongue's tree?" she asked.

Fenn grinned, all the humor riding in his eyes. "But he's been dead a hundred years or better, of course. It's the other wizard that's bound in there now. The one that came after Puretongue."

"And what was his name?"

"That's part of the riddle and why you're needed. Learn his name and you have him."

"I don't want him."

"But if you free him, then he'll finally let me go."

Somehow, Angharad doubted that it would be so simple. She didn't trust her companion. He might appear to be the brother she'd never had—red hair, witcheyes and all—but there was something feral about him that made her wary. The oak tree caught her gaze again, drawing it in like a snared bird. Still there was something about that tree, about that house up in its branches. Silence hung about it, thick as cobwebs in a disused tower.

"I'll have to think about this," she said.

Without waiting for Fenn, she crept back through the weeds, keeping low until the first outriding trees of Avalarn Forest shielded her from possible view.

"Why should I believe you?" Angharad asked.

They had returned to where she'd first found him and sat perched on stones like a pair of magpies, facing each other, watching the glitter in each other's eyes and looking for the spark that told of a lie.

"How could I tell you anything but the truth?" Fenn replied. "I'm your friend."

"And if you told me that the world was round—would I be expected to believe that, too?"

Fenn laughed. "But it is round, and hangs like an apple in the sky."

"I know," Angharad said, "though there are those that don't." She studied him for another long moment. "So tell me again, what is it you need to be freed from?"

"The wizard."

"I don't see any chains on you."

Fenn tapped his chest. "The bindings are inside—on my heart. That's why I need your song."

"Which can't be sung until the wizard is loosed."

Fenn nodded.

"Tell me this," Angharad said. "If the wizard is set free, what's to stop him from binding me?"

"Gratitude," Fenn replied. "He's been bound a hundred years, treewife. He'll grant any wish to the one who frees him."

Angharad closed her eyes, picturing the tree, its fat bole, the lofty height to its first boughs.

"*You* can't climb it?" she asked.

"It's not a matter of what I'm capable of," Fenn replied. "It's a matter of the *geas* that was laid on me and the wizard. I can't stray, but I can't enter the house in its branches. And the wizard can't free me, until he himself is free. Won't you help us?"

Angharad opened her eyes to find him smiling at her.

"I'll go up the tree," she said, "but I'll make no promises."

"The key to free him—"

"Is in a small wicker basket—the size of a woodsman's fist. I know. You've already told me more than once."

"Oh, treewife, you—"

"I'm *not* a treewife," Angharad said.

She jumped down from her perch on the stones and started for the tree. Fenn hesitated for a long heartbeat, then scrambled down as well to hurry after her.

"How will you get up?" Fenn whispered when they stood directly under the tree.

Though the bark was rough, Angharad didn't trust it to make for safe handholds on a climb up. The bole was too fat for her to shimmy up. She took a coil of rope from her pack and tied a stone to one end.

"Not by witchy means," she said.

The boy stood back as she began to whirl the stone in an ever-widening circle above her head. She hummed to herself, eyes narrowed as she peered up, hand waiting for just the right moment to cast the stone. Then suddenly it was aloft, flying high, the rope trailing behind it like a long bedraggled tail. Fenn clapped his hands as the stone soared over the lowest branch, then came down the opposite side. Angharad untied the rock. Passing one end of the rope through a slipknot, she pulled it through until the knot was at the branch.

Journeypack and staff stayed by the foot of the tree. with only her small harp on her shoulder, she used the rope to climb up, grunting at the effort it took. Her arms and shoulders were aching long before she reached that first welcome branch, but reach it she did. She sprawled on it and looked down. She saw her belongings, but Fenn was gone. Frowning, she looked up and blinked in amazement. Seen from here, the wizard's refuge was *exactly* like a small house, only set in the branches of a tree instead of on the ground.

Well, I've come this far, Angharad thought. There was no point in going back down until she'd at least had a look. Besides, her own curiosity was tugging at her now.

She drew up the rope and coiled it carefully around her waist. Without it, she could easily be trapped in this tree. Her witcheries let her talk to the birds and the beasts and to listen to their gossips, but they weren't enough to let her fly off like an eagle, or crawl down the tree trunk like a squirrel.

She made her way up, one branch, then another, moving carefully until she finally clambered up the last to stand on the small porch in front of the door. She laid a hand on the wooden door. The wood was smooth to her touch, the whorls of the grain more intricate than any human artwork could ever be. She turned and looked away.

She could see the breadth of the forest from her vantage point, could watch it sweep into the distance, another sea, green and flowing, to twin the darker waves of gorse and heather that marched westward. Slowly she sank down onto her haunches.

She remembered the foxfire flicker in Fenn's eyes and thought of the lights of Jacky Lantern's marsh-kin who loved to lead travelers astray. Some never came back. She remembered tinker wagons rolling by ruined keeps and how she and the other children would dare each other to go exploring within. Crowen's little brother Broon fell down a shaft in one place and broke his neck. She remembered tales of haunted places where if one spent the night, they were found the next morning either dead, mad, or a poet. This tree had the air of such a place.

She sighed. One hand lifted to the harp at her shoulder. She fingered the smooth length of its small forepillar.

The harp was a gift from Jacky Lantern's kin, as was the music she pulled from its strings. She used it in her journeys through the Kingdoms of the Green Isles, to wake the Summerblood where it lay sleeping in folk who never knew they were witches. That was the way the Middle Kingdom survived—by being remembered, by its small magics being served, by the interchange of wisdom and gossip between man and those he shared the world with—the birds, the beasts, the hills, the trees. . . .

Poetry was the other third of a bard's spells, she thought. Poetry and harping and the road that led into the green. She had the harp and knew the road. Standing then to face the door, she thought, perhaps I'll find the poetry in here.

She tried the wooden latch and it moved easily under her hand. The door swung open with a push, and then she stepped through.

The light was cool and green inside. She stood in the middle of a large room. There were bookshelves with leather-bound volumes on one wall, a worktable on another with bunches of dried herbs hanging above it. A stone hearth stood against another and she wondered what wood even a wizard would dare burn, living here in a tree.

The door closed softly behind her. She turned quickly, half-expecting to see someone there, but she was alone in the room. She walked over to the worktable and ran her hand lightly along its length. There was no dust. And the room itself—it was so big. Bigger than she would have supposed it to be when she was outside.

There was another door by the bookshelves. Curious, she crossed the room and tried its handle. It opened easily as well, leading into another room.

Angharad paused there, a witchy tickle starting up her spine. This was impossible. The house was far too small to have so much space inside. She remembered then the one thing she'd forgotten to ask Fenn. If the wizard had caught him, who had caught the wizard and laid the *geas* on them both?

She wished now that she had brought her staff with her. The white rowan wood could call up witchfire. In a place such as this that had once belonged to a treewizard, fire seemed a good weapon to be carrying. Returning to the work bench, she looked through the herbs and clay jars and bundles of twigs until she found what she was looking for. A rowan sprig. Not much, perhaps, but a fire needed only one spark to start its flames.

Twig in hand, she entered the next room. It was much the same as the first, only more cluttered. Another door led off from it. She went through that door to find yet one more room. This was smaller, a bedchamber with a curtained window and a small table and chair under it. On the table was a small wicker basket.

About the size of a man's fist. . . .

She stepped over to the table and picked up the basket. The lid came off easily. Inside was a small bone. A fingerbone, she realized. She closed the basket quickly and looked around. Her witcheries told her that she was no longer alone.

Who are you? a voice breathed in her mind. It seemed to swim out of the walls, a rumbling bass sound, but soft as the last echo of a harp's low strings.

"Who are you?" she answered back. No fool she. Names were power.

She felt what could only be a smile form in her mind. *I am the light on a hawk's wings, the whisper of a tree's boughs, the smell of bell heather, the texture of loam. I dream like a fox, run like a longstone, dance like the wind.*

"You're a wizard, then," Angharad said. Only wizards used a hundred words where one would do. Except for their spells. Then all they needed was the one name.

Why are you here?

"To free you."

Again that smile took shape in her mind. *And who told you that I need to be freed?*

"The boy in the forest—the one you've bound. Fenn."

The boy is a liar.

Angharad sighed. She'd thought as much, really. So why *was* she here? To spend the night and see if she'd wake mad, or a poet, or not wake at all? But when she spoke, all she said was, "And perhaps you are the liar."

The presence in her mind laughed. *Perhaps I am,* it said. *Lie down on the bed, dear guest. I want to show you something.*

"I can see well enough standing up, thank you all the same."

And if you fall down and crack your head when the vision comes—who will you blame?

Angharad made a slow circuit around the room, stopping when she came to the bed. She touched its coverlet, poked at the mattress. Sighing, she kept a firm hold of the basket in one hand, the rowan twig in the other, and lay down. No sooner did her head touch the pillow, than the coverlet rose up in a twist and bound her limbs, holding her fast.

"You *are* a liar," she said, trying to keep the edge of panic out of her voice.

Or you are a fool, her captor replied.

"At least let me see you."

I have something different in mind, dear guest. Something else to show you.

Before Angharad could protest, before she could light the rowan twig with her witcheries, the presence in her mind wrapped her in its power and took her away.

The perspective she had was that of a bird. She was high in the oak that held the treewizard's house, higher than a man or woman could climb, higher than a child, among branches so slender they would scarcely take the weight of a squirrel. The view that vantage point gave her was breathtaking—the endless sweep of forest and moor, striding off in opposite directions. The sky, huge above her, close enough to touch. The ground so far below it was another world.

She had no body. She was merely a presence, like the presence inside the treewizard's house, hovering in the air. A disembodied ghost.

Watch, a now-familiar voice said.

Give me back my body, she told it.

First you must watch.

Her perspective changed, bringing her closer to the ground, and she saw a young man who looked vaguely familiar approaching the tree. He looked like a tinker, red-haired, bright clothes and all, but she could tell by the bundle of books that joined the journeypack on his back, that he was a scholar.

He came to learn, her captor told her.

Nothing wrong with that, she replied. *Knowledge is a good thing to own. It allows you to understand the world around you better and no one can take it away from you.*

A good thing, perhaps, her captor agreed, *depending on what one plans to do with it.*

The young man was cutting footholds into the tree with a small axe. Angharad could feel the tree shiver with each blow.

Doesn't he understand what he's doing to the tree? she asked.

All he understands is his quest for knowledge. He plans to become the most powerful wizard of all.

But why?

A good question. I don't doubt he wishes now that he'd thought it all through more clearly before he came.

Angharad wanted to pursue that further, but by now the young man had reached the porch. He had a triumphant look on his face as he stood before the door. Grinning, he shoved open the door and strode inside. The presence in Angharad's mind tried to draw her in after him, but she was too busy watching the footholds that the young man had cut into the tree grow back, one by one, until there was no sign that they'd ever been there. Then she drifted inside.

Look at him, her captor said.

She did. He'd thrown his packs down by the floor and was pulling out the books in the treewizard's library, tossing each volume on the floor after only the most cursory glances.

"I've done it," he was muttering. "Sweet Dath, I've found a treasure trove."

He tossed the book he was holding down, then got up to investigate the next room. After he'd gone, the books on the floor rose one by one and returned to their places. Angharad hurried in after the young man to find him already in the third room, dancing an awkward jig, his boots clattering on the floorboards.

"I'll show them all!" he sang. "I'll have such power that they'll all bow down to me. They'll come to me with their troubles and, if they're rich enough, if they catch me in an amiable mood, I might even help them." He rubbed his hands together. "Won't I be fine, won't I just."

He was not well-looked upon, her captor explained. *He wanted so much and had so little, and wasn't willing to work for what he did want. He needed it all at once.*

I understand now, Angharad. *He's—*

Watch.

Days passed in a flicker, showing the young man grow-

ing increasingly impatient with the slow speed at which
he gained his knowledge.

It was still work after all, Angharad's captor said.

"Damn this place!" the young man roared one morning. He flung the book he was studying across the room.
"Where is the magic? Where is the power?" He strode
back and forth, running a hand through the tangled knots
of his hair.

Can't he feel it? Angharad asked. *It's in every book,
every nook and cranny of this place. The whole tree
positively reeks of it.*

She felt her captor smile inside her mind, a weary
smile. *He has yet to understand the difference between
what is taken and what is given,* he explained.

Angharad thought of ghostly harpers in a marsh, Jacky
Lantern's kin, pressing a harp into her hands. Not until
she'd been ready to give up what she wanted most—as
misguided a seeking after power as this young man's
was—had she received a wisdom she hadn't even been
aware she was looking for.

She watched in horror now as the young man began to
pile the books in a heap in the center of the room. He
took flint and steel from his pocket and bent over them.

No! Angharad cried, forgetting that this was the past
she was being shown. *We can't let him!*

Too late, her captor said. *The deed's long past and
done. But watch. The final act has yet to play.*

As the young man bent over the books, the room
about him came alive. Chairs flowed into snake-like shapes
and caught him by the ankles, pulling him down to the
floor. A worktable spilled clay jars and herb bundles
about the room as it lunged toward him, folding over his
body, suddenly as pliable as a blanket.

Flint fell with a clatter in one direction, steel in another. The young man screamed. The room exploded
into a whirlwind of furniture and books and debris, spinning faster and faster, until Angharad grew ill looking at
it. Then, just as suddenly as it had come up, the wind
died down. The room blurred, mists swelled within its
confines, grew tattered, dissolved. When it was gone, the

room looked no different than it had when Angharad had first entered it herself. The young man was gone.

Where. . .? she began.

Inside the tree, her captor told her. *Trapped forever and a day, or until a mage or a witch should come to answer the riddle.*

Before Angharad could ask, the presence in her mind whisked her away and the next thing she knew she was lying in the bed once more, the coverlet lying slack and unmoving. She sat up slowly, clutching basket and rowan twig in her hands.

"What is the riddle?" she asked the empty room.

Who is wiser, the presence in her mind asked. *The man who knows everything, or the man who knows nothing?*

"Neither," Angharad replied correctly. "Is that it? Is that all?"

"Oh, no, the presence told her. *You must tell me my name.*

Angharad opened the wicker basket and looked down at the tiny fingerbone. "The wizard in the tree—his name is Fenn. The boy I met is what he could be, should he live again. But you—you live in the tree and if you have need of a name, it would be Druswid." It was a word in the old tongue that meant the knowledge of the oak. "Puretongue was your student," she added, "wasn't he?"

A long time ago, the presence in her mind told her. *But we learned from each other. You did well, dear guest. Sleep now.*

Angharad tried to shake off the drowsiness that came over her, but to no avail. It crept through her body in a wearying wave. She fell back on the bed, fell into a dreamless sleep.

When Angharad woke, it was dawn and she was lying at the foot of the giant oak tree. She sat up, surprisingly not at all stiff from her night on the ground, and turned to find Fenn sitting cross-legged beside her pack and staff, watching her. Angharad looked up at the house, high in the tree.

"How did I get down?" she asked.

Fenn shrugged. He played with a small bone that hung around his neck by a thin leather thong. Angharad looked down at her hands to find she was holding the rowan twig in the one, and the basket in the other. She opened the basket, but the fingerbone was gone.

"A second chance," she said to Fenn. "Is that what you've been given?"

He nodded. "A second chance."

"What will you do with it?"

He grinned. "Go back up that tree and learn, but for all the right reasons this time."

"And what would they be?"

"Don't you know, treewife?"

"I'm *not* a treewife."

"Oh, no? Then how did you guess Druswid's name?"

"I didn't guess. I'm a witch, Fenn—that gives me a certain *sight*."

Fenn's eyes widened slightly with a touch of awe. "You actually *saw* Druswid?"

Anghard shook her head. "But I know a tree's voice when I hear it. And who else would be speaking to me from an oak tree? Not a wet-eared impatient boy who wanted to be a wizard for all the wrong reasons."

"You're angry because I tricked you into going up into the tree. But I didn't lie. I just didn't tell you everything."

"Why not?"

"I didn't think you'd help me."

Angharad gathered up her harp and pack and swung them onto her back. Fenn handed her her staff.

"Well?" he asked. "Would you have?"

Angharad looked up at the tree. "I'm not dead," she said, "and I don't feel mad, so perhaps I've become a poet."

"Treewi—" Fenn paused as Angharad swung her head towards him. "Angharad," he said. "*Would* you have helped me?"

"Probably," she said. "But not for the right reasons." She leaned over to him and gave him a kiss on the brow. "Good luck, Fenn."

"My song," he said. "You never gave me my song."

"You never needed a song."

"But I'd like one now. Please?"

So Angharad sang to him before she left, a song of the loneliness that wisdom can sometimes bring—when the student won't listen, when the form is bound to the earth by its roots and only the mind ranges free. A loneliness grown from a world where magic as a way of life lay forgotten under too many quests for power. She called it "The Weeping Oak" and she only sang it that once and never again. But there was a poetry in it that her songs had never had before.

Thereafter, as she traveled, that poetry took wing in the songs that she sang to the accompaniment of her harp. It joined the two parts of a bard that she already had, slipping her into her life as neatly as an otter's path through the river's water. She continued to range far and wide, as tinkers will, but she was a red-haired witch, following a bard's road into the green, which is another way of saying she was content with what she had.

And so she was.

GULLRIDER

by Dave Smeds

Much of sword and sorcery fiction, as mentioned in the Introduction, deals with a reshuffling of time-honored elements; to find a story with a genuinely original gimmick is rare. So when I started this story, I was deeply intrigued. I've read stories of women with telepathic links to many (too many) dragons, unicorns and teddy-bears; even a society of lesbian priestesses with mental and emotional links to sapient purple rhinoceroses (this particular story was wildly original, but so amateurishly written that I couldn't possibly buy it.)

Unfortunately new writers with really original ideas can seldom express them with professional fluency; which is why I often start off a rejection slip with, "This is a good idea, but stories aren't about ideas, they're about people."

Fortunately Dave Smeds managed to make his people as interesting as his idea; and I can seriously recommend "Gullrider" as a good story.

(I still regret the purple rhinoceri. . . .)

Dave Smeds is a commercial artist who hopes to switch to fulltime writing. So far he's published a novel, THE SORCERY WITHIN, (1985) and a sequel, THE TALISMANS OF ALEMAR (forthcoming). He's also published a generous handful of short stories and novelettes; mostly sword and sorcery. We'll all be the gainers when he does make the switch to fulltime writing.

S erla glided over the ocean, the body of her gull warm and steady beneath her. They had left the coastal fog behind. They were out over mer waters now, where few people other than gullriders went. Ahead lay the spires, their thin, volcanic tips enveloped in a cloud of nesting sea birds. Rhysas led them in a circle around the highest of the crags, evoking memories of their first long flight a year earlier, when Serla was still a raw apprentice.

This time, the maneuver was easy and smooth, her control precise. Screech knew her touch; all it took was a light pressure of her knee against his feathered neck to make him turn, no reins at all. Her bird matched Longbeak's every dip and angle, the two gulls maintaining perfect formation, the large white and gray in the lead, the somewhat smaller, pure white in the rear. As they came out of the circle, Rhysas pulled Longbeak up in a sharp, skilled evasive tactic. Serla, who had expected the test, countered it. Rhysas glanced back, smiling and nodding at her performance. They headed farther out to sea.

Serla rubbed the back of Screech's neck, pleased with herself. Her flights with Rhysas were no longer a matter of master teaching apprentice. It was more two gullriders enjoying a flight together as equals. Realistically she knew that, in spite of his advancing years, there were few gullriders that could hold a feather to Rhysas when he decided to challenge their ability, but the great gap was gone. She did not have to constantly ask him what to do, or receive daily lectures. Instead, they simply practiced, and at times such as this, she could pretend that they were comrades. The day before he had actually complimented her.

They headed for the sea lanes. They were, after all, technically on patrol, observing the boats as they sailed through mer waters to the fishing banks. To Serla's delight, one of the first they passed was her family's own trawler. She guided Screech down and passed by them at mast height. Her father, at the tiller, yelled an inaudible greeting. Her sister and brother-in-law waved from the bow. She gave them the sign of good fishing.

She doubted she could be happier than at that moment. Her sister might have been the pretty one, the one who had caught one of the best husbands the village had to offer, but there she was in a boat dealing with smelly fish, while Serla had the skies. Dainty arms and a petite build might be fine for attracting a man, but they weren't meant for the joy of commanding a gull.

It was as she and Rhysas were leaving mer waters, entering the territory where, by treaty, humans owned the fishing rights, that they spotted the merman. He was gesticulating wildly, riding the crest of a swell, showing off the bluish white of his belly to make himself more visible from above.

This was an odd sight. Mermen rarely surfaced so close to the border. Furthermore, if there was anything a merman preferred to avoid, it was the giant gulls. Serla's first impulse was to be suspicious. But that was unjustified. Humans and mer had been at peace since the year she had been born.

Rhysas signaled, and they descended. As the gulls approached, the merman sank further into the ocean, but he did not stop gesturing. Serla realized that his movements were not random. He was speaking in the sign language that mer and human traders used between themselves. She knew a little of the speech: the two dozen symbols that were useful to a gullrider trying to communicate while in flight. She doubted she would understand him, then she realized that the merman was not making sentences. He was repeating a single word.

Kraken.

Rhysas comprehended it at the same time. "Hurry to the fishing grounds!" he shouted.

They left the merman behind. She urged Screech on. The wind of their passage beat at her face, threatening to untie her hair from its bun. The gulls usually glided, stiff-winged. When they flapped, the ride was rough, awesome, and swift. Serla struggled to keep her eyes open. A feather, blown off Screech's head, stung her cheek. Rhysas was not waiting for her. With her lesser experience and smaller mount, she could not pace him. He and Longbeak shrank into the distance.

They passed two boats, and, seeing nothing amiss, sped on. Rhysas was almost out of sight before she saw him whirl and dive. She opened the slits of her eyes wider. The water was churning. As Screech ceased pumping his wings and settled into a smooth final approach, she saw the monster, its tentacles locked around a fishing vessel.

The kraken had already torn the rigging off the deck, and was tearing the hull into shards. Mast, sails, and halyards floated in the ocean. Serla could see the fishermen cowering against the gunwales or in the hatchway, praying to their patron god to deliver them. They cheered the arrival of the gullriders. Their craft was already half demolished, shipping water, doomed. Just as Serla arrived, the kraken squeezed, snapping the remnant in two. The hold spilled its catch. The fishermen plunged into the waves—into the dead fish, rope, netting, and splinters of wood.

Rhysas dived first, aiming at the man in greatest danger. Longbeak emitted a cry of distress as they darted past the flailing tentacles, but held steady, plucking the fisherman from the ocean with his modified feet. The others were swimming for their lives.

Serla chose her man and dived. Halfway down Screech stiffened, resisted, and finally fought off her guidance. They overshot the target. Serla was furious. She veered to the left, yanked hard on the leather, bringing her bird around for a second try. Rhysas and Longbeak were carrying their burden to a safe distance, which she should have been doing by this point. There were three more men to save. The gulls could not afford to be afraid of the kraken.

Serla plummeted in. Screech struggled, but she didn't allow him to falter. She felt the sudden lurch and decrease in speed as her mount grasped the fisherman. She could have wept.

The kraken lashed out. Serla felt the impact through Screech's body. The bird screamed. Serla saw tail feathers scattering out behind. It was several seconds before she could calm Screech down; by that time they were high, out of harm's way.

Screech did not appear to be seriously hurt, but she knew she'd have a difficult time rescuing the next man. She glanced back, and her breath caught in her throat. The kraken seized one of the fishermen and dragged him under. Rhysas was approaching, but he would not be in time.

She bit her lip. There was nothing she could do but carry away the man she had already rescued. She watched Rhysas dive toward the fourth and last man. He came in directly over the kraken. As they passed, the monster seized one of Longbeak's ankles. Rhysas was wrenched off his perch, saved only by the safety strap. Longbeak nipped at the tentacle. The kraken recoiled, releasing its grip. Gull and rider skimmed the surface, catching spray in their faces, barely avoiding a dunking.

Serla quickly dropped her man in the ocean next to the one Rhysas had rescued, and hurried back to the wreckage. She saw Rhysas circling. She kept expecting him to dive, but he did not. As she neared she saw why.

There were no more men swimming near the kraken.

Something cold touched her, down deep, inside her rib cage. Like Rhysas, she circled aimlessly over the kraken, making certain that the last fisherman was truly gone, and not, for instance, swimming underwater. But no head bobbed to the surface. There was only flotsam and jetsam.

The kraken slapped the water, creating a loud crack. It was a defiant, almost smug gesture. It continued to destroy any piece of the craft larger than a cask. When there was nothing left, it submerged. One squirt of its jets, and it was gone. One last time Serla scanned the scraps of wood, the fish floating upside down in the swells, then hung her shoulders in defeat. Rhysas gestured toward an islet to the west. She nodded and they flew back to recover the fishermen they had dropped, before the kraken grabbed them, too.

They deposited the men just off the islet, to let them clamber out of the ocean onto the rocks. By that time both of the gullriders had landed and dismounted.

"Are you hurt?" Rhysas asked.

They said no. They looked bedraggled and uncomfortable in their drenched clothing, physically unharmed but wobbly with shock. Serla recognized the elder of the pair as a man from her mother's home village. "Herld? What happened?"

Herld waved numbly in the direction of the disaster. "It just came up, out of nowhere, and started wrecking us. We didn't even have nets out."

"Like the attack five years ago," Rhysas said. "The mer say it's a disease, like rabies. When kraken are in that state, they'll attack any large object on the surface."

Serla had heard the tales, though the only kraken she had ever seen were the much smaller ones that were sometimes caught in the nets. "But—the other boats—"

"Anything on the water is in danger," her teacher said.

"We have to warn them," she said urgently. She had a brief, awful image of her father being squeezed to death by a tentacle.

"More than that," Rhysas said. "All the warning in the world won't do any good if the kraken catches up to them on their way back to the harbor. You saw how ineffectual we were just now. It takes more than a riding gull to handle a kraken. We'll have to tame a wild gull. With one of them, we can frighten the beast away, or kill it if we're lucky."

Taming a wild gull was the stuff of legend. One of the reasons Rhysas had such a formidable reputation as a gullrider was that he had accomplished it not once, but three times.

"Just us?" Serla asked dubiously

"We've no time to waste flying back to the coast for other riders. The kraken could attack while we're gone. We've lost enough people already."

Both the fishermen looked down. Serla felt her cheeks grow hot. Rhysas seemed to regret the statement. "Mount up," he told Serla. "We're off to Gull Island." He nodded at the men. "We'll get you off this rock as soon as we can."

Gull Island was a red, pock-marked mountain of lava to the north of the fishing banks, a favorite rookery for wild gulls, both great and small. Rhysas and Serla landed on a broad ledge part way up the side of the ancient caldera. Below, several giant gulls were milling about on a flat area.

The underarms of Serla's jacket were stained with sweat. Her buttocks were sore from the hard ride. They had made a rapid circuit of the fishing banks, warning as many boats as possible, ordering them to pass on the word and head for harbor. She stood stiffly where she had dismounted.

"Get your chin up," Rhysas said. "Not many gullriders ever get to see what you will today."

"I'm sorry, master."

The old man raised an eyebrow. Damn him, she thought. He knew her too well. "What is it, Serla?" he asked.

"The kraken. If I hadn't failed to make Screech dive the first time, I might have made it back in time to save the last man."

Rhysas gave her a wistful smile. "And here I thought you were ashamed of me for not saving him myself."

"Oh, no! Not at all!"

He shrugged. "We do what we can, Serla. We're gullriders, not gods. I'm trying not to think of how we failed this morning, but how we may succeed at midday. I suggest you do the same."

She nodded. She still felt the guilt, but it was better knowing that, at the very least, her teacher did not blame her.

Rhysas led her to a cleft in the rock. There, to her amazement, lay a sea chest securely anchored out of the way of wind and marauding gulls. He opened it. Inside she saw three or four gull bridles and safety straps, a bit larger than the ones worn by Screech and Longbeak. Several bright, sea green ribbons rested next to them.

"There's another chest on the far side of the island," Rhysas said. "If you use up anything, it's your responsibility to replace it with new gear." He made his selection and closed the lid. They walked together to the edge of the rock. Three gulls were preening themselves almost directly below. Even the smallest was more massive than Longbeak.

"This won't be anything like breaking Screech," Rhysas cautioned. "When the great sorceress Gerryjill bred the first riding gulls, she removed the ferocity from their nature, as well as adding a great deal of intelligence and loyalty. These are like those out there." Rhysas waved at a group of sea gulls fighting over a crab near the shore. "They're vicious, ill-tempered, and stupid. They're as much a danger to their rider as they are to a kraken.

"Still, people rode gulls before Gerryjill tinkered with the species. I confess that as a young man I was fool enough to believe the adage that a person isn't a true gullrider until he or she rides a wild gull. I hope you are never so unwise. Since those days I've only ridden them when I was forced to. They *will* attack a full grown kraken, and I don't know of anything else that will, unless it's another kraken."

It almost seemed as if there was a flicker of doubt in Rhysas' eyes. Serla had never seen that look before. Lack of confidence was not an emotion she associated with him. Still, it had been twenty years since Rhysas had ridden a wild gull. Since the war with the mer.

His uncustomary expression lasted only a moment. He held up the ribbon. "Try not to lose this. The damn wizards charge a full day's catch to make one." He pointed to a gray gull in the group below. "Lead that one under the overhang. I'll take it from there."

Not far away was a place where she could clamber down. She descended about thirty feet to the flat, and hugged the cliff all the way back to the base of the overhang where Rhysas waited. At this level the gulls towered over her. One swift peck and she would die. She stayed under the protection of the rock and flung the weighted end of the ribbon toward the gray gull. She wiggled it. Like the lesser species, the bird could not resist the shiny green snakelike object, particularly not when magic augmented the appeal. As she reeled in the ribbon, the gull followed with long, deliberate steps, cocking its head to either side to regard the bait first with one eye, then the other. It loomed so near that Serla thought she was going to lose control of her bladder.

Suddenly Rhysas was on its back.

The gull reacted instantly. "It bolted into the sky. Rhysas scrambled to its neck and locked his legs around the bird's collar bone with a nimbleness that belied his age. Before they gained the altitude that the gull needed to maneuver, Rhysas wrapped the safety strap around and secured it to his belt. Serla felt a rush in her fingers and toes. All he needed to do now was get the bridle in place.

The gull began to swoop violently. Rhysas clung with heels, hands, even teeth. The bird shook. It dived toward the surf. It found updrafts and rose in sharp, near vertical climbs. Rhysas' legs were shaken loose. The safety strap pulled taut. He regained his hold. On the island, Serla held her breath. He'd told the truth: breaking a riding gull was never like this.

The gull bucked, pitched, and tried to reach the man with its beak. For a quarter of an hour its efforts never ceased. Rhysas was shaken loose three more times, saved only by the strap. Finally, the gray began to tire. Rhysas finally had the respite he needed to let go with one hand so that he could seize the bridle.

He tossed the bit over the gull's beak. It shook free, and responded with a series of wild maneuvers that prevented the man from trying again for several minutes. Eventually, he reeled in the gear and flung it again. The gull dipped abruptly and the toss went astray.

Rhysas patiently gathered up the bridle, hanging on through more turns and twists. Finally the bird began climbing steadily. Rhysas threw. The bridle settled snugly in place. As he yanked on the reins, the gull turned. Serla burst into a smile. The critical part of the battle was over.

The gull plummeted, shaking its entire body. Rhysas pulled back on the reins, drawing its head back, making it level out. When it went left, he pulled in the same direction, as if that were his choice, not the bird's. When it went right, he did the same. In due time the gull ceased initiating movements. It waited for his directive. He tried simple changes, and when those met with success, he rode all the way around the island in a wide circle.

Serla climbed back to the ledge, where Screech and Longbeak waited. She waved as Rhysas came around the far side of the caldera. He waved back.

Suddenly the gull dived. Straight down, head first,

making no attempt to avoid the ocean. Rhysas tumbled straight down, the safety step sliding along the bird's neck and over its head. He hit the water just ahead of the gull. They both disappeared beneath the surface.

Serla's eyes went wide in horror. The splash had barely subsided when the gull burst up, shook its body, and climbed into the air, bridle still attached. Serla ignored it. She searched for signs of her teacher. At last a dark lump foamed to the surface. It didn't seem to be moving.

Serla leaped onto Screech's back. The docile bird was startled by the heels in his neck. They raced to the site. Serla recognized Rhysas by the color of his clothing. Just as she swept down over him, she saw him raise his head out of the water. Screech scooped him up.

She hurried back to the ledge, pulled Screech up in a hovering pattern, and deposited Rhysas gently on the rock. To her dismay, he unfolded in a limp pile and remained there. She dismounted and ran to him. He coughed up a small amount of water.

"What's wrong?" He seemed calm, but he remained unusually, disturbingly still.

"My back," he said. His breath hissed, a sudden release, like a man whose wound is being cauterized.

"Can you move your toes?" she asked.

He shifted one foot, then the other, wincing both times. "There's no paralysis. I have to stay still; otherwise it hurts too much."

Rhysas was a man who never complained about pain. The statement alone proved how badly he was injured. She pulled off his boots and stuffed her jacket under his head. He preferred to remain on his side, in a tucked position, facing the ocean and shoreline.

"A healing wizard owes me a large favor," Rhysas murmured. "It may be time to collect."

It was only then, as she acknowledged that he was not going to recover quickly or easily, that Serla began to consider the consequences of Rhysas's injury.

"What should I do now?" she asked, automatically deferring to her teacher. Should she try to get Rhysas to the healer? Should she fetch another gullrider? Should she go back and continue warning the fleet of the kraken? None of those courses of action seemed completely right.

"You have to tame the gull," Rhysas stated firmly, grunting as his back spasmed.

It was an option which she would never have considered. She was a one-year apprentice. "How could I if you—" She stopped short of saying "failed."

"Try with the same bird. It's tired. It's half-broken already."

"But what if I can't find it?"

He pointed. She turned. Below them, the gray gull had returned to the flat. It was preening its feathers several hundred yards away. "The bridle is still attached," Rhysas said. "And it won't fight you as hard as it did me."

"What if it tries the same move that threw you?"

"Keep tension on the reins at all times. Don't let it dip its head. I made a mistake when I waved. I should have kept a two-handed grip until he was completely broken. Go. You can do it. I have faith in you."

Rhysas was both a stern judge of character and an honest one. It was a shock to hear the sincerity in his estimation of her. She stared at the gull. Its feathers were still ruffled from the plunge in the ocean. It was so big. Rhysas might believe she could ride it, but she herself had yet to be converted.

"What will happen to you while I'm gone?"

"Longbeak will protect me. You know that. Go, while you still have the chance."

She was clenching her teeth so hard it made her jaw ache. Rhysas, even in all his discomfort, had kept a clear head. It was true that the gray might decide to leave at any time. What could she do then, try to overcome a fresh gull? She swallowed hard, picked up the ribbon that she had dropped, ran to the sea chest for a new safety strap, and paused at the top of the trail down to the flat area. She glanced back at Rhysas. He winked, the way he always did when she was about to attempt something she had never done before. She tried to smile.

In order to get to the gray, she had to walk between other wild gulls. They glared at her as she negotiated the rocky ground, making her worry but otherwise keeping their distance. She kept the ribbon hidden until she was near her goal.

The gray squawked and stepped away. Quickly, before it decided to fly, she uncoiled the ribbon and tossed it out. The effect was instantaneous. The gull ceased fidgeting and focused its gaze on the green material. Serla pulled the ribbon next to a boulder and abandoned it. The gull pursued with long, deliberate strides, oblivious to her or any other distraction. She climbed the boulder, checking to be sure that no other gulls had been caught by the ribbon's charm.

It was almost too easy. The gull reached the bait and began pecking it. The boulder gave Serla precisely the height she needed to leap onto its back. She almost wished it had been harder, so that she would have had an excuse to fail. She took one deep breath and jumped.

She landed low, and had to scramble to the gull's shoulders. It was already in flight. She had never felt such force. Her heart pounded and her breath came in staccato bursts—she was barely conscious of whipping the strap around the neck and fastening it.

She accomplished it just in time. The gull bucked. She was flung into the air. The strap caught her, slamming her pelvis back down against the bird's spine. She swallowed the pain, clenching hard with her thighs, calves, and ankles in order to stay in her seat. Holding on was all she could think about. She was not aware how long it took before the gull ceased struggling. Gradually she realized it was calm. She sat up. The reins, somehow, were in her hands.

The gull was gliding smoothly. Just in time, her suspicions were raised. She clamped hard on the reins with both hands.

The gull jerked its head downward, beginning a dive. But Serla's maneuver kept it from plummeting straight down, as it had done with Rhysas. She applied more pressure, bringing the head back, forcing the bird to level out. It obeyed, but seemed outraged at her temerity. It twisted, shook, and dived more violently than before, screeching until Serla nearly let go to cover her ears.

She rode it out. The bird was getting tired. It tried

again to make a vertical dive, but she was ready. This time, its protests were half-hearted. Her arms were aching from the strain. Her hands bled where the reins had rubbed completely through the skin of her palms. But she felt strong, energetic, and alert. She knew she was winning.

The gull apparently realized it, too, and abruptly conceded. It flew level and straight, unless she tugged the reins, then it went whichever way she indicated. The gray was a far cry from a trained, well-tempered mount, but it could be ridden.

She didn't try elaborate tests. It was enough just to stay aboard and get the gull to where it was needed. She flew past Rhysas. He waved feebly, moving only his hand. She, not trusting the gray, kept her hands tight on the reins. She whistled. Screech left Rhysas and Longbeak, following her and the gray in the direction of the fishing banks.

The gray, surprisingly, did not fly faster than Screech. Nor, in spite of its extra mass, was it as steady. Screech had been bred for speed and the comfort of his rider. But Serla could sense strength and a violent nature waiting for the proper moment to be unleashed.

They met the first boat just after noon. It was one of the ones she and Rhysas had warned earlier. It was already outside the banks, heading for harbor. It was unharmed. She continued on, wondering if the fishermen realized they were seeing a rider on a wild gull.

She began to relax. She passed over two more boats, one of which she and Rhysas had not warned earlier. Both were intact. Her task was not impossible, if she looked at it one piece at a time. First of all, she had the gull. The next priority was to get the fleet to harbor. Perhaps the kraken would not appear again. She could summon other gullriders—older, more experienced ones who could catch wild gulls. Half a dozen of them could bait the kraken with an empty boat, wait for it to strike, and deal with it. With any luck, she might happen across another rider soon. In perhaps as little as two hours she could abrogate her responsibility. She could assume a lesser task more in keeping with her desires, such as rescuing Rhysas from Gull Island.

Her hopes were shattered as she encountered a flotilla of four trawlers, including that of her family. The boat next to them was being ravaged by the kraken.

The monster had coiled several tentacles around the boat's rigging, pulling it until the port gunwales were at water's edge. Three crewmen were clinging to the starboard side; another was swimming away.

The gray screeched fiercely, startling Serla. She hoped it was the cry of the hunter—wild gulls fed on young kraken. She directed it into a swoop.

The gull screeched again, and flew past without touching its target.

Serla cursed softly. One problem was solved—the gull was not afraid of the kraken—but a new one had been created. The wild gull, being untrained, would not respond to her command to engage. She circled. The kraken was unwrapping itself. The men in the boat, which was still listing badly to port, cheered. Perhaps, Serla thought, the big bird had had some effect. She tried another dive.

Once again, the gray would not complete the assault. The kraken, however, slapped upward. The blow tore feathers and skin away from the bird's gullet. Had it been a little higher, Serla might have been knocked from her saddle. They flew past, the gull screaming. The kraken settled back to wait, ignoring the boats and the men.

Serla sped westward, unable to turn the gull. It shook, trying to dislodge her. She held fast, pulling with all her might to one side. Finally the gull responded. She pointed it back toward the fishing fleet. She knew now what she had to do.

She came in slowly, low over the ocean. The kraken was ripping planks off the boat, but stopped as soon as the gull approached. Serla unbuckled her safety strap, and as they closed in, she scooted rapidly forward until she was sitting on the bird's head.

The weight forced the gull into a sharp dive. Serla fell off into the water next to the kraken. The gull hit dead center.

The impact of the water nearly blacked her out, but she had tucked well. Her back stung, but she could bear it. She opened her eyes and saw nothing but bubbles. Currents churned, buffeting her. A tentacle grazed her. She kicked in the opposite direction, swimming as hard as she could. She hoped the surface was not too distant.

As she swam away, the body of the kraken became more distinct—the great mass of tentacles at the forward end, the squidlike body behind, eyes half as wide as she was tall. At the base of its tentacles a wicked, beaked mouth snapped, the clash audible even under water, severing one of the gull's ankles. But most of the blood staining the water was not the red of gull, but the black of kraken. Though her lungs were threatening to burst, she had the satisfaction of knowing that her tactic had succeeded.

Then she saw something that she couldn't believe. She broke the surface, grasped a lungful of air, and dived again to be sure she had not imagined it.

Hovering just above the kraken's back was a merman. He hugged the monster's body closely, manipulating the corrugated skin on its forehead. No sooner was she absolutely sure of his actions than he was knocked away. The gull's beak slashed through the water to dig deeply into the kraken's head, narrowly missing hm.

He turned and saw Serla. He did not have to be human for her to read the look in his eyes. He pumped his powerful webbed feet, moving toward her with the speed of a dolphin, drawing a jagged coral knife.

She knew she had little chance against him, although for a human she was a good swimmer and diver. She groped for her own knife, wrapped her palm fiercely around the hilt, and prepared to die hard.

When he was two arm-lengths away, a wild thrash of a tentacle caught him on the head and shoulders, knocking the knife out of his hands, leaving him stunned and motionless. Serla moved swiftly, aiming at his exposed throat, making the first blow count. She followed it with three stabs to the chest. He resisted none of them. She put a foot against his chest and kicked away. She needed air. The merman's body remained limp, surrounded by a cloud of blood.

She broke the surface, coughing water. A loose tentacle floated not far away, as well as many, many feathers. She heard the scream of the gray. A wave from the battle swamped her. As soon as she resurfaced, she whistled sharply.

Screech was there in seconds, pulling her out of the ocean and away from the struggle.

She watched the behemoths die from the deck of her family's boat, where Screech had left her. It was difficult to say which creature had suffered the most damage, the gray gull or the kraken. The only movement was the spasmodic jerking of a single tentacle. Sharks had already begun to gather, waiting to feast on the remains. Before long the wild gulls would come, too, since they relished kraken meat.

Serla was numb in body and spirit, though her sister had loaned her a dry cape. Her family did not attempt to make her talk, for which she was grateful. She had a great deal to ponder.

"The mer say it's a disease, like rabies."

"Father, move the boat in closer," she said abruptly.

Her sire frowned, glancing toward the carnage and back again.

"They're dead. It will be safe. I need *that,*" she said, pointing at the shape in the froth near the giant combatants. It was only vaguely manlike at that distance, but now that her father took a hard look, his face went pale. He did as she asked.

"Put us between it and the other boats," she said. The men and women in the nearest trawler, she was pleased to see, were preoccupied hauling a section of severed tentacle aboard as a souvenir.

Serla and her brother-in-law used the grappling hooks to pull the dead merman on deck. The sight nauseated her sister, who had never seen one up close before. The race was an odd mix of human and cetacean—two disproportionately long legs, ending in flippers; webbed fingers; earlobes that had become small fins. Serla paid attention only to the belt around his waist. The clasp was a distinctive design inlaid with mother-of-pearl. It designated a special caste of mer.

A sorcerer. She'd guessed it. It would take a magician to be able to ride a kraken as gullriders did their birds.

"These are knife wounds," her father said, gazing at the chest and throat. He turned to Serla, jowls stiffening, the mistrust and enmity clear. He had fought in the last war with the mer, had lost his own mother in the conflict.

"Now is not the time to explain," she said firmly. "I want you to do something for me. I know it will be against your liking." She paused. He was listening, as carefully as a common fisherman would with a gullrider. It startled her to think of their relationship that way. "I want you to hide the body in the hold. I want you to keep utterly silent about this until after I've talked with the high council."

"But, Serla, what happened?"

"I can't tell you yet," she insisted. "Just promise me." She glanced at her sister and brother-in-law. "You, too. Not a word back in the village—not until tomorrow. You'll have to trust me."

Her father pursed his lips, shoved a toe into the merman's ribs, and sighed. "You've always had a level head on your shoulders. I give my word."

Serla made sure the other two did the same. She helped slide open the hatch and dump the corpse within, her arms and legs jerky as a marionette's. Her mind was already racing ahead, toward what she had to do later that day, to what could happen to her world that season as a result of her actions.

"Once I leave, set a course for Gull Island," she said. She told them about Rhysas. It was best that, for his back's sake, he ride home aboard a ship. She used the bullhorn to ask the crew of one of the undamaged trawlers to fetch Herld and his companion from the islet.

"Just tell me, Serla," her father said as she prepared to call Screech down. "Is it war?"

"No," she said. "Not if I have anything to say about

it." She pressed his hand tightly, kissed his cheek, then quickly turned and whistled for her bird.

She couldn't wait to get back in the sky, back to the familiarity of gullriding. But even there, she couldn't escape the burden of decision. Would she be able to keep silent while she waited with Rhysas for her family's ship to reach the island? There *would* be war, if men like her father and her teacher, both veterans, learned too abruptly that a merman had guided the kraken to attack. Relations had been good with the mer since the year Serla had been born. There had been only two previous kraken attacks, years apart. She would not cause a conflagration when there was a possibility that a single mer, perhaps a bitter veteran himself, may have been the cause of all three incidents.

She thought back to the merman who had alerted them to the crisis that very morning. She was sure that there were mer, perhaps a great many, who were aghast at the actions of their wizard. It would take calm minds, careful diplomacy, and good will to see that the truth was revealed and justice done.

She prayed that when she brought her story to the high council, they would listen to all of it, and not simply to the parts they wanted to hear.

Rhysas was waiting where she had left him, Longbeak hovering paternally over him. He met her with an alert, interested glance.

"Well," he demanded, "how did it go?"

At the moment, she felt every bruise and strained muscle she had incurred during the gullbreaking and battle. "I'm afraid I lost a bridle," she said simply.

"Yes. Happened to me every time I rode a wild gull."

He began to laugh, and she eventually joined in. She had waited so long for such a level of camaraderie with him. Their casual humor said it all—Rhysas would never be her teacher again, even assuming he recovered the ability to fly. She had withstood a rite of passage. They were equals now.

But a new gulf had opened, as it had between her and her father years earlier, when she realized for the first time that some of his philosophies and decisions were not perfect, merely an individual's choice, and she, being a different individual, was not always going to agree with him. So she sat down beside Rhysas, her fellow gullrider, her old friend, and made sure that Rhysas the veteran— the headstrong hero of the preceding generation, so often praised as being the first to battle and the last to leave—remained unaware just how different the skies surrounding her gull's wings would be for her from now on.

BLOOD DANCER

by Diana L. Paxson

Diana Paxson's heroine Shanna made her debut in a story called "The Dark Mother" in Andy Offutt's SWORDS AGAINST DARKNESS, after having been rejected by a well-known feminist editor who stated that no properly feminist heroine should pay any attention to a curse of childlessness.

Since then, Shanna has appeared in many other places, including all four of the SWORD AND SORCERESS volumes, and has become a favorite with readers. Here Shanna survives a plague and experiences another kind of Goddess.

Diana Paxson lives in Berkeley, at "Greyhaven" (starring in the anthology by that name). A popular but understandable misconception made Greyhaven the home of Marion Zimmer Bradley; no, my house is named Greenwalls, because of the garden-high shrubbery surrounding it; it's not in the Berkeley hills, as Greyhaven is, but in the South Campus area. Greyhaven is within easy walking distance and is still the home of many writers; it's listed in the *"San Francisco Bay Area literary guide";* but I never lived there except briefly while househunting.

Diana, when not writing, plays an Irish harp.

S hanna of Sharteyn was five miles from Otey when she saw smoke, as if a dirty finger had smudged the pale sky. Distracted by her own memories, she thought only that some peasant must be burning off brush before the spring planting, for this was farming country, broad and flat, with stunted grass ruffled by a hot wind.

To a northerner the land seemed dry for this time of year, but perhaps that was normal here. Already it was too warm for the crimson cloak that lay rolled with her pack behind the saddle. As Shanna rode southward, the advancing season would soon force her to lay aside the jerkin of quilted red leather as well, and ride only in tunic and her vest of fine, gold-plated mail.

But it seemed unlikely that she would need armor in this land. The countryside was quiet—indeed, Shanna had passed only a few wagons going toward the city that day, and none returning. Not that she missed company. On her journey along the great road she had mostly camped out in the open or among the ruins of the posting stations built by the old Empire of Kath, content with the companionship of her mare, Calur, and the falcon, Chai, who had once been human, too.

She wondered if the three weeks spent in the company of a ghost in the dark labyrinth beneath the city of Fendor had left her afraid of her own kind, or only disillusioned with mortal men. . . .

The falcon perched on her saddlebow sidled impatiently. Then the wind changed, and Calur squealed and began to plunge. Shanna choked on the sudden reek of smoke and charring flesh and hauled back on the reins with one hand while with the other she tried to soothe Chai.

"What is it? Does the fire frighten you? I tried to tell you what it was like, in the world of men—" Chai's kin could take bird or human form, but the curse of the Emperor they had served had condemned them to bird-form outside of their own valley. Shanna's quest for her missing brother and Chai's pursuit of a pardon had made them allies.

Shanna's quick appraisal had already located the fire—the smoke was coming from a farmstead just off the road. A touch of the spur persuaded the mare, mincing and tossing her head, to turn down the lane. Shanna had thought to offer help, but the place was already burned to the ground, and though the earth was pocked by the prints of many feet, the only signs of life were the disconsolate bleating of a goat in a nearby field and the glittering black eyes of two ravens that waited in the oak tree for the ashes to cool.

Shanna's fingers curved involuntarily in the Sign against Evil as she felt their cold glance. Birds—unlike Chai, they were only birds, but the people of the Misty Isles believed that their goddess could take raven form, and after being cursed by the Dark Mother, Shanna had had enough of goddesses for awhile. She jerked Calur's head around and headed the mare back toward the road.

It's no concern of mine, she thought as they started south again. *If I stop to help every wretch on the road, my brother will be dead of old age before I reach Bindir. I've already been too long delayed. . . .*

She had left Sharteyn almost two years ago, the only daughter of a princely house, on her way to the Emperor's city to find her brother, hiding in her baggage her mail and her sword. Now she rode with no companion but Chai and the mare, a warrior-woman with only the oath she had sworn to bring her brother home to connect her with her past—

—only that, and the ache in her womb to remind her that the priestess of the Dark Mother had cursed her womanhood. That had been two months ago, and her blood had not answered the call of the moon since then. It could be natural, she thought—illness or activity had delayed her courses before—but Shanna felt an inner certainty that the things that other women longed for were now forever denied her.

"I do not regret the choice I made," Shanna said aloud, and straightened her tall body, leanly muscled and hardened by months on the road. Surely she should be grateful to be thus freed from human needs.

But even as she forced a smile, she heard cawing in the air above her, and as Chai called a harsh challenge, the two ravens flew past her toward Otey.

By the time Shanna had passed beneath the worn stone arch of the Wall of Otey and found an inn, dusk was leaching all color from the town. She saw Calur securely stabled and settled Chai in a corner of her chamber before venturing down to the common room for the evening meal.

And having done so, she thought that she should have eaten in her own room instead.

It was not that anyone was hostile—even the inn-keeper, seeing the black braids coiled around Shanna's head when she took off the steel cap she wore, had betrayed only by a widening of the eyes his wonder at seeing a woman armed and traveling as a man. Perhaps he thought her one of the Emperor's Valkyr guards, though she was really too dark and too thin. But mostly, he seemed too dispirited to care.

Shanna poked at the fat congealing in the bowl of barley stew and glanced around her. There were perhaps a dozen other people in the long room, sitting alone or in groups of two or three with large spaces between. The chamber was not unattractive, with striped cloths nailed over the plaster and racks of painted Essseyn ware—so why was there no singing, no laughter?"

She suppressed an impulse to ask her nearest neighbor, an old fellow in a drover's cap who was dozing against the wall. Perhaps they were worried about the drought, or maybe it was just the way of the place. Better to hold her peace; in the morning she would be gone.

There was a commotion at the entry and Shanna turned, noting the sharp sound of indignation in the voices there, or was it fear? She caught something about troops from the garrison at Karna . . . she strained to hear, but the words faded to a mumble and the door closed. The innkeeper came back into the common room and a man in a shopkeeper's embroidered gown asked a question.

"I don't know—" the host replied. "We asked for someone to help us, but can soldiers make it rain, or frighten away the Blood Dancer?"

"Ssh!" The other man made the Sign against Evil and the innkeeper shrugged, then paled as the man at the table near Shanna suddenly sat bolt upright and began to cough. In the firelight she saw his cheeks flush crimson as an actor's paint.

The other men saw, and stumbled to their feet, blessing themselves, reaching for cloaks and bags. "Blood Sign!" someone echoed the innkeeper. "Get him away!"

But the host was already scurrying, and as the drover slumped he grabbed him beneath the armpits and began to drag him toward the door.

"Wait!" Shanna found herself on her feet, going after him. "What are you doing? Can't you see the man's ill?"

Face averted, the innkeeper thrust the big door open with one hand and tumbled the limp body of his guest into the road. Trembling, with a face like dough, he turned to answer her.

"Ill! Where have you come from, that you don't recognize the plague?" He looked down at his hands and rubbed them against his apron as if to wipe off the contagion. "Gan! Tami!" he called to the kitchens. "Get that table outside and burn it, and the trencher he was using, too!" The other guests still huddled in the common room, afraid to stay there, more afraid to go past the thing that lay outside the front door.

"But you can't just leave him to die in the road!" exclaimed Shanna. "Is there no pest-house? Are there no healers in this town?"

"The Moonmothers have set up a hospice down by the square, for all the good it does anyone. So long as he doesn't do it in my house, the man can die as well in the road as anywhere! The gods have cursed us!" The innkeeper began to rub his hands against his sides again. "No one will come here now! What will I do?"

"Down by the square, you say?" Shanna pushed past him. "If the gods are angry, you will die no matter what you do—" she said over her shoulder. "You may as well try to act like a human being while you live!" She strode down the broad steps and bent to lift the drover, who was retching redly into the road.

"You're dooming yourself, you know—" the innkeeper began again. "What do you want done with your mare and that bird you've got up in your room? Don't think I'll let you through my door again, not after you touched *him* . . ."

Shanna peered up at him. "I'll make you a wager, then—take the bird down to the mare's stall and perch her there; feed them both well, though you'd best mind your fingers with Chai if you want to keep them all! If I die, free the bird, then sell the mare and keep the gold. If I return, you'll bear the cost of keeping them."

In the innkeeper's sly eyes cupidity fought fear. "How long before I can sell them, mistress? How long?"

"Three days?" Shanna grimaced, realizing that she had just committed herself to yet another delay. "Long enough to see if I have taken the pestilence." It was an annoyance, but she could always find another inn. "And if I find you've ill-treated them, or sold the horse before the appointed time, beware," her strong fingers caressed the hilt of her sword, "for you'll find there are worse ways of dying than the Blood Dance!"

The innkeeper was grinning now. Shanna supposed she should find his confidence about winning the wager ominous, but as she tightened her grip on the unconscious body of the drover and heaved it over her shoulder, she was more concerned with whether she would be able to get him to the Moonmothers in time.

"The Goddess bless you, my daughter. You may bring the man over here—"

Suppressing a momentary astonishment that the priestess had been able to discern her sex at one glance in that dim light, Shanna followed her, stepping carefully over and around forms huddled in the stillness of coma or tossing weakly as they fought the disease. Despite the innkeeper's skepticism, the Moonmothers seemed to have plenty of patients. For the first time, Shanna realized how serious the plague in this city must be.

The priestess lifted her lamp above an empty pallet, and gratefully, Shanna set her burden down. He stirred and whimpered then, and as he began to cough the Moonmother bent over him, wiping his face with a damp cloth and murmuring meaningless phrases like a mother soothing a sick child. After a little, the paroxysm passed, and the priestess sat back with a sigh.

She looked up at Shanna, and in the lamplight the warrior saw her face for the first time clearly, worn and weathered, but strong and in its own way beautiful as a Goddess-face carved from living stone.

"Thank you, daughter. He is no relation? Not many would have dared to bring him here . . ." Her voice held gentle dismissal.

Shanna shrugged. "I know . . ." She cast another glance at the fitful light that shone on the faces of the dying and the blood-spattered blue robes of the women that moved along them. These days she had no love for priestesses, but she saw weariness blurring the strength in the face before her. Was her courage less than theirs?

"My innkeeper's barred his door against me for fear of the contagion," she tried to smooth her tone to graciousness. "If you've a use for me, and a place where I can spread my cloak, I'll stay a few days to help you here."

The smile of the priestess was like the kindling of a lantern. "The blessing of our Lady Moon be on you, my daughter. I am Mother Elosia, and with what hospitality we can offer, I bid you welcome here."

Three days passed quickly, the distinction between light and darkness disappearing in the lamplit pest-house. At first Shanna simply lent her strength to assist the priestesses in lifting the bodies of the dead from pallet to the carts that would take them to the burning-ground, in washing blood-stained coverlets and laying them on the newly-stricken who had crawled to their doors or been brought by panicked relatives.

But soon enough she picked up the few procedures for nursing this disease that the Moonmothers had been able to devise. To keep the patient clean and comfortable, to sponge the body with a wet cloth and try to keep the fever down was nearly the whole of it. Some few survived the crisis and began to mend. Most died. Shanna soon realized that the Moonmothers did not pretend to cure—only to tend the burning body until it was purified or consumed.

"What would become of this world if the moon were always full?" said Mother Elosia. "She must wane and go into the darkness before she can be born anew. And so it is with humankind. The Blood Dance is a more painful death than most, but faster. We ease the transition as best we can. . .''

Despite her continued exposure, it did not occur to Shanna that she might take the plague. The Goddess had passed up so many chances to destroy her already—clearly she must live long enough to endure the curse that saving the boy Tomas from the altar of the Dark Mother had earned.

But she was not so absorbed in her labors as to forget her agreement with the innkeeper. On the morning of the fourth day, her weariness struggling with her relief at being done with her task, Shanna set off for the inn to reclaim her property.

The innkeeper's disappointment would have amused her if she had not been so tired. He eyed her as he might have looked at a roast chicken that suddenly flapped its wings and flew away. Smiling blandly, Shanna snapped shut the clasps of her jerkin and settled the steel cap over her hair, then slung her crimson cloak across her shoulders, for the sky was darkening and the air had the welcome smell of rain.

After four days without exercise Calur was well-rested. It was all Shanna could do to hold her to a walk through the streets toward Otey's southern gate. Fortunately most of the foot traffic seemed to be going in the same direction.

That, in itself, should have made her wonder, but it was not until she had to pull the snorting mare up short to avoid crashing into a knot of arguing townsfolk who were blocking the roadway that she realized that half the city seemed to be gathered before the gateway.

And the Gate was shut.

Shanna caught a glimpse of green near the wall and stood in her stirrups to see. There were soldiers there, wearing the dull green cloaks of the Provincial Forces. She saw the flash of green again as someone climbed the ladder to the watchtower. The crowd's growling grew louder as the officer reached the top. Then it stilled.

"*In the name of Baratir Abeiren, Emperor of the North and Monarch of the Middle Lands, Prince of—*" sonorous titles rolled from the man's lips in a litany of power. Chai bated restlessly on Shanna's arm, picking up the impatience of the crowd, and Shanna soothed her russet feathers with a gauntleted hand.

"*To his loyal people of the city of Otey—*" Now he was coming to it! The crowd settled again, watching with the patient attention of a cat below a bird-filled tree.

"*Having heard your petitions for relief in your time of trial, and being mindful of the security of the Empire, our gracious Lord doth decree that prayers and sacrifices for the salvation of your city shall be offered in Bindir in the great temple of Hiera and Pitaus; that wagonloads of grain shall be sent from the Imperial storehouses in compensation for the disruption of trade; and that the Gates of the city shall remain shut and guarded during the course of the pestilence, lest this curse of the gods spread throughout the Empire.*

"*Given this day—*" The proclamation's conclusion was lost in a sound like approaching thunder; the gathering protest of the crowd.

"We're trapped! Trapped here to die!" cried a woman.

"Get the soldiers—" shouted a man. "They can't keep us in here!"

The crowd rolled toward the Gate in a movement as mighty, as formless, as the swelling of a wave in the sea. Fitful sunlight flickered on steel, the crowd recoiled as spears bristled suddenly from the ranked men-at-arms before the wall. One of them dripped red, and a sudden ululation of mourning pierced the tumult of the crowd.

Forced back upon itself the crowd began to mill, a maelstrom of humanity swirling ever more swiftly as its fury grew. Again it rolled against the wall, again it was repulsed. Shanna shortened her reins and loosened her sword.

"The Emperor has abandoned us and the gods have cursed us. We are doomed!" came the cry. "The Blood Dancer strikes to purge us of our sins!"

"Goddess, have mercy!" shouted someone.

"The Blood Dancer must be appeased! We must be purified!"

"The Dancer burns through the city, consuming the impure!" more voices shrieked.

"The fire! Fire! Let us destroy the ungodly and purify the city with fire!"

Shanna knew that note—the hysterical howling of hounds that sight their prey. Calur snorted and began to paw the ground as she did before battle. *Maybe she's right,* thought Shanna. *Maybe she knows better than I.* The crowd's fear and fury were almost palpable now. Shanna stiffened her will against it as if she were raising a shield.

"We have been cursed for harboring the ungodly!" A woman's shrill voice pierced the roaring of the mob. "The Dancer has already marked them—burn them and the city will be cleansed!"

"The hospice! The hospice!" Many throats took up the chant as if one mind had possessed them all. "Burn the hospice! Purify the City, and the Dancer will be appeased!"

For a moment the crowd hesitated, then it focused and began to move as one being in the direction of the Moonmothers' hospice, gathering a slow but inexorable momentum.

"Fire!" it shouted. "Fire for the Blood Dancer, blood and fire!"

But even as the chanting began Shanna had wrenched the mare's head around and was spurring her ahead of them through the cobled streets of Otey.

"Peace, daughter—no, listen to me—" Mother Elosia's soft voice stilled Shanna's frantic pleading. "My sisters and I cannot run away and leave these folk here to die—" she gestured toward the dark doorway behind her.

"They will die anyway!" Shanna said brutally.

"Not all of them. And the time and manner of life or death is not mine to choose—either for myself or for others. I have served the Goddess when Her face was shining. I will not deny Her dark face now. It is She who must make the decision whether to save or to slay. . . ."

An echo of memory tugged at Shanna's awareness, her own voice raised in dedication before Yraine's holy fire—*"Lady of Wisdom, I am Thy sword to spare or to slay!"*

She turned, hearing behind her the muted roaring of the crowd like a distant forest fire. And as if a spark from that flame had lodged in her breast, Shanna felt the heat of excitement flare along every limb. Her heart was racing, and she took several deep breaths to steady it. Her promise to seek her brother should have sent her fleeing to whatever safety she could find, but an older oath governed her actions now

"Then let Her decide," Shanna said with a grim cheerfulness. For a moment the clouds parted and the ruby eye of the falcon that hilted her sword winked balefully as she drew the blade. "If She will give me the strength to use it, here is one sword to defend Her."

For a moment a frown clouded the love she saw in Mother Elosia's eyes. Then the older woman sighed and lifted her hand in the sign of blessing. "I forgot that you are not bound by our vows," she explained, "and surely, the Lady has many faces. May She bless you, my daughter, and if we meet in this life no longer, I will pray that you may one day find peace in Her embrace."

Peace! Shanna thought, *I hope not, but at least if I die now the blessing of the Moon Mother will balance the curse of Saibel!*

Then the Moonmother turned away. Shanna did not wait to watch her go. The sound of the crowd close now. She felt the vibration of their coming through the stones on which she stood. Chai gave a soft, harsh cry, and sidled along Shanna's arm, head swiveling nervously.

"Are you afraid?" Shanna said to the falcon. "I never meant to drag you into a war." she lifted her arm. "You are free—fly away if you will. Your oath does not bind you to help me here."

For a moment the falcon fixed her with one golden eye, then Chai moved up to Shanna's shoulder, where she stayed. Shanna shortened her reins, but though tremors of tension rippled across the mare's flanks, Calur stood still. Shanna controlled her breathing, deepening her awareness to encompass the falcon and the horse, the clouds that massed overhead and the stones of the square and the frenzied faces of the people crossing them.

Torches trailed banners of pallid flame through the

dull air; Shanna caught the gleam of weapons—knives, scythes, and here and there a sword. None of these people would have caused her a tremor as individuals, but now they had become that many-headed monster, the mob.

In her belly she felt the familiar churning of mingled excitement and fear. As she counted the faces, the surface of her consciousness told her it was hopeless. Shanna forced herself to ignore that message, striving for the deeper awareness in which the goal would be not survival, but the harmony of fighter and foe.

The crowd saw her still figure waiting there and for an instant it paused, then a man in the chequered garments of the Misty Isles led the surge forward.

"Warrior, stand aside," he shouted. "Do not interfere between the Goddess and Her sacrifice!"

"Surely She can claim Her victims without aid from men!" Shanna replied coldly. "Your own lives are forfeit if you invade Her sanctuary."

For a moment he seemed to listen, then the murmur behind him focused to a deep chanting—"Purify, purify! Appease the Blood Dancer with blood and fire!"

Abruptly the crowd's bloodlust intensified. Shanna flinched as if the blast of hatred had been a physical blow, and Calur, sensing her rider's fear, tossed her head and pawed at the ground.

As if the ring of steel horseshoe on stone had been a signal, the mob leaped forward. The air shivered to a many-throated baying—"Blood, blood, and fire!"

A cobblestone grazed Shanna's cheek and shattered against the facade of the hospice behind her. She glimpsed more missiles flying, dropped her reins on Calur's neck and urged the mare forward, guiding her with heels and knees while with her left arm she brought the brass-studded buckler into position and with her right she swung up the sword.

Something crashed into the side of her steel cap, nearly knocking her out of the saddle. Dizzied, Shanna felt the chinstrap give way, and as she struggled back upright, blinking away darkness, the cap fell free and clanged on the stones. Her vision still blurring, Shanna sensed, rather than saw the spear that jabbed at her. Automatically her blade circled and as Calur sprang forward, severed the hand that held the spear. There was another flicker of metal; again her blade sang.

The sun found an opening in the clouds and abruptly the air blazed around them. Chai launched herself shrieking from Shanna's shoulder and the loosened coils of Shanna's long black hair fell free, tossing as she recovered and struck again.

The blade bit bone, there was an anguished cry and then another shout. At first, Shanna did not understand. Then, suddenly, there was space around her. Breathing raggedly, she straightened, blinking at the brilliant sunlight that made her cloak one crimson glow and sparkled on her reddened sword.

"Marigan!" the cry came again in the accent of the Misty Isles. "See—her bird and the red cloak!"

"Marigan! Marigan!" came the deep echo, and "Mariganath! Anath!" in the accent of the southern lands. Shanna shuddered, buffeted by sound.

"Lady, we did not know You—receive Your sacrifice!" The crowd gave way before her, and Shanna reined Calur in a half-circle on her haunches.

"Marigan!" cried the crowd. The blood pounded in Shanna's ears. She felt the sound as a vibration rather than hearing the syllables of the name. Dark wings flapped around her, fire flowed incandescent through every vein. She was aware of horse and hawk as she felt her own limbs, but sight and sound were thunder and shadow. Only that repeated invocation reverberated in her brain.

"Marigan . . ."

The mare carried her forward. She must cut off the crowd from—Shanna no longer remembered who she was fighting or what she was defending. The red darkness beat in her ears like a great drum. Her arm rose and fell and rose again. Men screamed and begged and pled for mercy, but she had no mercy. The Goddess they had invoked had come upon them, and She hungered for the blood of fear.

*   *   *

Shanna stood up, fastened her belt, then began to snap shut the clasps of her jerkin, one by one. At last she was satiated, content as a tigress that has eaten her fill, no— her body glowed with a more luxuriant satisfaction, a sexual fulfillment, as if—

She heard a kind of stifled whimper and looked down.

A man was lying at her feet, the flaccid nakedness of his body exposed before her, as mingled shame and terror were exposed in his eyes. For a moment Shanna stared, bewildered. Then, unbelieving, her reviving mind began to evaluate the evidence of his body and her own. . .

"No, Lady, please—I cannot serve you again! Great One, have mercy—" seeing her eyes on him, he was babbling.

Shanna swallowed and stepped swiftly backward. "Cover yourself!" she said harshly, turning away. Her sword was safely sheathed by her side, but her buckler was gone, and Calur and Chai were nowhere to be seen. What had happened? How had she gotten here? Her right arm ached, and boots, breeches, hands and arms were splashed with red.

With blood—she stank of blood. Her gorge rose at the sick, sweet smell. She heard running footsteps and knew with dumb relief that the man she had forced to service her had fled.

She felt hot, and nauseous from the smell. There was a throbbing behind her eyes. What had she done? She remembered the crowds, and the fighting, and then only a crimson blur. The people of Otey had invoked the battle goddess, Mariganath, she remembered, but *she* served honor, she served Yraine!

Dizziness shook her. *I'm ill* . . . she thought dully then. Instinctively, her feet carried her through streets she no longer recognized toward the hospice. There were bodies in the streets—surely she had not killed them all—and it was very still. She felt a cool wetness on her cheek and wondered if it were tears. Then it came again.

Shanna looked up and saw a dark pall of clouds drawn across the sky. It was raining at last. The cold drops touched her face like a blessing, but it was growing steadily darker. She could not tell if the day were dying, the clouds getting thicker, or it was her own sight that failed.

She forced herself to focus, saw a familiar row of columns and staggered toward them. She had reached the hospice, but it, too, was still. Were they all dead here, too? She tried to call, but all that came from her throat was a raven's harsh cry.

Shanna set her foot upon the first step, but her muscles did not want to obey. Shadows swung dizzily around her and the ground came up to meet her, knocking the breath from her body. And then the darkness folded around her like black wings, and Shanna lay unknowing in the rain.

For three days it rained, soaking deep into the thirsty earth until cheerful rivulets ran in every gutter, washing away the dust of the drought and the seeds of the plague. But Shanna knew nothing of that—she struggled through dreams of fire and terror in which she killed, and killed, and killed. . . .

When she opened her eyes at last, the air was luminous with cloud-filtered light. From outside came the steady, gentle patter of rain. Shanna blinked and sighed.

"Are you awake, then, daughter? The Goddess is merciful," came a voice from nearby.

Some goddesses are merciful thought Shanna grimly. *Not the ones who favor me* . . .

"Have I had the plague?" she spoke aloud.

"I do not believe so," Mother Elosia replied with a frown. "Only a fever. Your horse and your bird found their own way to us, and they have been waiting eagerly for you to get well. You are the last of our patients. Some died, some recovered, and for three days no more have come here. Perhaps it is the rain. The soldiers opened the gates of the city yesterday."

Three days? Shanna tried to think back. She remembered the gates closing, and then the mob, and then—abruptly memory overwhelmed her, waking memory now that knew what had happened to her, what she had done. She groaned.

"Are you in pain?" asked the Moonmother. "Come now—here is an herb-drink that will ease you."

"No—" Shanna shook her head. "I am afraid . . . to dream again. How could you take me in? Didn't you see the blood on my hands?" She shuddered, remembering how it had covered her afterward, and rubbed her palms reflexively against the coverlet.

She felt herself held; a cool cloth was laid on her brow.

"I understand," came Mother Elosia's soothing murmur. "You are a warrior. But surely you have to had to kill before—"

"Not like this!" Shanna burst out. "Before it was in fair combat! But this time—it was a madness—I killed them even when they begged for mercy. I don't *know* how many I killed. But I *enjoyed* it!" she added, swallowing. "What can I do? How can I put on my sword again, not knowing if I—" Shanna's hands clenched, she felt tears of weakness roll down her cheeks. "I should have died!"

"I heard the Name by which they called you. The Goddess has many faces . . ." Mother Elosia's voice seemed to come from very far away. "Not all of them seem kindly to us, or beautiful. But I believe that all of them are necessary. I cannot judge Her, or you. If indeed the plague was the visitation of Her wrath upon Otey, perhaps you were the instrument She used to end it."

Perhaps, thought Shanna, *but it was no rape. There was something in me that welcomed Her. That is the knowledge that frightens me.*

"Did you think yourself immune from the Lady's frenzy, as your body was immune to the plague?" said the Moonmother as if Shanna had spoken aloud. "Remember this, my daughter—as you have slain, so shall you save. *All* the faces of the Goddess are implicit in you."

Mother Elosia bent over Shanna and set a cup to her lips, and Shanna did not resist her. As she slid into the cool sleep of healing, she felt the Moonmother's kiss upon her brow, and heard the words of a blessing that comforted her until the dawning of a new day.

KAYLI'S FIRE

by Paula Helm Murray

I get a lot of stories about dragons, but most of them are what I call "MacCaffrey clones" and simply get sent off *between* accompanied by the standard rejection slip. So I was delighted to find this story in my mail—it's always wonderful to find a writer who has a new slant on an old idea and can express it fluently.

Paula Helm Murray has been active in fandom for just over a decade and is currently the secretary of the Kansas City Science Fiction and Fantasy Society. She lives in Prairie Village, Kansas with her husband Jim. "Kayli's Fire" is her first professional fiction publication.

Kayli stood before her hearth in the dripping great hall, wondering if she should go to bed, to at least be under warm covers. She hoped the roof hadn't been breached in her bedchamber. It was almost the last dry room in the old castle.

She felt a light tug at her ankle. Then her silvery house dragon lightly climbed up to perch on her left shoulder, bracing himself with several curls of long, lithe tail around her right shoulder.

"Riders coming," he said, turning to look at her, nose to nose, with amber eyes that matched her own. "BIG horses, too, not the ponies from around here."

She reached up and patted the warm little being. "Thanks, Fyl." She gave him a gentle poke. "Get any fatter and you'll not fit up here. Been sucking eggs again?"

He drew up with an indignant expression on his little face. "You said the EGGS were OURS, as long as I

continued on next page

didn't hurt the hens. And I am NOT fat! Poof!" A little puff of smoke left his mouth, then a small flame.

Kayli ignored the fireworks. "Well, your heft tells me it's not fluff. Hold still." She wiped the yolk from the corner of his mouth with her sleeve. "You'd best lay low . . . you scare the yokels so. I hope they don't wake Ylgs." She gestured and the fire in the hearth blazed up warmer.

Fyl slithered away. *I don't want to deal with Ylgs today*, she thought. *He's senile, no reasoning with him, and the rain makes me cross.* The bridge dragon, a true dragon, had been a gift to an ancestor. Senility made it a liability.

Kayli opened one of the doors to the great hall and stood, watching for the visitors. Lightning cracked and illuminated the bridge over the river in front of her home. Two armored riders on great horses, westerners from their garb and ensigns, clattered quickly across the bridge. One slouched over the pommel of his saddle, clutching his right shoulder. They stopped before the steps up to the door, in the courtyard, dripping in the steady rain.

Lightning crossed the sky again. The wounded one's horse screamed and danced a little. Kayli went to him, ignoring the rain, and calmed him, stroking his muzzle.

"You're the wizard?" The unhurt man, stag head on helm, asked. His strong western accent confirmed Kayli's guess at their origin.

"I'm a fire mage," Kayli replied quietly, stroking the horse, "so I guess, yes, I am." The injured man's helm bore a bear's head figure.

"He's hurt," Stag head said flatly.

"I can see that." She could see bright eyes in the darkness under the stag's head, staring with fear.

"Our enemy has a wizard. Our chirurgeon said his wound needs a wizard to heal it. Villagers below said you're a wizard."

Kayli refrained from commenting on anyone "owning" the services of a wizard. She stood in silence, thinking. Healing, she knew; wise woman's skill, not magic.

Ylgs' head appeared over the side of the courtyard.

The huge old dragon, silver with age, looked warty with the moss he accumulated from sleeping beneath the bridge. Usually slow, he could only climb; his wings had withered with age and size.

"Goddess!" she said, "Come along, ride your horses into my hall." She threw the other door open wide and stood aside.

Stag head looked behind him as they passed through the doors. The horses needed no urging. Kayli heard "Sweet mother . . ." softly escape his lips.

Ylgs roared feebly, emitted a couple of puffs of black smoke, then slid back down. *Good, he'll settle, he's only irritated. I get tired of replacing these doors, but I can't move stone ones.*

She looked up at Bear head. "Can you get down?"

He moaned, then unsteadily obeyed. She helped him sit at a bench by her hearth, careful to touch him only lightly. Iron and steel burned her flesh.

"I must be away," Stag head said nervously, "I'm needed. Will your dragon. . . ?"

"If you gallop, he won't notice," Fyl chimed in, slithering up onto Kayli's shoulder again. "He's senile. He doesn't move quick, like me. Probably think it's just lightning."

The man made a pious gesture. "Then I'll be away. I'll be back for him." He grabbed the other horse's reins, wheeled them around and galloped away. Kayli winced. She didn't approve of galloping horses on pavement.

"I'll get your mail off," she said quietly. She slipped off her cloak and used it to take off the helm. It was lighter than it looked. She set it aside.

He had thick, curly red-gold hair, a blond, thick mustache, pale, fair freckled skin and a strong aquiline profile. An old, deep scar cut from above the corner of his right eye across the bridge of his nose down to beneath his left eye. He seemed dazed.

"Problems?" Fyl chirped.

"Taking off that mail shirt is a painful problem, little one."

The man stirred. Kayli found herself looking into deep blue-green eyes.

"Where am I?" he asked. Then, "Aye, must be a

wizard. No mortal has yellow eyes. I remember now."
He shifted his weight. "Aygh!" He clutched his shoulder
again. "It gnaws!"

Kayli wondered at the wound. The mail had no tear,
though blood oozed through near where he held it. She
took off his cloak and outer, insignia'd tabard, careful
not to touch the steel. Kayli found the double entwined
gold dragons on a blood-red field quite fascinating. *Later*,
she thought, *work to do now*.

"I need help," she said finally, "I'll do as much as I
can, but help me get your mail off. Do I pull it over your
head?"

"Clips here in front." He clumsily started unfastening
them left-handed. "Can't seem to move my right arm."

Kayli stood behind him when he finished with the
clips. "Now, hold still." She braced herself and grabbed,
pulling it off from behind as quickly and carefully as she
could. He held in a scream as it caught, then slipped off
his right shoulder.

She threw the shirt on the floor, then plunged her
hands into a mostly filled bucket of cold rainwater. The
faint scent of burned flesh, hers, lingered. The man
slouched forward again. Despite the immediate smarting,
her burns would heal quickly.

She went back to him and stripped off his undertunic.
It was bloody, but untorn. The wound in his shoulder
made her step back a pace. Bloody, big enough to fit
both of her fists inside, something writhed in it. "Yll-
worm," she said out loud. *Easily cared for*, she thought.

"Kay . . ." Fyl gasped, peering fearfully down at the
wound.

She startled. Sometimes she forgot she carried him. He
hadn't lived with her that long. "I may need help, little
one," she said softly.

"I'm here for it." He lightly nuzzled her cheek, a soft,
warm comfort.

Kayli braced again and grabbed the blood-red worm
hard behind its head, starting a live flame in her hand to
kill it. It turned on her and bit her thumb hard.

She cast it to the floor. Fyl leaped off and incinerated

the monstrosity with a minor "whuff," leaving only a small smear of char on the stones.

The man stirred again, then took a deep breath and looked up. "The pain . . . the gnawing is gone . . ." He stared as Fyl climbed back to Kayli's shoulder.

"Good lad," she scratched the little dragon's head. "Now please, fetch some clean rags from the kitchen."

"Yes, ma'am." He sped off with an unusual absence of discussion.

"It talks," the man said, staring.

"Aye," Kayli replied. "If you think you can walk, I want to get you to a bed."

"I . . . I think I can. I may have to lean, lady."

"I'm strong."

She walked him up to the only real bed she had and sat him on its side. He walked strongly, only leaning a little on the stairs. Fyl appeared at her side as he sat, rag bag in his mouth.

"Thanks, Fyl," she said, taking them and patting him gently. "You're especially good, to keep them dry." She paused and looked at the man. "I don't think your friend told me your name."

"He'd not, not to a wizard." He looked up at her, exhaustion and some fear showing on his face.

"I'm only a fire mage," she replied impatiently, "Would I live in this leaking pile of rocks if I were a wizard? My name is Kayli. I'll not harm you, you stupid sod!" She turned to getting rags out to make a bandage.

"My . . . my name is Hugh," he said softly, "Fitzhugh to my kin. My mother heals . . . I should know better. I'm sorry, lady."

She felt badly that he seemed ashamed. "You've been fighting with an evil wizard," she said gently, "I don't envy you and I don't blame your fears. He'll be here soon enough."

"What's that?" He looked at her sharply.

"The Yll-worm is . . . I don't know how to explain . . . it's part of him, somehow. He'll know it died without killing you. Here, let me look at your shoulder. It may hurt."

She carefully blotted the blood away. The flow had

slowed to an ooze. She wondered he wasn't screaming in agony. The wound was deeper and uglier than she'd thought at first, bone and deep tissues exposed. No muscle or tendon seemed left at the front of the shoulder, and some of the bones had been gnawed on.

"Can you feel your arm?" she asked.

"No. About the wizard . . ."

"Damn the wizard, man! You're badly wounded. That should be your concern for now. Leave the wizard to me." She hoped silently that the wound wouldn't prove mortal. "I've got to do something that will hurt."

"What?"

"I must sear the wound, so it won't go septic. It's so deep, if it did, you'd surely die."

"Then do it." He set his face and sat up squarely. Fyl squeaked and left the room.

Kayli made a free fireball the size of her palm, then braced herself and passed it lightly over the wound just long enough to blacken it. Hugh sweated and the veins stood out on his forehead and neck, but he sat still, silently. She dissipated the fireball when finished.

Then she bandaged his shoulder, bracing it so it wouldn't bend easily, and bound his upper arm to his side to prevent pulling on the wound. He sat in silence, a dazed expression on his face. She finished by binding his forearm to his body, making a close sling to support the weight.

"Come," she gently pushed to make him stand. He obeyed. She took his kilt and leggings off, then made him sit again on the bed. She finished with his leggings and pulled his boots off. "Now, lie down." She helped him so he wouldn't hurt his shoulder, then covered him tightly.

She sat beside him and touched his cheek. "Sleep, Hugh," she said softly, "sleep and heal." He shut his eyes.

She left him, wondering what this stranger made her feel.

Hugh stayed between sleep and half-trance for three days. Kayli made herself a pallet before her kitchen hearth. Fyl helped her stay warm at night.

She put the wizard to the back of her mind. *Does no good to worry*, she thought, *he has to be more powerful. Evil, too—no one with any sense of decency would use Yll-worms.*

The fourth morning after Hugh had come, Kayli killed an old hen for a stew. He'd seemed no better when she checked on him at dawn and she needed something to help keep her strength up. *At least the weather's turning*, she thought, starting to look to spring. She ached from sleeping on cold stone.

"Lady."

Kayli jumped. Her mind wandered while she plucked the chicken. Hugh stood in the doorway, leaning on the frame.

"So this isn't a dream," he continued. "Then, didn't think it was when I put on my shirt." He had pulled it over his hurt arm, not bothering with the sleeve.

"Come, sit down." Kayli laid the hen aside and went to him. "How do you feel?" She looked closely at his face.

"Well, and hungry." He sat at the table across from where she had been sitting.

"This hen'll be in the pot soon," she replied, "I've already started the potatoes, carrots, and turnips." She sat again.

"Smells good." He sniffed the air, then looked her over critically. "How long have I been here?"

"This is the fourth day." She looked down at the hen. "When I'm done, I want to look at your shoulder and change the bandages. How does it feel?"

"Doesn't. Oh, it aches a little on the chest side, but my arm and shoulder seem numb, don't move, either. How long before I can use my arm?"

She kept her face down. "I can't tell, it's too soon."

He reached across the table and made her look at him, left hand firmly under her chin. "Tell me that again, lass."

"You're lucky to be alive," she said stiffly, "I'm surprised at that, though you seem very strong."

"True, lady."

"You may never get use of it back. The . . . the thing

ate away too much. Much longer and it'd have gnawed through to your heart. That's what it's made to do." She pushed his hand away and turned back to her task.

"And your man? Where's he away to?"

"I . . . I don't have a husband." She felt the flush deepen. "The local folk fear me, and I . . . well, I know better than to try. All I have are my looks, and I've been told often enough that they're a pitiful lot."

"You're dead wrong on that," he replied. "Your looks show you're a strong woman, and capable. I thought you older, at first." He stroked her hair softly. "White hair, guess it goes with amber eyes."

"Feathers!" Fyl's gleeful squeal broke the mood. He galumphed into high speed from the doorway, dived into the pile on the floor and started sneezing. Feathers filled the kitchen.

"Fyl!" Kayli yelled and went for him. "You know better! I just cleaned in here!" She swatted his fat backside as he barely cleared the doorway ahead of her.

There were feathers everywhere. She went back to sit, head in hands, realizing how tired she was. *This is the last straw,* she thought. Then, a faint drip hit the back of her head. *Wonderful, the kitchen leaks now.* She couldn't hold back the tears.

"Ah, lass," Hugh said gently, "don't cry. It's just a few feathers."

She looked up through her tears. "Just a few feathers!" That did in the last shreds of her temper. "My blasted roof leaks, this nasty rockpile is cold and damp, I've a senile dragon to deal with, I'm weary to the bone with sleeping three nights on a cold, damp stone floor, and, to top it off," she stood, "I'm going to get myself killed over an ignorant peasant. Just a few feathers, indeed!" She threw the mostly plucked hen down on the table, scattering more feathers. "Damnit, I can't take any more!" She stormed out the door.

"Now you've done it," Fyl squeaked, head peeping around the door frame well after she left. "She's been cross since . . ."

"Looks as if you're the one who 'done' it," Hugh replied, "jumping into those feathers like a fool." He

looked around a moment. "Here I find myself, in the lair
of a mage, sitting and talking to a dragon. An idiot
dragon, at that."

"That's very good," Fyl fired back, smoking a little
from his nostrils. "Do you do this sort of thing often?"

"You'll cut the smart remarks and help clean up,"
Hugh said quietly, "or I'll help her beat your fat rear end
like a drum. The lady is upset and I don't blame her.
Come along."

Kayli returned when she realized she could hear nothing from the kitchen. The smell of dragonsmoke and
burnt feathers told her the fate of most of the feathers. A
few bits of down still drifted.

Hugh and Fyl sat, staring at the plucked, singed hen.
A knife lay beside it.

"What's wrong?" They both jumped at her voice.

"I just realized what being one-handed really means,"
Hugh said sadly, "I can't figure out how to hold it and
cut it up, too. I don't want Fyl to hold it, I'm unsteady
left-handed."

"Here," she said calmly. She took the bird to her
chopping block, pulled out a bigger knife and cut the
bird to pieces. "I thank you for cleaning up," she said,
putting the pieces into the pot.

Fyl slithered up to her shoulder, nuzzled her ear and
cheek. "Sorry I jumped in the feathers, ma. Wasn't such
a good idea after all."

Kayli stroked him. "I'm sorry I flew off like that,
Hugh, Fyl."

"Wizard's got you worried," High said quietly. "Don't
blame you for being on edge."

"I'm just a mage, Hugh," she said. "All I've got is my
fire magic. That comes from me, is me, Hugh. Wizardry
is a learned thing, usually more powerful than what I
have, or so I was taught."

"Aye, like my mother heals," he replied. "I understand, lady. It's just taken a while to sink into my thick
skull. Why did you help me? You must've known a
wizard was involved."

"You were hurt. I couldn't turn you away."

He stood and went to her. She stiffened, wondering what he was going to do.

"I'll not hurt you, lady," he said, very softly.

"I . . . I'm not used to other people," she replied, embarrassed. She felt herself flush again. This man threw her quite off balance. She didn't understand it at all.

He kissed her gently on the forehead, then gave her a very gentle one-armed hug. "You're risking a lot for me," he said gently, looking her over. "When the time comes, I'll do what I can."

"We both sleep clothed, usually," Hugh said, "though I woke up bare. But my clothes were clean, which explained that."

Getting ready for bed, they stood across her bed from one another. Kayli was getting her things, going to sleep in the kitchen again.

"I do," she replied shyly.

"Then you'll sleep in your own bed tonight," he said firmly. "End of discussion." He had a set look on his face. "If you fear me, I'll lay my sword between us."

"I fear the steel more, Hugh," she said softly.

"Pardon?"

"Because of my . . . my nature, steel burns my flesh," she replied soberly.

"Let me look at your hands, lady," he said gently, "before you put out the lights."

"Why?" she asked hesitantly. Her palms still bore the marks of touching the mail, though the soreness left the first day.

"I remember . . . taking my mail off, seems a bad dream, now. I remember smelling burnt flesh and wondering where it came from." He looked at her palms, then kissed them. "I wonder . . . how much would you do for a true friend, if you risk so much for a stranger?"

"We must sleep," she replied. "I'm very tired." She gestured and the candles died.

She woke a little before dawn. *The rain has stopped*, she thought. *Perhaps things'll dry out*. Then she heard a faint tinkle of horse gear. She sat up. Fyl was gone, as well.

She slipped out of bed, careful not to disturb Hugh, and pulled a dress over her undershift. Then she went down to the great hall. A sense of doom fell over her.

She opened one of her front doors to a surreal scene.

An army, gloriously armed and bannered with Hugh's double dragon ensign, stood on the far hill, just beyond the ramp of her bridge. Many archers stood at attention, armed and ready.

A tall man in ragged robes stood on the middle of the bridge. He turned as Kayli stopped in her doorway.

"Surrender my man." His magnificent voice carried over the distance, loud as if he stood near her. He ignored the troops behind him.

Kayli left the charm in it, seductive, luring. It held nothing for her. "Never," she said calmly. "The man belongs to himself, not to any wizard."

"I will have him, whatever you say, woman," he replied contemptuously. He gestured and six oval objects the size of her fist flew past her head . . . *Yll-worm eggs*, she thought, and wondered if that were his only spell.

She turned inside. "Fyl," she shouted, then saw him by the kitchen door, charred mouse in his mouth. "Go to Hugh now! No questions!" He wheeled and flowed up the stairs with a speed that surprised her. She turned back to the scene before her. The eggs would land and open near their intended victim, to attack and kill. From what she recalled about them, they could only be put on a victim, like Hugh, if the wizard could see him. She hoped Hugh was awake, though.

An irate roar, stronger than usual, rang from beneath the bridge. The wizard looked around him, surprised. Ylgs appeared beside him, flowing up one of the bridge piers and onto the bridge with a suppleness Kayli thought long past him. She wondered if, somewhere in his senile brain, he remembered his purpose and sensed the threat of the wizard to his castle and mistress.

Dragon and wizard faced off silently for a moment. Then the wizard started chanting and gesturing. When he stopped, a blossom of blood appeared on Ylgs' left shoulder. He screamed in rage. That he could be hurt by spells brought a chill to Kayli's heart. The wizard started to chant again.

"Not that I want you up against one," she recalled her grandmother saying, "but remember your fire. You can live in it, bathe in it. Wizards burn as mortal men, Kayli, remember that."

She started a sweeping gesture, but an arrow pinned her sleeve to the door beside her. Her heart nearly stopped when she saw it was made of steel. She tore her sleeve free and started again.

She finished her gesture at the same time as Ylgs finally worked up a fiery belch at the man who caused him so much pain. She heard the wizard scream as the combined fireball hit him.

Then Ylgs screamed, engulfed in a rain of steely arrows. His exposed neck and belly, soft and vulnerable, quickly turned into a pincushion of arrows.

"No!" Kayli heard herself scream. She ran toward her dragon as he fell writhing across the bridge atop the wizard's remains.

The archers started toward the bridge. Beside the great dragon, Kayli realized he was dead, an arrow deep in his right eye. She looked up at the advancing men.

"No, go back!" she shouted, "Go back! He's dead!" Another arrow whizzed by her head. She feared being a better target, but she didn't want them killed. "Dragons immolate when they die, you fools! Go back!"

A dull thud sounded as the fire in the old worm's belly ignited flesh that could only burn with its own fire.

"Troy, go back!" She heard Hugh shout behind her. "She tells the truth!"

The oncoming men halted, far enough back to avoid the fireball that bloomed around Kayli. She heard Hugh scream, anguished, and realized he had no way of knowing she lived. A wonder that he cared crossed her mind. She dismissed it, as she found herself standing beside the smoking scales and bones of her old dragon. The charred skeleton of a man lay beneath the dragon's breastbone.

The men, some slightly singed, stood at point-blank

range, staring at Kayli. Stag head, afoot and standing in front, gestured. Rain started again.

She started to run, but froze at the movement of a bowman. He aimed at her, steel arrow ready to fire.

"Troy, no!" As Hugh shouted, Kayli watched as, almost in slow motion, an arrow sped toward her. She moved, but not far enough.

She fell as her shoulder filled with the pain of the steel piercing her flesh. The smell of the dead dragon in her nose kept her from catching the scent of her own flesh charring. She shut her eyes, oblivious to all but her pain.

When she opened her eyes again, the pain still thrummed through her. Hugh stood over her on one side, Fyl on his good shoulder; Stag head, Troy, stood on her other side, sword bared.

"She saved my life, Troy, no!" Hugh said.

"She is a wizard, as he was," Troy gestured at the man's skeleton. He pulled off his helm, revealing a man as dark as Hugh was golden.

"She is as mother," Hugh replied. "Her talent is only fire." He crouched and sat her up. "Help me, Troy. The arrow burns in her flesh!"

"Your mother, not mine," Troy replied stiffly.

"Use your sword, man. Strike the head off so I can back the arrow out," Hugh ordered.

Kayli turned her face into Hugh's chest and shut her eyes as the dark man raised his sword.

"I trusted you," Hugh said quietly, "and I served you. My lady harmed no one, save your enemy. I can't help her one-handed. If you kill her, you'll have to kill me as well, half brother."

"I'll help," Fyl chirped, causing Troy to stare at Hugh oddly.

"No, little one," Hugh ordered, "you'll hurt yourself. Metal is stronger than your little teeth. No, Troy, you help."

Kayli cringed as the sword clattered to the ground beside her. She fainted as hands tugged on the arrow.

Kayli woke again alone in her bed. Her shoulder throbbed. She could hear people in her hall. She rose, washed her face and hands, and dressed. She could hear rain on the roof.

Hugh stood and argued with Troy by the hearth of the great hall; Fyl was still ensconced on his shoulder.

"She wakes," one of Troy's men said.

"Kayli," Hugh said, going to her side as she reached the floor of the hall. "Are you all right, lady?" Fyl started to climb to her.

"Aye, Hugh. No, little one, my shoulder'll not bear touching." The little dragon looked hurt.

"This little fellow saved me, you know," Hugh said, patting him. "Though he said you sent him, he didn't know why but he felt he must obey. Those worms . . . without him killing them, I couldn't have warded them off, not six at once, not one-handed."

"Burned 'em all," Fyl chirped, stretching up. "Hugh tossed 'em on the floor and I cooked 'em." He preened proudly.

"Will you come with us?" Hugh asked.

"No, Hugh, I cannot," Kayli replied flatly. She felt a strange pain in her heart. A sense of desolation started in her.

"Kayli, I must go back," Hugh said, "I've obligations."

"I cannot leave, Hugh." She looked away. "You say I'm like your mother, ask her. As we get older, we . . . we belong to a place." She crossed her arms and gulped. She refused to have tears before these strangers. "Do not ask me again."

"I'll go," Fyl chimed in, "Adventures!"

That caught in Kayli's heart. She wheeled. "Go, Hugh," she said angrily, to hide the pain that engulfed her heart. "Go and take that ungrateful little beast with you! I can live here alone, I've done so for many years." If she had anything in hand, she would have thrown it. "Go and get these people with their great horses out of my hall! Begone!"

Kayli tried to cast a cold fire, to scare, but it failed, making her reel with weakness. She staggered to the banister so she wouldn't fall. She gathered up her composure and walked back up to the solace of her bedroom. She didn't hear Hugh scold Fyl for unfaithfulness.

She fell into her pillow, weeping at last. She didn't turn when her door opened and someone entered. She didn't even look when Hugh's big, freckled hand touched her shoulder.

"Go away, damn you!" she sobbed.

"Lass," he sat and stroked her back. "Kayli, your dragonet will stay. And I'll be back. I've business to settle, that's all. I swear I'll return."

"Don't promise, Hugh." She gulped to quell the sobs and turned to look at him. "You just want me to stop crying. I'm sure you've women after you where you're from, all prettier than I."

He touched her cheek. "I can only prove by doing, Kayli," he said quietly, "I've no choice in the going, as you have none in the staying. I *can* promise you that you are fairer to me than any other woman I've known, and I've not promised myself to another yet. Look for me before the moon is in the same quarter again, half moon. I promise that, lass."

"I . . . I . . ." she thought a moment, looking up at his open face. "I will look for you, then."

"You've not much conviction in that," he said softly, smiling a little sadly. "For reasons I don't understand completely, I want to prove myself to you, want to come back to you. I must be away. Troy wants to be well underway before the sun rises more." He scooped her up one-armed and kissed her cheek. "I'll be back, lady, I promise."

She lay still as he left, wondering and thinking, even after Fyl came in and curled up beside her.

THE RING OF LIFARI

by Josepha Sherman

I rejected "The Ring of Lifari" for the first of these volumes, because of the inelasticity of typeface; but I remembered the story for more than a whole year, and when it came in again, I reserved a place for it. I think you'll find it memorable, too.

L ike all Uzkeni towns, Alakent was a maze of whitewashed mud brick walls and unpaved streets, though now lent a certain blued glamour by the early twilight. And, thought Khaïta, Alakent's honest folk, like those in all Uzkeni towns, would already be barricading themselves for the night, leaving out in the dim silence only thieves, fools, and this one small, slim young woman who'd just barely reached this desert town before the gates had been shut till morning.

Bad fortune to have arrived now. Worse fortune, though, to have had that storm separate me from the caravan. Ha, and after all, the trouble I'd had convincing them that a woman alone was neither wanton nor bad luck! Ai, well, at least I'm here alive and unhurt, only footsore. Who knows? I might even be able to find an employer in Alakent to help me refill this sad purse of mine.

The guards at the gate were watching her, peering through the twilight, puzzled. "Better get yourself inside, lady! Don't want thieves to get you!"

They meant worse than thieves, of course. Dark eyes alive with wry humor, Khaïta bowed, only too well aware that in her refined smallness she looked, for all the dust of travel on tunic and trousers and long black braid, like

123

some lost little palace lady. She glanced down at the gleaming bow in her hand and shrugged. Small and female wasn't necessarily weak, as the caravan folk had had to concede after her arrows had brought in game for the lot of them, and a professional archer can usually take care of herself.

But right now she didn't want to have to prove anything; she only wanted a safe, soft bed for the night. And, lovely thought, a bath. Back prudently to a wall, Khaïta checked to see if she'd enough coins for respectability. Copper, copper . . . silver? Hey, now, a silver *drahim!* But wasn't it . . . Yes. Khaïta's hand clenched convulsively. A Perishani *drahim,* with the head of the King stamped in clear profile.

The King. Her father. And Khaïta winced in unexpected pain at the memory of words that should have long lost their sting. Cripple . . . worthless outcast. . . . Even though her handicap was nothing visible, still it was there, and she'd been abandoned at birth, just like any other . . . imperfect child.

Ahh, Dzvina take it! Homeless I may be, but hardships or no, I like my life! I'd have been miserable in a royal harim! Eh, and musing like this is a good way to get knifed! Father here can just buy me dinner and—

A sharp, choked cry of pain from an alleyway just before her cut into her thoughts. The startled archer had arrow to bow and was moving warily to the alley's mouth before she'd stopped to think. Two men were there, dim shapes in the uncertain light, crouched over a third, motionless figure. Khaïta saw a dagger flash, thought, *I can't just watch murder being done!* She couldn't see clearly enough to hit a small mark like a dagger, but her arrow shot neatly between the two men, embedding itself dramatically in the mud brick alley wall.

Both thieves whirled, open-mouthed. They couldn't have made out the archer's size or sex or youth, but they certainly could make out the menace of the drawn bow and the second arrow aimed steadily at them, and they broke and ran. Khaïta stood waiting grimly, arrow nocked, till she was sure they weren't going to try circling around behind her, then lowered her bow with a sigh.

Had she been defending a corpse?

No. Not quite. The archer knelt by the man's side, wincing as she realized the severity of the wound. Ardhina's mercy, there wasn't going to be too much she could do for him. . . . And he'd been such a well-made man, tall for an Uzkeni, richly dressed and proud-featured, dark of hair and beard. Khaïta started as she saw him stir, then heard him murmur in a soft, quick, angry voice that wasn't really meant for her ears:

"What a stupid way to die! Stabbed in the back by common thieves— What a stupid, stupid way to die!"

Suddenly his hand shot out, closed about the shocked Khaïta's wrist. "Listen to me, girl! I know I am slain, and so I charge you to obey this my wish!" His eyes blazed. "Will you obey me?"

Shaken, the archer nodded. A command from the dying was sacred; she couldn't refuse. The man sighed, more in relief, she thought, than in pain or fear of approaching death. He released her wrist, fumbling with a ring on his left hand. But when the archer would have helped him, the man drew away, and those burning eyes held her again.

"No. You shan't take this ring. Not yet . . ." His voice faltered for the first time, and the fierce eyes closed. When he opened them again, his voice was hurried, strained. "Listen to me well. When I am dead, take this ring from my hand and go to the house that stands at the end of Griffin Street. There you will give the ring to the one who answers the door. Do you understand?" At Khaïta's uneasy nod, "One word of warning, girl. Don't try to cheat me. For I am the sorcerer Melik-Kar, and this is the Ring of Lifari, and should you do other than what I've commanded, I promise you, you'll regret it."

With that, quite simply, he was dead.

After a moment, Khaïta reluctantly reached out a hand. The Ring of Lifari slid into her palm with a smooth, subtly alarming ease, a broad band of what seemed gold so pure as to be almost too soft for the wearing. On it was traced a very peculiar glyph that made Khaïta not wish to study it any further. With a shudder she slipped the ring into her purse and rose, bidding a silent farewell to bed and bath and dinner.

A vow was, after all, a vow.

Griffin Street was small, featureless in the darkness, narrow lengths of whitewashed walls broken now and again by heavily bolted doors. Featureless, and still, so very still. . . .

Angry at her nervousness, Khaïta walked quickly to the last of the doors and rapped on it with forced bravado, ready, as it swung open, to simply hand over the ring and leave. But—

It was Melik-Kar!

No, no, of course it wasn't. Oh, there was a resemblance, good gods, yes! But this man's eyes were disturbingly blank, not blind but somehow empty of life. Thoughts of sorcery whirling through her mind, Khaïta quickly handed over the ring. The man wordlessly slipped it onto his hand. For a long moment he stood motionless, the archer just as frozen, helplessly fascinated.

And then Khaïta sprang back in shock, hand tracing a quite involuntary sign against evil. For life had flashed into those dull eyes—*Melik-Kar! Melik-Kar indeed! The— the ring held his soul, placed it in this new body— And I helped!*

The man was laughing silently at her wide-eyed horror. "I see you recognize me. Ah, no, don't back away! You've done me a great service! Don't you wish a reward?"

Khaïta, struggling desperately for poise, shook her head, tempering the refusal with a little hand gesture that said plainly it wasn't necessary. The sorcerer frowned.

"Come, come, can't you speak— Ahh, no, I see the way of it. You *can't* speak, can you?"

Khaïta sighed, shook her head. She was, as her royal kinfolk had quickly discovered, quite mute.

"Tsk, and here I was wondering what misguided timidity had kept you from calling for help when I was dying!" He stopped at her shudder and gave her a most charming smile. "Never mind. Would you like this to be your reward, then? Would you like me to give you a voice?"

Gods! Wild-eyed, Khaïta stared at him.

And that was a mistake. Despite the urbanity of his smile, there was a raw power in the man's gaze, and a suddenly dazed Khaïta found herself moving gently into his reach. Alarmed and furious, she tore her glance away to snap the spell— Aie, too late! He'd seized her, and he seemed to have all the powers of the Earth behind him! Dear gods, yes, this new body of his could only be a Construct, she'd heard of such things, a created body, hard and cold and impervious as stone!

Despite the best of Khaïta's struggles, Melik-Kar lightly picked her up in his arms and carried her into the house. The archer glanced wildly about, seeing one great, sparsely furnished room. A massive stone stairway led up to the second floor and down into darkness. What light there was came from an intricately wrought bronze chandelier, suspended from the ceiling by what looked like nine alarmingly thin silk cords woven together in nine intricate knots.

"Don't fight so, girl. I'm not going to kill you. You've rendered me too great a service; magic prevents me from bearing the weight of your death."

That was hardly reassuring.

"But I can't let you go, either," continued Melik-Kar calmly. "You saw me take this new body, and even mute young women can find ways to tell tales. The priests of Alakent have managed to tolerate me so far, but I'm afraid they'd find this transformation of mine a bit too near blasphemy." He sounded more like a merchant discussing finance than a sorcerer. "I can't afford to have them turn people against me. Business is bad enough in so small a town."

He'd carried Khaïta down the stone stairway as he'd spoken, and stopped there in the cellar before a pit whose circular mouth was sealed by a grating in interwoven metal bars. The sorcerer dropped Khaïta casually to one side, and the archer struggled to her feet, knife in hand. No time for niceties; she lunged upward in a killing blow—

But the knife snapped in two against Melik-Kar's Construct chest. He caught the archer easily, held her out over the now unbarred opening. And then, without saying another word, he let Khaïta fall.

Aching, dizzy, the archer worked her slow way back to her feet. She'd gone limp in the fall, miraculously escaping with nothing worse than bruises. Escaped, though, to what? She stood, still trembling with shock, looking about at darkness and up at the opening. The grating had been replaced; she could see the metal bars shining dully in the dim light from the cellar.

If—if this is his idea of trying not *to kill me . . . Ardhina's mercy, what is this place?*

A pit? No more than a narrow pit? Had he left her to starve? No. Even in the darkness she could sense a vastness about her, and the archer wondered, and even dared a little hope. After all, so much of these lands lay on beds of limestone, and limestone did tend to be honeycombed with tunnels. And might one lead to the surface. . . ?

Or—the gods help her, why had she thought of this? —only into eternal Night.

How long had she been walking? And how far had she come? Khaïta gave a small, weary sigh. Oh, she'd found her bow, she'd made a torch from scraps of wood and cloth. That much, at least, was well. The air seemed fresh enough. But this tunnel twisted and bent so maddeningly! The silence was so heavy it smothered even the sound of her own light footsteps. Was there no end to this?

There was, and so sudden an end that Khaïta nearly fell, clutching bow and torch frantically as she stumbled down an unexpected nearly vertical drop. As the breathless archer reached more level footing, she found herself surrounded by beauty dimly seen in the smoky light, a cavern of pink and purple and gold. In the center of the cavern stood a column, a slim pillar of smooth, unmarked crystal that gave back the fire from Khaïta's torch a hundredfold as she approached in wary wonder. What enchantment could have created— It *couldn't* be natural!

Eh, but there was, all at once, the faintest of sly movements behind her! Moving slowly for all the sudden fierce pounding of her heart, the archer carefully put down her torch and just as carefully reached for an arrow and fit it to the bowstring. She'd pinpointed the sound, but would there be time to aim. . .?

Khaïta had one quick, terrifying glimpse of blazing blue-white eyes, sharp fangs, a dark-furred body tensed to spring—then her arrow took the thing in the throat! Choking, it crumpled, talons clawing stone as it tried and tried to reach its slayer as it died.

Finally it was still, and after a time Khaïta managed to catch her breath. What in the names of all the gods? Was it an animal? Was it only an animal? The taloned hands lacked thumbs, those were the fangs of a predator. An animal, yes, and covered with smooth, shining, blue-black fur. And where there was one, there might still be another—

She hadn't finished the thought before a second of the things crashed into her! The archer twisted desperately aside as fangs snapped just short of her throat. In the struggle she lost her footing, the torch flying from her hand, but the snarling beast fell with her. Khaïta, frantic, brought her linked hands down hard on the back of the creature's neck, just as she would have done with a human opponent. To her amazed relief, the beast went silently limp, a heap of gleaming fur. Khaïta scrambled to her feet, meaning to put an arrow through the thing before it recovered!

But then she froze, eyes wide. Impossible, impossible! Her torch had fallen against the crystal column—and now that column was all aflame! But crystal didn't—crystal couldn't—

She staggered back, fell, arms flung across her face to shield her eyes as the blazing pillar all at once flared up—

And was gone.

As her vision slowly cleared, Khaïta sat up, blinking. Someone was bending over her! She grabbed frantically for her bow, because that someone was fanged and black-furred!

But there was now true intelligence in the animal eyes, and a voice, distorted but still understandable, was saying, "Oh, you killed the female! A pity! Here I'd put them down here in the quiet hoping they'd breed. Such an infertile species— Eh, gently, girl. I'm not going to hurt you."

Khaïta stared. She gestured wildly from where the column had stood to the being who crouched before her.

"Yes, my silent one. I—or my essence, rather—was indeed trapped in that. But you freed me, willy-nilly, with the flames from your torch. My original body is, alas, long gone, so I took the only one that was unoccupied." The being straightened, flexing clawed hands tentatively. "And an awkward body it is, too! But it will serve till I find some more suitable home."

The archer tried to gesture, stopped, tried again, frustrated at not being able to voice her hundred questions aloud.

"Tell me girl, how come you down here? Surely you weren't exploring! No. Who was it cast you down here, hoping you'd conveniently die? Melik-Kar? Oh, I thought as much! Typical of his lack of professionalism!"

There was such a gleam in the feral eyes that Khaïta knew the answer even before she signed, *You are enemies?*

The being smiled, an alarming flash of fangs. "Oh, no, nothing so very dramatic. We're business rivals, that's all. You see, I was the first to settle in Alakent. I always did prefer small towns. Well, that's neither here nor there. Suffice it to say, I found just enough—ah—clients to be able to live here very nicely. But then Melik-Kar came. Bah! I do believe he's nothing more than some refugee! Probably made an enemy of someone more powerful than he, the charlatan! And why he picked Alakent . . . there just aren't enough customers in a town this size to comfortably support two sorcerers. I hadn't the slightest intention of being driven from my home. But . . . well now, I'll admit it, I was careless. Overconfident. And Melik-Kar, damn him, trapped me in my very house. Oh, he couldn't kill me, I was far too strong for that! But he could, he did, trap my spirit in crystal." The feral eyes flashed. "Tricked by that—play-actor of a sorcerer! Ahh, but I'll trick him! I'll trick and trap him right out of his body!"

But Khaïta shook her head, indicating with eyes and hands that Melik-Kar was already out of his body and into one that seemed quite invulnerable.

"So! Is he wearing a ring? Yes? I thought as much! That ring is mine! Why, yes, girl. That is the Ring of Lifari, as I'm sure he was insolent enough to tell you. And I am Lifari."

Khaïta bowed, only slightly ironically, signing, *Well and good, but how do we get out of here? Is there an exit?*

"What's that? Oh, no, no. But don't worry about that. Do you want revenge against Melik-Kar? Aie, don't glare. I admit it was a foolish question! Or course you do! Come with me, back the way you came, and we'll see what we shall see."

Lifari glanced up at the metal grating overhead. "Can you hit that thing with an arrow, girl?"

Puzzled, Khaïta nodded. But what could one arrow do?

"The arrowhead's iron, isn't it? Shoot, and watch."

The archer eyed him doubtfully, but she obeyed. The arrow struck cleanly, there was one brief, white-hot flash and a scent of burning—and the grating was gone.

"You see?" crowed Lifari. "Nothing in this house can survive the touch of iron. I should know, I designed it that way! Come, let's be going!"

He caught her about the waist, murmuring a quick, alien chant under his breath. Before the astonished Khaïta could struggle, the floor seemed to dissolve beneath her feet. There was a rather sickening blurring of space about her. Then abruptly she was released, and found herself, dazed, in the main room of the house, facing a stunned Melik-Kar, his attention all on the dark-furred shape at her side.

"Lifari!"

"Why, my dear friend, I'm amazed you've the skill to recognize me!" Contempt dripped from every word. "Amateur!"

"How so? How so?"

"To let the girl live! You must have realized there was always a chance she might free me!"

"I had to let her live, fool! Else the backlash would have—"

"Amateur, I say!"

"Adept enough to trap you, Lifari!"

"An accident! Look you, there were safe ways to kill the girl and still ground the power. But those would have been far too sophisticated for a refugee like you!"

Melik-Kar's eyes blazed. He growled something that sounded suspiciously like, "Damned provincial wizard!" and insulted power glittered in angry sparks about him.

Two sorcerers bickering like merchants. *It was almost funny,* thought Khaïta. *It would be funny, if I weren't caught in the middle of it! So let me say a silent farewell to the two of them and . . .*

But when she tried subtly to move, the archer was thrown halfway across the room by someone's magic. By the time her head had cleared, Khaïta found herself cornered by two men who'd gone beyond insult. Battle was joined. Neither spoke, neither moved, but their eyes were terrible, and the tension of fierce magic weighed down the air. Khaïta watched them keenly. Surely they'd now forgotten all about her? If she could slip past them, make a run for the door— Oh, no. Melik-Kar moved far too swiftly. Aie, even if she did elude him, if he won here, he'd come after her, no doubt of it!

Yet Lifari seemed to be the older, the more experienced, of the two. Surely he was the stronger?

But Melik-Kar has the ring, and with it and his Construct's body he's tireless! If he wins, Lifari dies—and so do I!

Hints of weariness were already showing on Lifari's beast-face. Desperate, Khaïta snatched up her bow, determined she'd not just stand waiting to die! But what could she do? Her knife had broken against Melik-Kar's chest, an arrow would just shatter! Dear gods, there must be a way . . .

Yes . . . the ring. God, pure gold, almost too pure, too soft for the wearing . . . yes? Oh, by the light, yes! There'd be only one chance, but she'd take it!

Khaïta softly slipped an arrow from her quiver, short-ening her grip on the shaft, thinking it made a terrible dagger. The gods grant the two rivals would stay like that, matched mind to mind, motionless as statues, just a bit longer. The gods grant neither sorcerer would notice her creeping cat-smooth toward Melik-Kar. The force of magic crackling in the air made her skin prickle and her limbs ache, and the pressure was growing and growing as she neared the sorcerer. So close, so close. How could he fail to see— But by now both rivals were totally focused on their magic, blind to all else! Melik-Kar's arms hung limply at his sides, and there glinted the ring, the soft golden ring. . . . The archer clenched her awkward dag-ger of an arrow, brought it up slowly, slowly, judging distance, angle, with a desperate eye.

And she slashed down at the Ring of Lifari! She felt the iron arrowhead grate against stony flesh, catch briefly between hand and ring, slash free and out across smooth gold— Aie, aie, but at an angle, she'd scratched the ring, notched it, no more than that! Melik-Kar struck out, a wild, instinctive backhanded blow that would have crushed her skull if she hadn't thrown herself aside. The archer rolled, came up on her feet, despairing, sure she was about to die.

But the ring, the ring! Cold iron slashing it had weak-ened it, loosened it, and Melik-Kar's mindless swing had sent it flying from his hand!

As Khaïta stood poised in fierce suspense, she saw the sorcerer freeze, arm still half raised. For a moment noth-ing at all happened.

And then, Melik-Kar no longer, the lifeless Construct toppled, and broke apart on the stone floor.

As Khaïta stared, stunned, horrified, at what had been a living being a bare instant ago, she heard Lifari give a sharp, savage laugh as he snatched up the ring with clawed fingers.

"Beautiful! Beautiful! But did you hurt it? No, no, the glyph's still whole, the gold's only scratched. Nothing I can't put to rights. Pity the magic insisted on so soft a metal. But then you wouldn't have been able to do what you did! Hah, the fool! Slain by a magicless little bit of a girl! And now his spirit's lost, he no longer has a host body to bear it! Or . . . has he?"

At that abrupt change in tone, Khaïta turned to him sharply. And what she saw in Lifari's eyes— Gods, gods, how she'd misjudged him, lulled by his chatter! Dear gods, he was every bit as cold and ruthless a businessman as his late rival!

"I'm sorry for this, my dear. But Melik-Kar's spirit is still lingering. He can't get at me. But you—I *am* sorry."

Khaïta had never fit arrow to bow with greater speed. But she couldn't fire! Aie, she couldn't loose the arrow though she fought the sorcerer's will till he was gasping for breath!

"No, girl. You can't shoot me. Now please understand, this is nothing personal. But I really don't want Melik-Kar back again."

Khaïta looked about wildly. Yes! *He said I couldn't shoot at him, he didn't say I couldn't shoot elsewhere! And Lifari himself told me that nothing here can withstand the touch of iron!*

Even as the sorcerer gathered power swirling about him, Khaïta loosed her arrow—straight for the great bronze chandelier over their heads! Oh, and that iron arrowhead sliced right through the nine-fold silk cords as though they'd been mist! The massive chandelier fell with a roar.

And it crushed the sorcerer Lifari beneath it.

After a breathless moment the archer dared to look. There was blood staining the stone floor, but all that could be seen of what had been the sorcerer was one clawed hand protruding from the bronze weight. That hand still wore the ring, and Khaïta gritted her teeth and carefully removed the gold circle.

But no sooner had she taken it than there came a sudden blow, a terrible pressure on her mind, her spirit, a crushing force that brought the archer staggering to her feet, ring clenched helplessly in her hand. Sobbing for breath, she knew the cause: Lifari! He was here, he was still here! His spirit was beating savagely at her being, trying to kill, trying to cast her into oblivion so he could wear her body as a mortal shell! And the anguish of it— Aie, aie, she couldn't hold him off!

Then suddenly there was a fierce impact against the first force, and the immediate torment lessened. But there was no mercy in it; through the haze of psychic pain Khaïta realized the truth.

Melik-Kar! He'll fight Lifari for me, my body means life to the victor! I don't know what to do, I'm no sorceress, I can't hope to defeat either one of them! Whichever wins, I'll die!

But one clear, cool, sane little voice at the back of her mind kept insisting, *No. The Ring of Lifari keeps them here. You've a weapon against them. Use it.*

Khaïta painfully forced open her clenched hand and threw down the little circlet. Now, now, while their attention was divided!

Sobbing, shaking with exhaustion, the archer seized an arrow from her quiver. The glyph on the ring, Lifari had worried lest the glyph be harmed, surely it *could* be harmed! Gods, let that be so! She struck down at the ring, struck again and again with the cold iron arrowhead, sometimes hitting, sometimes missing, struck again and again and again! All at once the psychic pain returned in all its horror. They knew, oh, they knew what she was doing! They'd stop her by tearing her mind apart!

Khaïta struck down wildly one last time, all her failing strength behind the blow. A combined surge of sheer, impotent fury blazed at her and tore a scream of silent anguish from her—

And then, with shocking suddenness, the torment was over. And that which had been the rivals Melik-Kar and Lifari was gone beyond all returning.

How long had she been huddling numbly? The archer straightened slowly, wincing. The arrow's shaft had snapped and splintered, she noted dully, and her palms were bleeding, but that didn't matter yet. Only the ring mattered.

But the Ring of Lifari was no more. She'd torn apart the sorcerous glyph, and all that remained now was a flattened, broken thing that might or might not have been gold. And Khaïta, mind clearing abruptly at the sight, gave a sudden wild laugh, of relief.

Crippled, am I? she called in silent triumph to those faceless ones who'd abandoned her so long ago. *Helpless, am I? Ahh, thank you, gods, thank you!*

She sprang to her feet, snatching up her bow, and ran with all her strength from that dark house. But once outside, the archer stopped, weak with reaction, leaning against a wall, head thrown back.

For morning had come to Griffin Street, morning, the end of sorcery, and the blessèd, blessèd sunlight was beating down on Khaïta's upturned, laughing face.

RITE OF PASSAGE

by Jennifer Roberson

In general I tend to distrust the story of a swordswoman teamed up with a mighty man who is an even better swordsman—or is he?—but I make an exception for Jennifer Roberson's Sandtiger and Del, who made their appearance in the subtly-crafted "Lady and the Tiger" in the second of these anthologies. In the meantime, Jennifer has published many books, four in her Cheysuli series, beginning with SHAPECHANGERS (DAW, 1984); and she has written a novel about Tiger and Del, SWORD-DANCER, (DAW, 1986) which I read in manuscript and found so good that I turned the pages with mixed feelings, eager to see what happened next and simultaneously never wanting it to end. My son Patrick, grabbing each page almost as I read it, liked it as much as I did, which is *very* rare!

Here is another adventure about these same two characters, and I will only warn you that it's not what it seems to be.

But then, one of Jennifer's greatnesses is that she never writes *quite* the story you expect.

The woman moved like a dancer. Her feet sluffed through the warm sand with the soft, seductive sibilance of bare flesh against fine-grained dust. Wisps rose, drifted; layered our bodies in dull, gritty shrouds: pale umber, ocher-bronze, taupe-gray.

But the shrouds, I thought, were applicable; the woman could kill us all.

I watched her move. I watched the others watch her

move. All men. No women here, at this moment, under such circumstances; never.

Except for Del.

I watched her move: detached appreciation. Admiration, as always. And pride. Two-edged pride. One: that the woman brought honor to the ritual of the dance within the circle, and two: that she was my right hand, my left hand; companion, swordmate, bedmate.

Edged? Of course. Pride is always a two-edged blade. With Del, the second edge is the sharpest of all, for *me*, because for the Sandtiger to speak of pride in Del is to speak also of possessiveness. She'd told me once that a man proud of a woman is too often prouder of his possession *of* her, and not of the woman for being herself.

I saw her point, but . . . well, Del and I don't always agree. But then, if we did, life would be truly boring.

I watched Del and the men who watched her as a matter of course, but I also watched the man she faced in the circle. I saw the signature pattern of his sword flashing in the sunlight, Southron-style: dip here, feint there, slash, lunge, cut, thrust . . . and always trying to throw the flashes and glints into her eyes. With precise purpose, of course; ordinarily, a shrewd ploy. Another opponent might have winced or squinted against the blinding light, giving over the advantage; Del didn't. But then, Del was accustomed to manufacturing her own light with that Northern sword of hers; the Southron one the man used was hardly a match for her own.

He was good. Almost quite good. But not quite. Certainly not good enough to overcome Del.

I knew she would kill him. But *he* didn't. He hadn't realized it yet.

Few men do realize it when they enter the circle with Del. They only see her: Del, the Northern woman with blond, cornsilk hair and blue, blue eyes. Her perfect face with its sun-gilded flesh stretched taut across flawless bones. They see all of that, and her magnificent body, and they hardly notice the sword in her hands. Instead, they smile. They feel tolerant and magnanimous, because they must face a woman, and a beautiful woman. But because she is beautiful they will give her anything, if only to share a moment of her time, and so they give her their lives.

She danced. Long legs, long arms, bared to the Southron sun; Del wears a sleeveless thigh-length leather tunic bordered with Northern runes. But the runes were now a blur of blue silk against dark leather as she moved.

Step. Step. Slide. Skip. Miniscule shifting of balance from one hip to the other. Sinews sliding beneath the flesh of her arms as she parried and riposted. All in the wrists, with Del. A delicate tracery of blade tip against the afternoon sky, blocking her opponent's weapon with a latticework of steel.

Del never set out to be a killer. Even now she isn't, quite; she's a sword-dancer, like me. But in this line of work, more often than not, the dance—a ritualized exhibition of highly-trained sword-skill—becomes serious and people die.

As this man would die, regardless of his own particular skill. Regardless of how many years he had apprenticed with a shodo or how many skill levels he had attained. He still danced, but he was dead.

She is simply that good.

I sighed a little, watching her. She didn't *play* with him, precisely, being too well-trained for such arrogance within the circle, but I could see she had judged and acknowledged her opponent's sword-skill as less than her own. It wouldn't make her smile; not Del. It wouldn't make her careless. But it *would* make her examine the limits of his talent with the unlimited repertoire of her own, and show him what it meant to step into the circle with someone of her caliber.

Regardless of her gender.

"Sword-dancer?" The question came from a man who stepped up next to me outside of the circle, slipping out of the crowd to stand closer to me than I liked. "Sandtiger?"

I didn't take my eyes from the dance, but I could see the man. Young. Copper-skinned. Swathed in a rich silk burnous of melon orange, sashed with a belt of gold-freighted bronze. A small turban hid most of his hair, but not the fringe of dark brown lashes surrounding hazel eyes.

"Sandtiger?" he asked again, hands tucked into voluminous sleeves.

"Sandtiger," I agreed, still watching the dance.

He sighed a little and smiled. The smile faded; he realized my attention was mostly on the circle, not on him. For just an instant, anxiety flickered in his eyes. "My master offers gold to the sword-dancer called the Sandtiger."

Well, Del could win without me watching. I turned to face the young man at once. "Employment?" I asked smoothly.

A bob of turbaned head. "Of great urgency, my lord Sandtiger. My master waits to speak with you."

I didn't answer at once. Too much noise. All the indrawn breaths of the onlookers reverberated as one tremendous hiss of shock and disbelief. Well, I could have warned them. . . No doubt he was too overcome by the fact he danced with a woman, even a woman who was quite obviously dangerous. No doubt he grew lazy. Or desperate. And now he was plainly dead.

I glanced at Del, automatically evaluating her condition. Her face bore a faint sheen of sweat. She was sun-flushed, lips pressed together. Blond hair, disheveled and damp, hung around her shoulders. But her breathing was even and shallow; the Southroner had hardly pressed her at all.

She turned and looked at me. The Northern sword, blood-painted now, hung loosely in her hand. She hunched one shoulder almost imperceptibly—a comment; an answer to my unspoken question—and then she nodded, only once; an equally private exchange.

I turned back to the turbaned messenger. A servant. I thought, but not just any servant. Whoever his master was, his wealth was manifest. And in the South, wealth is synonymous with power.

"Well?" I suggested.

The hazel eyes were fixed on Del as she cleaned her sword of blood. The onlookers huddled and muttered among themselves, settling bets; none were winners, I knew, except for the one wise man who knew the woman better than most. Many drifted away from the circle

entirely; away from the woman who had killed one of
their number in a supremely masculine occupation with
supremely "masculine" skill.

Sword-dancing isn't for everyone, any more than assas-
sination is. The profession carries its own weight in legend and superstition. And now Del, once more, turned
Southron tradition upside down and inside out.

I smiled a little. The servant looked back at me. He
didn't smile at all. "A *woman.*" Two words: disbelief,
shock, a trace of anger as well. Underlying hostility: *a
woman had beaten a man.*

"A woman," I agreed blandly. "About that job. . . ?"

He pulled himself together. "My master extends an
invitation for you to take tea with him. I am not author-
ized to inform you of the employment he has to offer.
Will you come?"

Tea. Not one of my favorite drinks. Especially effang
tea, gritty, thick, offensive, but customary in the South.
Maybe I could talk the man into some aqivi . . . "I'll
come," I agreed. "Where to?"

The servant gestured expansively, one smooth hand
sweeping out of its silken sleeve. "This way, my lord
Sandtiger."

And so I left Del behind, as I so often had to when we
rode the Southron sands, and went with the servant to
see what the master had to offer.

Damp hair tumbled over her shoulders. Her skin glowed
apricot-pink from the bath-water's heat. Dressed in a
fresh tunic—this one bordered with crimson silk—she sat
on the edge of the narrow cot, bending to lace sandals
cross-gartered to her knees. "Well?"

Del was never one to waste her breath on two words
when one would do. But then, she knew she didn't have
to, with me. Enough time spent together in deadly situa-
tions had honed language down to only a few necessary
words.

I shut the door behind me. The inn wasn't the best;
we'd spent the last of our coppers a couple of weeks ago
searching for the man Del had just dispatched in the
circle. Since then our only income had been wagers won

from unsuspecting Southron men betting against the Northern woman. Hoolies, the only way we could pay *this* bill was to use all the bets I'd just won, leaving us no extra. That's the lot of a sword-dancer: rich one day, broke the next.

Today was a rich day, thanks to the job I'd just accepted.

"I said I'd have to check with my partner," I said, "but, frankly, we needed the money, and I didn't dare tell him about you."

One shoulder moved in a negligent shrug. "We agreed I'd keep a low profile while we were in the South, Tiger, to make things easier." She didn't so much as glance at me as she said it, but her even tone was eloquent; in the South, women aren't due the respect men are. Women bear children, tend the man, tend the household. They don't enter business. They *certainly* don't enter the circle.

"Yes, well . . . Del, this was a little different."

She waited in silence for the explanation.

I sighed. "It's like this," I told her. "Our employer is a *khemi*."

Del merely frowned.

I sighed again, heavily. "It's a religious sect. An offshoot of the Hamidaa faith. Hamidaa hold majority here."

She nodded, but the frown didn't fade.

"*Khemi* are zealots," I explained. "They take the word of the Hamidaa'n—the sacred scrolls of the Hamidaa—rather literally."

"And what does the Hamidaa'n say?"

"That women are abomination, unclean vessels that should not be touched, spoken to or allowed to enter a *khemi's* thoughts."

"Pretty conclusive," Del observed after a moment. "Can't be too many *khemi* left, if they don't have congress with women."

She was taking it better than I'd expected. I imagine they've figured out a few loopholes, since the job involves a son. Ordinarily I'd have turned it down, of course, since I do have *some* sensibilities, after all, but we really *do* need the money."

"Just what *is* this job?"

"We are expected to negotiate the release of this son, who was kidnapped two months ago."

"Negotiate." Del nodded. "That means steal back. Who, how and when?"

"Name's Dario," I said. "Soon as possible."

Del combed slender fingers through damp hair. Her attention seemed divided, but I knew she listened intently. "That's the who and the when. What about the how?"

"Haven't gotten that far. I wanted to leave something for *you* to contribute."

She smiled briefly. "I imagine this *khemi* had an explanation for the kidnapping."

"Says a neighboring tanzeer had the boy taken to force trade concessions."

Pale brows slide up. "Trade concessions? Tanzeer? That means— "

"It means our employer is the tanzeer of *this* domain, bascha, and he's more than willing to pay handsomely." I pulled the leather purse out of a pocket in my russet burnous and rattled the contents with pleasure. "Half up front, half after. *This* is enough to last six months, depending on how extravagant we feel once the job is done. Imagine how rich we'll be when we're paid the *other* half."

"You and your gold . . ." Del's attention was mostly on the sword she unsheathed and set across her lap. "Sounds easy enough. When do we leave?"

"About a half hour ago."

Rez. Small enough town, was Rez, capping a domain not much larger. No wonder the tanzeer had deemed it necessary to go to such dramatic lengths as kidnapping to get concessions from Dumaan's tanzeer. Dumaan had been a rich town, rich domain. Dumaan had wealth to spare.

Some of it was in my purse.

Del and I did a careful reconnoitering of Rez, locating the puny palace and paying strict attention to the comings and goings of palace servants. It is the servant population that forms the heart of any tanzeer's palace; subsequently, it is the servant population that forms the heart of any city, town, village. You don't see a tanzeer without first seeing his servants, any more than you break into a tanzeer's palace without first figuring out how to get past his loyal servants.

A day spent loitering outside the ramshackle walls of the dilapidated palace with the rest of the bored petitioners did get me a little information. I now knew one thing was certain: Rez's tanzeer didn't subscribe to the same religion Dumaan's did. Or there wouldn't be female servants on marketing expeditions. And there *certainly* wouldn't be harem girls.

It was Del who came up with the idea. I mostly watched the silk-swathed women spill out of the palace gates, giggling among themselves like children. Hoolies, for all I knew they *were* children; the silk burnouses hid everything save hands and sandaled feet, and the hands clutched at bright draperies eagerly, as if unwilling to share with the petitioners what the tanzeer saw any time he wanted. They were accompanied by three men in correspondingly bright silks and turbans; eunuchs, I knew, judging by bulk and Southron custom.

As I watched, Del considered. And then she dragged me off into the labyrinthine market stalls and made me listen in silence as she explained her plan.

Since she wouldn't let me talk, I did what I could to dissuade her. I shook my head repeatedly, vehemently rejecting her suggestion.

Finally, she stopped and glared. "Have you a better idea? Or *any* idea at all?"

I scowled. "That's unfair, Del. I haven't had time to think of one."

"No. You've been too busy ogling harem girls." A hand plastered across my mouth kept me from replying. "Wait here while I get the things we need." And she was gone.

Disgruntled, I waited in the shade of a saffron-dyed canvas awning, out of direct sunlight. The Southron sun can leach the sense from your head if you stay out in it too long; I wondered if it had finally gotten to Del's Northern brains.

She came back a while later lugging an armload of silks and spent several minutes laboriously separating them until she had one suit of masculine apparel and one of feminine. And then I began to understand.

"*Delilah*—"

"Put the clothes on." She plopped a creamy silken turban down on top of the pile in my arms. "We're going into the palace as soon as we're dressed."

"You want me to masquerade as a *eunuch*—?"

"You can't much masquerade as a harem girl, can you?" A smile curved the corners of her mouth. "Get dressed, Tiger—we'll be in and out in no time with Dario in tow."

"The *khemi* may have the right idea," I muttered in disgust, staring at the clothing in my arms. "How does a eunuch act?"

"Probably not much different from the Sandtiger." Her words were muffled behind the multitudinous robes she was bundling herself into. "Ready?"

"I haven't even started."

"Hurry, Tiger. We have to insinuate ourselves into that flock of Southron sillies. And they're due to come by here about—*now*. Tiger—come *on*—"

Silks whipping, tassels flying, Del hastened after the women as they bobbed and weaved their way through the narrow stallways on their way back to the palace. Hastily I jerked on my eunuch's robes, slapped the turban on my head and went after her.

As always, the fist clenched itself into the wall of my belly as I passed guard after guard on my way into the palace. Del fit in with the other girls well enough—though a head taller than most—but *I* felt about as innocuous as a sandtiger in a flock of day-old goat kids. Nonetheless, no one paid much attention to me as we paraded down the corridors of the musty old palace.

I wasn't certain I *liked* being taken for a eunuch so easily.

I watched as Del in her rose-colored robes allowed the other girls to move ahead of her. Now we brought up the rear. I saw Del's quick hand gesture; we ducked out going around the next bend and huddled in a cavernous doorway.

"All right," she murmured. "We've passed four corridors—Dario's supposed to be in a room off the fifth. Come on, Tiger."

Sighing, I followed as she darted out of the doorway and headed down the appropriate corridor at a run. I *didn't* run, but only because I decided it was not in keeping with a eunuch's decorum.

I caught up to her outside yet another doorway. This one bore a large iron lock attached to the handle. "Dario?" I asked.

Del shrugged. "The women said it was. No reason not to trust them."

I glanced around the corridor uneasily. "Fine. *You* trust them, then. But did they slip you a key as well?"

"I already had one." She displayed it. "I borrowed it from the same eunuch who donated his clothing to you."

"Borrowed" key, "donated" clothing. Borrowed *time*, more like. "Hurry up, Del. Our luck can't hold forever."

She turned and inserted the key into the lock. Iron grated on iron; I wished for a little fat to oil the mechanism. But just about the time I was opening my mouth to urge a little more care, the lock surrendered and the door was ours.

Del shoved; nothing happened. I leaned on it a little and felt it move. Rust sifted from all the hinges. But the door stood open at last.

The room, as we'd hoped, was occupied. The occupant stood in the precise center of the little room—cell, really—and stared at us anxiously. He was, I judged, not much past ten or twelve. Dark-haired, dark-skinned, brown-eyed, clad in silken jade-green jodhpurs and soiled lime-colored tunic; two months had played havoc with all his finery. He was thin, a little gaunt, but still had both arms, both legs, his head; Rez's tanzeer, it appeared, didn't desire to injure Dumaan's heir, only to arrange a more equitable trade alliance.

And now the leverage was gone.

"Here, Dario." Del, smiling encouragingly, reached under a couple of layers of silken harem robes and pulled out more clouds of the stuff. Orange. It dripped from her hands: a woman's robes. "Put these on. Use the hood and modesty veil. Walk with your head down. Stay close to me and they'll never know the difference." Her warm smile flashed again. "We're getting you out of this place."

The boy didn't move. "Hamidaa'n tells us women are abomination, unclean vessels placed upon the earth by demons. They are the excrescence of all our former lives." Dario spoke matter-of-factly in a thin, clear voice. "I will touch nothing of women, speak to no women, admit nothing of women into my thoughts. I am *khemi*." His eyes ignored Del altogether and looked only at me. "*You* are a man, A Southron; *you* understand."

After a moment of absolute silence in which all I could hear were the rats scraping in the wall, I looked at Del.

She was pale but otherwise unshaken. At least, I thought she was. Sometimes you can't tell, with her. She can be cold, she can be hard, she can be ruthless—out of the circle as well as in. But she can also laugh and cry and shout aloud in an almost childish display of spirits too exuberant to be contained.

She did none of those things now. I thought, as I watched her looking at the boy, she had never met an opponent such as this son of the Hamidaa'n.

And I thought she was at a loss for what to do and how to answer for the first time in her life.

Slowly I squatted down in the cell. I was eye to eye with the boy. I smiled. "Choices," I said casually, "are sometimes difficult to make. A man may believe a choice between life and death is no choice at all, given his preference for staying alive, but it isn't always that simple. Now, something tells me you'd like very much to get out of here. Am I right?"

His chin trembled a little. He firmed it. "My father will send men to rescue me."

"Your father sent *us* to rescue you." I didn't bother to tell him his *khemi* father had no idea my partner was a woman. "A choice, Dario. Come with us now and we'll take you to your father, or stay here in this stinking rat-hole."

Something squeaked and scrabbled in the wall behind the boy. I couldn't have timed it better.

Dario looked down at his bare feet sharply. Like the rest of him, they were dirty. But they also bore torn, triangular rat bites.

"Choices, Dario, are sometimes *easy* to make. But, once made, you have to live with them."

He was shaking. Tears began to gather in his eyes. Teeth bit into his lower lip as he stared resolutely at me, ignoring Del altogether. "Hamidaa'n tells us women are abomination, unclean vessels—"

He stopped talking because I closed his mouth with my hand. I am large. So is my hand. Most of Dario's face disappeared beneath my palm and fingers. "Enough," I told him pleasantly. "I have no doubts you can quote scripture with the best of them, *khemi,* but now is not the time. Now *is* the time for you to make your choice." I released him and rose, gesturing toward Del and the silks.

Dario scrubbed the heel of a grimy hand across an equally dirty face. He stretched the flesh all out of shape, especially around the eyes; an attempt to persuade imminent tears to go elsewhere immediately. He caught a handful of lank hair behind an ear and tugged, hard, as if hoping *that* pain would make the decision itself less painful. I watched the boy struggle with his convictions and thought him very strong, if totally misguided.

Finally he looked up at me from fierce brown eyes. "I will walk out like *this.*"

"And be caught in an instant," I pointed out. "The idea here, Dario, is to pass you off as a woman—or at least a *girl*—because otherwise we don't stand a chance of getting you out." I glanced sidelong at Del; her silence is always very eloquent. "Decide, Dario. Del and I can't waste any more time on you."

He flinched. But he made his decision more quickly than I'd expected. "*You* hand me the clothes."

"Oh, *I* see—from my hands they're cleaner?" I jerked

the silks from Del's hand and threw them at Dario. "Put them on. *Now.*"

He allowed them to slither off his body to the ground. I thought he might grind them into the soiled flooring, but he didn't. He picked them up and dragged them over his head, sliding stiff arms through the sleeves. The silks were much too large for him, but I thought as long as Del and I stuffed him between us, it might work.

"Now," I said to Del, and as one we each grabbed an arm and hustled Dario out of the cell. The brat protested, of course, claiming Del's touch would soil him past redemption; after *I* threatened to soil him, he shut up and let us direct him through the corridors.

We reached the nearest exit. I leaned on the door and it grated open, spilling sunlight into the corridor—

—and came face to face with four large eunuchs.

Armed eunuchs.

For a moment I thought maybe, just *maybe*, we might make it past them. But I don't suppose my face—stubbled, scarred, lacking excess flesh—looks much like a eunuch's. And although I claimed the height, I had none of the customary bulk. At any rate, they each drew a sword and advanced through the door as we gave way into the corridor.

"Hoolies," I said in disgust. "I think our luck just ran out."

"Something like," Del agreed, and parted the folds of her silken robes to yank her own sword free of its harness and sheath.

I shoved Dario behind me, nearly grinding him into the wall in an effort to sweep him clear of danger. Like Del I had unsheathed my sword, but I wasted a moment longer tearing the no-longer-necessary silks from my body.

Four to two. Not bad odds, when you consider Del and I are worth at *least* two to one when it comes to sword-dancing, probably more like three to one. Sword *fighting*, however, is different; it showed as the first eunuch lumbered past Del to engage me and discovered discounting Del was as good as discounting life. He lost his.

I heard Dario's outcry behind me. I spared him a

glance; he was fine. Just staring gape-mouthed at Del in
shock. Grimly I smiled as Del engaged another eunuch
while the remaining two came at me.

When involved in a fight that may end your life at any
moment, you don't have much time to keep tabs on what
anyone else is doing. It is deadly to split your concentration. And yet I found mine split twice. There was Dario,
of course; I was certain the eunuchs wouldn't hurt him,
but it was entirely possible he might not duck a sword
swipe meant for *me*. But there was also Del. I knew
better than to worry about her—Del had proved her
worth with a sword already, even as she did again—but a
partnership is precisely that: two or more people engaged
in an activity or form of commerce that should profit
both or all. If it's a *good* partnership, none of the parties
involved bothers to wonder what makes it that way. It
just *is*.

So I didn't *worry* about Del, exactly, but I did keep an
eye on her just to make sure she wasn't in any trouble.
I'd learned that was all right in the parlance of our partnership; often enough, and even now, she did the same for
me. It's an equality two sword-dancers *must* share if they
are working together in the circle. Ours was an equality
fashioned by shared danger and shared victory, in the
circle and out of it. And I'd learned that in the circle, in the
sword-dance, because of Del, gender no longer mattered.

Simply put: you're good, or you're dead.

Two men. My blade was already bloodied; I'd pinked
one man in the arm and the other in the belly. Neither
wound would stop either guard. So I tried again.

Behind me, I heard Dario breathing noisily. In pain?
A quick glance; he seemed to be all right. Just shocked
and frightened by the violence.

Beyond the eunuchs, I saw Del in rose-colored robes. I
heard the whine and whistle of her Northern sword as
she brought it across the corridor in a two-handed sweep
intended to relieve her opponent of his head. She is tall.
She is strong. I have seen her do it before.

I saw her do it again, although it was only in a series of
disjointed glances; I had my own head to concern myself
with at the moment. It remained attached, but only just;

one of the eunuchs parried my sword while his partner slashed at my neck. Braced, I jerked my head aside and leaped sideways even as I used the strength of my wrists to smash aside the other sword. My size is often a blessing.

My shoulder rammed into the corridor wall, sticky, smelling of blood. As I pushed off the wall, I realized I also was sticky and smelled of blood; the beheaded body had drenched me.

"Son of a dog!" one of the eunuchs shouted at me.

He'd have done better to save his breath; Del, working contrapuntally against my own sword-song, killed the man with the mouth while I took out his fellow guard.

Four dead, two standing: Del and I.

And one more slumped against the wall in shock, brown eyes nearly as wide open as the mouth: Dario.

I spat blood. Mine; I'd bitten my lip. But the blood splattered across Del's face as well as mine—Dario had been missed entirely—belonged to the beheaded man.

Del reached out and caught a handful of the silk swathing Dario. "Come." She dragged him toward the open door.

When she takes *that* tone, no one argues with her.

We stumbled out into the sunlight, blinked, squinted, determined our precise location in relationship to the palace entrance; once determined, we started running. Even Dario.

Without Del's help.

No more fluttering past the gate guards like a clutch of colorful hatchlings. But there were only two of them, after all; Del took one, I the other, and a moment later we were running again, Dario in tow.

Horses waited for us in the market, but only two. I sheathed my sword and threw Dario up on the rump of Del's horse even as *she* sheathed and swung up, then jumped aboard my stud and headed him through the winding alleyways with Del—and Dario—in the lead. Hooves clicked against stall supports; I gritted my teeth and waited for the anticipated result—

—and heard the shouted curses of the angry merchant as voluminous folds of canvas collapsed into the alley.

Ahead of me, Dario was an orange bud against Del's

full-blown rosy bloom. Silk snapped and rippled as she took her gelding through the alleys at a dead run, putting him over handcarts, bushel baskets, piles of rolled rugs and water jugs. Dario, clinging, was engulfed in clouds of silk. But somehow, he hung on.

Hung on to a *woman*.

We stopped running when we left Rez behind and entered the desert between the two domains. We stopped walking when we reached the oasis.

"Water stop." I unhooked foot from stirrup and slid off my stud, unslung the goatskin bota from the saddle and headed for the well. "Can't stay for long, Dario— drink up, now."

The boy was exhausted. His stay in the dungeon hadn't done much for his color or spirits, no matter how hard he tried to show us only fierce determination. Del, still in the saddle, offered him a steadying hand as he tried to dismount; he ignored it. And I ignored his startled outcry as he slid off the horse's rump and landed in the sand on *his*.

Del unhooked and jumped down. Sunlight flashed off the hilt of her Northern sword. I saw Dario staring at it as well as at Del. No more shock. No more gaping mouth. Consideration, instead. And doubt. But I didn't think it was *self*-doubt.

Del was at the well with her own bota. Dario still hunched on the sand: a gleaming pile of orange silk. "You're burning daylight," I told him as I levered the bucket up. "Do your share, boy—water the horses."

"*Woman's* work." He spat it out between thin lips.

"*Boy's* work, if he wants to drink."

Dario got up slowly, tore the offending silks from his bedraggled body and marched across the sand to the well. He snatched the bucket out of Del's hands. An improvement, I thought, in willingness if not in manners. But as he tipped the bucket up to drink, I took it out of his hands.

"Horses *first*."

He was so angry he wanted to spit. But, desert-born, he knew better; he didn't waste the moisture. He just marched back to the horses and grabbed reins to lead them to the well.

That's when I saw the blood.

"Hoolies, the boy's *hurt*—" I threw my bota down and made it to Dario in two steps. Startled, he spun as I grabbed a shoulder. He lost the reins, but the horses, smelling water, only went as far as Del and the well. "Where are you cut?" I asked. "How badly?"

"But—I'm *not*—" He twisted, trying to see the blood. "The man she killed spurted all over the corridor—"

"But not all over *you*," I said flatly. "Dario—"

"Leave him alone." Del was at my side. "Tiger, turn your back."

"What—?"

"Turn your back." Almost without waiting for my response, she locked her hands in the waistband of Dario's jodhpurs.

"No!" Dario *screamed* it; I spun around with Del's name in my mouth as I heard the jodhpurs tear.

"A *girl*," she declared. *"A girl—"*

Dario clutched jodhpurs against belly. He—*she?*—was yelling vicious *khemi* epithets at Del. Also at me.

"Del—" I began.

"I *looked*, Tiger, and unless the *khemi* have taken to mutilating their boys, *this* boy is not a boy at all." She glared at the quivering Dario. "How in hoolies can you spout that *khemi* filth, *girl?* How do you justify it?"

"I am *khemi*," Dario quavered. "The Hamidaa'n tells us women are abomination, unclean vessels placed upon the earth by demons. They are the excrescence of all our former lives." Tears spilled over.

"That is no excuse—" But I wasn't allowed to finish.

"Tiger." Del cut me off with a sharp gesture. Her expression had altered significantly. Gone was the anger, the shock, the outrage. In its place I saw compassion. "Tiger, it *is* an excuse—or, at least, a reason for this masquerade. And now I want you to go away. There is something Dario and I must attend to."

"Away—?"

"Away."

I went to the far side of the well and sat down to wait.

It didn't take long. I heard the sounds of silk being torn, low-voiced conversation from Del, muted responses from Dario. He—*she*—had undergone a tremendous change in attitude.

Well, I might, too, if someone discovered *I* was a woman instead of a man.

Especially at *my* age.

"Water the horses," Del told Dario, and then came over to the well and motioned me a few steps away.

I went. "He's—*she's*—not hurt?"

"No. Not hurt." She was more serious than usual, almost pensive. She hooked sunbleached hair behind one ear. "Dario is not a boy; neither is Dario a *girl.* Not—anymore."

I opened my mouth. Shut it. "Ah," I said after a moment. There seemed to be nothing else left to say.

Del dug a hole in the sand with a sandaled foot. Her jaw was rigid. "When we get to Dumaan, I'm going with you to see Dario's father."

"Del—you can't. He doesn't know you're a woman."

Her head came up and I looked directly into a pair of angry blue eyes. "Do you think *I* care? His beloved *son* is a woman, Tiger!"

I glanced over at Dario, patiently holding the bucket for two horses in competition for its contents. But I could tell by the rigidity of her posture that she knew full well we were discussing her. It would be hard not to, in view of Del's shout.

I looked back at Del. "There's a chance we won't get paid if you come with us."

"What has been done to Dario transcends the need for money," Del said flatly. "At least—it does for *me.*"

I sighed. "I know, bascha; me, too. But—Dario seemed willing enough to spout all that *khemi* nonsense."

Del's smile wasn't one; not really. "Women do—and are *made* to do—many strange things to survive in a man's world."

"Like you?"

"Like me." She unsheathed her sword with a snap of both wrists and automatically I moved back a step. "I want to go with you to see Dario's father because I intend to put him to the question."

I looked at the sword uneasily. "With that?"

"If necessary. Right now, I intend only to tell Dario how I learned to kill."

"Why?" I asked as Del turned away. "So she can learn, too?"

Del's answer was whipped over her left shoulder. "No. Because she *asked*."

Del came with me as I took Dario back to her father. I hadn't bothered to argue the point any longer; Del's mind was made up. And I was beginning to think she'd made Dario's mind up for *her*.

It wasn't easy getting in, of course. The palace servants were men, naturally, and the sight of Del striding defiantly through their halls was enough to make them choke on their prejudice. I imagine the sight of *any* woman might have done the trick, but Del—beautiful, deadly Del—was enough to fill their *khemi* nightmares with visions of blond-haired demons.

Dario walked between us. In a complete change of gender allegiance, she'd turned away from me on the ride to Dumaan to give Del her exclusive attention. Poor girl: all those years spent in a *khemi* household with no women—*no* women—present to answer questions.

At first I'd wondered if Dario had even known she was female rather than male; when I'd asked the question, she told me only that a sympathetic eunuch had admitted the truth of her gender only after swearing her to eternal secrecy. It was a *khemi* rite to expose female children at birth, thus removing all excrescence from the Hamidaa faith.

"But you exist," I'd protested. "Your father bedded a *woman* in order to get you!"

"A son. A son." She'd answered me very quietly. "Once a year a *khemi* lies with a woman in order to get a son." Brown eyes had flicked sidelong to mine. "*I* am my father's son."

"And if he knew the truth?"

"I would be taken to the desert. Exposed. Even now."

I hadn't said much after that. Dario's muted dignity moved me. All those years . . .

Now, as the three of us walked down the marble corridor toward the audience chamber. I knew what Del intended to do.

Which she did. She stood before the enthroned *khemi* tanzeer of Dumaan—the richest man in this finger of the Southron desert—and told him she was taking his daughter from him.

He flinched. He *flinched.* And I realized, looking at the expression of abject terror on his face, he'd known all along.

"Why?" I demanded. "Why in the name of all the gods did you never tell *Dario* you knew?"

He was not old, but neither was he young. I watched his young/old face undergo a transformation: from that of a proud Southron prince with an eagle's beak of a nose, to that of a tired, aging man surrendering to something he had hidden from for too long.

His hands trembled as he clutched the arms of his throne. "I am *khemi,*" he said hoarsely. "Hamidaa'n tells us women are abomination, unclean vessels placed upon the earth by demons." His brown eyes were transfixed on Dario's ashen face. "They are the excrescence of all our former lives." His voice was a thread of sound, and near to breaking. "I will touch nothing of women, speak to no women, admit nothing of women into my thoughts. I am *khemi.*" Then he drew himself up and, with an immense dignity, stared directly at Del. "How *else* am I to cherish a daughter while also remaining constant to my faith?"

"A faith such as this *excrescence* does not deserve constancy." Del's tone was very cool. "She is a girl, not a boy; a *woman,* now. No more hiding, tanzeer. No more hiding *her.* And if you intend to force Dario from her true self, I swear I will take her from you. In the North, we do not give credence to such folly."

He thrust himself out of the throne. "You will take her *nowhere,* Northern whore! Dario is *mine!*"

"Is she?" Del countered. "Why don't you ask her?"

"Dario!" The tanzeer descended two of the three dais steps. "Dari—surely you *know* why I never told you. Why I had to keep it secret." He spread both hands in a gesture of eloquent helplessness. "I had no choice."

Dario's thin face was pinched. There were circles under her eyes. "Choices," she said, "are sometimes difficult to make. And, once made, you must live with them." She sighed and scrubbed at a grimy cheek, suddenly young again. "You made yours. Now I must make mine." She looked at Del. "Tell him what you told me—how it is for a woman in the North. A woman who is a *sword-dancer*."

Del smiled a little. She faced the tanzeer squarely. Over her left shoulder, rising from her harness, poked the hilt of Northern sword. "There is freedom," she said, "and dignity, and the chance to be whatever you wish. *I* wished to become a sword-dancer, in order to fulfill a pact I made with the gods. I apprenticed. I studied. I *learned*. And I discovered that in the circle, in the sword-dance, there was a freedom such as no one else can know, and also a terrible power. The power of life and death." Again, she smiled a little. "I learned what it is to make a choice; to choose life or death for the man who dances against me. A man such as the Sandtiger." She cocked her head briefly in my direction. "I don't kill needlessly. That is a freedom I do not choose to accept. But at least I know the *difference*." She paused. "What does Dario know?"

"What does Dario *need* to know?" he countered bitterly. "How to kill? Needlessly or otherwise."

"In the North, at least she will have a choice. In the South, as a *khemi*—as a Southron *woman*—she has no choice at all."

Dario stared at her father. In a whisper, she asked what *he* could offer.

He stared at Del for a very long moment, as if he tried to decide what words he had that would best defeat her own. Finally, he turned to Dario. "What you have had," he told her evenly. "I have nothing else to give."

Dario didn't even hesitate. "I choose my father."

I thought surely Del would protest. *I* nearly did. But I said nothing when Del merely nodded and turned to go out of the tanzeer's presence.

"Wait," he said. "There is the matter of payment."

Del swung around. "Dario's safety is payment enough."

"Uh, Del—" I began. "Let's not be *hasty*—"

"Payment." The tanzeer tossed me a leather pouch heavy with coin. I rattled it: gold. I know the weight. The *sound*.

Dario stood between them both, but looked at Del. "Choices *are* sometimes difficult," she said. "You offered me the sort of life many women would prefer. But—you never asked if I thought my father loved me."

I saw tears in Del's blue eyes. Only briefly; Del rarely cries. And then she smiled and put out a callused hand to Dario, who took it. "There is such a thing as freedom in the mind," Del told her. "Sometimes, it is all a woman has."

Dario smiled. And then she threw herself against Del and hugged her, wrapping thin brown arms around a sword-dancer's silk-swathed body.

When the girl came to me, I tousled her matted hair. "Take a bath, Dari . . . for all I know you're a Northerner underneath the dirt."

We left them together, Del, and I, and walked out into the Southron sunlight with money in our possession. A *lot* of money, thank the gods; we could enjoy life for a while.

I untied the stud and swung up. "Aren't you even a *little* upset?" I asked, seeing Del's satisfied smile. "She made the wrong choice."

"Did she?" Del mounted her spotted gelding. "Dario told me I'd never asked her if I thought her father loved her. I didn't *need* to. The answer is obvious."

It was so obvious, I waited for it.

Del laughed and yanked yards of silk into place as she hooked feet into Southron stirrups. "Her father knew she was a girl from the moment she was born. But he never had her exposed." She laughed out loud in jubilation. "The proud *khemi* tanzeer *kept* his abomination!"

The stud settled in next to her gelding. "As a *khemi*," I pointed out, "what he did was sacrilegious. The Hamidaa could very well convict him of apostasy and have him killed, if they knew."

"Choices are sometimes difficult to make," Del quoted. "But sometimes *easy*, Tiger."

THE EYES OF THE GODS

by Richard Corwin

One of the things which gets an almost automatic rejection is an attempt to retell folk legends or fairy tales; but a story which attempts to re-create the world in which such legendry takes place is something else.

With a distinct atmosphere of Indian mythology, Richard Corwin has told a story which relies on his own imagination and invention.

Richard Corwin is the pen name of a fan who's better known as "Corwin" than by his own name; a costumer of high professional caliber, who has recently transferred from a career directed at early childhood education (which is a loss to the children of this country—we need much more male input into education) to a career in architecture. He made his writing debut with "Red Pearls" in S&S II; we wish him luck in whatever career he finally adopts, but hope he doesn't abandon writing.

B lacker than black, she stole silently into the darkened temple. Looking slowly back and forth across the echoless expanses of the cold aisles, she tugged her hood tighter about her head and crept deeper into the shadows. Moving cautiously, she crossed under the ornately carved dome within a few minutes, and arrived at the frozen targets of her night's work. Her soot-blackened hand moved upward to the face of Vishnu and scratched out his eyes.

Her targets were gilded, life-size statues of the gods, posed in various yogic positions, with their open hands symbolically pouring out manna for the whole of humanity. The statues themselves were not her prey. But their jeweled eyes were.

Pocketing Vishnu's emeralds, she moved a few feet to the votive statue of Shiva. Incense still smoldered at his feet, and fresh garlands of flowers draped his chest. The incense had a pleasant scent, and gave off a slight amount of precious heat as she crawled up his body to reach his face. She plucked out his eyes and then moved cautiously down the line to Krishna, Arjuna, Indra, Rama, and Yasoda, dropping the jewels into her pockets as she went.

She had come here to the monastery of the Great Abodes, the holiest of holies, placed by the hands of the gods on the slopes of Dhaulagiri, high in the Himalayas. It was a huge monastery of angular white terraces that would have been considered a mountain on their own, were they not climbing up the side of an even bigger, snow capped mountain. At the top of the highest terrace of the monastery stretched the huge, golden-roofed temple of Holy Audience, the temple in which the spirits of the entire pantheon were said to watch over the affairs of mankind with the very eyes that she was now tearing out. It was the perfect crime in the perfect place because the temple was unguarded by any sort of militia. Only the peace-loving priests resided here. And they would be no threat to her.

As she reached up to grasp the eyes of Ganesha, the soft voice of an old man rose unexpectedly from behind her. "Why do you steal from those who forever give unto you?"

She froze instantly.

"Come my child, there is nothing to fear. I will not harm you. It is not my place to mete out the divine justice of the great ones. Step down from our beloved Ganesha, giver of all wisdom, and tell me why you do this."

She turned her head slowly, almost imperceptibly, and saw that the voice belonged to the unimposing figure of a balding, orange-robed priest. His eyes glittered in the gloom of the temple. How had he come up from behind without her hearing?

She quietly climbed down from the platform and looked at the priest with an even stare. "I do this because I have nothing to fear from painted wood, old man," she said, "Times are hard, and my belly is empty. These here have never done anything for me, except make my life hard. They hate me. They mock me with their fate. I am already doomed by the sins of my past to spend my next life on a lower plane, so I do what I can to make this life more bearable."

"But you steal the eyes from which the gods look out into the world. Without these eyes they cannot see. The world would be plunged into darkness if they could not see."

"But if they could see into the world through these eyes, why then did they not stop me?"

He mused for a moment, then replied, "Surely they willed me to intervene on their behalf. I was meditating here, leaning against the column, when the scrape of your foot on the pedestal brought me back to consciousness. This could not have happened by mere chance.

"Come, give me back their eyes. I will re-affix them. Then we will go into the monastery kitchen and get you a simple meal to warm your cold belly. Surely this will make amends from the gods to you. Then you must make amends to the gods for their generosity. Give your life over to their care, here in the monastery, and you will never know want of any kind ever again."

"What I want, you, your monastery, and your gods cannot give me," she hissed, stepping down from the pedestal.

"Then the gods must give you another gift," he said. With a slashing movement, his arm swept upward, cuffing her jaw just below the ear, sending her spinning to the floor. "They must give you retribution."

Crab-like, she scuttled backward on her back, trying not to tangle herself in her black clothing. He closed the distance between them, and swept at her with his foot. She managed to dodge it, but her evasion suddenly wedged her between two statuary pedestals, cornering her. She rose quickly to her feet, and squared off against the old one. He hesitated for a moment, then swung his fist wide at her. She cut inside the swing and rolled her elbow squarely into the side of his head, using her body as a fulcrum to redirect his movement toward the floor.

He collapsed on the flagstones, and she turned to flee before their scuffle attracted attention. Perhaps she had underestimated the resistance of the priestly caste. But as she attempted to flee, his legs tangled in hers, and she was sent sprawling back to the earth.

He rose before she did. "You are indeed a poor fool," he said. "Give me the stones."

It was then that she noticed that his proportions had changed. His bulk was no longer that of an old man. It was somehow more than that now.

She leapt to her feet as he came nearer again. His movements were more supple, more sure. He reached to his belt and began unwinding his robe from his body. Then, with a reverse-bolero movement, he threw his raiment at her, snarling her in its folds. She found herself blinded and trapped by cloth that seemed to expand as it knotted itself about her. Then a crashing blow to the head sent her spinning down the aisle in a tangle of fabric.

Desperately, she clawed at the fabric to no avail. It refused to yield to her in an unearthly fashion. She heard the sound of his footsteps approaching. Groping among her own clothes, she found a means of escape.

With a slash of blackness, a long, serpentine dagger rent the robe into a thousand pieces. Shrugging it free, she bounded up to meet her attacker. He was much taller now, over six feet in height. The musculature of his nearly naked body seemed flawless in the dim light. Brandishing the knife before her, she snarled, "Who are you?"

"The one sent to stop you. I told you that," he said, edging backward.

"They sent some shape-shifter to stop somebody as strong as I am?"

"You are not that strong."

"Oh?" she queried.

"And they did not send a mere shape-shifter." He paused for a moment. "They sent me." Then he reached up toward one of the statues that lined the aisle and gently wrested from its normally unbending fingers a sword that it was carrying. "You may call me Lord Yama."

She felt her stomach plummet. They had anticipated her. But apparently not too well, because they did not stop her before she entered the temple. This gave her courage. "Then you know why I came?" she tested.

"Of course. And I know that you will not gain what you want here. And that you will not leave here alive." With that, a thin arc of flame leaped from the tip of his sword to her neck, burning the hood from her head. Her long dark hair tumbled to her waist.

"Now I know who you are, my lovely. Do you know that I am who I say that I am?" he asked.

"Yes."

"That is good, because it would be a sad thing if you did not know who was sent to destroy you."

"If you can destroy me," she muttered. With a deft leap, she sailed through the air, planting one foot in his jaw while bringing her dagger down onto the sword. Giving her wrist a twist, she wrenched the sword from his hands as she landed feet first on the ground, sending the blade clanking across the temple floor.

He smashed both fists into her chest in return, slamming her backward into a pillar. She shook her head to clear it in time to see Yama procure a spear from another statue and hurl it at her. With a flick of her eyebrow, she sent it away on another course before it could come near her. He threw another. She deflected it again, nearly turning it back against him. A third spear came at her. This time, she shattered it into splinters of flame with more intense concentration. Why was he relying on spears, when he, too, had great powers? Then a fourth spear came at her, but it came from behind her.

She turned her head to see something unexpected. The

gilded statue of Yama had risen from its pedestal and thrown it. He had been stalling for time while he wove his spell. Another spear came at her from Yama at the same time that the statue let one fly. She clapped her hands, and both fell to the floor. She was in a cross fire, and she could not stand up against more statues if he roused them at her. And she estimated that he could rouse them.

She concentrated for a moment, then formulated a plan. She dived to the floor, retrieving one of the spears that had fallen at her feet, then hastily threw it at Yama with her left hand. She continued rolling, grabbing another spear to hurl at the statue. Because it had no magical extension of its own, and because Yama had been distracted by the first spear, her missile hit home in the statue's chest. The force of the blow sent the light wooden statue backward, toward the row of other statues, where the blade of the statue of Kali rose up and sliced the statue of Yama in half.

"Two can play at that game, Yama," she said.

"Yes, two can," he replied. He pointed both of his hands toward her, and those statues that had eyes hurled all the weapons that they had at their disposal at her. The air of the temple was sliced in a thousand fragments as a thousand golden weapons sped toward her.

She closed her eyes and screamed. And suddenly the weapons froze in flight, then tumbled to the ground in silence.

"Are spears and swords your only weapons, Great One?" she baited.

"Even you aren't that stupid, O Slave of the Black One," he said, taking a sword from the floor. "I know full well that you could deflect or bounce back any magic that I could throw at you. And anything deflected in here could damage the eyes of my dear friends." He gestured to the statues. "But you, anything you throw at me, I will simply deflect away from the statues. Or perhaps absorb it. I also know that you are here to steal the staff of Kali to free her from her prison within the earth. You cannot win. Give up."

The statues. He was foolish to let it slip from his lips. It was more than a case of him trying to stop her, he was here to protect the statues as well, particularly their ever-watching eyes. She now knew that the statues were the key to his defeat. She smiled for a moment, and then spoke as she began to circle him. "Why should I give up?" she said, "I am here to set free the one who will end the rule of you and your incompetent statue-friends. Your whole age has been a waste of an eternity. You cannot make decisions, you cannot intervene in the affairs of man, you cannot even quell the demons who ride along the back of the night winds. You have accomplished nothing in this age except entropy. You are worse than useless."

"I suppose you prefer chaos to what you see before you?" he asked, feinting to her left.

She parried with her black dagger. "Yes. At least it will weed out the weak, the slow, and the indecisive . . . like you. The Kali-Yuga, too, will eventually be overthrown. And that will bring about a new age of order and strength. That is what I prefer to your boring and tedious Yuga. You have neither order, nor chaos. You have both, and can make a rule of neither. It is time for you to come to an end. Especially if all you care for is a few pieces of gilded wood."

With that she flung her free arm outward, causing a searing gout of flame to engulf the entire wall of statues. She laughed, "Now your weaklings don't have eyes. Can they intervene in this world now?"

Yama began to scream uncontrollably, clutching at his face. She sent a jet of fire boiling toward him, sending him reeling down the aisle. As his hands came from his face to steady himself, she saw that his eyes had been burned from their sockets.

She smiled. She knew that she had beaten him. She reached into her pocket and withdrew two random jewels, then threw them as far behind her as she could.

"There are two eyes for you Yama. If you are quick enough to find them. And if you find them, you just might be able to stop me," she called.

As she predicted, he stumbled blindly past her in the

direction that they had skipped upon the flagstones. She
ran to the main altar where the huge, eight-spoked wheel
of Law stood. Flanking its sides were the four pillars of
the Ages of the Law. Raising her dagger she hacked the
column of the First Age of Law in half in a single blow.
Then she made the column of the Second Age of Law
into rubble. Then the column of the Latter Days of the
Law fell to the floor with a thundering crash that began
to send chips of plaster falling from the high roof. She
assessed the final column, the column of the Kali-Yuga,
the Age of Darkness. The skull-capped staff of Kali
would have to be in it, since it had been in none of the
others. With deft strokes, she pared away at the column
until she heard the ring of metal on metal. Then, chip-
ping around the wand, she freed it from its bondage.

Down the aisle, Yama still fumbled at the ground,
seeking a pair of eyes that might let him see. She turned
to him and raised the serpent-entwined staff. "Prepare to
meet a new existence," she said as she let a bolt of
lightning free from the hollow eyes at the end of the rod.
The bolt wound itself around Yama, lashing at every
nerve he possessed until he fell lifeless to the floor.

Then she turned to the Wheel of Law. "Now I will free
you, Dark One," she said, pointing the staff the Wheel.
Lightning sprang from the tip and crashed against the
Wheel of Law, sending its orientation askew. Slowly, it
turned itself, until the spoke that indicated the beginning
of the Kali-Yuga tilted to the top. Beneath her, there
was a thundering sound as the floor of the temple flew
upward toward the rafters. Amid the explosion, Kali
stepped forth from her prison in the bowels of the earth.

"You have done well," Kali said in a voice that was
like the finest silk. Taking the staff from her servant, she
stepped before the Wheel of Law. Wrenching it from its
anchoring, she threw it across the nave of the temple,
sending it crashing against the far doors. The roof of the
temple began to collapse about them.

"The Dark Times have begun," the Queen of Blackness said as they lifted into the air on her nightwings.
Darting through a gap in the temple roof, they sped
upward. Below them, the monastery tumbled into the

abyss that she had created when she strode from within the earth. As the last stone sank beneath the snow, she laughed to herself and then turned and flew into the darkness.

FATE AND THE DREAMER

by Millea Kenin

One of the ideas which turns up regularly on the desks of editors is an attempt to modernize some approach to the Three Fates who spin destiny. Nine times out of ten—that really should be ninety-nine times out of a hundred—it doesn't work; I spot the incipient rehash on page one, and head it off at the pass via rejection slip.

The hundredth time, the story has an original twist which really works.

Millea Kenin is a local commercial artist and small-press editor, married to an entertainer; she has two teenage children.

I was Spinner that day. The rains were late that year, and I sat cross-legged outside the entrance to the cave, at ease in the balmy air and in the lithe, graceful body of the Spinner. The sky was a blue dome over the ocean, clear and hard as glass. I kept the spindle spinning; the fibers glittered in the sunlight as they coalesced to yarn.

A winged shadow passed over me, and I looked up, turning my head toward the dark cliffs of Takonia that rose sheer at my back, to eastward. There a *théiakon* caught the wind on her wings, a sea-hawk of the cliffs. (Some say, these days, that Takonia was named for the hawks who dwell here; but my two sisters and I remember an older meaning which we do not tell.) The sea-hawk's mate launched himself from their rock-ledge nest, and they soared out in a great arc over the sea. A thin plume of smoke rose from the natural vent in the rock roof above our kitchen alcove, straight up for many yards in stillness before it bent to the wind aloft.

Footsteps crunching on the pebble beach called my attention back below. Few come to consult our oracle, and it is the least part of our labor, but I found myself looking forward to the change in routine with the Spinner's childlike eagerness, glad that I would be the first to greet a stranger and that I was the one with a fair outward form that day.

A traveler was coming toward us from the south. Surely she was seeking the oracle, for otherwise she was far astray; no road leads past our cave. She was as slim and young as the Spinner seems, but more wiry and angular of build, with bold, proud features in a dark, narrow face. Her steps were slow as if she'd come a long way without rest, and her back was bent beneath the pack she carried; her sheathed longsword struck against her thigh with each awkward, weary step.

All this while, wherever my eyes had looked, my hands had not faltered in their spinning; and now, still spinning, I rose to greet her. She straightened and drew a deep breath; we stood eye to eye. "Be welcome," said I in the sweet soft voice of the Spinner, "to the shrine of That Which Must Be."

"Hail, Lady," her lower, huskier voice replied. "I am Erialthi of Hiónath, and I have come to consult the oracle on a matter of the gravest need."

"Do you seek the counsel of That Which Must Be on behalf of any of the powerful of this world?"

She shook her head and gave a short bitter laugh. "I am here on my own errand, and if I had any power, I doubt I'd need your help!" Then, as if she feared she'd been rude, she added, "Though doubtless it is of value to anyone." She was really very young.

This made me laugh, knowing what I know; but I laughed gently. "No, I mean that here you must ask your own questions. If the Emperor of the South, or of the West or of the East, should send us a messenger, we'd send back word that the Emperor himself must come."

"I see. And do I ask you my question, Lady?"

"You need not speak it aloud unless you wish. It is

asked of fate." Again I could not help smiling. "Come inside, and my sisters and I will show you what to do."

She followed me into the cave and laid her sword and her pack where I showed her, inside and by the doorway. No weapon may be brought within reach of the loom. After the bright sunlight, the cave looked dim and green. The shape of my sister, who was the Weaver that day, was like a shadow before the loom, the picture she was weaving too tenuous to be seen. "Welcome, Erialthi," she called out in the Weaver's rich warm voice. Erialthi gave a start, for till then she'd had no way of learning that what one of us knows, all of us know.

My other sister, who was Snipper, shuffled forward with shears in hand, her frame stiff and bent with the aspect of age. With her other hand she drew her black cowl about the face that no mortal may look upon, save one who is already changed. "Time to pay your fee, dearie," she said in the cracked, trembling voice of the Snipper.

Erialthi tried to speak, cleared her throat and said, "What is the fee, Lady?"

"A lock of your hair."

So she uncoiled the long braid from behind her head and unplaited it. My sister cut a lock and gave it to me, and I fed it into the strand, forming a dark place in the shining yarn. Erialthi stood still, her hair falling loose in glossy black waves below her waist.

Neither the Weaver nor I may pause in our work till sunset, so, slowly, with short faltering steps, the Snipper brought out the heavy jar of lots. The Snipper shook the jar to mix the stones within, then set it on the floor, grunting with the effort. "Kneel here, dearie," she quavered, panting a little. "Now I've got to blindfold you, and then you just think hard about the question you want answered, while you reach in and take out all the stones you can hold in one handful."

Erialthi nodded silently and knelt before the big clay jar. The Snipper tied a scarf around her eyes, then took off the lid. Erialthi put her slim brown hand in, then drew it forth, stretched taut and paler-knuckled around a fistful of stones. The Snipper whisked off the blindfold, covered the jar and slid it aside.

"Drop your stones right here, dearie." Pebbles rattled on the stone floor. Still spinning, I looked over, and the Weaver passed the shuttle between the warps and turned her head to look. Her motherly face stiffened with concern.

The stones had fallen in a group, without much of a pattern. All of them were dark gray, wave-smoothed slate, save four small white quartz pebbles in the center of the group.

"The chances of success for you are small," said the Weaver.

"Very small," quavered the Snipper.

"Is there anything you can tell me to help me know what those chances are and how to take them?" Erialthi's arched brows drew together over the narrow bridge of her nose, and her full lips tightened to a thin line.

"Seek along the cliffside till you find a way to climb," I said; "there are ways, though no easy ones."

"When you get to the top," the Weaver went on, "search in the highlands of Takonia till you find a small sky blue, five-petaled flower, growing low amid the rocks. This late in the autumn, there will still be some in bloom, but not many."

"You will know it when you see it," I added, "for there is nothing else like it growing in those parts."

"Pick seven perfect blossoms," said the Weaver, "no more, no less."

"Then bring them back to us, dearie," finished the Snipper, "and *then* we'll see!" She crowed with cracked, ancient laughter, for so the one of us who is Snipper may do; but the Weaver and I remained grave-faced and attended to our work.

Erialthi's strong fingers swiftly braided and coiled her hair. "Will you give me water before I go?" Such a request could not be refused. Nor could we warn her of the omen: only the Snipper's hands were free. She brought the young woman an earthen mug filled with the cold, clear water that wells from a spring in the rocks not far above our cave. Erialthi drank it thirstily, then shouldered her pack, belted on her sword, and set out upon her quest.

The rest of the day passed without event, till the sun sank beyond the ocean, turning the air and water to a cauldron of fire and blood. I laid the day's last skein of yarn in its place. The Weaver tied off her threads, and the Snipper cut them. In one minute her day's work is done, yet it is as necessary as the daylong labor of the other two.

Then we looked at the day's weaving, and saw it was without flaw and as it must be, and laid it in its place. After that we did the homely tasks that we, like mortal women, must perform—bringing water from the spring, gathering herbs and roots and taking fish from our traps in the stream, and cooking supper. The Snipper put aside her cowl, and as we ate we told over some of the old tales we know so well, of what has been, and what will be, and laughed together at the brief follies and griefs of mortals.

Then we lay down to dream, and change.

It was sunset again on the eighth day when Erialthi returned, so I was Weaver, just finishing my stint and preparing to knot off. My sister laid aside her spindle and went to greet the woman. If Erialthi's steps had been weary before, they were weighted now with exhaustion; and if her pack had been heavy, now its weight was almost more than she could bear, though it must have been lighter by a week's provisions and heavier only by the weight of seven flowers. Her clothes were dusty, and torn here and there, and there were grazes and scratches on her hands and along her cheekbone. Yet she was smiling calmly, as if the accomplishment of that task had given her confidence of victory.

We did not yet know any of the particulars of the task that lay before her—not even as much as herself could know. And even if we had, it was not for us to disillusion her. The Spinner and I smiled at her. The Snipper, whose face may not be shown, snipped the threads and laid aside her shears, then went up and took Erialthi's hands in her own bent and knotted ones.

Then we all made supper together, and shared it. The Snipper had to turn aside to eat, that Erialthi might not see past her cowl; for even yet, there was a chance that what was planned would not happen. Such night-edge matters as this are in the tied-off end of the day's weaving. They are never certain; they may ravel.

Last of all we steeped those seven flowers in hot water in a cup of hollowed stone. Now, and only in veiled terms, we must warn Erialthi.

"If you would learn the several paths that lie before you," I said, "you must drink from the same cup with us, and dream together."

"But it is laid upon us to warn you," said my sister in the Spinner's soft voice, "that if you do, you will never be the same. You will Change, as we do."

"What does that mean?" Erialthi sat erect and cross-legged; her face was calm, but her hands lay tense upon her thighs.

"We may say no more; but you must think on the warning we have given you, before you decide."

"Oh, I do hope you go through with it!" quavered my other sister, she who had woven when I spun. "It's so long since anything has happened to us, and we have never been anyone like you!"

"Sister," I said coldly, "you have said too much!"

"It doesn't matter. I must do this. Otherwise I can see no path at all before me." Erialthi reached out, and I put the cup into her hand. She took it in her two hands and sipped; her face remained impassive, not reacting to the bitter flavor. The Spinner reached for the cup and sipped in her turn, wrinkling her lovely nose, then passed it to me. I drank half of what remained and passed it to the Snipper. She flung back her cowl and drained the cup, slurping loudly.

At the sight of that face, Erialthi drew in her breath in a sharp hiss between clenched teeth. But she did not flinch when the three of us surrounded her and hugged her tight. Instead, brave woman, she hugged us back as if she were already our sister.

Then we lay down to dream, and change.

*   *   *

It was not like an ordinary dream. Although it was more vivid, more like waking reality, I never forgot that I was dreaming, though for a long while I did not remember where my body lay or why I was dreaming so. I knew it was on purpose, though.

My cousin and I rolled together in the dust; he was getting the worst of our rough-and-tumble. With a burst of energy he broke away and ran sobbing to my uncle.

"Daddy, Daddy, Erialthi's beating me up!"

"I am not! We're just wrestling! Degi's just a sore loser." I stood scowling, drawing circles in the dust with one bare big toe.

"Degi, heroes never cry, whether they win or lose. And Erialthi, you must learn to behave like a lady. Princesses don't wrestle. Really, Miúnis," my uncle said to my mother, who approached slowly, twirling her parasol, "you must start teaching your daughter some deportment."

"Come, fluffbird," said my mother, but she did not hug me, dusty as I was. "Let nana wash you and put a pretty dress on, and I'll give you my jade butterfly to wear around your neck." How well she knew how to bribe me; how well she knew I loved that pendant and would climb in her lap and stroke it whenever she wore it.

I remembered that I have it yet; I'm grown, and it hangs around my neck always, under my clothes, against my skin. I wear it in her memory. She's dead! I panicked, in the dream, and it shifted.

"Ah," Master Úlua said, "that was a pretty stroke, child. You may rest."

I put down the practice sword and mopped my brow.

"You'll be a fine swordswoman, my princess. If only Degi had half your application."

"They tried to make me stop studying with you. They only gave in after I didn't eat for three days. Mama and Uncle Athor don't think a princess *ought* to be a swordswoman."

"All things considered, perhaps a princess oughtn't— don't lose your temper, child, it'll put you off your stroke!

But a talent like yours deserves to be given its rightful skill, be it given to boy or girl, princess or beggar."

I flung my arms around Úlua and hugged him. The sword he gave me—I bear it to this day. Even when I sleep it's never far from me. I reached out my hand— Where is it? I can't find it! Ah, yes, I'd left it by the door of the cave. I relaxed.

"Why must you be so stubborn?" My mother's voice was fretful, and tears smeared the kohl around her huge dark eyes. Even as she lay dying, she had her maids carefully paint her wasted face; and I, with my stubbornness, was attacking this pitiful gallantry. And so I must, in self-defense.

She wanted me to do what custom demanded: marry her brother's son, Degi, and secure the succession. My father, dead so long ago I could not remember him, had been the last survivor of a dwindling royal family. All my life, almost, my uncle Athor had been regent. In a year I would come of age; it was my intention to fight for my right to rule in Hiónath.

It was my mother's dearest wish to see me settled before she died: married to Degi, Athor confirmed in power. No matter that she knew as well as I what Degi was: flabby and bleary-eyed from drink, though he was no older than myself. No matter that she, as well as I, had tried to help the bruised, unfortunate women who had been forced to serve his pleasure.

No, Mama, I wouldn't cut off my hand to make you die content; I wouldn't put my eye out; and I wouldn't marry Degi.

The dream flew swiftly past her funeral, past my coming-of-age ceremony, to the night when Ilani, Degi's current concubine, came to warn me that he was sending half a dozen men-at-arms to seize me and force me on pain of death to marry him. She crept away, before her absence should be noted. I had asked her to do one more brief thing for me, but I hadn't known if she would dare take the time. It would have been as much as her life was worth, if Degi found out it was she who'd warned me.

All I could hope to do for the moment was escape. I left the palace by a secret way that was unguarded; I had not discovered it, thank all the gods, until a year or two after I'd stopped trusting Degi with any of my secrets.

Outside the palace gates, as I'd dared to hope, a cloaked figure waited. I'd asked Ilani to tell Úlua, if she dared, if she had time. Here he was, with a pack of provisions and my sword.

I gripped the good old armsmaster's hands in mine. "Thank you, Úlua. Protect Ilani if you can."

"I'll try, child. What will you do now?"

"I will go to Takonia to consult the Oracle, first of all. Then perhaps I will find out what to do."

Ah. Now I remembered where I was and what for, and why I was reliving my life in this dream. But I had reached the present, and the dream had not ended.

I saw myself returning to Hiónath in disguise, seeking out people disaffected with the Regent's growing inability to keep in check his debauched son's ravages upon the populace. I saw myself leading an insurgent army. I saw the Regent's troops crushing us, my comrades slain, half of Hiónath in flames, myself dragged in chains before my uncle's throne.

I saw my troops marching victorious to claim the palace, myself enthroned, Athor and Degi kneeling in chains before me.

I saw myself setting out northward, living from hand to mouth, finally hired to help guard a caravan by a merchant desperate enough for anyone at all, that he would hire a female sword. I saw a troop of bandits springing out from behind the rocks, and myself falling in combat with them.

I saw myself emerging unscathed from victorious battle against the bandits, reaching finally the capital of the Empire of the West and vowing my service to the Empress, herself the general of a great army about to set forth to conquer other lands.

I saw myself heading east into the mountains, climbing to a temple in the heights and asking to join the holy sisterhood. I saw myself, at the High Priestess' command, dedicating my sword to the Goddess and surrendering it upon her altar, and retiring to a cell to pray daily in silence, for years, never given leave to do anything else.

I saw myself coming down from the mountain with a group of my sister priestesses, all robed in blue. We were quiet but full of excitement, for we were returning to the cities of the world to heal and teach.

I saw myself returning to Hiónath, confessing myself penitent, marrying Degi, swallowing the bile that rose in my throat as I submitted meekly to whatever he wished of me in bed. I waited till he seemed fast asleep, then took out my knife to stab him. I saw him waking, struggling, desperation lending him strength to break my wrist, seize the knife and stab me.

I saw him waking, struggling, too drunk and weak even to slow me down, the terrified appeal in his eyes as I stabbed him to the heart—then fading, glazing over. I saw myself sitting with the knuckles of my clean hand pressed against my mouth, the bloody palm of the other massaging my stomach as I fought its heaving, watching Degi die.

I saw myself, in despair at all the possibilities, climbing the cliff once more and flinging myself off the heights of Takonia into the sea.

No, I didn't believe that. It was all a dream; none of those things had happened. I was free to choose, up to a point, and from all the other choices defeat or victory might come. But I was certainly not about to kill myself. I sighed, relaxed and sank into a deeper sleep, to the memory of endless rounds of days, spinning, weaving, snipping. That was reality; the short life as princess of Hiónath was the dream.

Morning was here. Gray light filtered into the cave; I felt it through my eyelids. The first birdsongs sounded softly outside. I smiled. I had enjoyed being Erialthi.

I was the Snipper, fixing the limits of each mortal day, and my joints ached with weariness that had been old before the world was new . . . but I would spin tomorrow.

I was the Spinner, who would rise and gather the mist of sea and mountain and the thoughts of mortal minds, twisting out of nebulous diversity a single wiry line; I'd sing and dance with joy even as I spun, and look forward joyously to weaving tomorrow.

I was the Weaver, interlocking the strands in all their crossed directions, making a web as firm as the needs of worm and bee and flower, strength and quietness in my hands; till, grown weary, I'd wait to snip tomorrow.

I was Erialthi, a thread of the weaving, ready to rise and make my small choice of peace or murder, wisdom to act or power to refrain. I, who had spun and woven with my sisters since time began, I was now young, mortal Erialthi, going forth to victory or doom, never to spin or weave or snip again.

We were four, and we were one.

THE NOONDAY WITCH

by Dorothy J. Heydt

To me, one of the high points of editing these anthologies is to bring back, year after year, such "well-known" heroines as Diana Paxson's "Shanna" and Dorothy Heydt's "Cynthia." Cynthia, in the period of Classical Greek antiquity (or is it?) is not just another reteller of folk legends; her sorcerous adventures are always just a little *different*, so that I'm not quite sure they don't take place in some alien dimension or other. But they are done with such a sure hand for psychological truth that it really doesn't matter *when* or *where* they take place. . . .

Dorothy Heydt's first appearance in print took place as co-compiler of the original Star Trek Concordance; she has also written Star Wars fiction, and has appeared in this and other anthologies. She has a superb (and classically trained) soprano voice, and her household is an assorted melange of cats, computers, children and other necessities of life.

Syracuse, 271 B.C.

The fishing fleet had gone out from the Lesser Harbor, and no one remained on the sheltering Mole of Dionysos but the usual handful of loafers, boys, and trash fishermen. A few gulls still wheeled overhead, but one by one they spiraled down to land on pilings or winchheads and tuck their heads into their back feathers. The weather was not unduly warm, the sun had not yet risen into noon; but already it was a day on which to get nothing much done.

The sun was almost at the zenith when the little boat came limping in from the northeast. Her fresh paint couldn't disguise her frayed sheets and tattered sails, and the worm had been intimate with her planks. It was probably only by the favor of the gods that her young master had managed to get her as far as Syracuse before her leaking bilges had overcome his companion's ability to bail her out.

Now the companion, her bailing bucket tossed to one side and her black stole to the other, was crouched on the dock unloading her belongings. Bundles wrapped up in bits of clothing lay dripping beside her, and she tugged with determination at an iron-bound chest that had got wedged into the prow. Her rust-colored gown was sodden, her hands and forearms were scratched, and the curses she muttered under her breath did not speak of a sheltered life.

The young man at the tiller—he could be no more than sixteen—bent down to touch what looked like a pile of sea-soaked finery in the bilges. It stirred, and took shape as an old man in a scarlet-embroidered cloak, his white beard tangled with wind and water, his eyes wide and blank as a baby's. "Come on, now, Father. Time to go ashore," said the young man. His father sat up, clasped his arms round his knees, and shook his head.

The boy made a face, and glanced up as if to seek sympathy from on high. Beside his companion there were two disdainful pelicans and a dark-haired Syracusan, about his own age, wearing a faded blue khiton and mended sandals. "You, there, could you give a hand? Father was struck on the head and he's gone simple."

The youth in the blue khiton reached down a hand, but the old man paid no attention, He sat in the bilges like a sack of grain, hard to get hold of and very hard indeed to lift.

"Come, Palamedes," the woman said softly. "Come to Cynthia." The old man looked at her and smiled, but made no attempt to move. The woman was younger at second glance than the Syracusan had thought, not much more than twenty, hardly middle-aged. She had sleek black hair and the dark eyes of an Egyptian queen, but her strong nose and chin spoke of a queenly temper and more than her share of stubbornness.

The youth dismissed her from his mind and turned back to the old man who sat like a lump in the rapidly filling boat. His son was still struggling to shift him. But instead of lending a hand, the Syracusan shouted, "I've got it!" and ran away.

In a moment he was back, dragging a rope and a pulley used for off-loading heavy cargo, and threw it over a beam. "Put this under his arms," he commanded. "Right. Now look out above!" Digging his heels into the dock, he hauled away on the rope. The old man rose smoothly into the air, and the woman Cynthia snatched his feet and brought him ashore. The pelicans took off. The boat rocked, and shipped more water, and the son of Palamedes leaped to the dock as she went under.

"O Zeus!" the woman cried. "The books!"

"Did you say *books?*" The Syracusan flung off his clothing and dived into the water. A great bubble burst at the surface; the boat was now quite out of sight. The youth's head reappeared, shouted "The rope!" and disappeared again. Cynthia dropped it into the water, and hauling at the free end pulled out the Syracusan with the loop of rope under one arm and the iron-bound chest under the other.

He set it carefully on the dock. "O Apollo, don't let the ink have run," he muttered. "What books are they?"

"They should be all right," Cynthia said. "I stopped the seams with wax to keep out the spray. We have books on philosophy, poetry, medicine, mathematics, and— Ouch!" Her companion had stumbled over a coil of rope and kicked her in the shin. "Mmm, yes. We have an exposition on the elements of geometry by my father's cousin, Euklides of Alexandria."

"Oh, marvelous," the boy said. "May I read them? Do you have a place to stay in Syracuse? Where do you come from? What's your name?"

"Demetrios son of Palamedes, of Corinth," the fair-haired youth said. "This is my brother's widow, Cynthia, and—"

"From Corinth? But you're among kinsmen here: Will

you stay with us? I'll ask my uncle Loukas, but I'm sure it will be all right. He's selling wool in the market. If you'll come with me . . . oh, sorry." Bending down to pick up the bookchest, he saw the blue khiton lying forgotten on the dock, and belted it about his body again. "Arkhimedes son of Pheidias, at your service." He shouldered the bookchest and led them down the jetty into the confusion of the market crowds.

For its size, the marketplace was quiet, surprisingly so; Cynthia could make out the words of individual voices. From a henwife's ramshackle coop built against one wall of a carpetweaver's booth, a rusty black cock put up his head and crowed once, uncertainly, and settled down again to sleep.

Palamedes was beginning to notice his surroundings now, just enough to shy at noises and balk when someone crossed his path. This made it necessary for both Cynthia and Demetrios to lead him, one on either side; Cynthia took the opportunity to whisper, "Kick me again and I'll break your leg."

"I didn't want you to mention the books of magic," Demetrios said. "Arkhimedes seems very nice, but he's terribly curious and I don't want him getting into Father's books. You should know by now that it isn't safe to meddle with things you don't understand."

"And how many times have I saved all our necks by meddling, while you stood around and wrung your hands?" she retorted. "I grant your point, but you've no cause to leave marks on me. You're not my husband."

"I still think—" Demetrios began.

"No," Cynthia said firmly, and took a better grip on Palamedes' elbow to guide him round a cart full of hay.

Their situation was a strange one, sure to win the world's reproaches if ever they were such fools as to let the world know about it. They had fallen in together three days before, escaping from the little city of Margaron as it fell to the Romans. Having few resources, and with old Palamedes still stunned out of his wits and needing care, they had thought it best to stick together. But what Hellene was going to believe in any woman traveling with two men, without being the wife or the whore of at least one of them?

They made their way through the flower market at the foot of the old Temple of Apollo and Artemis, with its double row of columns and brightly painted cornices. Over to their right stretched the narrow causeway that connected Ortygia to the rest of Sicily. The sun was fierce overhead now, the air all the closer for the dampness left by yesterday's rain. Somewhere a voice was singing, a shrill monotonous sound like a cicada, some mother singing a lullaby perhaps to a child fractious with the heat. The city sparkled in the sun, all its colors fresh-washed, but its people were beginning to droop, declining gently into the prospect of the afternoon's nap.

Demetrios had offered to let Cynthia stand as his wife, purely for the public's consumption of course; Cynthia had preferred to put round the story that her late husband Demodoros had been Palamedes' elder son. Cynthia had her way, as she usually did, but her position was still precarious: what if Palamedes suddenly came back to himself and said, "Who's *that?*" Well, she would just have to keep an eye on him.

"Come, father," Demetrios said, guiding Palamedes round a muddy rut in the street. "Come, father," Cynthia echoed, to get the old man used to the sound of it.

Loukas was a little, wiry man of about thirty, with no hair at all left on the top of his head, and he was asleep with his head against the wheel of his cart. Against the other wheel slept a man taller than Loukas, with a broken nose and a face that still scowled as he snored. Arkhimedes raised an eyebrow. "That's Gellias," he said. "When they wake they'll start fighting again, and then they'll have a few jars. We'll talk to him later." He led them away. "I'll bring him round, and he'll bring Grandmother round. Did you say you had books about medicine? Do they tell how to draw a tooth?"

"I can draw a tooth if there's need," Cynthia said. "My father was a physician and taught me a bit."

"Can you deliver babies and cure the cough?"

"Usually," Cynthia said cautiously.

"Then you'll be well settled with Grandmother. Have

you been in Syracuse before? I'll show you round the island today; you can see the rest of the city later. How long were you at sea? Are you hungry? Uncle brought some bread and olives, but—"

"We have a little money," Cynthia said. She reached into her bodice and brought out a small purse of faded embroidery. She took out a couple of coppers; that should be enough, unless the fortunes of war had sent prices farther up than was decent. (She had a considerable sum of money as well, sewn into the hem of her gown, but she wasn't about to let Arkhimedes or his fellow-citizens know that.)

They bought bread, and small green onions with the morning's dew still on them, and a flask of wine that Arkhimedes recognized as not so bad at the price, and a cup to mix it in. "We'll get water from Arethousa's spring," Arkhimedes said, "It's a great marvel, and besides she is a patroness of the city and one should pay respect to her. It's at the other end of the island—you can walk that far, can't you? It's less than ten stadia* and you'll see many fine things on the way." They set off down a wide street that ran down the island's spine. The first colonists from Corinth had settled on Ortygia, just off the eastern shore of Sicily, and only later spread into the smooth slopes of the Akhradina on the larger island. A causeway connected the two islands now, with a fortress on it to guard the passage between them and overlook the Little Harbor.

All the buildings that lined the street had once been very fine, and some still were. Here was a great house, its stones freshly plastered to cover cracks and graffiti, but the house next to it had been cut up into a warren of little rooms and let out to the poor. Both buildings had a drift of humanity round their bases, like the line of foam and trash left by the sea along the shore: merchants, peddlars, beggars, thieves, street boys with their eyes out for a chance at a quick copper or two. All were growing quiet and drowsy with the heat. Old Palamedes was lulled into docility, making him easier to lead.

---

*Ten stadia come as close to an English mile as makes no difference.

They stepped inside the great Temple of Athene for a moment, to admire the beauty of its paintings and to enjoy the cool shadows under the forest of pillars that held up its gilded roof. The temple was the richest in Syracuse, and probably the most splendid throughout all Greater Greece. Its great doors, carefully formed of gold and ivory, were unmatched anywhere in the world. The interior walls were painted with scenes of the wars of the tyrant Agathokles against the Carthaginians, and with portraits of the kings of Sicily.

When a junior priest strolled toward them, plainly in search of a donation, they stepped out into the heat again. High over their heads, a great figure of Athene stood on the roof, with her gilded shield that could be seen far out to sea.

Most of the aristocracy now had their houses on the Akhradina, Arkhimedes said, or up on the cliffs of the Epipolai overlooking the sea, but some still kept second houses on the harbor so that they could sail small pleasure boats. "That one there, for instance," he said, pointing to a large house on a rise of ground by the shore, its white walls brilliant in the sun. "That is the house of the noble Leptines. I've been inside it, and it's so beautiful. All the floors are mosaic, with patterns of sea creatures. My Uncle Hieron married into the family."

"Cleverly done!" Demetrios said. "That's a big step upward."

"Not so very far," Arkhimedes said; "Uncle Hieron—oh, smell the fish!" An old fishwife was grilling the odds and ends of the day's catch over a little charcoal fire. They bought half a dozen tiny fish, still sizzling from the grill, and as they walked away the old wife yawned, and covered the fire and settled down for a nap. There were no more customers anyway. The whole island was quiet, and above it Cynthia could hear that humming cicada lullaby song. Maybe it was a cicada? Ortygia was thoroughly built up, but there were still some trees and gardens, in the grounds of Leptines' house for instance; leaves fluttered over its roof. Except that Cynthia could almost make out words in it, not Greek words but some kind of barbarian jargon she'd never heard in all her travels. She set the thought aside and concentrated on the task of getting Palamedes down the green bank that surrounded the Fount of Arethousa where it poured out of its rocky grotto. There were a dozen people lying on the grass round the spring already, all of them asleep. Cynthia could have sworn she saw a cutpurse creep up beside a citizen, hand stretched out to pluck, and then decide it was too much trouble and lie down to sleep like a child beside his intended victim.

They settled themselves at the edge of the spring and spread out the food on the clean grass. They dipped up water to mix with their wine, and poured a libation to the nymph of the island. Men said this spring was the same that went underground with the holy river Alpheios in Elis, far away in the Peloponnese, and that when they made sacrifice in Elis the blood welled up in the water here. But there was no blood today; the water was cold and clear, far down into the depth of the rocky grotto beneath.

It was very warm now, and Cynthia felt she might sleep herself if not for Arkhimedes and Demetrios, and their constant chattering.

"My uncle Hieron was a captain under General Pyrrhos; he was just thirty when Pyrrhos left Syracuse without a leader and went to defend Tarentum against the Romans, but he didn't succeed—"

"You needn't tell me! After the Romans took Tarentum they came and took Margaron, and we had to run for our lives—"

"—And Pyrrhos had executed Thoinon and the other aristocrats who'd sold us out to the Carthaginians, so the people elected Uncle Hieron general—"

"—And we had to cross open ocean in that leaky little boat, and we were nearly captured by a Punic warship—"

"—And Uncle Hieron married Philistis, the daughter of Leptines, practically the only one of the noble families that's survived this long. We're all so proud of Uncle Hieron, he may make all our fortunes, and that's why Uncle Loukas keeps arguing with Gellias, because these days it's the aristocracy against the army and Gellias was a sergeant—"

Palamedes was asleep. Cynthia settled her back comfortably against a stone and looked down into the depths of Arethousa's spring. Cool, dark and green.

Cold water closed over her head, and instantly she was awake; awake for the first time since morning. That song! That shrill cicada lullaby, there was some magic in it, a spell to put the whole island to sleep and her with it. And now she had fallen in. She tried to throw off her stole, kick off her sandals and swim back to the surface; but she could not move. Far above her head the little silver disk of the sky turned blue, went dark, dwindled out of sight.

Belatedly she realized that she was still breathing—breathing air? water? a thing against nature either way, and surely the work of some god. The spring was a holy place. Sucked down into the earth like Persephone. She folded her hands before her face and waited as the waters bore her downward.

They laid her down on a bank of sand and pebbles, dropped there like herself in an eddy of the current. The waters swirled round her on every side, shining with a cold blue light. There was no light overhead, the sunlight could not penetrate this deep, but the water was full of a cold brilliance, shading back and forth between blue and green like the feathers of a peacock, dazzling as his Argus-eyed tail. There was no living thing to be seen at all, but Cynthia knew she was watched. As one who walks singing through the forest hears his own voice fall silent, and feels eyes upon his back, and turning, knows by his trembling that his mortal flesh beholds immortal things, so Cynthia trembled, and clutched at her drifting stole to draw it over her eyes. So Odysseus, washed up on an unknown shore, heard the laughter of young women and knew the fear of the nymphs who haunt the mountain peaks, the springs of rivers and the grassy meadows. Cynthia bent her body down to the bank and hid her face in her hands.

Get up, woman. You have nothing to fear.

Cynthia obeyed. Still she saw nothing, only the swirl of color in the water.

I am Arethousa who inhabit this spring, the voice said.

(She could have left it unsaid. Through clever fakery or the skills of temple craftsmen one may mistake a mortal's voice for a god's, but no one hearing an immortal's voice will mistake it for a mortal's.) *Ortygia gave me refuge when I fled my native Elis. When the men of Corinth came here and built a city round my spring, and a temple to far-shooting Artemis, I was pleased, and claimed the city for hers and mine. Now impious mortals threaten the peace of my city, and would fill it with strife and hatred and violent death. Not yet is it time that Syracuse must be overthrown by the children of Aphrodite. I will protect the city from division, and you shall be my instrument.*

A hand parted the light like a curtain, revealing the shape beyond.

She might have been the size of a mortal woman, seen close to, or very large and far away; the eye could not fix her in place. Her limbs were smooth, almost transparent, like a jellyfish or a piece of glass barely visible in the water and likely to appear or disappear at a whim. *Hold out your hand.*

Cynthia did so, and the nymph touched one finger with her own, a touch like cold fire or the chill of a deadly fever. A dark shape appeared on the finger, not instantly but like a shadow developing on the street when the sun comes out of a cloud. It was a ring, a plain ring of black iron with no ornament. *This will protect you. Go toward my Lady's temple, and you shall see what you are to see. Return to me at sunset.*

All at once the waters reversed themselves and bore Cynthia upward like a cork bobbing to the surface. She clutched at the bank and hauled herself out, lay panting for breath on the soft grass.

But if I was breathing water down there—was I?—it would have been hard to breathe. Could I have spoken, if I had dared? This gets me nowhere. O Zeus, O Artemis, what am I now to do?

Someone is preparing an act of violence against my city, she heard from a great way off. *Go and prevent it.*

"How?" Cynthia said aloud, but there was no answer. Already that voice was so far distant that to expect it to answer was like asking Homer to speak again, or a bird to sing that sang in Agamemnon's garden.

She got to her feet. Everyone around her was still asleep, and the cicada song still shrilled in her ears. Her clothing was dry, and her hair had come unbound. She pinned it back in place, picked up her skirt, and climbed up the bank to the street.

Every living thing lay still in sleep: even the seagulls; even the flies. As for the men and women, it seemed the spell had come on them slowly, for they had taken the time to lie down or at least to find a comfortable seat. Here was a horse asleep on its feet, and its groom propped against a cartwheel, asleep with the reins still in his hand. Here were three little street boys curled up together like a basketful of puppies, and here an iron-jawed matron, her stole embroidered in gold, her head pillowed on the shoulders of the slaves who carried her baskets.

I am like Gyges who found the ring of invisibility, she thought, *and stole everything he wanted, even to Kandaules' wife and kingdom*. Sokrates had said any man would do the same, given the same opportunity, but somehow Cynthia was not tempted. Gyges, after all, could not be caught in the act by anybody—that was the whole point of the story—but Cynthia had Arethousa to answer to.

Go to my Lady's temple. But which Lady? Ah, well, both temples lay north of here. *You shall see what you shall see*. She set off to the north at a good pace, as fast as she could go without making much noise. *An act of violence*. The word *hybris* carried the sense, not just of blood and destruction, but of an outrage against the natural order of things, such as the gods never let go unpunished, but would always avenge—eventually. Sometimes too late to be any help to men. The cicada song grew stronger. She could see the bright roof of the Temple of Athene now, and the road across the causeway, pointed like a dusty arrow straight at the distant palaces on the Achradina.

Something was moving on the causeway road, a human figure or so it seemed, little and black against the heat-shimmering air. Cynthia ducked quickly behind a cart. Had he seen her? If he had, he made no sign, but kept

walking in her direction, the little black speck growing
slowly, not fly-sized now but beetle-sized, the size of a
thumb, the size of a hand. Cynthia crouched down behind the cart's solid wheel—*if I can't see him he can't see
me*—and peered at the approaching figure through a tiny
crack. The flutter of a scarlet cloak, the confident stride
of a warrior, a glint of metal in the sun. But this was no
soldier, no man at all but a woman, walking alone through
the silent street like one who knows exactly where she is
going and what she intends to do, and still coming this
way. Cynthia settled herself against the wheel as though
she had fallen asleep there, and pulled her stole forward
just enough to shadow her face. The sound of footsteps
was now quite near.

As the woman passed by, Cynthia got a good look at
her back but none at her face. Her scarlet stole was rich
with embroidery, her gown dyed with saffron, and her
jewelry jingled with every step. A rich woman, who
would surely never be permitted out on the street by
herself if anyone were awake. And she spared not a
glance for the sleeping marketplace; she had expected it,
planned for it, and now under its shelter she was setting
out to carry out whatever plan she had. And none awake
to watch her but Cynthia, armored by Arethousa's ring.
She needed no bolt of lightning, no flight of doves to tell
her who her target was—but what was her task? What
violence did this woman have in hand? Cynthia slipped
off her sandals, got to her feet, and followed the scarlet
figure at twenty silent paces' distance.

She came to the house of Leptines, and pulled the
door open with a gold-ringed hand. The slave who kept
the door lay asleep across the threshold, and the woman
stepped over him, carefully, as though her touch might
wake him. Cynthia did the same. The man shifted in his
sleep, and settled his shoulders against the stone. He was
smiling.

The hall was floored with smooth blue tiles, cool against
Cynthia's bare feet, and the light reflected from them
shimmered against the walls like water, like the cool light
in the hall of Arethousa.

Cynthia followed the woman by the sound of her jewelry, through the great house full of sleeping servants and out onto a terrace in the sun. The floor tiles were the color of burnt cream, the walls were brilliant with white-wash, and a low outer wall looked out over the brilliant turquoise of the Greater Harbor and the emerald of early summer on the hills. The air was blisteringly hot now, but there was a little breeze out of the west, enough so that the man lying under the blue canopy could sleep comfortably. All around him the sunlight lay thick as amber.

A peasant of Corfu, to ward against the stings of scorpions, will carry a little flask of oil in which a scor-pion has been drowned. In its slow death the beast lets out its poison into the golden oil, misty and dark as the smoke from a damp fire, and this extraction (it's said) will cure the sting as easily as the prick of a thorn. Now the woman in the red cloak paused, suspended in the thick sunlight, and stretched out her arm slowly like the drowning scorpion. There was a dagger in her hand, long and thin-bladed, with a ruby in the hilt like the scorpion's heart, and around her hung a mist of hatred that Cynthia (Arethousa's ring cold on her hot hand) could see almost with her eyes.

She drew in her breath, sharply, and the woman turned at the sound and looked at her coldly. "Who are you?" she demanded. "How are you still awake? Who sent you?"

"Arethousa," Cynthia said. "She says you must not kill—"

"That be damned for a tale," the woman said. She took the loose end of her stole and threw it over her shoulder, and took a better grip on her dagger's hilt; and all at once Cynthia realized why it's said the gods help those who help themselves. She might have virtue on her side, and Arethousa's mission, and even Arethousa's ring that warded off the sleeping-spell and maybe other bale-ful magics. But it wasn't likely the ring would ward off the sharp edge of iron, and plainly the easiest way for the woman to get her business done was to cut Cynthia's own throat before she cut Leptines'.

She seized the end of her own stole and wound it

around her forearm for a guard; it was heavy wool at
least, better than that silk. Wasn't there anything here
she could use as a weapon? Leptines had nothing by him,
only a bronze bowl on a little table with nuts and early
cherries in it; not even a fruit knife. Pity it wasn't apple
season. She held her padded forearm before her throat
and retreated slowly as the woman advanced. (How far
behind her was the parapet?) She slipped away to the
side, and the woman turned to follow her, smiling. "You
can't escape," she said.

"I wouldn't think of it," Cynthia said. "Why do you
want to kill Leptines? Is it just to stir up the city, like a
little boy with a stick in an anthill?" She circled again,
backing toward the sleeping man. (How solid were those
canopy poles? Could she pull the canvas down over the
woman's head?) "Or is it personal? Did he betray you?
Men were always deceivers. Or did he only cheat you out
of your price?"

"Be quite, slave's garbage," the woman hissed, and
thrust the dagger toward Cynthia's face. Cynthia deflected it with her stole. (The woman did not seem really
sure of what she was doing with that blade. Had she used
one before?) "Or I'll kill you slowly, I'll take hours at
it." But she glanced uneasily toward the sun. Perhaps she
didn't have hours; perhaps the cicada would run out of
breath before then. (Could Cynthia distract her long
enough for the household to awaken? Unlikely at best;
and the canopy poles were firmly planted and too strong
to break.)

There was a pendant round the woman's throat, baked
clay it looked like: marked with a little red ochre, hanging from a leather thong, unsuited to lie on that smooth
breast surrounded by gold. It had the shape of an eye,
wide and staring, and the woman's own eyes were round
and wide and seemed hardly to blink.

Cynthia reached behind her with her free hand. The
table's edge; the rim of the dish, a handful of nuts. She
caught up a fistful and threw them into the woman's face.

She dodged, and lunged forward; Cynthia took the
dish by the rim and skimmed it like a skipping stone to
the floor; the bronze rang like a bell and the woman

went down in a rattle of nuts and a shower of cherry juice. Cynthia leaped and came down heavily on her back, pinning her down like a wrestler, and what she lacked in skill she made up, thank the gods, in weight.

The woman cursed quietly, lacking breath, and raised the dagger, but Cynthia grabbed her wrist and struck her elbow twice, thrice, against the tiled floor. The woman screamed, and her hand released the hilt; Cynthia caught it up before it could fall and held the point to the woman's throat. "Now then." She took a deep breath, her first it seemed in several minutes. "Indulge my curiosity, I ask again: who are you, and why Leptines?"

"You barbarian bitch—" the woman squirmed, trying to throw Cynthia off her back. Cynthia let the dagger's point press her throat a little closer, and she lay still.

"I am a pure Hellene and the daughter and grand-daughter of scholars in Alexandria," Cynthia said, exaggerating only a trifle. "Answer my question."

"The crows take you!" Cynthia eased the dagger along a little further. "I'm Phano daughter of Thoinon. Leptines—aagh!—Leptines delivered my father up to Pyrrhos, to his death; Pyrrhos and that slave's bastard of a general. I'll have their lives for it—" but Cynthia settled her weight a little more squarely onto Phano's shoulders, and she fell silent.

Violence against the peace of my city. Yes, the murder of a leading figure like Leptines could hardly avoid causing turmoil among the citizens, a power struggle within Syracuse, and they had war abroad already, did they not? And here Cynthia sat with Phano's own dagger against her throat, and the day was wearing on. Sometime the spell must fail, and the city and Leptines' household awake—and who were they likely to put their trust in then: the daughter of the rich Syracusan (never mind what had become of him since), or the tattered stranger with the dagger in her hand? No, she must stop Phano now and make her escape before anyone awoke, and now the sweat began to run down her spine, one could drop after another, as she realized that the only way to stop her was to kill her.

Take the dagger and push it into her throat. The edge is sharp; it will be no effort at all. But she could not do it.

Her hesitancy must have spoken down the blade of the dagger, for suddenly Phano got her hands under her and reared like a wild horse, throwing Cynthia to one side. Her arm thrust convulsively, and then the blade was jerked from her hand. She fell to the ground, all her weight painful on the point of one shoulder, and tried to roll over to meet Phano's attack.

But there was none. She sat up, favoring her shoulder, and looking around her. Phano lay full-length on the pavement, and the dagger was in her hand with its point toward Cynthia; but she lay still. Had she killed her after all? There was no blood, and in the deep silence her breathing came small and regular. With her left arm Cynthia turned her over, and saw the clay medallion fall away from her throat, its thong cut by that hasty dagger-stroke. Cynthia picked up the cut ends, reluctant to touch the thing with her fingers, and let it dangle at arm's length. The silence was profound; yes, the cicada-song had stopped, and now in the distance she heard footsteps. She got to her feet and took a step backward. There were her sandals, where she dropped them; she turned them over with her toe and slipped them on.

The figure that appeared in the doorway was old and bent, as one might have expected, and swathed in rusty black like Cynthia herself, and nearly toothless and marked by a ferocious squint. Her narrow glance took in the whole scene in an instant. "Good afternoon, grand-mother," Cynthia said to her, as courteously as she could. "I'm sorry to have interfered in your business, but you see I was under orders. I do hope she paid you in advance— "

The old woman raised her hand. "Give me that," she said, and Cynthia's hand that held the medallion began to tingle. The sunlight seemed to darken, and the hot air close in around her. Her shoulder ached, her fingers were growing numb, and the muscles of her arm twitched as if with cramp; against her will they contracted and raised her arm to hold out the medallion. The old woman reached out to take it; and Cynthia raised her arm a little higher and jerked it downward, and smashed the thing into the floor. It broke in two, and the old woman clutched at her breast and staggered back.

The sunlight rushed back into her eyes, and Cynthia took a step toward the broken medallion. She stumbled and nearly fell, but caught herself, and laid the sole of her sandal over the broken pieces. "I'll break it to powder," she whispered.

The old woman raised her hands. "No, no. One for you." She bent down and shook Phano's shoulder. "Get up, you." Phano yawned, and got slowly to her feet. Her eyes were half-closed, and she glided over the pavement like a sleepwalker. The old woman led her away. "Yes, I was paid in advance," she said over her shoulder, and sharply, "Mind you, I'm not done with you." She disappeared through the doorway.

Leptines muttered something in his sleep, and turned over. Inside the house someone coughed, and a baby cried, and there was a faint clatter out in the street. Cynthia picked up the clay pieces in a fold of her stole, and the dagger in her other hand, and fled. Both arms ached and tingled. *I have just faced down a professional witch and come out, if not ahead, at least even.* But she didn't feel triumphant, or even relieved, but only frightened and tired and sore. She got out of Leptines' house before anyone noticed her, and made her way through the slowly rousing crowd back to Arethousa's spring.

As soon as her arms would work again, she threw the pieces of the witch's charm far out into the harbor, and watched them disappear in tiny splashes. Then she sat at the edge of the spring again, and took the dagger between her hands to examine it. It was a fine piece of work, with garnets in its pommel, and a hilt of fine braided wire, and along the base of the blade was engraved, "Arkhias made me for Philip."

"Where did you get that?" Arkhimedes demanded, peering over her shoulder and rubbing his eyes. "I thought it was lost for good."

"You know this?"

"Everybody knows it. It belonged to Alexander once, but Pyrrhos gave it to my Uncle Hieron when he left

Sicily. It was stolen a month ago; more like two months. We'd given up hope on it."

Everything came together at once in Cynthia's mind; yes, even in little Margaron one had heard something about Arkhimedes' Uncle Hieron. There had been something about his birth—a servant's by-blow, that was it, and exposed at birth, but bees had come and fed him with their honey, and his father had accepted the omens and acknowledged him. A typical hero's story. Plainly the gods had something in mind for little Arkhimedes' Uncle Hieron; but if Leptines had been found killed with his dagger it would have set the city on its ears.

"Give it to me," Arkhimedes was saying. "Grandmother can keep it till Uncle gets home."

"No," Cynthia said. (If it could be stolen once it could be stolen again.) "We'll offer it to the nymph, in gratitude for her protection of the city. I'll explain later. Is there any of that wine left?"

Most of the citizens had risen from their naps by now, and gone off about their business, but a few lingered to watch the little ceremony, a courtesy to their city's patroness. Palamedes, as elder, poured the libation of wine (Demetrios guided his arm); Arkhimedes, who was native there, sang the hymn in a voice that had not quite finished cracking.

> "Muse, sing of holy Arethousa, the nymph of Elis,
> who sheltered Sicily from the wrath of queenly Deo,
> when she was seeking her trim-ankled daughter, whom Aidoneus
> rapt away, given to him by all-seeing Zeus the loud-thunderer.
> Trinacria more than all the rest she blamed, where she found
> the marks of her loss. So there with angry hand she broke
> the plows that turn the soil; in her rage she gave to destruction
> farmers and cattle alike, and commanded the fields
> to betray their trust, and the seed to lie sterile. . . ."

Cynthia held the dagger high to flash in the westering sun, and then let it slide into the cool darkness of the water. It turned as it fell, like a leaf falling; then it was gone. Deep beneath the water something shone blue-green.

"Then, Elean desired of Alpheios, you lifted your
    head from the pool
and brushing your dripping hair back from your temples,
you said, 'O mother of the maiden sought over all the
    earth
and mother of fruits, cease your great labor and do not
    task
the land that is true to you with such violent anger.
I dwell in Sikania as a pilgrim, but now this land
is dearer to me than any other; this is Arethousa's
    home,
here is my sanctuary; spare it, merciful goddess. . . .' "

There was a marble railing over the head of the grotto, carven with acanthus leaves and a row of lilies; a handful of citizens leaned over its rim to hear the song. Looking up suddenly, Cynthia recognized Loukas, awake now, and smiling. He looked a reasonable man with his eyes open, and Arkhimedes glanced up, too, as he paused for breath, and they exchanged smiles. *Good*, Cynthia thought. *We'll have shelter for the night.*

"Wearied with hunting, nymph, returning from the
    Stymphalian wood,
you found a stream flowing without eddies or ripples,
crystal clear to the bottom, in which you could count
    every pebble,
and silvery willows and poplars nourished by the waves
of their own will gave natural shade to the sloping
    banks. . . ."

She knelt at the water's edge and twisted at the ring on her finger. It wouldn't come loose. She rubbed the finger against her nose, to oil it, and tried again, but the ring slipped round and round and wouldn't come off.

*   *   *

"Then Alpheios called from his waters, 'Why do you
    flee, Arethousa?
Why do you flee?' he called you in his roaring voice,
and you, worn with the effort of flight, 'O help your
    armor-bearer,
far-shooting Artemis, pure maiden whose shafts are of
    gold,
to whom so often you gave your bow to bear and your
    quiver
with all its arrows!' "

She looked up again. Behind the smiling Loukas stood
Phano, her stole wrapped close round her head, her eyes
cold, her vengeance thwarted. Next to her stood the old
witch; she caught Cynthia's eye and smiled slightly. It
was the smile she had seen once on the face of a skilled
fox-and-hounds player in Alexandria, just after his opponent had put him in check and just before he broke out
to sweep the board; the smile of an old campaigner who
has met a temporary setback.

"Cold sweat poured down your frightened limbs,
and the blue drops fell from all your body.
Wherever you put your foot a pool sprung up, and
    from your hair
fell dew, and sooner than I now can tell the deed
you were changed into a stream. Then Alpheios
    recognizing
in the waters the shape he had loved, cast off the man's
    shape
he had taken on, to mingle his waters with yours.
But the bold-hearted goddess split the earth, and you
    descending
through the dark caverns came hither to Ortygia,
which you love because it bears her name,
and first received you into the airs above the world."

I would have slain that wretch while I had the chance,
Arethousa said from deep within the water. *Human lives
are so short it hardly matters one way or the other, does*

it? But I am not ungrateful. Keep the ring, you may need it. Now go away.

> "Hail, nymph! Keep this city safe, and govern my
>   song;
> and now I will remember you and another song also."

If I were a god, the poet says, I would have pity on the hearts of men. A cool wind had sprung up; she wrapped her stole closer around her and watched the light fade away.

REDEEMER'S RIDDLE

by Stephen L. Burns

Steve Burns made his first professional sale to SWORD AND SORCERESS I, with the delightful thief-outwits-thief foolery of "Taking Heart," which seems to have attracted more attention than any other "first story" in the volume. Since then he's sold to many other magazines, including the very prestigious ANALOG, but we're delighted he still has time to turn out thoughtfully constructed and subtle stories like this one.

He lives somewhere in upstate New York, (the address looks as if he were somewhere in the Thousand Islands) is unmarried at last word, and calls his residence "Mathom House." We know just what he means.

The fire Captain Karenai al-Ibranin sought was yet some distance ahead, the ruin and horror she had escaped in Irkingu still dogged her steps, and the moon seemed to peer down at her through the leafy canopy in silent judgment. An owl landed on a branch nearby with the beat of heavy wings.

The midnight forest was alive with sound; the rustle of leaves, the buzz of insects, the lorn cries of night-birds. Out of it all her ears sieved the terrified squeakings of a mouse caught in the owl's sharp beak. She had to clamp down on a sudden urge to hunt the owl down and make it give up its tiny captive so that at least one lost thing might find freedom by her hand.

She hunched her shoulders and plodded grimly on, weary and footsore. Her thoughts were darker than the night, torchless, and unlit by moon or stars. For her the dawn would not end the darkness, it would be but a cruel joke of appearances; a smile painted on a hanged man's face.

Karenai limped into the firelit circle, and though her feet felt as leaden as her heart, none there had marked her approach. She was among them before they realized she had returned, and those pitiful few were sent groping for their weapons. One, young Barth, managed to get up and face her, clumsily gripping his sword in his left hand. Of his right only a stump wrapped in bloody rags remained. His brown eyes burned with such fear and pain that it was long moments before he recognized her.

Karenai tried to make herself smile, failed. That had been scourged from her, along with laughter, along with hope. She felt shaped of mud and cinders, of dust and ash; and tired, so very old and tired.

"Peace," she said, dropping heavily to the dew-damp ground near the fire. She watched Barth sway, then sit down abruptly, his beardless face averted so she could not see the tears his effort had cost.

She knew she should reward him with a kind word for his valiant, pitiful attempt to protect the others around the fire, most of them more sorely wounded than he. But it was not in her heart to affirm his bravery; part of her cried out that she should order him to run away as far and as fast as he could, to seek some land beyond Irku's borders where the dread name *Dral* was yet unknown, his works a nightmare yet undreamed.

She shook her head, trying to put such thoughts aside. "Peace," she muttered, gazing briefly at the human wreckage strewn around the fire, remnants of the once-proud White Guard of Irkingu. "You will have nothing to ease your pains and lighten your dreams if I tell what passed this day."

"W-we were o-overmatched again, then?" Old Shen whispered.

Karenai marked the wet bubbling sound in her breathing and the bloody froth gathered on lips gone bluish. She knew Shen would probably not live to feel the heat of another day's sun warming her bones. Karenai's hands knotted into fists and she wondered if any lamentation could be great enough to sing this further loss bound to all the others.

"Overmatched? We might as well have been a brave and desperate army of rabbits throwing ourselves against a pack of wolves. The Hell-spawned things which serve Dral scythed us down like wheat and trampled us under, howling and gobbling, painting their teeth and faces with our blood. As it was the first time, to strike one is to strike living stone. I hewed the claw from one, the only reward for all my blows other than a notched sword.

"We knew that if we did not win through, Irkingu's fate would be sealed, and we fought without reserve. We had no lack of valor. The White Guard's honor, at least, remains. High Captain Jasare fought his way through the swarming abominations somehow, his sword shining like a beacon. He forged his way to within a spear's-throw of the monster Dral before . . ."

Karenai fell silent, the memory too foul to pass her lips.

"As before, Captain?" Barth asked quietly.

"Aye. As before. Dral stood waiting undaunted. Nay, more than undaunted; his laughter filled the air like poison smoke, like a rain of knives. He pointed one scabrous finger at High Captain Jasare and the cess-pit of his mouth formed a single Word. The Black Rot—"

Those that could still move shifted uneasily, each faced with his or her own recollections triggered by that dire phrase. Karenai stared into the twisting flames, but behind her eyes burned the never to be forgotten sight of brave Captain Jasare's skin beginning to bubble, turning green-black and liquid, skin and flesh coming off him in stinking drops and gouts as he wailed and tore at his own rotting flesh with hooked fingers which unraveled to melting bones even as they flew and gouged, reduced in a dozen agonized heartbeats to a limbless keening thing leaking from its armor, collapsing into a foul black puddle in the space of a dozen beats more.

"That tore the heart from our charge. I cried for a rally of the few left standing. But a dying, fear-maddened horse knocked me down and trampled me so I know not if any heeded my call. I went down, the horse atop me."

Karenai paused. Gods, she felt cold telling this, the blood in her veins iced with shame and despair. She kicked a log deeper into the fire, sending up a shower of sparks.

"I came to my senses still under the dead horse, near to drowning in the curdling pool of its own blood. I pulled myself free and found the battle ended. Lost. Our dead were . . . the fortunate ones. Dral's unholy servants had dragged the few survivors to the White Plaza to be within sight of the High House and Dral. Torches had been lit. Iron pins had been driven through the hands and feet of the survivors and into the spaces between the marble flags. They—"

She shook her head, swallowing hard. One of the wounded passed her a cup of water and she drank. It wet her mouth but the terrible taste of her words remained. No water could ever be sweet enough to wash it away.

"They fed on those still living, with gleeful howls and wet tearing sounds, with the screams of their victims and their awful gobbling laughter." She hung her head, seething with loathing, much of it directed at herself. She spoke again, her words as cold and heavy as clods thrown into a grave. "I crawled away."

Some dark thing like laughter boiled out of her then, caustic as acid, bitter as gall. "The last brave Captain of the White Guard slunk away on her belly, her mouth full of vomit, her—"

"*Captain!*" Karenai's teeth clacked together on the curse she was about to call down on herself. Young Barth stared at her, his face horror-stricken. "Y-you f-forget yourself!" he stammered.

She nodded once, sharply. "Perhaps." She sighed. "Would that I could. Then I would know the gods care at least that little."

This was no profit to any of them. She pulled her cloak closer about herself. "Enough ill tidings. Sleep now, if you can, and pray to wake tomorrow and find the past days only a bad dream."

* * *

Karenai came awake choking and gasping as the dream-Dral's leprous finger swung toward her and the pit of his mouth formed her name. One of the Guard was snoring, another moaned in his sleep. The fire had burned low; reduced to dying embers and cold ash like the White City Irkingu's glory, like yesterday's dreams of freeing it from Dral's foul, smothering grasp.

"Ashes. Yes, child, in the end all becomes cold ash and wind-blown dust." The unexpected low voice answering her thoughts brought her to full wakefulness in an instant. In less than three beats of her suddenly-hammering heart Karenai had come to a crouch, her knife already in her hand. Her other hand found her notched sword as she sought to separate the intruder from the gloom.

A vague gray shape across the firepit came a step closer. A handful of leaves and twigs were thrown into the fire by an unseen hand. The fire blazed up, crackling and popping.

The new ruddy light dazzled her eyes, but still she was able to see a rag-robed old woman leaning on a long gnarled wooden staff. The intruder shook back the sleeve of her free hand, baring her bone-thin arm and showing her empty hand.

"No weapon, child. No death come creeping out of the night like the mists. No enemy—perhaps even a friend." The woman met Karenai's gaze squarely. "Stand ready to gut me if you wish, but I intend to sit." She grunted as she lowered herself to the damp ground, bracing herself with her staff. Karenai could hear the woman's bones creak as she sat, and allowed herself to sit as well while she watched the old woman fussily rearrange her rags against the night's chill.

"Who are you?" Karenai pitched her voice low so that the others might sleep on. She let go her sword within easy reach but kept her knife.

"Now there is a question. Better you might ask what I know; it would be more useful to you," The old woman cackled at some private joke, showing her ruined teeth. "And more certain, as I am scarcely what I used to be, or who. My knowing remains; well do I know the night, and her bright sister the day, and most things which happen inside them. The strength to act may be lost to me, but little escapes my notice. Aye, little escapes." The old woman stirred the flagging fire with the heel of her staff, then cast in some small branches with a hand as thin and knotty as the twigs she fed the blaze.

Karenai said nothing, remaining silent and watchful. Thus far there was no need to interrogate the stranger. She would let her ramble on and assay her danger or harmlessness in that way.

"You will not ask what I know? Well." She grinned at Karenai, her eyes glittering in her seamed face in a way which made the Captain wonder if the crone was mad. Her talk hinted at such.

"Then I will tell you just one thing I know. A boy yet shy of seventeen summers pretends to sleep behind me, clutching the knife in the one hand he has left to him. He listens, this boy, ready to slip his blade between these brittle ribs if he senses any threat to you from me." She raised her voice slightly but did not turn.

"Come to the fire, young Barth am-Sordann. Young though you are, you must know that there is a better thing to stick in a woman than a bronze blade—even one so well-forged as that. Come, let me tend your arm and the fever that burns in it, or you will not live to enjoy such pleasures and seed children to live after you."

The old woman winked at Karenai and slapped her knee. "Come, my son, you need not fear."

Karenai shifted her weight so she sat more comfortably but maintained her guard. "If you are awake, obey her, Barth," she said. "I watch, and if she makes one move I doubt, you will sleep with her severed head for your pillow. I swear it." She stared hard at the old woman, letting her see the truth of what she said.

She heard Barth stir; watched him come into the light at the old woman's side. She marked the taut and shiny look of of his face, some coming from trepidation, but not all of it. Something clenched like a fist inside her and she knew the intruder spoke rightly; the boy had the Wound Fever, the Warrior's Bane.

Barth shot her a pleading look, sharp as an arrow. She could only nod curtly in answer. There could be no unbending until she knew more of the old woman and her intentions. Barth looked stricken but did as he was ordered, submitting to the old woman's touch. She began stripping away the black, blood-crusted rags. Her touch was sure and tender, that Karenai could see. But her words were not.

"What time is it, Captain Karenai al-Ibranin? The High House of Irkingu is become an unemptied chamberpot, a vessel filled with filth. Its former High Lord hangs from a hook on its walls like a gutted sheep at market. The others of the blood hang beside; those not eaten by the Black Rot are food for flies and crows. Dral is near invincible behind the bulwark of his troop of monsters, and the new-forged circle of those corrupt enough to please and serve him. The once-proud White Guard is now reduced to a few broken husks and living fodder. Irku is become a stockyard and Irkingu an abattoir; the people shiver lamb-helpless and hide in the new darkness which stains the white stones, and for them there will be no mercy and no escape."

The old woman turned eyes suddenly hawk-like and piercing on Karenai. "Is it time to run, Captain? To know that you alone cannot prevail where the whole White Guard failed, to hide from what you cannot right and will never forget?"

Karenai stared back at the woman, feeling the frayed strands of her temper stretch tight; who was this crone to speak to her so? She forced her words out through clenched teeth. "You know less than you think if you believe that. I will do my duty and help these poor few find safety and shelter, then I return to Irkingu. My blade is notched, not broken."

The old woman was undaunted. "Ah, well. A hero." She turned to face Barth, pulling a small skin flask from the folds of her rags. "This will burn like fire when I put it on, son. But it will consume the cause of the fever which has begun. Will you bear it?"

Barth met the old woman's gaze. Karenai could see that he was near tears in his pain and trepidation. He tipped his head slightly. "My Captain has ordered it." he whispered harshly.

The old woman's face softened. "My apologies," she replied solemnly. "I mistook you. You are a man, not a boy, Barth am-Sordann."

Karenai's feeling of pride lasted only a moment. She was taken back by the speed with which the old woman moved, catching Barth's ruined arm in one surprisingly strong hand and pouring the clear liquid from the flask over the raw stump with the other. Barth's jaw clamped down on a scream as the liquid burned away the dead flesh from his hastily cauterized stump, then his eyes rolled back in his head and he mercifully fainted.

The old woman did not let him fall. She supported his slack body as she cleaned his arm with more of the liquid, then dressed it in a clean cloth. She laid him down carefully, tender as a mother with a new-born babe. She brushed the sweat-soaked hair back from his brow, sighed deeply, then faced Karenai once more.

"Only you and I now, Captain, as it should be. Do you trust me now?"

Karenai did feel a little trust, but too grudging to be told.

"Your name," she said. "If you must hide that, then I must wonder what else you conceal."

"That again? Well. Call me Manmi. Many have."

Karenai stared at the old woman coldly. "You bait me. Manmi is worshiped by some quiet few, just a name from old tales to most, supposedly the wise and beautiful young goddess it was said helped Shazu found Irkingu so long ago and acts as its guardian. Manmi is a chipped statue in a dry fountain in Irkingu's oldest quarter."

The old woman snorted. "You would have me be cracked and faceless marble if I am to be at all? Well. Truly my prime passed me by long ago. Too long ago, maybe, and though I still live, is it no wonder that I look old? That my guard fails? The years swarm around me like midges, and though each tiny bite only costs me a single drop of blood, they are so thick I am nearly bled dry. Wise? Well," She hung her head, her gray tangles falling to cover her face as if hiding from a vast sorrow.

That sorrow's shadow touched Karenai, and she felt the merest touch of the uncountable years gathered about her strange visitor, a touch like the wind off hundreds of small wings. In the matter of her age, at least, the old woman spoke truly.

The intruder shrugged, looking up and pushing back the errant strands of tarnished silver from her eyes. "Wisdom is a precious prize, won only at the cost of learning from one's mistakes. I should be wise after all these years, after all my errors and failures, after all my mistakes."

Manmi—if that was truly who she was—suddenly changed before Karenai's eyes. She sat up straight, regret falling away from her face like a veil, revealing a stern and lordly visage. Her bearing became regal and power seemed to radiate from her like heat from the sun. Karenai's breath caught in her throat and she knew that it was no mere trick of light or pose which made her look younger, greater, and awesome.

The old woman's voice had gone as deep and ringing as a bell, and she said, "But I make no mistake in this. The loyalty and trust Barth pays you shines as true as the Guide-Star; to him you are a hero. Irkingu is in dire need of a redeemer, a hero. Otherwise, it will be a cold marble necropolis haunted by ghosts, and all Irku an empty wasteland. Dral will take his dark pleasure from sucking the life out of it like marrow from a bone. Unless he is stopped."

The old woman searched Karenai's face, she felt the empty sack her heart had become searched as well and she feared she would be found wanting.

Manmi spoke again, her voice deep and portentous. "You, Karenai al-Ibranin, are the last Captain, and twice now you have been driven off by Dral. You doubt, you despair, you feel shame for your failure, and yet even so reduced you still command loyalty and trust. Your hope is gone, but you are not yet defeated. There is great strength in you. Strength and wit and courage alone might make you a hero equal to the need of less certain times. But more is needed; you are forged, but your tempering is not yet complete. As you are, you cannot prevail. Yet there is a way. Will you hear Manmi's counsel?"

Karenai's heart rang with awe and the faint glimmerings of a new-kindled hope. Manmi was not some fancy spun by the story-tellers after all; she was as real as the cuts and bruises put on her body by yesterday's battle. More than that, she remained Irkingu's protector and offered help.

"I will, Manmi," she said humbly, bowing her head.

Her head snapped back up and anger crackled through her at Manmi's cackling laughter. Manmi held up her hands, palms out.

"Peace, child, I mock you not. It tickles me to feel belief and awe after so long." She smiled, then her lined face grew serious.

"Listen, closely now, for some matters are harder to hold onto than dreams. For everything on this earth there is an opposite; good to evil, day to night, beauty to ugliness. Not only is Dral in this land, so is his opposite for that balance of opposition is one true thing in this world, and what affects one affects the other."

Manmi lifted her hand, pointed off to her left. "Less than an hour's walk from here is a stream. At its head is a hill, and atop the hill is a grove where dwells Dral's opposite. Find it."

"And then," Karenai prompted, expecting more.

Manmi shrugged. "That is up to you."

Karenai felt anger unsheathe itself inside her, felt tricked and let down. "That is all you give me? High talk and a damned riddle? You would dangle help and offer only this? Tell me, am I to kill this opposite of Dral's? Or—"

Manmi silenced her with a single glance. "To be a hero you must make a hero's decisions, not play the puppet's part. Go now and find your own answer. Suffer fate or act as its hand."

Karenai found herself rising and strapping her weapons and leather armor back on, her thoughts in a whirl. Manmi's reproof could no more be argued than the wind. She had no sense that the old goddess was controlling her; it was more like those moments in the heat of battle when the body knows what must be done and acts while the mind straggles behind, helplessly trying to catch up.

But she was still a Captain, still had duties and responsibilities. "What of these wounded ones?" she asked.

"I shall care for them," Manmi replied. "If you succeed I will see to it that they are returned to Irkingu, will take them away if you fail. Peace, pride and fair days to you, daughter."

Karenai ducked her head. "And to you." Then she turned and limped off into the night once more.

Before long the forest swallowed up the fire behind her. Not so long ago she had arrived at it filled with despair. Now she put it in the distance, telling herself that an uncertain hope was better than none at all, and that a riddle was at least better than the sentence of certain death she would have brought down on herself in the lone assault she had earlier planned.

By the time the sun had begun rising from its nightly embrace in the earth's bed she had found the stream and made some progress in her solitary march along it. The bruised stiffness of her body had abated some and her limp was all but gone.

The polished copper disk of the sun seen rising through the snow-trunked birches lining the eastern bank suffused the drifting morning mists with a soft pearly light, but such beauties were lost on Karenai. Her mind still restlessly played with Manmi's oracular riddle, turning it over and over like a purse that was certain to hold a hidden gold coin.

The sun rose higher, burning off the mists fleecing the ground. Brightly colored birds embroidered the morning with color and song. Bees hummed with contented industry among the low flowered bushes growing between the trees and the water's edge, and just ahead of her a fish gave an exultant leap, flashing silver and landing with a gleeful splash.

The morning's peace and beauty at least touched Karenai a little, but for the most part she found herself resenting it. Irkingu writhed in the tormented death-agonies of a snake on a griddle, but here, in the same land, no pall was cast.

Yet, she amended. That thought made her take a closer look about her, Irkingu's beauty had not so long ago been unstained and seemed unviolable. This, too, could be fouled by Dral's fell hand.

Dust and ashes, Manmi had said. Was that Dral's plan? To make the once-gleaming marble city the capital of a land of dust and ash, spreading desolation and despair outward as far as he could reach? Would he move on once all Irku was in ruin? If so, then what scourged corpse of a land had he come from?

No matter. If Dral and this thing she sought were bound together as closely as Manmi had said, then it would die by her hand to begin Dral's downfall. It must be beautiful to counterbalance the abomination that was Dral. Well, so was the city beautiful before his coming, and now it was surely dying. As a soldier Karenai knew that everyone and everything dies sooner or later. This beautiful thing would just die a little before its time, that was all.

Karenai's hand fell to her notched sword, her answer to the riddle. She quickened her steps and carried all Irkingu in her thoughts.

The land climbed slowly toward the cloudless sky. Now the stream she followed chuckled and tumbled over its rocky bed, giving way in places to wide pools where foam-cloaked waters whirled and spun. The eastern bank, on her left, had risen to become low steep cliffs heaving straight up from the water's edge. She had been forced to cross to the other side, crossing by leaping from one wet and slippery stone to the next.

Coming at last to the end of a long eastward bend, she caught her first glimpse of the hill she had been told to seek. Its long green slopes were close enough for her to make out the huge old oaks dotting its flanks and the high crown of trees at its crest. Beyond the hill the land rose steeply; it was but a foothill of the CloudHerds, the range of low mountains which formed Irku's southern border. True to their name, the peaks had clouds gathered around them like sheep.

Though she was yet too low and distant to see it, she knew that the stream sprang from a wide rocky opening part way up the hill. The Mouth, it was called, and the glade she sought known, unsurprisingly, as Manmi's Lap. She had been to the hill's foot before, but had never approached it from this direction.

Karenai knelt and drank, staring at the hill as she sipped the clean clear water. Her mission was simple now; she would do the deed at the hill's crest, then a league's march would take her to a farm where a horse might be commandeered. With luck and a hard ride, she might reach Irkingu by the sun's setting.

Once there, her notched blade would taste Dral's blood or be broken in the attempt.

She reacted to the sound instinctively. It might have been the snap of a twig or the rustle of leaves crushed by a booted foot, the only warning whisper of steel against leather. She knew it only as the sound of threat.

Karenai dove to one side and rolled, a grunt escaping her lips as her shoulder struck a stone thrust up through the grass.

A knife grew out of the turf like a deadly flower in the place where she had been standing. She rolled to her feet, damning herself for not thinking that Dral might have prepared to defend his vulnerability. The knife had come from behind the wide bole of an oak not ten strides from her. She heard a muffled curse as she drew her own knife.

Her position was bad; she was only two-thirds of the way up the hill's slope, the nearest other oak was forty strides away, and there was no cover larger than a blade of grass between herself and the tree behind which her foe lurked.

Karenai's lips drew back from her teeth and she coiled into a tense crouch. She was damned tired of running. By the White Crown, yesterday's flight from Irkingu had been her last retreat.

Forward then. *Attack!* She sprang toward the knife in

the ground, throwing her own knife just before she reached it. Her blade whistled past the tree's right-hand side, planting itself in the grass beyond. She snatched up her foe's knife, sprinted farther to the right and flung it at the moving something of which she caught a fleeting glimpse just around the tree's curve.

The moment the blade left her hand she dodged toward the tree's left-hand side, her sword hissing out of its sheath. She swung it up, over, and brought it down in an oblique slash, the notched blade coming to a sudden stop as it chopped into the shoulder and back of her foe as he stumbled back into its deadly arc. The man let out a strangled scream and toppled, his right arm half-severed, his shoulder and back opened to blood and bone like a mouth which would suck the life out of him.

Karenai was on him in an instant, slamming her booted foot down on his throat and damming up any cry he might have made.

"How many others?" she panted, staring down at him, her face grim and her eyes cold as a winter night.

The man writhed like a worm on a hook under her foot. He was tall and gangly, garbed in a motley collection of dented plate and outsized leathers, like a child playing at war. His thin, wisp-whiskered face darkened with pain and terror as he fought for air. Karenai knocked his good hand away from her ankle with the red-splashed flat of her blade, then rested its point on the center of his forehead.

"How many, I asked." She let off his throat a little so he could answer.

"T-two m-m-more," he gasped. His bulging eyes took in the cold metal poised to pin his head to the ground, then turned toward Karenai's face. He moaned at the look she wore, the pitiless stare of an executioner.

"Dral sent you?"

The man began to sob. "N-no—I d-dare not! H-he—"

Karenai put more weight on the sword. Its point grated against bone with a small ugly noise. "Tell me!"

"Y-yes! Protect the hill or die! *T-the Rot!*" He sobbed harder, his whole body shuddering. "The rot, the rot!"

Under him the blood from his wound spread, painting the grass crimson.

She glanced at the jumble of things by the tree. "You have a horn. How many blasts to summon the others?"

"Two! Mercy, Captain! Have m-mercy on me!" His eyes were wide and beseeching, filled with tears.

Karenai stared down at the pitiful thing she had captured, and her teeth clenched at the thought that any man could be so corrupt as to serve Dral. Her gaze fell on the gold Captain's badge strung on a string around his neck, looted from one of her own dead. *Mercy?* She should feed him his own guts until he strangled on them, make him feel some of what the others endured—

Images as dark as a flight of bats flitted before her eyes; screaming men and women struggling against the iron pins driven through their hands and feet, begging to die while hulking, misshapen things gnawed and tore and gobbled. No mercy for them, tormented, tortured—

Karenai's breath whistled through her teeth as she drove her blade through the man's throat, granting him a faster, cleaner death than he deserved.

"Mercy, then," she muttered, taking the Captain's badge from around his neck and wiping her blade clean on his ragged scarf.

"For my good, not yours."

She waited, concealed among the lower boughs of the oak, the bow at ready, one arrow nocked. Had the corpse on the ground been one of her soldiers she would have had him flogged for his stupidity; to throw a knife when a good bow and full quiver were at hand. Had the man been a well-trained soldier, or something other than an overconfident fool, she would have been the one growing cold on the grass.

Was it a sign that Manmi watched over her? Was her fortune the work of the old goddess' hand? Divine help was new to her and she had no way of judging.

She was given no more time to think of it. On her left a short, heavy-set man approached, drawn by the horn's call. She drew back on the bôw and took careful aim. *Come closer,* she beckoned silently.

The man did, and fell clutching at the arrow in his throat.

Karenai rolled over her third foe with the toe of her boot. The two bolts in the woman's broad back twisted and broke under her weight. The one in her heavy belly had broken earlier, when the woman with the pox-scarred face had fallen. This one she recognized, the robber Murgurre, and that she was free told Karenai that Dral had recruited help from the prisons.

She turned away from Murgurre and gazed up at the hill's crest. One more death to bring, and with it the beginning of Dral's downfall. Sweating from the high sun's heat, she wiped her face, took a deep breath, and headed up the hill, wondering what she would find there.

Whatever it was, its doom had arrived.

There was an outer vanguard of pines circling the hill's crest like spires of a crown. Their trunks grew straight and clean as the shafts of spears, their lower boughs not starting below half their height and spreading to form spearheads of rich green. Head-high bushes lushly adorned with fragrant multi-hued blossoms clustered around the trees' bases like brightly-dressed beggar-children swarming around a rich stranger at market. Needle-carpeted paths meandered through the spaces in between.

Just as she was nearing one such opening, still outside the palisade of trees, the sound reached her ears. It drifted on the breeze, sweet, beguiling and unexpected, making her breath catch.

It was a low warbling music, haunting harplike trills which reached inside her and warmed her like strong wine on a bitter cold night. The sound beckoned her on, drew her through the living pine gates, along a blossom-decked hall of thriving green and inward as if a subtle spell had been cast over her.

The bushes gave way to a wide sward, the vivid green of the lush grass dotted with small white flowers, their glossy petals shining like stars in the night sky. In the glade's center there rose a rocky spring surrounded by a small blue pool.

But the spring and pool received no more than a moment's glance from Karenai; her eyes were drawn like lodestones to the source of the song which wrapped her in silken enchantment.

The song came from a bird perched on a stone before the pool, a bird the like of which she had never seen or even dreamed could exist. To say it was beautiful no more described it than saying the sea was wet. She had seen a peacock once, and had thought it the most beautiful thing to ever wear wings. Compared to the creature preening itself before her that peacock was but a gaudy vulture.

Gold it was, bright burnished living gold that caught the sun's rays and flung them back in a thousand aureate gleamings. It spied Karenai's approach with its bright ruby eyes and spread wings of brilliant yellow flame, its song becoming a thrilling anthem of welcome and delight.

Karenai's steps faltered. The song caressed her more sweetly than mother or lover, and the slow flashing beat of its perfect wings sent gilded arrows of light flying, some to pierce her heart with awe and wonder.

She dropped to her knees, clapping her hands over her ears and turning her dazzled eyes to the ground. The solid ground of her purpose crumbled under her, pitching her into a deep chasm where the plans of her mind were set against the plucked strings of her soul. What she had found was truly as beautiful as Dral was terrible; he was nightmare enfleshed, raging through the day, and now before her sang a dream the gods would covet, born in beating heart and unfurling golden wing.

A moan escaped her and she shook her head from side to side, her eyes squeezed shut and her hands still clamped over her ears. How could she kill such a perfect thing? She had to kill it if Dral were to fall! To snuff out such a light would be evil! Yet as it throve, so did evil. . . .

Round and round it went, a dizzying dance of damnations.

"My soldiers, my city . . ." She whispered her pledge, trying to turn the eyes of her mind away from the bird's burning afterimage and toward the blood-fevering remembrances of the High Captain's cruel and loathsome death, how the White Plaza had become a gore-spattered feeding ground for monsters, of the acid insanity of Dral's mad, malevolent grin.

"*I must!*" she wailed, drawing it out into a heartsick battle cry as she lurched up off her knees and flung herself toward where the bird placidly waited.

At the last instant she unstoppered her ears, whipping off her cloak and daring to squint through the tears in her eyes at the blurred glow of her mark. She threw herself at it, her cloak held before her like a net.

Moments later she lay on the ground gasping for air, feeling as if she had just fought an hours-long duel. The bird lay trapped beneath her cloak, silent and still. Yet she knew it to be alive for she could feel the rapid beating of its heart through the cloth.

Working one-handed, she rolled some stones onto the cloak's edges to keep it netted, and once she was certain it could not escape she rolled off gladly, for its touch reminded her what was hidden by the cloak, huddled and waiting for her stroke.

She stood wearily, licking her lips and feeling heat and dampness in her eyes. So much pain and ugliness of late, so much death. That such evils could be combatted by the destruction of such a beautiful thing seemed a cruel mockery of all that was right and honorable and just.

And yet . . .

Her hand shook as she drew her notched blade. She had to wipe away the sweat—or was it tears?—which stung her eyes and blurred her sight. Her arm trembled as she lifted her sword, its weight suddenly seeming too immense to be borne.

She thought about Dral destroying all that was beautiful in Irkingu, about herself destroying beauty to serve other ends, perhaps for more noble reasons, but becoming like him to defeat him.

"My soldiers, my city . . ." It came out more an apology than a pledge and promise. She clenched her teeth and gathered her strength. One stroke, swift and clean . . .

That hideous face, the hand of desecration . . . helpless prey . . .

Her blade moved in a whistling arc that ended with a

scream of rage and frustration as she flung her sword as far away as she could. It turned end over end in the air then struck rock and the notched blade shattered, along with all her hopes. The pool swallowed the pieces like raindrops, like tears.

She fell to her knees once more and hung her head, feeling old, tired and empty; a lamp with all its oil burned away, its vessel cracked and its wick charred beyond reuse. Too dry for tears, all fuel for other than dry despair gone.

"I am sorry," she said to no one in particular, her only answer to all her failures.

"And I am proud," she was answered. "I made no mistake in you, brave Captain."

Karenai looked up, startled. Manmi sat on the grass before her, smiling back at her.

"No mistake. Worthy I thought you, and worthy you proved to be. If Irkingu is to be redeemed, it will be by you, daughter."

Karenai shook her head, bewildered. "But I *failed!*"

Manmi patted her hand. "No child. Had you killed what you found, then you would have failed. No hero could have destroyed a thing so good and beautiful, no matter the need or the end it served. No one who could do such a thing would deserve to return to the White City under Manmi's blessing. A warrior without mercy— mercy you showed against much temptation—and without any consideration other than her own goals, worthy though they may be, would be no better than the soulless monsters which serve Dral. No better than Dral himself."

Karenai struggled to understand. "You—saw all?"

Manmi chuckled. "Little escapes me, did I not tell you that? Now lift your cloak, daughter."

Karenai did as she was told, rolling the stones away and lifting the spread cloak carefully. The bird was gone, and in its place lay a golden sword.

"Pick it up," Manmi said. "You earned it; it is yours now."

She closed her fingers around it, and it came to her hand like a part of her which had been missing up until that moment. Hope flowed into her in a heady rush which rang inside her like the song the bird had sang. Her weariness and despair washed away in an instant, leaving her feeling new, strong and complete.

The sword was a marvel; its blade long and shaped like a feather, chased with marks like vanes. The hilt was shaped like a bird's neck, the pommel its head, formed open-beaked and set with two bright ruby eyes. Wings spread from where hilt met blade, curving back to form the guard.

She lifted it then, surprised to find it as light in her hand as the feather it had been shaped to resemble. The sun caught it, transforming it into a brilliant tongue of golden flame. She turned toward Manmi, her eyes wide with wonder. "It is the bird . . ."

Manmi nodded. "Aye, and the beauty you spared will serve you now and ever. You must tarry no longer; Irkingu cries out for deliverance. Neither Dral or his creatures will be able to stand against that blade if a true heart wields it. It is no divine protection, but wield it well and you shall win through. Redeem the city. Cleanse it. But remember what you learned in gaining it, or it will fail in your hand. You are ready now. Go."

Karenai did as she was bidden. But before she reached the edge of the glade she turned back to face Manmi.

She was answered before she could ask. "Those you left in my care are more healed than you might expect. They await you outside the city. You will find them and lead them once more."

Karenai ducked her head. "I thank you Manmi. I—I shall remember you, and the people will know that you still live and watch over them. Offerings will be made, and—"

Manmi's laugh cut her off. "On your way, blast you! Send wine if you must offer, but for now stop dawdling!"

Karenai found that she could still smile after all. She saluted the goddess, then turned and left the glade.

Manmi watched her go. "Well," she said, "A warrior-queen I think you shall be, and a long life to you! But some day you will find the crown pinching and constricting, and then you will find yourself here and this tired old guardian can at last take her rest, leaving a young strong replacement. And about time, too!"

Cackling to herself, Manmi pulled a flash of wine from inside her rags, took a long swallow, and settled back to wait and watch.

Karenai stepped out of the shadows and into the bright sunlight. She took a deep breath of the sweet piney air and held the golden sword—Manmi's staff—aloft. It blazed like a beacon, like a glowing promise of redemption.

"My city! For Manmi!" she cried, clear as the call of a silver horn. She laughed aloud for joy at her release from despair. Then sheathing the golden sword she started down the hill on her way toward Irkingu, her footsteps as light as hope.

THE TREE-WIFE OF ARKETH

by Syn Ferguson

This story came in quite late in the selection process; and when I read it, I said "Oh, no; not *another* story about dryads!" But then I read it again, and decided that since stories tend to come in cycles, maybe this was this year's Singular Coincidence, or should I call it the workings of the law of Synchronicity?

Whatever you call it, I thought it was too good a story to reject and I'd have to squeeze it in somehow.

She says of herself that she is an Oregonian with "a high tolerance for rain" (she's lucky; I spent fourteen years as a Texan with no tolerance at all for heat, dust, glare and Fundamentalists), "and a low tolerance for traditional employment which is lucky because there's no employment at all here, traditional or otherwise"; she speaks of writing as her "secret vice" in the intervals of being an Air Force paramedic, a reporter, a Yukon territory cook, etc. She has won workshop awards from Ursula LeGuin and others, and "refuses to fit a pigeonhole." That's an occupational hazard with writers, so that we could pigeonhole her as "classic nonconformist writer." Like all the rest of us, Ms. Ferguson. You're recapitulating all our life stories.

A tree cracked the pavement where the cobbles met the wall and grew up as tall as a woman. To the woman who watched from the deep window or the arched doorway across the alley, it seemed to happen apart from the ebb and flow of Arketh traffic, outside time.

222

One day there was nothing but the whitewashed wall, scarred by over-burdened carts and stick-wielding boys, then the young tree was woman-high, swinging its green and silver leaves, its copper bloom.

The watcher had no illusions. When a club was needed, or a fire, the living tree would be slain; yet it was the tree in the alley she watched, not the plantings in her watered garden.

Hillmen trod the narrow alley from the north gate to the free quarter of the city, as any free soul was wise to do. Khansmen policed lesser forms of life from the wider ways the nobles took. All the travelers from the steppes passed this door, marching south for adventure, bringing their beasts and barter and stories.

It was the stories the woman bought, paying round silver coins for tales of the wild clans who lived up on the edge of the world. In the day she cried her need to the crowd, at night she visited the nearby inns, draped in black, listening to travelers' tales as if she believed them.

This night the sun set in a bloom of sulfur and brass. The sky faded to red-brown dusk as the first wind blew the fine, fine dust in from the desert. When the light was gone and the traffic with it, the woman left off watching and went to prepare her meal. She had no servant to intrude on her solitude. She closed the door to the house but left the gate open that led from the alley into the garden.

Water was wealth in these lowlands. She would not hoard it. Many hillmen, descending the stone passes and canyons from the Edge where water was free, would have suffered want of it in Arketh but for that unlocked gate. At first the lowlanders had stolen from her—a little, not enough to make her move—but she had ignored them. Now there was less thievery.

When she heard the uneven rush of running feet and a tattered figure skidded through her gate, she turned to face the intruder without alarm. A long knife leveled at her breast she ignored. The runner was a girl dressed in the long woolen shirt of the hill clans. A belt at her waist held an assortment of gear and weapons. Her brown legs were bare to the knee where her soft boots tied, and her eyes, greenish amber, were bright with pain. The snapped-off shaft of a throwing stick protruded from the back of her thigh and hampered her stride. Blood ran down her leg into the fur-lined boot. Other running feet clattered over the cobbles—the hard-shod feet of city dwellers.

"In here," said the watcher, with a slight inclination of her head toward the arched entry to the house.

The runner hesitated, her knife still poised for action; then she jumped for shelter as her pursuers spilled into the garden giving tongue all at once, like a pack of hounds that tolerate each other for a chance at the prey.

They were sons of the city's lesser nobility by the clothes they wore, too young to be Khansmen yet, but eager to grow into it. Each of them held a weapon pointed at the watcher.

The leader silenced them with a snarl. "A running girl, where is she?"

The watcher studied each face in turn, seeming not to see the threat. Finally she shrugged. "You must have lost her. No one but you is here uninvited. Search if you wish, but don't trample my herbs."

The leader's voice cracked in indignation. "Be glad she's not, then! She's killed three Khansmen. She'd as soon cut your throat as give you good evening."

The watcher made no reply, and one of the pack plucked at the leader's arm, looking askance at the bladders and coiling strings that glowed faintly atop the water tanks. "She wouldn't go to ground right here in Spenarr; let's watch the north gate."

With an insolent nod and no apology for their intrusion, the leader consented. The watcher followed them and, for the first time in many years, closed the garden gate and barred it. Then she returned to the tank and stood watching the small life there until all sound had died away. Gossamer fins fanned the water among bladder-stems. Dark eyes dreamed watery dreams.

"You can come out," she said at last. "They have gone."

The girl came limping out, her weapon still in her hand, but under the watcher's eye the blade wavered and fell. With a sigh she sheathed it again. Her breath was still coming fast, but even wounded she moved with assurance. She rubbed her forehead with the back of her hand and offered a left-handed apology.

"I didn't mean to bring them down on you. I'll go now."

"You are welcome to stay."

"You'd be a fool to let me. What he said was true. I might cut your throat, and the Khansmen certainly would if they knew you'd sheltered me." Her hot, bright eyes brooked no compromise with truth, but her lips were thinned to a bitter line.

"If you do not tell them," the watcher said, "I will not."

The girl looked a little startled. She frowned, but before she could speak again, the watcher went on.

"How were you wounded?"

"Breaking out of the slave pits. My mother told me never to turn my back on a dead man unless I'd cut his throat myself."

"Your mother is a warrior?"

The girl's face closed again, controlling emotion. "Was. She's dead."

"A great loss to her people." It was the ritual phrase of condolence, but the girl refused it, lifting her chin a little.

"No. She was clanless, as I am."

In Arketh that was damning. Loss of clan affiliation was a death sentence on the Edge—worse, because the clanless died in two worlds at once, flesh and spirit. No name survived them in the realm of the dead. The girl's control as she spoke showed what that loss meant to her, but her mane of dark hair shaken back, her level stare, warned that there would be no pity asked or accepted.

"And I," said the watcher quietly. "Your wound needs care. Will you trust my skill?"

The feral stare faded. The girl relaxed and sighed. "I'd be glad of help. It burns like fire."

Without comment, the watcher led the way to the kitchen and silently offered fruit, cheese and bread. The girl wolfed the food and watched with interest as her hostess lit the lamps and put two kettles on the fire, one

with herbs, one with knives, tongs and needles in it. Her
chewing slowed as she watched the preparations, and at
last she shoved the food away.

"I hope I don't heave when you cut me. It's the first
time I've had enough to eat in a week. You must be rich
to have a house this big. Don't you have any servants?"

"No."

The girl's quick eye inventoried the wealth of pots and
food in the room. Ignoring her wound and a tendency of
her leg to drag, she got up and made a circuit, fingering
the wooden bowls and pitchers. Restlessly she swung
around and studied the watcher.

"A clanless woman, but rich. No friend of the Khan's,
since you put that pack off my trail—yet you're free.
Why aren't you working in a slophouse or the baths? My
mother said that was all there was for an honest woman
here."

"The Khan does not know where my treasure is hidden. If he kills me he will have neither that nor my tax.
On the Edge silver would not buy equal safety. I am not a
warrior."

"No," said the girl. "We don't enslave strangers; we
kill them. But you'd be free while you lived. Cities stink.
I was warned to stay out of them."

"What does a clanless woman do with freedom?" The
watcher seemed intent on her kettles, but her slow stir-
ring stopped until the girl answered.

"I don't know. Stands in the light, as long as she can."

The watcher began to stir again, and they were quiet
until she pulled the simmering pots off the fire and put
them on the wide table. The girl helped clear the remains
of her meal, then eased herself up onto the dark wood
and stretched out, belly down, pillowing her head in her
arms.

The watcher hung a lamp on a long cord from a hook
over the table, and wrung out a rag in her kettle of
herbs. "First I must clean the wound."

"You sound like my mother. Clean the dishes, wash
yourself, pick up this pigpen." There was no real resent-
ment in her tone.

The watcher set about her task with a light, firm touch.

The stick had entered the thigh from above, striking down into the tendons at the back of the knee. The skin had been torn—probably when the girl broke off the hampering shaft. She lay still now, but the racing beat of her heart had started the bleeding again, and rhythmic tremors of pain or chill tensed the muscles in her leg as the blood was wiped away.

When the wound was clean, the watcher brought a length of cloth and slid it under the girl's thigh, and knotted it tightly, then almost in the same motion she reached up as if gathering shadows and scattered a handful of leaves over the girl's head and shoulders. At their touch, the tense form slumped into unconsciousness.

Working swiftly now, the watcher cut deep into the flesh, following the shaft of the stick to find the barbed point. It was lodged against the bone and slippery in her fingers, but she freed it, rotated it to bring the barbs up through the incision, and had it out. Dark blood trembled and welled from the wound, but there was no bright arterial gush. She had fashioned her curved needles herself, from aged and dried hardwood. She sewed the wound closed with painstaking care—muscle, fat, skin—with fine fibers from the stems of the bladder plants. She made a neat job of it, like any woman who has learned to rely on her own handiwork. When she had wrapped the wound in a clean bandage, she brushed the leaves from the girl's head and shoulders. The leaves fell into shadow and were seen no more.

The girl came swearing and panting back into consciousness.

"I fainted! But it's not so bad now, just aches like the devil. Did you put tar on it?"

"Tar?"

"Clan Davin's healer packs a wound with hot tar to stop the bleeding."

"I used no tar. Tell me how to find your friends."

The girl raised herself on her elbow and shook her hair back to look up at her hostess with narrowed eyes. She was sweating and pale—and refusing to acknowledge her weakness.

"I have no friends. Clan Davin might do me a service if I asked. Why?"

"You do not wish to stay in the city."

"Oh. No. But they wouldn't trust you—" She ran a hand over her eyes, obviously trying to clear her mind and come up with a solution to the problem. She had the air of being used to solving them.

"You could take a message to The Hanged Man. Show the barkeep this—" She fumbled at her neck and pulled something dangling on a thong over her head with an effort. The supporting elbow trembled. In the very act of holding out the object she dropped it and slumped over the edge of the table. Quick hands caught her. As if it were no burden to her strength, the watcher lifted the limp form and carried it thorough a curtain into a room where a narrow bed and a low brazier were the only furnishings. The room was warm, a concession to the second wind, which would blow chill off the Edge as the night turned toward morning. The watcher knelt, stretched the girl out on the bed and pulled a padded quilt snug under her chin.

The young face was strong, full of impetuous life even in unconsciousness. The lips were even and narrow, the soot-dark lashes cast a ragged shadow on the brown cheek. The closed eyes had been the green of glades not entirely hidden from the sun.

The watcher returned to the kitchen and removed the traces of her surgery, then found the talisman where it had fallen. It was heart-shaped, ribbed and notched like a linden leaf, but red as copper, red as fire. From her own breast she pulled its mate. The two leaves lay on her palm like flakes of fire, no more identical than two snowflakes, yet the same, from the same source, and she was that source. Two leaves, two flakes of fire, and one wild girl whose mother was dead.

The effort it took to realize those facts disoriented her, like the growth of the tree. Over her rushed the river of time, and it was the same river that washed other shores less durable. A tree can grow up in a night. A daughter be born and grow to womanhood. Her hand closed over the leaves, and the slow, slow beat of her own heart

sounded in her ears. Her feet felt the dirt floor under-
foot, her arms lifted away from her body and her hair
rose on her scalp . . . but no, not yet. There was work to
do.

Forgetting the cloak that hung by the door, the watcher
let herself out into the night, locking the door behind her
as if it guarded the one thing of value in the world.

It was morning when the girl woke. The second wind
was dying. Across the room the watcher sat against the
wall, her eyes gleaming out of shadow. The look was
intense, yet the watcher's words, when she spoke, were
quiet.

"The men of Clan Davin will bring a cart for you soon.
They will take you out of the city. Many were concerned
for you."

"For Sarveth. They are glad to have him out of the
slave pit today. In a year they will have forgotten." The
girl's tone was bitter.

"You do not value friendship?" The watcher's voice
was as soft as wind in a raintree, and the girl responded
to the detached tone.

"I want no one's friendship. Believing that lie killed
my mother."

"Then I will not insult you with the offer of what you
do not want."

Quick color flushed the girl's face, and her brusque
tone faltered. "I didn't mean—you have been more than
kind to me—I—"

Amusement warmed the watcher's face. "No apology
is necessary. Like you, I have found friendship—a haz-
ardous venture. And my cooking may be another. Yet
you should eat. Will you try my soup?"

"I can't repay you for any of this," the girl said
ungraciously.

"I collect stories. You can tell me the tale of a clanless
woman who died for believing in friendship—after you
have eaten."

"And if I survive?"

"That, too."

The girl ate almost enough to satisfy her hostess, then

handed the bowl back. "I haven't eaten many things that green, but it was good—better than my story, I'm afraid."

"Why?"

The girl's face sobered and she picked at the hem of the quilt as she answered. "My mother was a fool or a liar. What story is there in that?"

"You are not a liar, so I think she was not. Did you really think her a fool?"

"Not while she lived. She said she came from beyond the ice, from a clan no one had heard of. She refused clan standing again and again. Even for my father's sake. She said it was against her law."

"Must it be a lie because it did not suit you?"

"No. But the friends she expected never came for her."

"Perhaps they did. Perhaps they could not find her—one woman alone on the Edge. Perhaps they had to look in secret."

"'Secret. That's what she always said. What secret is worth a woman's whole life? She was a warrior. She could have *led* a clan, but she would not take a name—so I have none."

"You do not know what she had before," the watcher said. "Perhaps—perhaps it was enough to justify the price."

"Not to me," the girl said, glaring from her lion-colored eyes. "If her friends came now and offered gold enough to walk on, I would spurn them. They caused her death."

"How did they do that?"

"She was always looking for someone, always expecting to meet someone—in every patch of willow by the river, every tangle of brier. She spoke of *forests* where trees grow thick as spears in battle. There are none on the Edge, nor in this town. She would travel days to meet a stranger. Word came of such a one captured by Khansmen and she went after them, up by the ice. I wasn't with her. She was getting old. They—" the girl swallowed and got it out, "they put a spear in her gut and left her to die. She was gone when I found her. I have sent those Khansmen cowards after her into hell,

and as many others as I can, I will send to follow them!"
She bent her head. "I need no friends."

The watcher let the silence stretch. "Yet you risked
your life to free the son of Clan Davin's chief from the
Khan's slave pits."

"Not for friendship, but to pay a debt. He helped me
trail my mother's killers. And if he asks me to join Clan
Davin, I will."

The girl looked toward the window, a gray square in
the darker wall. She shook her hair back and breathed
the air off the Edge like a wild horse scenting water.

"Cities and crowds are not for me—stale air, stale
laws. I need the open. If I shed blood again, it will be for
a clanbrother or sister who must aid me when I am in
need."

"Isn't that friendship?"

The girl shook her head. "All know what clan owes
clan. If you fail, the clan will know that, too, and take
your name away. It is *that* people fight to protect—not
each other. Friendship—" her face twisted with pain,
"in all the years they did not come, my mother did not
blame them." She pushed the cover away, impatient, a
little embarrassed at revealing so much.

"A poor story, as I warned you. I should have told
about the three-year winter, or fighting the worm from
the ice, or how she rode an ice-flow into the camp of
Clan Innon, but you have heard of that, surely?"

"Traveler's tales—many of a dark-haired outlaw—but
none that gave name or place, none that said she had a
daughter. None told how she died—" the watcher's voice
faltered, "or if she was happy."

The girl's keen gaze raked the watcher's figure, seeing
for the first time how tall this woman was, how seamed
her face, how the straying tendrils of her hair were like
lichen-roots or moss. The leather thong of the girl's talisman hung down from fingers knotted together like roots.

"She died fighting—and I think she was happy, most
of the time. She didn't grieve, but sometimes she would
stand and stare—as you did, in the garden—dreaming in
daylight. Sometimes—when I was small, she told me of
flame-dancers and tree-wives in kingdoms beyond the

ice— *How long have you been asking travelers for these tales?*"

The watcher rose and went to the window, looked out, far beyond the walled water garden on which it gave. Her voice was low, no louder than a snowflake on a bare branch. "Twenty years," she said, as if it were nothing, the time it took a leaf to fall, a tree to grow.

"For her?" It was an incredulous whisper.

"No," said the watcher like a woman who discovers a truth, like a tree who finds a nest in her boughs, and a fledgling in the nest. "Not for her. For myself."

Tears rose in the girl's eyes. "If she could have lived one year longer, if she had only known— You would have taken her back to the clan beyond the ice?"

"If she desired it."

The girl threw back the cover and limped across the room on her bandaged leg. She reached out, hesitated, then placed both hands on the watcher's bowed shoulders. The watcher started, as if the touch pained her, but she did not move away. She did not look back.

"I'm sorry. I'm sorry I said what I did about friendship. I didn't know. I was wrong."

Slowly the tension under the girl's hands eased. After a moment she moved back. A cart turned into the alley, loud in the silence. The watcher turned and looked again at the tall girl with the dark mane of hair, the stubborn jaw, and the eyes green as witchfire in the wood. The slightest smile curved her lips.

"I think your friends have come."

Relief warmed the girl's face. "Yes."

Together they walked through the house and out the door. The watcher helped the nervous hillmen hoist the girl into the bed of the cart. They were anxious to go. The girl silenced them with an imperious wave of her hand. The watcher held the talisman up.

"You could keep it—it was hers."

"I know," said the watcher. "She meant you to have it. You might call it—the sign of her clan. I will think of you wearing it."

"But I'd like to give you something—" At the actual moment of parting, the girl was finding it difficult to go, but every heartbeat increased the danger to driver and guards. Then her vitality flashed forth, pleasure in giving pleasure. "You never asked my name. It might mean something to you. It was one of her clan's words."

"I would be honored to know it."

"Linden. My name is Linden. Good fortune. Thank you." She laughed, and the hillmen started the cart, and the laugh was the only thing she left behind as they clattered around the corner and out of sight.

"Linden," the watcher said, with her hand on the heart-shaped leaf she wore around her own neck. "Linden." She listened until the last rattle of the cart faded away. The sun came up, spilling brilliance over the Edge, from the high country the girl was bound for, the bare, brown steppes she found beautiful. Freedom, she had said, was standing in the light.

For the last time the watcher studied how the tree grew so abruptly up into the alley, making its place in the world. Each branch, each leaf, was edged with light. The tree's dark shadow was an elongated, angular twin of itself that stretched twice the tree's length down the wall, but they sprang from the same source, and when she walked across the cobbles and broke off a leaf—just before she reached into the morning and pulled down a vortex of spinning yellow leaves and vanished from Arketh forever—both trees, bright and dark, trembled to the root.

SPELL OF BINDING

by Richard Cornell

In general I am very hesitant about pseudonyous stories; if a story isn't good enough for a writer to stand up and admit he wrote it, why should it be good enough for us to print? A writer even had the gall to tell me that she wanted to use a pen name on her science fiction and fantasy in case she did some serious writing some day.

However, Richard Cornell is a pen name with the best possible reason for using one; his real name is the same as that of another well-known writer in this same field. The reason I found as valid as the young tenor whose real name is Charles Anthony Caruso; he sings at the Metropolitan Opera under the stage name of Charles Anthony.

"Cornell" first came to my attention as a fine writer when he sent me a story for an anthology I was editing on the subject of "Women in Crisis." That anthology never found a publisher, and I finally had to release some very fine stories for the authors to find print elsewhere. But this writer had such a fine way with words (and also he lives in the Bay Area) that I kept in touch with him and he finally sent me a story I could use for this anthology.

And here it is.

M aris woke huddled against cold stone, her right side numb with pain. She lay still, listening for any sound of her captors, then moved slowly, testing her arm, her shoulder, her ribs. Nothing was broken. She shuddered as she recalled the fight in the tunnel, the scaly fingers clutching at her body, the touch of something hard and smooth where flesh should be.

On her knees, she felt about in the darkness.

The pit was an inverted funnel, its walls sloping up to the narrow mouth at the apex. She leaped, and could just reach the heavy slab that lay across the opening. The damp walls were jagged and rough; a cool draft seeped through the cracks in the stone.

She removed one boot, left it at the base of the wall, and crawled around the perimeter of her prison. Along the way, she found several hard oblong objects that could only be pieces of bone.

The chamber was no more than ten feet across; the only way out was above. Maris put her boot back on, then tore a strip of cloth from her blouse and wound it around the end of the longest bone. Resting it in her lap with the wrapped end outward, she took a deep breath and uttered the Spell of Fire. Pale sparks danced in the air, then died.

Nothing.

Stone ground against stone. Pale green light flooded the chamber. Maris hid the useless torch behind her and stared up at the round opening. Something stared back at her, its naked chest hard and flat like the underside of a turtle, its head set low against its shoulders and covered with bony protuberances.

Sorvan help me! she cried out mentally. There came no reply.

She took a deep breath, then uttered a Spell of Striking. Amber pinwheels flared in the darkness of her mind, then—

Nothing.

The creature leaned forward.

"What do you want with me?"

Small dark eyes peered at her from beneath the bony ridges of its eye sockets. The creature grunted, then backed out of view. A moment later, a bucketful of water came raining down on her. Then the slab slid back into place, sealing her in darkness.

*   *   *

She was deep inside the mountain, below Stone Top itself—if she was still in this world at all. Boundaries were uncertain in the Half Lands; you could pass from one world to the next without knowing.

Maris shivered in the cold draft. She moved to the drier center of the chamber, then sat, back straight, legs folded in front of her. Sorvan had carved his keep out of Stone Top, he'd said, because there he "already had one foot in *keris*." Very well, then; if the worlds ran together, she ought to be able to slip from one to the next, even if she was trapped in the Underworld.

Closing her eyes, she turned her awareness inward and prepared to enter *keris*. As her concentration grew, she sensed the band of fire at her crown, and let herself float toward it till the blazing light engulfed her; then her consciousness broke free of her body like a ship breaking mooring and she hurtled upward.

Starpoints exlpoded into trails of light as she streaked toward the blackness . . . the dark point swelled into a huge hole, an open mouth waiting to swallow her. She fell toward it, no longer able to turn back . . . fell . . .

And entered *keris*.

She was standing in a circular arena, enclosed by a wall of golden light. Her bare feet pressed against hard, brown dirt. Above was only blackness. Her body was slender beneath a soft brown shift, and not yet scarred by battle; in *keris* she was still a girl.

"So, Maris, you have returned to me."

Sorvan stood before her, a towering figure wrapped in a crimson cape. His hair clustered in dark locks about his neck, his eyes gleamed in the golden light. The faceted jewel embedded in the base of his throat sparkled with reflections.

"You've taken my magic," she said.

"I take only what is mine."

"When I came to you—"

"You came seeking knowledge. I gave freely."

"But my magic—"

"Your magic is my magic. You are bound to me, Maris; I have uttered the Spell of Binding." He extended his arms toward the arena. "Even here, in *keris,* you go only where I allow."

She turned quickly and ran toward the wall. Her hand met no resistance as she lunged forward. For an instant, she was wrapped in the dazzling light. Then her vision returned. She was standing before Sorvan in the center of the arena.

"As above, so below," he smirked. "Leave Stone Top, and your power will diminish with each step you take. Even the lesser magics will fail you—as perhaps you have already discovered."

"Those spells were mine!"

Sorvan only smiled and moved toward her. Maris stared into the black depths of his eyes, felt his hands on her shoulders pushing her downward . . .

. . . and awoke shivering on the damp floor, deep in the bowels of the mountain.

Damn him! she thought, retrieving the makeshift torch in an angry frenzy. Focusing on the end bound with cloth, she uttered the Spell of Fire once more. Nothing happened.

She pulled off her boots, then stood with her legs apart, pressing her feet against the floor of the chamber. She sought the cool green energy of the earth beneath her, but found only gray stone. Calling on the Mother to help her, she began the spell again, concentrating more deeply on the words, turning them over and over in her mind till she entered and became them. . . .

. . . *Jagged crystals of frozen flame burned fiery orange and tore at her throat.* . . .

The spell words stuck in her throat like hot coals. She choked and struggled and and finally spit them out. The cloth sputtered and smoked, but would not burn.

Maris sank to the floor, exhausted, her body drained dry like an empty skin.

In her dream, she stood outside the Half Lands. Ahead, the trail plunged across a desolate plain pocked with foreboding holes, mist-shrouded rivulets and dark bulging mounds. *The twisting trail became a white rope, coiled round her neck. Sorvan held the far end, and was slowly pulling her in.*

No! she cried, struggling in vain against the steady tug of the rope. "Amaris," a voice whispered. She saw a face atop the mound of earth beside her. "Father!" He couldn't hear her, he was sinking into the earth. She began climbing. "Father!" At the top she found only a deep hole. Her father was gone. She leaned over to search the darkness below and felt someone push her from behind. Laughter echoed through the empty cavern as she fell. She looked back. Sorvan smiled down on her. "Amaris," he mocked. "Amaris. . . ."

She woke with a start as icy water splashed over her. Sorvan's face was gone; instead, she glimpsed the beaked profile of one of her captors, silhouetted against the pale green light. Her name still seemed to echo in the chamber—the sound of stone against stone as the heavy slab slid back into place.

Betrayer! she thought bitterly. She'd entered the Half Lands freely, a proud warrior who could cast spells, who'd fought for the King at Calinth and Dakkar, who'd seen the Blue Marshes beyond the mountains of Jarl and the sea that stretched from Borona. She'd come seeking Sorvan, to offer what she could in return for his teachings, a free woman, his equal.

Well, not quite free, she admitted to herself, wincing at the grandiose image she'd painted. Truth was, she was weary of battle, weary of drifting alone through the world, weary of fearing any attachment lest it be violently sundered. Weary and troubled.

She'd come hoping Sorvan might help her understand her . . . gift (even now, she shied from calling it that, the pain of disappointment still strong in her heart—and beside it, the growing fear that she might never understand it). At first he'd been kind. Though he said nothing of shapes and colors when he began teaching her spells, he was curious when she spoke of them. How happy she'd been, to find someone with whom to share her burden! But he soon grew impatient, dismissing her visions as useless distractions and growing irritated with her difficulty memorizing the words. She endured many months of this, until finally she admitted to herself that Sorvan did not hold the answers she was seeking. When she announced she was leaving, he demanded payment for his teachings; when she suggested that her months of service at the castle were fair recompense, he became enraged and drove her away. That, she now realized, was when he'd taken her magic.

She thought of her father, who'd left home to fight for the King's honor at Corin's Forde when she was still a young girl. He'd been searching for something, too—at least that's what her mother had said.

How odd that she should remember him now! She relived the dream in her mind. Wasn't that just how it was, that he never seemed to hear her? What was he seeking that was so important, that he could leave them and never want to return? And yet . . . isn't that just what she'd done? Her mother's voice echoed in her memories. "You're just like your father," she'd said, on the day Maris left home to be a soldier. "Just like your father. . . ."

Damn them all! Maris stood and stretched her stiff limbs. She'd lost everything—her food, her weapons, her magic, her illusions. But not her pride. She could curl up and wait to die, or fight her way out of the hole she was trapped in. It was up to her. Alone.

Her anger focused on Sorvan. So he'd taken her magic. Soon he would find she had other skills!

But first she had to escape from her prison. Without food, she would weaken. Her only chance was to strike soon, when the stone slab that capped her cell was withdrawn.

Maris crawled through the chamber, gathering the fragments of bone she'd discovered. She sorted out the sturdiest pieces, and chose the longest, the one she'd tried to make into a torch, for a tool. Then she searched the walls of the chamber till she found a piece of rock she could loosen, and scraped around it with the bone until it pulled free. This she used to hammer the smaller pieces

of bone into cracks and holes in the wall, making a series
of hand- and foot-holds.

When she was done, she tried scaling the wall. Because of its backward slope, she had to climb facing the
rock. It took all her strength to stay pressed against it;
even then, she couldn't hold on for long. She would have
to pray for some luck.

She dropped back to the floor, and began sharpening
the long bone against a smooth stone. Then she sat back
and waited.

"Mother, You who hear all things, hear my cries!" she
whispered, as minutes or hours or days passed. "As my
tears drop upon the ground, look upon me!"

She was beginning to doze when she heard something.
The slab was moving! She jumped up and climbed the
wall, the bone knife clenched in her teeth.

Clinging to the wall, she leaned her head back and
gazed at the shaft of green light pouring through the
round opening. The muscles in her calves began to ache.
Mother, look upon me! Finally, when her left arm was
beginning to cramp and she knew she couldn't hold on
much longer, the guard stuck its head into the pit and
peered around. They faced each other, both upside down;
then Maris leaped with what strength she had left and
grabbed onto its head. For an instant, she hung there,
clinging to its neck. Then the creature lost its balance
and toppled forward, and they crashed to the floor in a
tangle. Maris rolled to her feet, the bone knife clenched
in her right hand, but the thing lay still. She kicked at it
cautiously, then stepped lightly onto its back, sprang
upward, caught hold of the stone lip and pulled herself
through the opening.

She was in a narrow tunnel, illuminated by the pale
light of phosphorescent lichen that covered the walls. A
stone bucket filled with water stood next to the pit; she
drank eagerly, then considered pouring the rest down on
the creature, but stopped herself—no use waking it. Knife
in hand, she stepped carefully down the narrow passage,
ducking beneath the fantastic dripstone formations that
covered the ceiling. After twenty paces, the tunnel veered
left—and ended at a pool of dark water.

Her mind raced with possibilities. Was the passageway hidden by spells, like the one she'd fallen through when they took her? If so, she might never find it, especially with her magic gone. Worse yet, it might no longer exist—the earth itself was malleable here. She might be trapped beneath the rock forever.

A sudden splash of water ended further contemplation. A long hand curled round her ankle as another creature emerged from the murky pool. Maris wheeled and stabbed down at its soft neck, too late; its head was wedged tightly against its shoulders and her bone knife glanced off the hard shell. The thing rose to its feet quickly and crushed her against its chest. She kicked and elbowed as it carried her back up the passageway, unhurt by her blows.

As they turned the corner, she went limp and sank heavily to the floor, taking her captor with her. As they sprawled on the floor, she felt for the base of its skull and pried at it with her fingers, opening an inch-wide gap above its shoulder—enough to ram the bone blade deep into the soft flesh. The thing made a throaty, clucking sound and rolled off her. Viscous fluid dripped from its neck.

Maris jumped to her feet, her back to the pool. The thing stood in the passageway, no longer concerned with the wound in its throat. Its small dark eyes watched her struggle to catch her breath. It began to advance.

She couldn't defeat it. Knowing it had risen from the pool, she clenched the knife in her teeth, turned, and dove into the black water.

A current rushed out through a narrow hole in the rock, Maris pushed through it, scraping her back on the rough stone, and swam blindly through the water. Then something caught hold of her foot.

The creature had followed her! She kicked at it, but couldn't break its grip. She struggled to pull herself through the water—there was no time left to fight!—but the thing was dragging her back.

Time began to slow down. Her arms ached. She was swimming in black ink with no up or down or forward or back. She was going to die here, she thought. The water would claim her, she could rest at last—just open her mouth, let it rush to fill her, become one with the darkness. . . .

Ahead she saw a starpoint of light—the gleam from the jewel Sorvan wore at his throat. She wanted to swim for it, but was dragging a great weight. She turned and saw clinging to her a huge turtle. Each time she started to speak, its head withdrew deep into its shell. "Look at me," she cried, twisting and turning to make it face her. Finally she grabbed its head before it could hide—but it was horrible! The beaked humanoid face of the thing in the cave—what else had she expected? It clutched at her legs, pulling her back from the light. she bent her knees upward, then kicked with all her might. The thing loosened its grip. She twisted free, but it came swimming back at her. She kicked at its face again.

The starpoint of light had grown to a sun and came rushing toward her, but she was too weary to duck and could only wave her arms weakly as the light exploded around her. . . .

Maris woke beside a chasm at the foot of the mountains. A torrent of water bubbled and splashed as it rushed down the channel. Every inch of her body ached; her chest was so sore it hurt to breath.

Her head throbbed. She remembered battling the thing in the water and could only hope she'd escaped it. The mountains were spinning around her. She dragged herself to the base of the hill and found shelter in a small crevice. Exhausted, she sank back into darkness.

When she woke again, the sky was bright gray. Though her body hurt, she could move, and stood stiffly to stretch. Her clothing stuck to her flesh where her skin had been cut and scraped; she peeled it off carefully, cleaned herself as best she could, then dressed again.

She was on the far side of the mountains. Stone Top was somewhere above her. With a trail to climb, she might make it by nightfall. But first she had to eat.

She dug up a handful of roots on the hillside, inadvertently uncovering a startled *zrill* that she caught and dashed against the ground. The lizard would provide a few ounces of edible meat. She gathered tinder and dry twigs and made a small fire by rubbing stick against stone—which served to rekindle her anger at losing her spells. Then she roasted the *zrill* and feasted on her meager meal.

She reached Stone Top by late afternoon. Behind her, the sky was turning from gray to black, pocketing the mountainside with shadow. Ahead, the trail ended at a blank face, a gray curtain of rock between two humps of ridge, too steep to climb. Travelers seeking to cross the ridge would turn back.

Maris continued climbing. As she approached, the spells that encrusted the wall began to waver. She glimpsed the faint outline of a window in the rock, and above, toothy crenellations. Sorvan's lair was half-castle, half-cave, sculpted from the stone by sorcery. Passageways led from these outermost chambers to forbidden caverns below.

A portal opened in the rock. As Maris passed into the courtyard of the castle, the wall sealed silently behind her. She looked back and saw only solid rock, and above, empty ramparts.

Sorvan was waiting in the tower, a frail old man hunched over a scroll spread on the table before him and anchored with glittery fragments of quartz. The room was cluttered with parchment and paper, great wooden chests, and racks filled with earthen jars and glass vials. He looked up as she climbed from the spiral stairway, and she was suddenly aware how ragged she looked. Sorvan seemed not to notice. His ancient face came alive, each furrow and crease animated by the smile that spread from his thin lips. "Maris! You've come back to me."

He absentmindedly brushed aside wispy locks of long white hair as he stood. Or was he deliberately displaying the sparkling gem that hung on a thin strand of gold at his throat, to remind her of his power?

"Sorvan, release me."

He shook his head sadly. "I hoped it could be as before, when you were so eager for knowledge."

"Release me." she repeated, her voice trembling. Even now, she wished it could be the way she'd envisioned.

"I cannot," he said softly, and she saw, or thought she saw, his own pain. "The Spell of Binding cannot be undone."

"I don't believe you."

"What you believe matters little. I tell you what is."

"Then what choice do I have?"

"Go, and leave your magic behind, or stay and share the secrets I've discovered." He smiled. "Or discover a Spell of Unbinding."

She had come seeking more than techniques or sorcery; she had come seeking peace, some calm beyond the turbulent waters of her mind, endlessly churning with questions. Only amidst the shapes and colors of the Spells had she found a hint of that calm; nothing else had come close. She could not let him take that from her.

"I will stay."

Sorvan nodded. She remembered the towering figure who'd taunted her in *keris*. Anger swept through her like a cold wind, clearing her mind. If he meant to teach her, she would never have left. He'd bound her because he had nothing more to offer, and intended only to use her. Damn him! She would fight rather than submit to his chains.

Her only advantage was physical prowess, which he could quickly neutralize with magic. She must act now when Sorvan least expected it; in the few instants gained by surprise, she must somehow even the odds against her.

She looked away, as if overcome with emotion. Sorvan came toward her. "You will learn to accept it," he promised. As he put his hand on her shoulder, she turned, carefully concealing the blade of bone in her palm. If she could seize the crystal that hung at his throat, his magic would be hindered.

Her hand moved toward his neck. The strand of gold would yield to her blade—it had to! In the tiny moment in which her muscles first tensed, she heard Sorvan laughing.

Something smooth and slippery and incorporeal reached

*into her skull and yanked her from her body. What a fool
I am! she thought, as he pulled her roughly through the
gateway. Sorvan had anticipated every move. He'd been
watching from* keris *the whole time, manipulating his
body from afar and undoubtedly enjoying the performance.*

She was standing in the arena, clad in leather hauberk
and vest of light mail. A short sword hung in its scabbard
at her side; in her hands she held flail and spear.

Sorvan stood before her clad only in loincloth, taunt-
ing her with the illusion of vulnerability. He grasped a
huge broadsword with both hands, but her eyes saw only
the gleaming jewel embedded in the base of his throat.

"Well, Maris," he chuckled. "You sought to even the
odds, did you not?"

She stepped forward and hurled the spear at his heart
before he had finished speaking. A bolt of blue-white
flame shot from the gemstone to meet it. The spear
disappeared with a crackle.

"Come, Maris, let's not be impatient. At least we can
enjoy the battle." He hefted the broadsword above his
head and charged; Maris barely had time to draw her
own sword before he was upon her. As he brought his
blade down, she raised hers to block it. There was a flash
of light as the two swords met, then Sorvan's passed
through and sank into her shoulder.

Maris dropped her useless blade and scrambled away
from him, clutching the wound that gaped open where
he'd cut through her mail.

She could not defeat him, not here in *keris*. If only
they were on the physical plane . . . that was it! How
could she be so blind! This was *not* the physical world—
hadn't his sword passed through hers? Sorvan had set
this combat to mock her, knowing her skills would be
useless. They were not even in their physical bodies!

She looked at the wound; in the real world, he might
have cut off her arm. The pain seemed real enough . . .
but hadn't he boasted that he controlled this domain?

Sorvan had discarded the broadsword, and stood across
the arena, his arms folded, watching her. "I expected
more from a warrior soul," he taunted.

Her only hope still lay in the crystal. Sorvan believed
he was invincible in *keris*; perhaps she could use that
against him. Things not possible in the physical realm
were possible here. If she could catch him off guard. . . .

Maris rose to her feet, holding the flail in her good
arm. As she charged, whirling the heavy spiked ball
above her, she reminded herself she was not in the physical world, but in *keris*; as she brought the flail down
toward the side of his skull, watched the shaft of fire
shoot from the crystal, and the iron ball disintegrate, she
told herself she was not a physical body, only a body of
light. Sorvan was watching the flail evaporate, his attention not on her but the weapon. She dove toward him, a
mere wisp of spirit, less substantial than the air. She
heard him grunt in surprise as she flew toward his throat—
and then she entered the crystal.

*A jumbling kaleidoscope of colors and shapes . . . jag-
ged lightning, purple and gold . . . wispy pink ribbons
fluttering in a lavender web . . . lambent globes of pale
blue fire, speckled with threads of darkness . . . vast purple fields spiked with pyramids of dark blue stone . . . a
dappled streamer of pomegranate red, tossed by the soft
green wind. . . .*

*She was in a repository of spells. No time to waste—
Sorvan would soon realize what she was doing. One thought
only: the Spell of Binding . . . she moved through the
shapes and colors like a sigh . . . then, before her, a ring
of golden light, binding a circle of darkness. . . .*

*She held the ring with both hands like a mirror, and
saw in the center dark reflections of herself . . . she was a
streak of light chasing herself round in an endless circle
. . . and the ring of light enclosed an arena, and Sorvan
stood in the center, clutching the gem that choked at his
throat . . . then the golden ring was a circle of words, each
linked to the next, and she moved among the words and
sang them, and her song was a song of freedom and
binding. . . .*

They were in the study. The sharpened bone fell from
her hand. Sorvan reached to his throat and felt only bare

flesh. His eyes met hers, then looked below, where the faceted jewel sparkled on its thin strand of gold.

Maris grasped the gem between her fingers, as if to convince herself it was real. It was cool and hard as it rested against her; in *keris,* it would be part of her flesh.

"You have succeeded at last," Sorvan whispered. He shuffled across the room to a window cut in the stone. Below, the courtyard was empty and silent.

Maris pushed the piece of bone to the center of the room with her foot, then uttered the Spell of Fire. She felt a tingle along her spine as the familiar current surged upward; then the room seemed to jump as the force hit the crystal and the bone burst into flame.

"The Stone is mine," she said, still reeling with the impact of it.

"The Stone has passed to your keeping," he corrected, his voice weary. "Be it burden or boon."

"Perhaps that is for me to decide."

First surprise, then amusement, perhaps even pride flickered in his dark, melancholy eyes. "I have grown fond of you, Maris."

He'd wanted her to defeat him!

"It is the law of the Stone, that he who would claim it must first be Bound. Others have tried to break its hold; only you succeeded. How, Maris?"

"You told me the Binding could not be undone, not that it couldn't be *reversed.*"

"But how?"

She told him how she'd searched among the spells in the crystal to find the Spell of Binding, then let herself be absorbed by it. When she finished, he shook his head in amazement. "I found only words in the Stone."

Maris was as dumbfounded as he. If he couldn't see the spells in the crystal, how could he enter and change them? Then suddenly she realized he couldn't change them, that sorcery for him had been a lifelong search to acquire existing spells. In that dizzying moment, she understood the power of her gift.

Sorvan was smiling. Everything he'd wanted had come to pass. But Maris could not understand.

"You welcomed your own defeat? Why?"

"What news do you bring from the Middle Lands?" he asked.

"Armies on the move, rumors of war in the south, this king seeking to expand his realm, that one rising to resist him. Each side accusing the other of sorcery, or worse."

He smiled at her oblique humor.

"Nothing ever changes in the world, Sorvan."

"Exactly," he whispered.

Her mind was filled with all the old questions.

"I grow old, Maris. I no longer wish to take sides." He looked at her with sad, round eyes. "You will find there are many who want what you have, and will try to take it from you."

A new thought dismayed her. "The Spell. I have reversed it. If I leave—"

"My strength goes with you. With each step you take, my power will diminish, as yours did when you left me."

She thought of the Underworld creatures who'd held her captive, and others she'd glimpsed in the Half Lands. Her mind swam with confused emotion. Sorvan her mentor. Sorvan her tormentor. Sorvan at the mercy of the things from the Underworld. He'd left her to fight for herself, hadn't he? Shouldn't he expect the same?

Maris remained at Stone Top through the winter. Sorvan taught her what he knew of the crystal, while she used her power to discover secrets that had eluded him. She saw a new side of him, a gentleness she'd glimpsed during the first months of her apprenticeship, but forgotten in light of their later antagonism—painful, she now saw, but necessary for her to claim her full power. And that was what Sorvan had wanted all along, she realized. With it came the realization that not only she had suffered.

As they worked together, their affection grew. The thought of her leaving weighed heavily on both of them. Then spring came, and with it, the time for their parting.

She found him among his scrolls in the tower. His eyes became moist when he saw her.

"You will go?" he asked, and she nodded. "Go safely, Maris."

"I cannot leave you defenseless," she said.

She sat cross-legged on the stone floor, hands resting on her knees, and turned her awareness inward. The room and Sorvan faded from her mind; she sensed the familiar crown of light above her, and below, something new: a radiant lattice. She floated downward, and once again entered the crystal.

. . . drifting through pockets of soft blue darkness, and then: the bright ring hovering before her. . . .

She held it by the edges, then brought her hands together and twisted. She let go and stood back to see what she had created, and there in the darkness saw two golden rings, separate yet bound together: the Sign of Infinity . . . two rings of gold, one circle of light . . . one endless circle of light. . . .

In the study, he gasped, and Maris smiled to see his amazement. Around his neck was a thin strand of gold, like the one that cradled the gem at her throat. He felt it in disbelief.

"You are bound to me," she laughed, her eyes sparkling. "Though I travel far, you will remain within the circle of my protection. Your magic is my magic; it will endure."

STORM GOD

by Deborah Wheeler

I dunno how Deborah Wheeler does it; she's a health care professional (a chiropractor) and a martial-arts expert, with two young daughters; yet somehow she's found time to appear in every anthology I've published. Early this year she sent me a long story I couldn't use—it seemed to me to be science fiction—and I really felt it belonged elsewhere; then she sent me this one, which fits superbly into the format without being in the least bit hackneyed.

(Being choosy about format and category has its hazards; I still remember a cartoon in one of the writer's magazines which showed a bemused writer staring at a rejection slip which read "We want fresh, original stories which exactly fit our formula." This puts an intolerable burden on any writer, to say nothing of the editor, who must walk a tightrope between stories which are too far off the wall and stories without a grain of originality, treading so close to the formula that the editor is two pages ahead of them at every turn.)

Deborah wrote this story while awaiting the birth of her second daughter; a period spent mostly in bed because the infant was far too restless and wanted to get into the world much sooner than her allotted time. We were delighted to hear, just before the deadline, of the healthy birth of Rose Helene Wheeler, strong and full term; the time in bed gave her mother plenty of time to think up this good story for us. One kind of creativity leads to another—I wrote my first novel while pregnant with my first son. Yet some yahoos still say creativity and motherhood don't mix.

S evens. *Damn!* Dov stared at the dice and pushed Rion's shoulder aside, as if a closer look could change the result. The mage's teeth glinted in the shadow of his purple hood as he swept in the wager pile, and she saw her flame-opal disappear under his hand. The watching inn-rabble grew noisy in disapproval; mages were not popular in these parts.

"It isn't possible," Rion groaned. "He must have cheated."

"He didn't and you know it," snapped Dov, tossing a mop of lanky ginger hair back from her eyes. "Oh, how could I have let you talk me into this? You're always taking ridiculous chances and now you've lost my opal! Why did I ever listen to you?"

"It was your idea as much as mine. An easy mark, you said. I was ready to go home an hour ago, but you insisted we stay for one more throw. Just one more throw as long as our luck held." His dark eyes glittered in the inn's smoky light.

Dov jumped to her feet. He was right, of course, but that did not change anything.

Rion relented. "Love, I'm sorry. I know how much your mother's opal means to you, and I wouldn't have— There's nothing I can do about it now. It's done with, over."

"There're a few other things that are over and done with." She turned toward the inn door and the crowd drew back from her in sympathy.

"In the interest of domestic felicity," the mage said in his precise, dry voice. "Perhaps we could continue the game . . ." He moved his hand and the flame-opal sat alone on the rude wood table, shimmering crimson and gold.

Dov halted, keeping her eyes from Rion's stricken face. She had not anticipated arousing the mage's interest, but there might be some advantage for her in it. As long as she could keep him talking, she had a chance of maneuvering him into a bargain. He was not mortal, but that should make no difference. She sat down again.

"I suppose we could, if you made it interesting enough."

"Dov," Rion hissed, "we've nothing more—" She silenced him, still keeping her eyes on the mage.

"Games of chance do not interest you?" asked the sorcerer.

"Not nearly so much as contests of skill."

"Ah!"

"For instance," she leaned forward, resting on her elbows and studying the soot-grimed ceiling, "you've been boasting there are some things mortals just can't do. If you made it worth my while . . ."

"Are you proposing to turn lead into gold?" The dry voice reeked with amusement.

Dov shrugged. "Do I challenge you to shape honest iron, which you dare not touch lest you lose your arcane talent? No, I had in mind something I could do without the aid of magic."

"Then it's hardly worth the betting—"

"How about crossing the Turgian Marshes in a single day?" Dov raised her voice to make sure the inn-rabble could hear and witness her.

The mage's spine straightened perceptibly. "You can't do it. No mortal can."

"I will—for my opal and ten pieces of gold."

"Don't do it," Rion sputtered. "No stone is worth the risk. You'll never make it alive. Don't you know the horrors that lurk in the swamps?"

"Of course I do, the same as you. Whip-plants, werefoxes, quicksand, vampire trees. Isn't that so?" she demanded of the mage.

"A crude approximation. The vampires are mythical and you omitted mention of the trap-spiders."

Dov blanched. She hated spiders and had blissfully forgotten them.

"You see how impossible it is," said the mage.

"These goodfolk heard my offer and they heard you say I couldn't do it," Dov replied. "Will they also hear you back down before a mere mortal?"

Slowly the mage shook his head. "If you survive and meet the time deadline, the opal is yours . . . and the gold."

*   *   *

Dawn filtered wan and yellow through the straggler trees bordering the Turgian Marshes as Dov adjusted the laces of her running boots and checked her knife in its hidden sheath. Rion shifted from one foot to the other, holding his tongue with visible effort.

"It isn't as if I'd never *been* in the Marshes before," she continued. "When I ran messages for Old Hammach over in Deever, I used to cut through them all the time. Most of the horribles aren't nearly so bad as their reps." She straightened up, shrugged her leather jerkin into a more comfortable position, and began a final inspection of her belt pouches.

"Listen, Dov—"

"Listen, yourself. I may have gotten out of condition since I took up with you and your crazy trading schemes, but I can still outrun anything in the swamps. Why do you think they call them swamp *crawlers?* Not, I assure you, for their fleetness of foot. Besides, I know a trick or two."

"That's just the problem. You can't fool a swamp crawler the way you can a human mark. You think you're pulling one on that mage, but he's the one who has you, not the other way around."

As if conjured by his words, the mage, robed as before in dusted purple, came striding over the grasses. The voice which issued from the darkened hood was brittle like aged parchment.

"Human, you are either foolhardy or extraordinary, possibly both. I will await you at sundown on the other side of the Marshes. Whether you arrive is another matter entirely." Then he vanished in the usual puff of smoke.

"Dov, it's only a game to him," Rion insisted. "He probably cheated us out of your opal just to force you into this ridiculous wager. It's not worth your life."

"This makes it all the better. Remember when you brought ice to Verbourg just because Rainold said it was impossible? The five bags of gold were nice, but you would have done it anyway."

"I didn't risk being eaten by a werefox!"

Dov laughed. "Rion, I promise you that if anything

out there eats me, it won't be a werefox. One couldn't catch me if it tried." She leapt lightly across the borders of the swamp and called back, "They haven't any feet!"

Dov made good time through the morning, keeping to the threadwork of game trails that laced the Marshes. She had no difficulty avoiding the patches of quicksand with their coats of light earth and certain, sucking death. The sun rose higher, pale through thickening clouds. Desolate though the swamp might appear, it teemed with subtle, carnivorous life, no place for the unwary.

She glimpsed a werefox curled near some brierbushes. Its whimpering, pitched to lure a predator to its end, aroused her pity at first. It looked exactly like a small wounded animal as it regarded her with bright, pleading eyes, its poison sucker-pads carefully hidden beneath furry sides. She laughed at its pretentious vulnerability and went on her way.

The whip-plants were another matter. She had just finished eating her midday meal, sitting on a patch of salt-grass and congratulating herself on the excellent time she had made. Descending from the hummock, her ankle turned on the slippery grass, and she stumbled into a tangle of branches. It took her a moment to realize that the grip on her arms and hair was not accidental. By then she was firmly held.

Dov lashed out at the bramble with a booted foot.

"You idiot plant, let go of me!" The pliant vines curled around her, tough and resilient, well beyond her strength to break. She felt a slight, irresistible pull toward the central trunk.

"Of all the stupid—," she gasped. *Just when things were going so well, to be eaten by a plant!*

She twisted against the branches, feeling them yield and then tighten. They lifted her slightly and her boots slipped on the dry earth, her traction broken. Glancing toward the trunk, she saw a pulsating bulge appear in the dark brown bark. A slit of serrated pink appeared and dilated, puckering avidly.

Realizing that she had to act quickly, Dov raised her right knee to pull her knife from its sheath. The plant took advantage of her movement to draw her in closer, and she lunged at it, breaking its hold. It was designed to keep creatures from pulling away, not rushing toward it.

Screaming, Dov plunged her knife into the reddish heart of the whip-plant. Its branches lashed out with sudden, wringing violence, and tendrils fell from her as it rent the air with whistling wails. She scrambled to her feet, stunned at her luck. Resistance was what the plant was prepared for, and she had saved her life with outright attack.

Still gripping the hilt of her knife, Dov ran until her breath came in painful rasps and she could no longer hear the plant's torment. She hunched over, sides burning and heaving, staying on her feet despite the trembling in her thighs. Gradually her breathing quieted, and she inspected her blade before replacing it in its sheath. There was no trace of the plant's sap on the metal, but she wiped it carefully on a patch of herbweed before putting it away.

From then on she went more carefully, her spirits somber. The cloud cover kept off the heat, and later it began to grow chilly. Dov again moved vigorously, jog-and-run as she had been taught, and the exercise kept her warm. She began to think that she might win the wager after all, if only to avoid spending the night in the Marshes. It would be a long time before she scoffed at their dangers again.

She did not see the earth-colored plasmoid lying in its rough trench until it was too late and she went slithering down the unnaturally slick slope. *Whomp!* The bottom ground met her with a tooth-jarring shock. The bars of the trap closed silently around her right thigh.

Dov pushed herself to her elbows, ears ringing with the impact of her fall. It was uncomfortably reminiscent of the time Rion had challenged her to cross the Whelan Ice-Lake (source of the ice they had shipped to Verbourg) and she had cracked two ribs falling on its uncompromising surface.

Her hip stung where she had landed on it, but the plasmoid trap held her so tightly she could not roll to ease the pain. She managed a sitting position, looking around her, and realized with horror where she was.

For the first time, Dov began to think Rion was right, that she had been risking her life foolishly. This was not her idea of a fitting end, dying alone in a trap-spider's den. She thought she was getting the better of the mage by counting on luck and her meager experience, amplified by boundless self-confidence. But she could not bargain her way out of *this* trap.

A roll of thunder sent her eyes heavenward. *All this, and a brewing storm, too!* she thought in disgust. The shallow pit in which she lay would give her scant protection against wind or rain.

Dov choked down a sob of anger, as much at herself as at the semi-living trap, and thrust her fingers at it. The plasmoid felt soft under her push, but its coarse suction-surfaces gripped her leather breeches still tighter. If she could slip something beneath it, she might be able to loosen its hold, but she had no lubricant to ease that process, nor could she reach the knife hidden in the boot top of her trapped leg.

Thunder again. "Oh, shut up!" Dov cried, her fingertips as well as her temper beginning to fray. "If you can't help, then keep your blasted nose out of it!"

"What's that you say?" rumbled a voice from above.

She squinted upward. "You didn't say that."

"Oh, but I did, small one. Haven't you heard of Kronk, the great and glorious Storm God?"

"Storm God, huh? I don't suppose you could get me out of this accursed thing before its owner comes to collect me?" Trap-spiders, according to those few who had lived to tell about them, were ten-legged, the size of a mastiff, and carnivorous.

"Ha!" clapped the thunder. "As if you were big enough for me to bother with."

Dov narrowed her lips to hide a smile. After Rion and the mage, how difficult could it be to manage a mere weather deity? "Of course," she agreed. "I'm only an undersized mortal, scarcely worth noticing. But then you aren't a *real* Storm God."

Thunder boomed across the sky, darkening as clouds

massed to hide the sun. "Not a real Storm God? I'll show you who's real!"

Dov waited until the racket died down and her voice could be heard. "I'm only a powerless human, ignorant of the dealings of the mighty. But I've always understood that real gods do things like crack mountains and move oceans. You couldn't even move a small thing like me."

"Move you? A piddling little lump of flesh like you? I've swept whole armies away! Easiest thing in the world."

Wind hit her without prelude, bringing blood to her cheeks. The plasmoid, however, was securely anchored to the bottom of the pit, and even Kronk's single-minded blasting could not budge it. Finally the gale died down enough for her to shout, "O great Kronk, now I believe in your power. It is not for the likes of me to challenge the gods. Punish me for my impudence in any way you like—blast me, thunder upon me—"

The first few raindrops hit her like pellets. Then more fell, plummeting to sting her face and arms, but they were not enough to soak her leather breeches into slipperiness. Water began to drip from her nose.

Dov threw her head back. "O mighty Kronk, do anything to me you wish, but please not that! Anything but getting me wet!"

"Wet? I'll show you wet!"

Rain came down in sheets, quickly soaking her. Dov held her hands out, cupping them to splash her trapped thigh. The thin leather slid a little under the softening plasmoid.

The pit began to fill with water, and Dov's fingers slipped beneath the bars of the trap.

Only a few more seconds now . . .

Half-floating, she braced herself against the pit wall and looked up to see the trap-spider looming black and hairy, clacking its mandibles above her head.

Terror shook her. She'd played her gambit, relying on the pride and stupidity as well as the raw power of Kronk—and lost. Her death towered above her, insectile and odorous.

"Curse you, Kronk, you old rain-bucket!" she shrieked.

"You're nothing but a weakling charlatan! You haven't moved me yet!"

The answering torrent lifted her on a swelling wave, and Dov gave a last thrust to slip the trap from her leg. She held her breath and curled beneath the water, reaching for her boot knife. The water carried her to the edge of the pit just as the spider leapt down and began to wade toward her.

As Dov struggled upright, the monster slipped on the slick mud, going down in a windmill of frantic legs. She hesitated for a moment before realizing that even if she could scramble out of the pit, the spider would soon be on its feet and after her. No escape lay in that route. She'd have to deal with it directly, just as she had the whip-plant.

Dov forced her way closer despite the stench of a thoroughly drenched creature of unclean living habits. Its wet, globular body gleamed like an obscene pearl encrusted with tortuous red veins. One hairy leg struck her below the diaphragm. She gasped, spitting bile, but she grabbed the foul limb with her free hand and kept her eyes on her target.

The trap-spider, as if guessing her intent, redoubled its thrashing. It lashed out at her with its poisoned fangs, straining to reach her. Dov twisted in even nearer and plunged her blade into its exposed abdomen. A quick jerk through the tender, unprotected vitals, and the giant arachnid lay twitching, the rain already washing its blood from her blade. She stood there trembling, scarcely able to believe how easily the creature had been killed.

Long moments later, Dov replaced her knife and wiped tears of relief mixed with rainwater from her face. She began to consider the benefits of a judiciously orchestrated weather-deity cult. But first, a small test . . .

"O worthy Storm God! O great Kronk! Hear the words of this small mortal! You would be truly mighty upon the earth, but for one small failing. Your devoted worshipers will get terribly tired of being wet all the time. It's a pity you're powerless to stop what you start."

Rainbows hailed her as she ran laughing on her way to reclaim her flame-opal.

DIE LIKE A MAN

by L. D. Woeltjen

I don't usually like stories about thieves; I'm almost always on the side of Law in battles between Law and Chaos. But I will break every one of my unwritten laws and prejudices for a writer who can keep me turning the pages, and a character who catches my attention so strongly that I want to keep reading instead of merely dutifully turning manuscript pages. A writer like that can have a heroine who's a harlot, a harem girl or even a horse.

I know nothing about Linda Woeltjen except that she appeared in S&S III with the heart-wrenching "More's The Pity"—and that she has a way with a plot . . . and character.

And that's all I really need to know about her.

H*e's going to take my hand*—Arista thought, struggling as he grabbed her shirt at the back of the neck.

"I saw 'im put 'is hand in your purse," the vendor shouted, almost gleefully. "Chop off 'is hand, it's your right. The law says so."

She watched her intended victim rest his hand ever so lightly on the hilt of his sword. Swallowing hard, she considered throwing off her disguise. He'd surely show more mercy for a woman.

"Please," she begged as her hand reached toward the front of her shirt. Her captor paid her no heed.

"He's only a lad," the man was telling the merchant.

"Just gather up my purchases." The vendor scowled as he followed his customer's instructions.

For the first time, Arista was aware of the crowd that had gathered to see her punishment. Their faces, too, wore disappointment. She searched the crowd till she spotted two ragged children pushing through the throng. Taz, her friend and mentor, held his little sister's hand. Seeing Arista's questioning gaze, he shrugged and bit his lip.

Beside Taz, the tiny girl's eyes grew wide as she saw Arista collared by an angry stranger and surrounded by glaring town folk.

"Oh, 'Rista . . ." Anja wailed before her brother clapped his hand over her mouth, smothering the last syllable.

"Wrists, is that what they call you?" asked her captor. He bore himself like a soldier, but wore no uniform. "Just the name for a pickpocket."

"By rights, that's all 'e should be left with," said the vendor as he handed the soldier a bundle. He held out his palm and received two of the silver coins that had lured Arista into this predicament. She hung her head, hoping a repentant demeanor might get her off with a kick or two.

Suddenly, the soldier jerked Arista's shirt collar. She looked up at him, ready for a scolding, a beating . . .

"Well" he said grinning wickedly, "you do owe me a hand." The crowd had begun to disperse, but his words caused several people to pause and look back hopefully. "I thiink it'll do me more good attached to that scrawny body of yours. Come on, boy."

Ignoring the grumbling of the onlookers, the soldier, still holding fast to Arista's shirt, dragged her down the street to the stable. Her captor shoved her through the stable door, making her stumble. She slid across the straw-strewn floor, landing with a thud against a stall wall, next to a stack of provisions. The man added the vendor's bundle to the pile.

"We leave at sunup, Wrists," he announced, then brought an armful of large leather pouches. "Start filling these saddlebags."

"Yes," she sought for an appropriate title, "Master."

He snorted, then knelt beside her and showed her how to pack the saddlebags. She looked at all the provisions he had laid out.

"There's enough here for an army!" Arista exclaimed.

The soldier laughed aloud. "Just a scouting party, lad. My nine comrades are waiting out in the hills for these supplies. Mind what you're doing."

Arista had worn herself out stuffing the preserved meats, dried fruits and hard cakes into the saddlebags. Any thoughts of escape were driven from her mind by the need to sleep. She had curled up in the straw, hardly aware that the soldier was laying out his own bedroll nearby.

When someone grabbed her shoulder and shook her awake, Arista assumed it was her captor, wanting her to do more work. She opened her eyes, but the stable was dark.

"It's me, 'Rista," came Taz's voice from the dark form crouched beside her. "Come quick! He's gone to the privy. Now's your chance to escape."

Taz was pulling at her sleeve, but Arista brushed his hand away.

"No, Taz. This is my chance to get away from the city."

"But we've kept you safe here. Whoever you're running away from hasn't caught you yet. Six months it's been. Do you think they're still looking for you?"

"Probably not, but there's always a chance I might be recognized. If I leave, I can be free. I'll miss you and Anja, and the others, but I've always planned to leave town when I could."

They heard footsteps outside.

"Go quickly," Arista whispered. She felt Taz squeeze her arm, then listened as he crept past the soldier in the dark. If the man heard anything, he probably took it for the stable cat, or the mice it hunted.

Arista lay still as the man got settled on his bedroll.

I will miss Taz, she thought. He had found Arista the day she ran away. She was hiding in an alley, not because she feared pursuit. Her in-laws would be glad to be rid of her. She had not thought beyond escaping the house. Once out in the streets, clad in a servant girl's rags, Arista did not know where to go. How would she eat? Where would she sleep?

A ten-year-old boy with a small girl in tow, came through the alley where Arista had taken refuge. Looking for useful rubbish, the boy was amused to find a young woman crouching among the cast-offs. He had befriended her, giving her food and inviting her to stay with his family.

Family! Arista was amused, remembering her first sight of the collection of street waifs Taz shepherded. Though some of the children were older, Taz was the cleverest. He served as leader of the group, assigning duties and overseeing them. Some of the children, the cute, yet pathetic-looking ones, like Anja, went begging. Those with quick hands stole, those with agile tongues resold the loot that the children had no use for. Fleet-footed boys hired themselves out to deliver messages.

Taz trained Arista to walk and act like a boy. He helped find a loose costume that would hide her small bosom, and womanly hips. He forced Arista to live as a boy, scolding her if she coughed daintily into her hand, mocking her if she spoke too politely. Taz also took stock of Arista's abilities and found she had the speed and dexterity of a first-rate pickpocket.

Sending the other children out to perform their tasks, Taz stayed with Anja. While the little girl wailed heart-wrenchingly, Taz kept his eyes and ears open. He spotted potential marks for the thieves, found customers for the runners, and watched for trouble. Taz would have helped Arista escape capture earlier, that day, but the victim had not been a target chosen by Taz.

Taz would never have let me attempt to rob a soldier, Arista realized. *He only picks out fat merchants and old dowagers. I should have at least let him know what I was doing. He could have caused some kind of confusion and helped me get away.*

Arista had participated in several rescue attempts herself. Taz might have knocked over a package from the vendor's stall onto Anja. She would have screamed like she was dying, and attention would have been drawn away from Arista.

The risk I took was foolish, Arista thought. She remembered the sight of a punished thief, his hand lopped off and laying in the dust, *but I am going to use this chance to leave the city, at last.* She smiled into the darkness.

The sun was just rising when the soldier dragged her from sleep. She rubbed her eyes, trying to wake up. Blinking them open, she saw four mules already loaded with the saddlebags she had filled.

"Don't suppose a street spawn like you knows how to ride," said the soldier.

She shook her head.

"These beasts are slow, graceless creatures. Just hold tight and I'll lead. He helped her scramble onto the back of the mule with the lightest load. "Don't think you'll break his back," the soldier chuckled. "How old are you?"

"Twelve," she lied. Taz had told her it was safer to roam the streets as a boy of twelve than a girl of fifteen.

"Well, you've still got plenty of time to grow, then." He looked up and seemed puzzled. *Has he seen through my disguise?* she wondered.

"Where I come from, there're few redheads," he said at last. "Those that are, well, they're like royalty."

"You're not used to it here, are you? Else you'd a lopped off this," she said, lifting the guilty hand. "Copper-headed kids are as common as pennies in this city."

He wouldn't have had time to notice this wasn't quite true. The soldier was mounting his horse. Soon they would leave the city, and Arista's past, behind. *Forever,* she hoped.

No, she did not regret this twist of fate. Perhaps she would miss Taz and Anja, but she would be safe. The days of fearing she would be recognized and sent back to her family were over.

The name, Arista, she left behind, with the city. Now

264 L. D. Woeltjen

she was Wrists, a thief, a servant, or, if she was cagey
enough, perhaps a fighter's apprentice.

Arista spent her first day of travel hunched on the
back of the mule, clinging to its neck as she was jolted
from side to side.

"Straighten up," the soldier commanded, "hold with
your legs, and balance. Watch me."

Arista watched the way the man poised himself on the
horse's back. He made it seem so easy. She tried to copy
his form, straightening her back, but suddenly found
herself slipping. Grabbing a handful of withers, Arista
wriggled back to her original position.

"I guess I'm no riding master," her companion confessed.

She continued to study him. There was grace in the
way he straddled the horse and controlled it with just the
smallest movements.

He's actually a handsome man, she thought, now that
she had lost some of her fear of him. He was dark, like
the men of the coastal clans, with eyes the gray-blue she
imagined the seas to be. *I'd wager he's seen the ocean,
and mountains, deserts . . .*

"Master?" she said, emulating the tone her little brother
had used when he begged Larvin, his tutor, for tales of
adventure. The soldier turned his head toward her. "Tell
me about the places you've been."

Obviously flattered, the horseman puffed up his chest,
taking in a deep breath. Briefly Wrists was reminded of
the public orators who stood on street corners, speaking
on behalf of the king. Soon she realized he was no
storyteller. His list of trips to Mountains of Ice, through
deserts in the West and over vast seas, was flat and
colorless. Instead of describing the places he had visited,
he counted the number of men he had killed and the
techniques he had used. Only once did he actually capture her interest.

"While I was fighting in the sea colonies, I came face
to face with one of the warrior women of the wetlands.
She did not give up her life easily, I tell you. Till then I'd
thought that the female armies were legend."

"You mean women fight? Just like men?"

"Not as well as men, perhaps," he boasted, "but they make a good attempt at it. That one was the only swordswoman I've actually fought, but since then, I've seen them in other armies. Served with some, in fact. They usually travel in groups and keep to themselves when they're on a campaign."

"But where was I?" the soldier asked himself. He resumed the account of lives he had taken. Wrists did not want to make him suspicious by asking more about the warrior women. She had heard Larvin mention them in his tales. *So women can be fighters,* she thought, with an elation she did not quite understand.

When he finally finished his cataloging of kills, Wrists dredged up memories of her little brother and tried again to imitate his excited fascination with danger.

"And what kind of quest are we going on?" she asked her companion.

"No treasure hunt, boy," he said with a laugh. "We'll not be saving any fair maidens, sad to say, nor fighting dragons, if that's what you had in mind." His face became serious.

"Do you know what a mercenary is, boy?"

Wrists shook his head.

"We're soldiers, but not the type you're used to seeing in that city you came from. We don't sign away our souls for a uniform and the honor of serving our country. We'll hire out our swords to the side that's willing to pay us the most."

Before Wrists could think of a response to his explanation, the man changed the subject.

"Here now, you're looking more like a horseman. Mayhap tomorrow, I'll let you try my mount."

"Could you let me try your sword, too?" Wrists begged eagerly.

"Just like me, when I was a boy," the man laughed. "Why not?"

"Master," though they both knew the title was no more than a flattering jest, kept his word. When they stopped for a meal, he took out his sword and handed it to Wrists.

"You should know the basics," he admitted. "If we are forced to fight, you may need to defend yourself."

Wrists liked the feel of her fingers gripping the sword hilt, but the weapon seemed too heavy for her. As she swung it the way he instructed, something in her wrists popped. The pain made her wince, but after feeling for the bones, and flapping her hand back and forth a few times, her teacher reassured her.

"It's nothing serious," he said as he tore a rag into strips. He bound the throbbing wrist tightly.

"This happens sometimes. My sword is too heavy for you, especially with those thin wrists. Slim as a woman's," he commented.

Wrists looked away and the man clapped her on the shoulder. "Nothing to be ashamed of, lad. You're still growing. Working out with my sword might even help build them up. Just make sure to wrap your wrists, tight like this, every time you practice. Wrapping'll give your wrists some support."

Wrists wheedled him into letting her use the sword every time they stopped. Her body ached, from the riding as well as the sword work, but she persisted. By the time they reached the camp, on the fifth day, she had impressed her teacher with her agility and her determination.

"Don't call me 'Master' here," he warned as they rode into camp. "I'm just one of the men. Call the captain, 'Captain'; otherwise, stick with names."

As he spoke, he nodded toward a thickset old man who strode toward them. When the man got closer, stopping next to her companion, Wrists realized he was only middle-aged. The lines that tracked his face made him seem older. She could not tell where the scars ended and the wrinkles began. His gray hair was unkempt and his chin bore several days' stubble. The man did not fit Wrists' image of an officer, but he spoke with authority.

"Did you get the provisions?" he asked curtly.

"Aye, but at a higher price than we'd expected, Captain. This job isn't going to leave us much profit," the soldier complained.

"Is that why you brought along another mouth to feed?" snapped the leader. "Where'd you get the kid?"

"Hey, Pell," called one of the soldiers who had come to unload the mules, "I didn't know your tastes ran into that direction."

Pell glared at the joker, unamused, then answered the captain.

"Caught the lad dipping into my purse. They wanted me to whack off his hand." His lips curled into a sneer of disgust. "That's what those price gougers call justice!"

"Barbaric," the captain said, shaking his head. He strode over to Wrists who fumbled with the ropes that held the packs on the beast she had ridden.

"Well, son," said the Captain, looking her up and down once, "you're a soldier now. Keep your hands busy with chores, understand?"

Wrists nodded and sniffled, wiping her nose with the back of her hand. It had been one of her brother's most annoying habits.

The captain turned and walked away.

"Over here, Vidow," Pell whispered to the joker once the captain was out of earshot, "let the boy unload. I want to tell you about this whore I, uh," he paused, noticing Wrists was listening, " 'visited' in the city."

"I knew I should've volunteered to get the supplies," Vidow grumbled.

Wrists' duties around the camp gave her little free time, but no matter how tired she got, she forced herself to practice daily. Often Faron, one of the younger men, would watch as she ran through the exercises Pell had taught her. Having an audience made Wrists nervous. Was he finding fault with her sword work, or could he see through her disguise?

One day Faron approached her as she tried to match her footwork with the moves of the blade Pell let her use.

"I admire your diligence," he said. "You're coming along, lad. Do you think you're ready to try using a shield?" Faron held his out toward her, angled so she could slide her left arm into the straps.

At first Wrists held herself away from Faron as he positioned himself behind her and used his own body to frame the movements she must make. "Thrust, block with shield, regain your stance, drop shield and thrust," Faron chanted as he pushed her limbs through the actions. She relaxed when it became obvious that Faron was caught up in the role of instructor. Wrists enjoyed the lesson then. This was one more opportunity to learn about the craft of fighting.

Maybe I'll get good enough to become a mercenary, too, she daydreamed. *I wouldn't have to steal to live. I could earn a proper wage, and see the world at the same time.* Memories of hours spent hidden in her brother's closet returned. Her mother had disapproved of her interest in old Larvin's stories. Boys could waste time on tales of heroic adventure. Girls needed to learn practical things. *What good is being able to embroider, now?* she wondered, looking down at her grimy, blistered hands.

While she did her chores around the camp, Wrists listened to the men, asking questions when she dared. The fighters all enjoyed bragging about their exploits. She listened closely, seizing opportunities to ask them to demonstrate the sword technique being discussed, or explain a tracking method that had been mentioned.

"And what is it exactly that we're supposed to be doing here?" she asked Faron one morning as they rested after a mock duel.

"We," Faron emphasized the word to remind her that she was not being paid for this outing, "have been hired by Baron Dusert to keep an eye on the road. The Baron plans to lay siege on Mountainhold, and depose its ruler. We're supposed to keep the holdmaster from forming any alliances before Dusert can move in his troops."

"What claim does this baron have to the city?" she asked.

"An army, that's all he needs," Faron said. When he saw Wrists did not find humor in his comment, he became serious. "Actually, it's his own brother he's trying to overthrow. Their father divided his kingdom between his sons, rather than giving all his holdings to his elder son, the baron."

"Isn't Mountainhold a rather poor prize to begrudge his brother?" Wrists asked without thinking.

"And when did you become an expert on politics?" Faron teased. "The Baron's just greedy. He accuses his brother of plotting rebellion."

"Does the holdmaster know what's about to befall him?"

"Dusert hopes not," Faron replied. "In case the holdmaster does get wind of it, the Baron has mercenary units like these guarding all the routes down from Mountainhold."

"So if they try to send to . . ." she paused, balking at the name of the country which had bred her, "to their allies for help . . ."

"We'll stop them," Faron answered, drawing a finger across his throat and smiling. She was appalled at his bloodthirstiness.

"Isn't that a rather unworthy cause to risk your life for?" Wrists asked finally.

"A job is a job," was his only reply.

I shall never understand men, she thought. *How can I pretend to be one? I can pass as a boy, but as a man?* Her training had included more than cooking and sewing she realized now. Her mother had taught her to revere life. A woman's purpose was to bring life into the world, to nourish it, to preserve it. A woman must hate war. *And yet she must be willing to send her husband, or her sons off to give up their lives for their country.*

Suddenly Wrists felt confused. The idea of becoming a soldier had excited her. She had forgotten, in all the fun of swordplay, that its true purpose was death. She had not been taught from the cradle to be brave, to thirst for her opponent's destruction, to think of death as glorious.

I now know how to handle a sword, she thought, *but could I ever use one?*

The following day, the lookout reported a small party, half a dozen horsemen, coming east from Mountainhold.

"No mercy, men!" the Captain ordered as they left camp. "If one escapes, we may have an army to deal with."

Alone at the camp, Wrists could hear the high-pitched neighs of distressed horses, the shouts of men, the clash of steel. She was glad she did not have to witness the battle.

Perhaps I have become too fond of Pell, she thought. *I do not want him to die.*

Several long hours passed before they returned. Even with her lack of experience, Wrists knew something was wrong. When the men began to return, she felt relief, in spite of their battered condition and blood-spattered bodies. She saw an injured man being half-carried, half-dragged, into the clearing and went to help care for the wounded.

"Pell," she called out, as she saw the soldier stumble into the clearing, "are you hurt?"

"No!" he growled. His eyes flashed fury. "An ambush!" he raged toward the captain. "Why didn't the lookout see the second party?"

"He's paid for his mistake," the captain answered calmly, wiping blood from his arm to see how much of it was his own. "They must have suspected the road was watched. The second group was deliberately maintaining a distance."

"We lost three, in all, Captain," Vidow reported. "Two more are hurt bad."

"Still, we did ourselves proud," Faron said. "Only one or two got away with their skins intact."

"All it takes is one survivor to spell our doom," the captain reminded them. "Two days at the most and they'll be back to wipe us out."

"I'll start breaking camp as soon as I finish with this bandage," Wrists volunteered.

"Hold, young one. We're not going anywhere," replied the captain.

"But.. . ." she began to argue.. Pell's glare shut her up.

Later, Faron joined her as she cooked dinner. "Listen, kid," he said quietly, prodding at the fire with a stick. "No one will blame you for running away. This isn't your fight, and you're hardly more than a child. Take one of the mules tonight and get out of here."

"You're all going to die," she said, keeping her voice cold, so she wouldn't cry. "Why?"

"It's our job."

"So some greedy Baron has a few more days to steal his brother's inheritance? Is that worth giving your life for?"

"Quiet," he hissed. "Don't talk our fate into being. Until it happens, we don't know for certain what will be."

"Answer me," she insisted. "Is this Baron's greed worth the risk?"

"No. But honor is. A man lives by a code of bravery, sometimes he dies by it. That's what it means to be a man. One day, you'll understand."

No, I won't, she thought. *That is something I can never understand.*

Wrists did not attempt to leave.

I know how to use a sword, she thought. *I can fight, and out of love for Pell and loyalty to Faron, I will. Those are things worth dying for.*

When Faron saw Wrists had not left, he took her to the road where the battle had been. At first she thought he intended for the reality of the butchered, reeking corpses to frighten her off. Faron led her among the bodies, not noticing how she kept her eyes averted. The young soldier stooped by a lifeless form and removed the dead man's weapon.

"Here, try this sword," he said, handing it to her. Wrists waved it back and forth a few times, but they both decided it was too heavy for her. Testing several more, at last they found one of lighter weight. Its owner had been a youth, probably a year or two older than Wrists' true age.

"Should I find a shield, too?" she asked.

"No, child. There's not time enough to teach you to use one properly. It would only encumber you. You'll have enough to do today just learning to use that pricker. It's finely crafted," Faron told her. "I'd wager that lad was kin to the Master of the city. Perhaps even a son. An

envoy like this would need a member of the royal family
to show its earnestness."

Both Faron and Pell helped Wrists practice with the
new sword. The latter reminded her to keep her wrists
bound. She also tended the sick and prepared what they
all knew would be their last meal together.

Dawn came and the eight fighters went to wait in
ambush for the attackers they knew would be coming.
Surprise might give them the edge they needed to survive. Since their horses had been lost in the first battle,
they would have to unseat their opponents to better their
odds. A trip wire was laid across the road for this purpose.

Several hours passed before the sound of galloping
hoofs told them battle was imminent.

Two dozen riders came down the road. At the last
moment, the wire was raised. The two lead horses bolted
forward, throwing their riders into the air. The following
ranks could not rein up quickly enough. Three more
pairs of horses fell. The pile-up of men and beasts forced
the entire company to dismount. Eight ambushers set
upon the confused warriors before they could react. Seven,
in truth, for Wrists hung back at first.

Two of her comrades had fallen as she watched, then
the captain had sunk to the ground, his head all but
severed, before Wrists was engaged in battle. Desperate,
with no time to remember what she had been taught,
Wrists fought for her life. Holding the sword before her,
she fended off the blows of her attacker. Her lack of
training proved to be his undoing. So unskilled were her
moves that the soldier relaxed and was unprepared for
her sudden thrust. Finding himself skewered, the man's
eyes widened in surprise and he stumbled toward her.
Wrists jumped back, losing her grip on the sword.

She stood staring as he died. Then, ignoring the blood
that gushed onto the ground, Wrists crouched beside the
dead man, wrestling the blade from his body. Once she
had it, she looked around. Only Pell still fought, and he
was ringed by fighters. A hand's count of blades slashed
into him, all at once. Wrists screamed, then realized her
cry had drawn attention to herself. She fled toward the
trees.

"Let him go," someone ordered. "He's only a boy. We've had our revenge, and made the road safe." But Wrists did not stop running until she reached the clearing. She found a half-filled saddlebag and thrust the sword she still carried into it. Hastily tossing the pack onto the mule and slinging a waterskin over her shoulder, Wrists mounted.

Three days traveling south, and no sign of pursuit, Wrists thought as her trail through the woods intersected a main road. *I think it is safe for me to stop hiding. I'll make better time on the roads.*

Wrists had driven the horror of battle from her mind. It had been what she expected, and uglier, but not terrible enough to dampen her ambition. From the moment Pell had placed a sword in her hand, she had wanted to be a fighter. She needed training, and in the days spent fleeing the Mountainhold men, she had decided how to get it. Old Larvin had told her brother stories of warrior women from a kingdom in the southern swamps. Pell had called their home the wetlands.

I will find that kingdom, Wrists vowed, *and train with the swordswomen. There I'll learn to fight, and die, if I must, like a woman.*

Wrists urged the mule out onto the road and headed south.

Her masquerade as a boy was ended.

DEATH AND THE UGLY WOMAN

by Bruce D. Arthurs

I've known Bruce Arthurs—or B.D., as he's often called in Phoenix fandom—a long time; ever since I started attending conventions in Phoenix; a place with a wonderful climate and a beautiful zoo and botanical garden. His first story ("Unicorn's Blood" in S&S II) was actually begun on my typewriter, while Bruce and his wife, (my good friend Margaret Hildebrand) were visiting us at Greenwalls some years ago. This year, very early in the selection process, Bruce sent me a long and complicated adventure story which for some reason or other failed to captivate me. I'm sure it will sell somewhere else, and I'll be looking for it; but I couldn't use it here, and reluctantly returned it to him. Bruce then sent me this poignant little masterpiece of a fable; fantasy or allegory. Anything which can make this hard-boiled editor choke up is pretty unusual, and I'm proud to present it here.

In those years when snow falls lightly upon the distant mountains, the river Gorquin flows slowly, the water low in its bed. Water trapped in pools stagnates. Warmed by the lengthening days of summer, the slow water of the shallows becomes dark with growth and ringed with scum.

On cool mornings a faint and odorous miasma can be seen rising from the surface. Drifting, the faint mist wafts its way, reaching into Easur, Rist, En, the other villages and towns along the Gorquin.

It is in such years that young children are watched with

extra care for the beginnings of fever, dizziness, nausea. Such are the first symptoms of bonecrush fever.

It was said that Death rode the Gorquin in a black skiff. Tall, pale, dark of hair, he traveled in the fineries of a lord. Black opals adorned the rings on his fingers, and black diamonds studded the hilt of the long and slender-bladed knife at his side.

It was said that he entered the homes where children lay sick with bonecrush; no locks or bars could prevent his entrance. And Death would stand over the feverish children, and smile, and draw the knife from its sheath, and thrust the thin blade, woundlessly, into their bones and joints.

And the children would die, screaming.

The two sons and the daughter of Dur, a fisherman of Easur, lay sick with fever. The daughter, Resti, lay awake, teeth chattering with fever and fear. She was old enough to have heard tales of Death and his knife. She tried to focus on the darkness before her. She could hear the troubled sleep of her brothers across the room, and, faintly, the snores of her father in the next room as he slept, finally, after caring for them all day.

The night clouds drifted away from the moon, allowing the pale rays to illumine the plain but clean room.

Death stood before her, Death with his jeweled knife held in a jeweled hand.

He tilted her head back with one cold hand, shifted to one side so the moon would light her face. He made a disgusted noise, deep in his throat.

Resti knew what he saw. "Pig-face," other children called her, her with her pushed-up nose, her bulging eyes, slack lips failing to hide the twisted teeth behind, the thin lank hair. Beneath the covers, her body was squat and thick, the curve in her spine twisting one shoulder higher than the other.

"One like you, I do not want," Death whispered, and turned away.

Resti closed her eyes against the pain in her heart. To be rejected even by Death. . . . A tear rolled down her sweat-filmed cheek.

Ross, her eldest brother, began to scream as Death's knife thrust into him, again and again. Resti threw back her covers, staggered up, lurched forward. She laid ahold of Death with fever-weakened hands.

Death barely paused as he smashed her away with a frigid, ice-hard hand.

Resti toppled back against her own bed, falling to the floor beside it. The last she saw that night was her father rushing in, his arms reaching out in hopeless comforting toward Ross, reaching through the Death invisible to him.

Later, Fren, too, began to scream. But Resti was not conscious to hear it.

Dur had taken the boat out of the harbor and into the open sea, far from the other fishing boats. The weighted sacks containing his sons lay on the deck. The ship slowed in the sun-sparkled water as he lowered the sail.

Resti was still weak, but the fever was gone. Her mind was clear, but heavy.

"Resti." Her father called her to him, and she helped lift the sacks, one by one, over the rail. The dark shapes vanished quickly as they sank beneath the surface.

Dur stared down into the depths long after the sacks were gone. Finally, sighing, he turned to Resti.

"When I die," he began, "and go to join your mother and brothers, this boat will be yours." He regarded the twisted figure of his daughter for several long seconds. "You will have no one to share it with, no husband to man it for you. It is time you learned the ways of the sea.

Dur died when Resti was sixteen, swept overboard when a squall caught them before they could reach the safety of port. By then she had learned the handling of the boat, the ways of catching fish, the skill of market bargaining. Years of hauling in nets and manning tiller and sail had put firm muscles on her squat frame.

In the Festival Days of the year she turned eighteen, she was walking toward her rooms after selling her catch. The streets were heavy with celebrants dressed in their brightest and best, and children ran wild.

"Sea-cow! A sea-cow's come out of the water!" A child was shouting and pointing at her. The other children around him laughed. *"Sea-cow! Sea-cow!"* they all began to shout.

Resti turned quickly and walked into an alleyway. She had never grown used to the taunts and calls, even after all the years of it. The shouts faded behind her as she traveled the narrow, gloomy backways.

She passed where the alley widened temporarily to form a small courtyard. A group of men, strangers to her, sat on a doorstoop, passing a bottle back and forth between them. Their loud talk stopped as Resti entered the courtyard, and they stared as she walked past. She heard muttering and a burst of coarse laughter from them as she re-entered the alley on the other side.

A moment later, she heard the running steps behind her. A glance back showed the men coming toward her. She ran, twisting and dodging through the maze of alleyways, but the men stayed with her.

She was becoming short of breath, and stopped, reaching for the fishing knife on her belt as she turned.

The bottle smashed into her arm, bounced and shattered on the cobblestones. The knife slipped from stunned fingers, and then the men were on her.

Two grabbed her arms, a third tossed his jacket over her head and held it there, muffling her screams and bites. Two more grabbed her legs and forced them apart. The sixth fumbled and tugged at her trousers, then cut them loose with a knife. They were all laughing.

There was a ripping pain between her legs, a heavy grunting weight on top of her, long seconds of painful thrusting, and a spurt of hot liquid inside her.

"I said I could fuck the ugliest woman on the whole Gorquin," the man said, laughing as he withdrew. "Who's next?"

Resti named the baby Pearl. The child was perfect in form, except for a brown bar in the blue iris of her left eye.

Others stared disapprovingly as Resti took Pearl with

her on the boat each day. She disregarded the stares. The taunts of children became ignorable.

Pearl's first steps were taken on the swaying deck of the boat. The first word she spoke was "fish."

When Pearl was three, the Gorquin lowered and grew slow, and a faint mist would rise from its surface on cool mornings.

Resti sat silently in the unlighted room, listening to the restless tossing and turning of Pearl. The bright moon shone through the window, gleaming from the fear in Resti's eyes, flashing from the blade of the knife she held.

Death entered through the locked and barred door. Resti rose to stand between the dark figure and Pearl.

Death barely glanced at Resti as he moved forward. Her knife rose up in a slash across his chest. The blade moved silently, effortlessly, through the dark fabric, the dark unknown beneath it.

Harmlessly. There was no sign of a tear or cut.

Resti stepped back, thrust toward where Death's heart, if heart he had, would be. The blade slid in again, then stopped as Resti's fist thudded against the chest of Death.

Death grunted, surprise on the pale face. He grabbed Resti's arm and squeezed the wrist with chill strength. The knife dropped from her fingers, falling through Death and onto the floor.

She struggled against his frigid grasp. Death tossed her to one side, the chair smashing as she fell over and onto it. She scrambled on the floor, grabbed one of the dark-clad legs, bit into it ferociously. Death roared with pain as a taste of bloody ice flooded Resti's mouth.

He seized her by the shoulders and threw her violently against the wall. Resti fell, stunned and almost senseless, into a heap on the floor.

She barely saw as the dark figure limped to Pearl's bed.

The tailor had just finished sewing the shroud tight around the small body when someone in the small crowd outside sighted Resti returning.

Her lank hair was plastered tightly to her broad skull,

and water dripped from her sodden clothing as she walked slowly, blindly, down the street. Her eyes, too, were wet, but not from river or ocean water.

The crowd parted silently as Resti passed within. The tailor stood as Resti entered.

"He would not take me," Resti said, dully. "I held the stone tight, and jumped into the deepest part of the Gorquin, and still he would not take me. I woke in the shallows, my face out of water, still alive. Breath still in me."

The tailor gathered up his needles and thread, the bolt of dark material. "I have other children waiting for me," he said, and left.

The season of sickness passed. The next year the Gorquin flowed at its normal level, and the year after that, and the year after that.

Resti lost herself, seemingly, in work. The usual labor of a one-manned fishing boat could fill the day's hours, but she did more. She began to use a larger net, straining to haul the catch aboard. When that net became too easy to use, she switched to a larger one still.

The other fishermen tapped their heads and called her mad when she fitted a long sculling oar to the stern of her boat. When they returned home from the day, sails full, they would frequently pass Resti as she pushed the oar back and forth, sweat dripping from her as the oar pushed the heavy, cumbersome boat through the water. After selling the catch, she would plod to her rooms, to fall into an exhausted sleep.

Her arms, and most of her body, grew ridged and knotted with muscle. To others, she became more grotesque, uglier than ever.

Festival. Again the streets of Easur were filled with traders, travelers, performers and rabble.

Resti walked toward her rooms, lost in her private thoughts. Many who saw her shied away and made room for her to pass.

One man, talking with another as he walked, struck her with his shoulder. "Damn y—" he began, then stopped as he looked down at her. He gave a bark of rough laughter, and walked on.

Resti stood motionless. Seven years might have added that touch of gray to his beard, those lines around his eyes. "Might" was not certainty, however.

But one of his blue eyes had had a bar of brown.

She followed the two men to a tavern several streets away. It was smoky and poorly lit inside. Some of the men knew her from the docks, and became silent when they saw the look in her eyes.

The man she had followed was at the bar, raising a mug of beer to his lips. She moved behind him and spoke.

"I recognized you, too."

He turned, slowly. He was big, nearly a head taller than Resti, and strongly muscled. His face twisted into a sneer.

"What do you want . . . hunchback?"

"Tell me the name of your daughter," Resti answered.

He stared at her blankly for several seconds, then laughed and slammed the mug into the side of her face.

She grabbed the front of his shirt as she stumbled back, blood pouring into one eye. Recovering, she yanked him off his feet and threw him into a table.

He came up at her with a knife in his hand. The blade burned against her ribs. She clamped his knife-arm under her own, used her other arm to yank his elbow across her chest. He screamed as tendons ripped.

Resti pushed him back, then wrapped her arms around his chest and squeezed. The muscles in her arms and shoulders strained with effort.

A hoarse, low scream hissed from the man's mouth as air was pressed from his lungs. His ribs made a sound like cracking knuckles as they broke. There was a louder crack as his spine snapped. His eyes rolled up into his head, and he went limp in Resti's arms.

She dropped the body to the floor and stood over it, panting. Blood soaked her side, and dripped from her face onto the dead man.

"Now I am ready," she whispered. "Now."

*   *   *

The Gorquin was low the next year. Resti walked the empty streets of Easur at night, alert for the sounds of the sick and restless, the lights of lone candles as parents watched over their children.

She met Death close to the docks.

"I can touch you," she told him as she barred his way. "I can hurt you."

"You have no cause to impede me," the dark figure replied.

"Memory is my cause."

"I am strong."

"I, too, am strong," she said, and attacked.

Death lay in the street, writhing, gasping in pain as he tried to move his useless legs.

"You have broken the back of Death," he groaned.

"Little enough payment for my heart," Resti panted.

Death's hands twisted together, despairing. "Have mercy, then," he said, "and finish me." With both hands, he held out his jeweled knife, hilt-first, to her.

Slowly, Resti reached to take it.

Like a serpent, Death struck. The knife dropped as he seized her hand. Before she could react, Death had twisted the object hidden in his hand onto her finger.

She jumped back as Death released her, and stared at the black opal ring on her hand. She tugged and twisted, but the ring was firm.

Death lay back upon the ground. He gave a quiet laugh and died.

Resti watched as the clothing and flesh of Death dissipated into a pale smoke. A skeleton of ice lay in the street, melting quickly in the warm night air.

She turned and walked away, down the empty street, toward her rooms.

She stopped when she saw the light as she passed a row of houses. She moved silently to the window, listened to the labored breathing behind it.

The door opened at her touch and she entered, moving past where the child's mother sat by the candle. She stared down at the young child for long moments.

Finally, she leaned down and pressed the small lips with her own.

It is said that, in the season of bonecrush fever, Death rides the Gorquin in a black boat fitted with a long sculling oar. Death is twisted in shape, grotesque and scarred of face. She wears a black opal ring upon one hand, and carries a sharp fishing knife at her side.

But the knife is never unsheathed.

And the children die, gently, in their sleep.

BLOODSTONES

by Deborah M. Vogel

It's curious to realize that I became a novelist because I didn't have the skill or craft to write short stories. I think that happens to a lot of people. Difficult though it may be to believe it, it's much easier to tell a story in 65,000 words than in 5,000.

Brevity is the most difficult thing to achieve. (Listen to any political speech.) AND THE FORM OF THE SHORT-SHORT STORY IS THE MOST DIFFICULT OF ALL. While I feel that the short story, the elegantly crafted tale of an idea embodied in readable characters, is the finest literary achievement in our field, I've seldom been able to do it; ninety percent of my own short stories were not worth the paper they were printed on and fortunately did not survive the short-lived pulps where they were printed.

But for the average writer, it's more profitable to write longer stories—since pay is always by the word. So every year I have to reject fifteen or twenty stories at 8,000 words or longer, and am *always* ready to make room for a good story at 1500 words or less.

Deborah Vogel sent this one in just under the wire.

She's the daughter of Barbara Armistead, whose story "On The Trail" appeared in FREE AMAZONS OF DARK-OVER.

Sounds like a good beginning. And I always try to wind up an anthology with something short and wry . . . with a nice little twist in the tail. And so it's a good ending, too, for this time around.

The fire illuminated her face as she danced. The night was cold, with just a hint of winter snows. Into the white sand, beside the glowing coals, a drop of blood fell. The dance went on, and soon another drop of blood fell beside the first. Across the fire, the look of greed deepened on the face of the man sitting there. He held in his hand a small white stone that glittered with inner fire. And still the woman danced.

A third and fourth drop of blood landed on the sand. The night grew colder; a pale moon rose slowly into the sky. The woman gleamed with exertion, but her dancing did not slow.

Presently there were six drops of blood in the sand. The dance slowed down, and the woman began a chant that kept time with the steps. Slower and slower she moved; louder and louder she chanted. Then she stopped moving altogether. She stood at the edge of the sand facing the fire with her head bowed.

She raised her hand, dropped to her knees and slowly set her finger in the center of the first red drop, now a glimmering stone.

"Power," she said softly. Then the witch said the man's True Name. She moved on to the second stone.

"Woman," and again she said his Name. At the third, "Riches," the fourth, "Strength," the fifth, "Loyalty," and after each, his True Name seemed to linger and reverberate under the trees. And at the sixth, she said only his Name twice.

Slowly she sat back on her heels and stared at the fruit of her labor. Across the fire, the man smiled in triumph.

"Give them to me," he said. The witch looked at him without any expression on her face.

"First," she said, "you must give me back my soul."

The man laughed harshly. Across the fire he threw the glowing white stone. It flew over the witch's head and into the cold night beyond. Her face did not change. Scooping up the bloodstones, she handed them to the man. Then she rose to her feet and left the fire. In the trees at the edge of the clearing, she picked up the glowing stone and ever so gently pressed it to her chest.

The stone melted into her body, and the glow moved to her eyes. The man laughed again as he got up and walked away from the fire. In his hand, the red stones burned with an inner radiance. He rapidly untied his horse and swung into the saddle.

From the edge of the clearing, the witch spoke.

"I must tell you something important," she said softly.

"Speak up, woman! What do I need to know about these stones except that with them I can take my brother's throne, his life, his wife, and command the loyalty of his best men?" He threw back his head and laughed aloud. "And the fool will be powerless to stop me!"

"It is as you say, Man," said the witch, "but remember this." She started to fade from sight, and she smiled a truly happy smile. "If you invoke the Sixth of the Bloodstones, the power of that Stone will eat the flesh from your bones and drink your soul."

The man snorted. "Then all I have to do is avoid the sixth stone, and I'll be safe."

The witch faded from sight entirely, but her laughter hung in the cold air of the clearing.

"Tell me this, Man. Which one is the Sixth Stone?"

DAW

BESTSELLERS BY MARION ZIMMER BRADLEY

THE DARKOVER NOVELS

The Founding

☐ DARKOVER LANDFALL   UE2234—$3.95

The Ages of Chaos

☐ HAWKMISTRESS!   UE2239—$3.95
☐ STORMQUEEN!   UE2310—$4.50

The Hundred Kingdoms

☐ TWO TO CONQUER   UE2174—$3.50

The Renunciates (Free Amazons)

☐ THE SHATTERED CHAIN   UE2308—$3.95
☐ THENDARA HOUSE   UE2240—$3.95
☐ CITY OF SORCERY   UE2332—$3.95

Against the Terrans: The First Age

☐ THE SPELL SWORD   UE2237—$3.95
☐ THE FORBIDDEN TOWER   UE2373—$4.95

Against the Terrans: The Second Age

☐ THE HERITAGE OF HASTUR   UE2238—$3.95
☐ SHARRA'S EXILE   UE2309—$3.95

THE DARKOVER ANTHOLOGIES
with The Friends of Darkover

☐ THE KEEPER'S PRICE   UE2236—$3.95
☐ SWORD OF CHAOS   UE2172—$3.50
☐ FREE AMAZONS OF DARKOVER   UE2096—$3.50
☐ THE OTHER SIDE OF THE MIRROR   UE2185—$3.50
☐ RED SUN OF DARKOVER   UE2230—$3.95
☐ FOUR MOONS OF DARKOVER   UE2305—$3.95

NEW AMERICAN LIBRARY
P.O. Box 999, Bergenfield, New Jersey 07621
Please send me the DAW BOOKS I have checked above. I am enclosing $_____
(check or money order—no currency or C.O.D.'s). Please include the list price plus
$1.00 per order to cover handling costs. Prices and numbers are subject to change
without notice. (Prices slightly higher in Canada.)

Name _____

Address _____

City _____ State _____ Zip _____
Please allow 4-6 weeks for delivery.

DAW

DAW PRESENTS THESE BESTSELLERS BY
MARION ZIMMER BRADLEY

NON-DARKOVER NOVELS

☐ **HUNTERS OF THE RED MOON**   (UE1968—$2.95)
☐ **WARRIOR WOMAN**   (UE2253—$3.50)

NON-DARKOVER ANTHOLOGIES

☐ **SWORD AND SORCERESS**   (UE1928—$2.95)
☐ **SWORD AND SORCERESS II**   (UE2041—$2.95)
☐ **SWORD AND SORCERESS III**   (UE2141—$3.50)
☐ **SWORD AND SORCERESS IV**   (UE2210—$3.50)
☐ **SWORD AND SORCERESS V**   (UE2288—$3.50)

COLLECTIONS

☐ **LYTHANDE** (with Vonda N. McIntyre)   (UE2154—$3.50)
☐ **THE BEST OF MARION ZIMMER BRADLEY** (edited by Martin H. Greenberg)   (UE2268—$3.95)

NEW AMERICAN LIBRARY
P.O. Box 999, Bergenfield, New Jersey 07621

Please send me the DAW BOOKS I have checked above. I am enclosing $_____
(check or money order—no currency or C.O.D.'s). Please include the list price plus
$1.00 per order to cover handling costs. Prices and numbers are subject to change
without notice. Prices slightly higher in Canada.

Name _____

Address _____

City _____ State _____ Zip _____
Please allow 4-6 weeks for delivery.

DAW

Savor the magic, the special wonder of the worlds of
Jennifer Roberson

THE NOVELS OF TIGER AND DEL

☐ SWORD-DANCER   (UE2376—$3.95)
Tiger and Del, he a Sword-Dancer of the South, she of the
North, each a master of secret sword-magic. Together, they
would challenge wizards' spells and other deadly perils on a
desert quest to rescue Del's kidnapped brother.

☐ SWORD-SINGER   (UE2295—$3.95)
Outlawed for slaying her own sword master, Del must return to
the Place of Swords to stand in sword-dancer combat and
either clear her name or meet her doom. But behind Tiger and
Del stalks an unseen enemy, intent on stealing the very heart
and soul of their sword-magic!

CHRONICLES OF THE CHEYSULI

This superb fantasy series about a race of warriors gifted with
the ability to assume animal shapes at will presents the Cheysuli,
fated to answer the call of magic in their blood, fulfilling an
ancient prophecy which could spell salvation or ruin.

☐ SHAPECHANGERS: BOOK 1   (UE2140—$2.95)
☐ THE SONG OF HOMANA: BOOK 2   (UE2317—$3.95)
☐ LEGACY OF THE SWORD: BOOK 3   (UE2316—$3.95)
☐ TRACK OF THE WHITE WOLF: BOOK 4   (UE2193—$3.50)
☐ A PRIDE OF PRINCES: BOOK 5   (UE2261—$3.95)
☐ DAUGHTER OF THE LION: BOOK 6   (UE2324—$3.95)

NEW AMERICAN LIBRARY
P.O. Box 999, Bergenfield, New Jersey 07621

Please send me the DAW BOOKS I have checked above. I am enclosing $_____
(check or money order—no currency or C.O.D.'s). Please include the list price plus
$1.00 per order to cover handling costs. Prices and numbers are subject to change
without notice. (Prices slightly higher in Canada.)

Name _____

Address _____

City _____ State _____ Zip _____
Please allow 4-6 weeks for delivery.